Fireflies IN SACRED *Shadows*

LOST AND FOUND BOOK 2

TONYA B. ASHLEY

Published by Scrivenings Press LLC
15 Lucky Lane
Morrilton, Arkansas 72110
https://ScriveningsPress.com

Printed in the United States of America

Paperback ISBN 978-1-64917-551-9
eBook ISBN 978-1-64917-552-6

Editors: Amy R. Anguish and Suzie Waltner

Cover by Linda Fulkerson, www.bookmarketinggraphics.com

All characters are fictional, and any resemblance to real people, either factual or historical, is purely coincidental.

*Home is the place where hope glimmers
in the darkness.*

To Jesus, who sits with me in suffering and shows me how to face the darkness instead of fleeing from it.

Chapter One

Van Buren, Arkansas
Late September 1853

As Rebecca Hogue handed her older sister, Ivajohn, a box in exchange for a blue bellflower stem, the ladies sitting around the parsonage parlor leaned closer. How many times had Ivajohn's wedding been postponed? Rebecca worried a leaf between her thumb and forefinger, holding her breath. Its rough texture and dark color complemented the blooms' delicate beauty. With careful planning, the group had managed to organize a surprise bridal tea in Ivajohn's honor.

The close-knit sewing circle had gathered for weeks, stitching to ensure the Hogue family would be sharply dressed for Ivajohn's upcoming ceremony. Somehow, they successfully catered to each sister's request while respecting Ivajohn's desire for simplicity. Cordelia demanded something pink with ribbons, while Martie wanted no frills and absolutely no pink. Nellie, sweet girl, wished to embellish her bonnet with ribbon and lace.

Edie pleaded for boy's knickers underneath her skirt so she could climb trees when the ceremony concluded.

Rebecca smiled inwardly. Dressing Pa and three brothers had proven far simpler.

Ivajohn lifted the lid and hummed with delight, admiring the simple cream-colored bonnet. Rebecca's instinct had been correct despite Mrs. Pratt's urging to obtain a more elaborate adornment from Brandt's Tailor Shop. She exhaled as Ivajohn's mouth curved in a demure bow.

"It's exactly what I hoped for."

Rebecca exhaled, some small weight lifted from her chest.

Across the room, Mrs. Pratt's arched eyebrow and pursed lips signaled her displeasure. Rebecca squeezed Ivajohn's shoulder. "We'll add yellow bush pea stems and a blue ribbon on the wedding day, as Mrs. Pratt suggested."

Mrs. Pratt's expression softened as she drifted closer with a cluster of women, bright chatter filling the parlor. Rebecca moved to the window. A playful breeze stirred the oak across the road, scattering shadows across the grass, and her eyes caught a trace, a shape resisting the sway of the shifting leaves. She leaned closer to the glass, but a gust tossed the branches wide again, and whatever she thought she saw disappeared. Perhaps it was a trick of the light.

Yet, a faint unease laced through her as she turned away. The hum of laughter pulled her back into the moment. She returned to her seat, twisting the flower stem between her fingers.

"Everything all right?" Eliza Dawn settled beside her.

"An overactive imagination, I'm afraid." Rebecca masked her concern with a smile. "Every time Dr. Dibrell and Dr. Pernot leave, I half-expect a frazzled messenger at the door. I don't mind helping, but our little town would benefit from another well-trained doctor. What if both doctors are gone and something happens on the wedding day?"

"Don't even think it." Eliza Dawn leaned closer. "You made

it here this morning without any issues. And Dr. Pernot will be back soon."

"Yes, but I can't stand being called away and causing more delays."

Eliza Dawn grinned. "It has been an unusually long courtship."

"It's understandable with both of them involved traveling regularly into Indian Territory for missionary work." Rebecca paused, swallowing hard as her gaze fell to the flowers. "And other unforeseen events."

"Your family has faced more than its fair share of trials." Eliza Dawn gently patted her hand. "I wish I could have met your mother before she passed away."

"Dawn, your arrival after we lost her was a blessing." The memory of losing Mama tugged at Rebecca's heart, and she squeezed Eliza Dawn's hand. "You and Justin have faced your own trials. How have you been?"

"We were holding dreams of a family in open hands." Eliza Dawn's expression dimmed. "But I think it's time we let it go. I can't bear the disappointment anymore."

"Would you consider embracing a child in need?"

"Maybe. After taking time to grieve."

"Of course." Rebecca rubbed Eliza Dawn's hand. "Of course, we've had reasons to celebrate as well. I gained a wonderful sister-in-law and friend when Justin opened his heart to you."

"I've received the greater blessing. You all made me part of a family once more." Eliza Dawn's voice grew gentler. "I'm curious, though. When will you open your heart again? You've never stopped grieving the loss of him. I see it in your eyes."

Rebecca's throat tightened. "He made his choice."

She turned slightly, the ache over losing him sharp and familiar as she dropped the bellflower onto her lap. Then, with a guarded smile, she pushed aside thoughts of Ben Ewing.

"No matter." She smoothed her skirt. "Today is about Ivajohn."

Eliza Dawn didn't press. She took the floral stem from Rebecca and placed it with the other flowers in the wide-mouthed jar on the side table. She squeezed Rebecca's knee. "It's time. You should call this gathering to order."

Rebecca stood, raising her hand. The conversation buzzed. She glanced at Eliza Dawn, whose expression warmed with support. Someone swished by, and something cool slipped into her hand. She turned her palm over to reveal a tiny bell. A backward glance met a warm smile from her friend Allie.

"A gift from my blacksmithing husband." Allie winked.

Rebecca rang it, and every eye settled on her.

"Thank you for sewing, mending, and stitching love into every seam. Thanks to your hard work, we finished ahead of schedule. We've spruced up our family's Sunday best, though it may have been handed down a time or two."

"Mine's been handed down more than that," blurted eight-year-old Edie, and the room rippled with laughter.

Rebecca smiled, cheeks warm. "Now a surprise for Ivajohn."

Eliza Dawn and Allie slipped into the kitchen. Rebecca turned to her sister. "Ivajohn, welcome to your bridal tea. We wanted to bless you and Pastor Turner as you begin your life together."

Ivajohn's cheeks flushed. "You didn't have to do this, but this explains why you preferred the last gathering at the parsonage."

"Yes, and it gave the men more reason to finish the parsonage repairs."

"I don't know how you managed it."

"Well, it helped that you didn't go with Pastor Turner and the missionaries on this trip to Indian Territory." Rebecca squeezed her sister's hand.

"I wanted the chance to settle in early." Ivajohn surveyed the room. "The parsonage is so bare without a woman's touch. It's silly, I know, but I want it to feel like *our* home when he carries me across the threshold. And I want to enjoy his company without having to worry about setting up house. Do you think Emil will like what I've done?"

"He'll love it." Rebecca fingered the crocheted lap blanket draped over Ivajohn's chair back. "Will he see it before the wedding?"

"No. He'll return the day before the wedding and spend the night at Levi's so they can finalize the ceremony notes since Emil can't officiate his own wedding." Ivajohn laughed awkwardly at the joke she'd made.

Rebecca resumed her address of the room. "All right, ladies, gifts may go on the table in front of the settee."

Packages wrapped in ribbon appeared from hidden baskets, and at Mrs. Pratt's insistence, Ivajohn rose to speak. Tall, slender, awkward as a heron, Ivajohn folded her hands tightly as her voice shook. Her words stumbled, but the sincerity in her face warmed Rebecca's heart.

"I—I—" Ivajohn's hand fluttered to her throat. "You caught me off-guard. I'm honored and humbled. And so, with my deepest thanks, I, um, thank you."

When Ivajohn finished her halting thanks, Rebecca folded her hands. "Let us pray." She bowed her head. "Lord, bless this union, the family You've knit together, and the food provided. Teach us to trust You, even when the future seems uncertain. Amen."

The blessing warmed the room as Rebecca led them to the refreshments. Muscadine strudel filled the air with its rich scent. Pies, pastries, nuts, and cheese filled the table.

"Rebecca, you've done a lovely job." Mrs. Pratt picked up a plate. "The simplicity is admirable."

"Thank you, Mrs. Pratt." Rebecca hid her amusement. Mama had taught her to accept Olivia Pratt's backhanded compliments with a heaping helping of grace. "Ivajohn values simplicity. A quality fitting a pastor's wife, don't you think? So, while we wanted to surprise her, we aimed not to overwhelm."

"Well done, dear." Mrs. Pratt added fruit and nuts to her plate. "I wish she had accepted the offer of a finer dress."

"She appreciated it." Rebecca lifted her cup. Little Edie fluttered in and danced around the two of them. "But she wanted something she could wear every day. The bonnet with fresh flowers and ribbon will dress it up nicely."

Mrs. Pratt's expression softened. "Mahala would have filled the room with vibrant blooms for such an occasion."

"I know," Rebecca whispered, the ache rising again.

Mrs. Pratt cupped Rebecca's chin. "You're the ribbon holding this family together, Rebecca."

Tears pricked the corners of Rebecca's eyes. "I want to give Ivajohn a wonderful beginning as she looks to the future."

"She'll be able to see so far into the future with my gift, you won't even have to worry, Becca." Edie grabbed two gingersnaps and dipped them into Bavarian cream. Rebecca shot her a warning glance. "That's why Ivajohn will like my gift best." Edie skipped out of the room, rejoining the parlor festivities.

A collective gasp swept through the parlor.

Allie appeared, breathless. "Rebecca, you'd better come. It's Edie."

Rebecca's heart dropped. "Oh, my."

Rebecca rushed into the parlor where she found Ivajohn holding a brass spyglass between her thumb and forefinger like a dead rodent. Hurrying across the room, she bit back a groan. She took it from Ivajohn, spinning on her heels and grasping Edie by the elbow.

She steered Edie into the now-vacant dining room, crouching to meet her eye.

"Where—" The word came out sharper than she intended.

Rebecca swallowed, easing her tone. "Where did this come from?"

Edie dropped her chin and clasped her hands in front of her.

"Is it Pa's? Did you take this from the mantle at home?"

Edie shook her head.

"Then where?" Rebecca folded Edie's hands in hers.

"I wanted Ivajohn to have something special." Edie's eyes reddened.

"Where did you find it, Edie?"

No answer.

"Go sit in the kitchen until we're done here." Rebecca placed her hands on her hips. "You'll have extra chores until you're ready to tell me."

"Am I going to miss the sleepover?"

Rebecca hesitated. She hated having to make decisions like this, but in the wake of their mother's death it seemed the responsibilities of motherhood landed squarely upon her shoulders, especially since Ivajohn traveled so frequently with the missionaries. The sisters had planned to stay at the parsonage, keeping Ivajohn company before her future mother-in-law arrived. Only Rebecca would miss it. Someone had to manage the boardinghouse. Mama would have found a way to offer grace without overlooking consequences.

"I'll speak with Dawn. If she agrees, you can stay, but you'll do chores before bed."

Edie sulked into the kitchen. Rebecca pressed her palm to her forehead, willing away the pressure building behind her eyes. When she lowered her hand, Eliza Dawn stood before her, bright-eyed and knowing.

"You know where it came from." Eliza Dawn plucked the object from Rebecca's hand.

Rebecca sighed. "The lost and found room. I wish Pa had never agreed to keep all the items left behind on the steamboats.

No one ever claims them." She sipped her tea. "Don't look at it that way, Eliza Dawn."

"You only call me Eliza Dawn when trying to rein in my curiosity." Eliza Dawn grinned, flipping the brass tube back to Rebecca. "I won't deny I'm curious. But I'll leave this one alone. There are enough mysteries in my journalism work. Like the new hotel owner, Ambrose Baas." She dropped her voice. "I suspect he came to Van Buren to do more than run a hotel. And with Justin leaving on ranch business, I want to investigate as many stories as possible."

Rebecca's brows furrowed. "I can't believe Justin and Pa are setting out now, of all times." She sighed. "The timing is ridiculous."

"They'll be back for the wedding." Eliza Dawn offered a half-smile.

"I'm glad Pa's going with him. There's no way he'd miss his oldest daughter's wedding. Sometimes Justin gets so wrapped up in horses he loses track of time." Rebecca turned the spyglass over in her hands. "A spyglass? Who would leave this behind?"

"Military scout, maybe, though it's hard to imagine one losing something so valuable." Eliza Dawn shook her head.

"Well, whatever its story, it's going straight back to the lost and found when I get home." Rebecca returned to her seat in the parlor and tucked the spyglass into her sewing basket.

"Mm-hmm." Eliza Dawn wagged a playful finger. "Mark my words, some things have a way of finding their way back out again."

Rebecca smiled dryly. "I refuse to give it another thought."

She patted the basket, leaving the spyglass and her unease in better hands than hers.

Chapter Two

Rebecca headed home, thumbing through her journal as she strolled up Main Street. Slightly larger than her hand, it fit easily into the pocket beneath her skirt. It had been her constant companion since Eliza Dawn gifted it to her last Christmas. She paused at the final few pages, running her fingers over the fishhooks anchored there. How long had it been since her last peaceful afternoon at Lee Creek? Too long. Her soul, like a parched field, ached for stillness.

"Been to the creek lately?" Allie smiled knowingly as she fell into step beside her.

"Balancing my family's needs and those of the boarders leaves little time for myself." Rebecca closed the journal, gliding her thumb across its soft leather cover before pressing it to her chest. Its worn pages offered a quiet place to ease her burdens, such a contrast to the weighty basket thumping at her elbow, a constant reminder of mounting responsibilities.

"I know how it is." Allie dabbed her forehead with a handkerchief. "Levi encouraged me to relax, but I had to check on the little ones before returning for the sleepover this evening at the parsonage."

"I appreciated his lending us the bell."

Allie giggled. "It's the only way to get the sewing circle's attention when they invite him. They find smithing projects for him, but when he arrives, they're all a-twitter, showing off their handiwork. He won them over when he filled in for me during a Christmas quilting project years ago."

"You and Levi have found a rhythm together."

"It's tricky, but we make time." Allie pointed to her uncle's store up the street. "My uncle keeps the children so we can steal a few hours for ourselves. It's a choice, intentional time together and intentional time to ourselves."

"I've half a mind to go to the creek right now." Rebecca smiled past her heavy heart. "But with Pa and Justin leaving for Missouri tomorrow, there's too much to prepare."

A wagon passed, stirring dust and a sharp whiff of manure. Rebecca wrinkled her nose and fanned the air with her journal. Digging in her basket for a handkerchief, her fingers brushed the smooth brass of the spyglass. A sudden jerk brought it to the surface, and she discreetly tucked it out of sight before Allie noticed.

"When I finish helping Pa, I'll prepare meals and tend to the few boarders we have left." Rebecca squinted against the sun.

"I hate you have to miss the sleepover."

"Me too." A twinge of regret. "But at least I'll have a bedroom to myself tonight."

"And a peacefully empty room next to yours." Allie winked. "That's rare in a house usually full to the rafters."

"Until recently." Rebecca dropped her journal into the basket, which landed awkwardly against the spyglass. "We're losing boarders left and right. The baker added rooms above his shop. Captain Cobb overnights on the steamboat to supervise repairs. Pastor Turner now lives at the parsonage. As for Dr. Ewing." She hesitated. "He's simply a fading memory."

"Is he?"

Rebecca tucked a strand of hair behind her ear. "I need to find new boarders soon."

"Surely business will pick up when the railroad comes."

"It could be years before it arrives here." A wave of relief brushed her at the change of subject. "I don't know what we'll do if things don't turn around soon."

"Could your family lose the house?"

"I don't believe so. We own the property outright, but feeding and clothing a family of nine is no small feat. And Cordelia has convinced Pa she should attend teacher college in the East." Rebecca sighed.

"Miss Hogue, may I have a moment?"

Rebecca and Allie turned as a short, stout man approached. His peppered hair, square jawline, and immaculate dark gray suit exuded a stony impression, though his accent lent a disarming charm.

"Yes?" Rebecca raised an eyebrow.

"Forgive the intrusion." He brushed the dust from his sleeve with a sharp flick. "I'm Ambrose Baas, the new hotel proprietor. I have a business proposal. I'm busy today, but we should talk tomorrow. I'll find you."

With a tip of his hat, he turned and disappeared down the street.

"Where did he come from?" Rebecca scanned the street. "Did he overhear us?"

"He seemed to appear from nowhere." Allie tilted her head. "Coincidence? Or providence?"

"He didn't allow me to tell him to speak to Pa instead." Rebecca jostled her basket, causing the spyglass to peek out. Masking a reaction, she nudged it deeper under her sewing supplies from the tea. "Something is unsettling about him."

"Strange encounter, that's for sure." Allie glanced at

Rebecca's basket. "What an interesting turn of events, Edie gifting the little telescope to Ivajohn."

"I thought it might be Pa's." Rebecca grimaced. "But it wasn't. I almost hoped it was."

Allie's eyes twinkled. "It came from the lost and found then?"

"Edie wouldn't say." Rebecca stopped. "It doesn't matter how she came by it because it's not hers to give and there must be consequences for taking it." She pressed her hand to her chest, soothing the dull ache. "It's times like this I would give anything to have Mama here. Justin and I used to talk things through. We helped each other recognize when one of us was being too hard on the younger siblings. But now he's busy with married life and starting his ranch."

"What about Cordelia and Simon?" Allie rubbed her shoulder. "They're old enough to help now."

"Cordelia is so self-involved. It's all I can do to get her to help with household chores, much less help manage a family. She fancies she'll marry well and be free of such things. And Simon—" She stared into the distance. "Well, it seems like just yesterday we caught him skipping school. I suppose I'm not used to the idea of him being grown yet."

"It's no secret he wants to be a lawman. He's grown to be a fine young man." Allie arched her eyebrows. "Responsible. Dependable. Sensible. You know he would help. All you need to do is ask."

"I don't know if I can step out of my role of protective older sister."

"You should try." Allie squeezed her shoulder. A sly grin emerged. "Now, what about this telescope?"

"I'd rather not discuss it." Rebecca continued up Main Street. "I don't have time for stray objects stirring up trouble. I'll put it in the lost and found when I get home." She rubbed her forehead. "I need a quiet afternoon at the creek. Far from problems, peculiar men, and spyglasses."

Allie snickered. "Maybe I'll swing by and brew you a pot of tea."

Before Rebecca could answer, a shout pierced the morning air.

"Miss Hogue! Miss Hogue!"

Seventeen-year-old Tommy Weston raced toward them, kicking up dust, panic etched across his face.

"Careful." Rebecca steadied herself as he grabbed her forearms. "You nearly toppled me."

"Yes, ma'am." Tommy panted. "Someone's been terrible hurt at the top of Main Street. Come quick."

Without waiting for permission, he seized her hand, almost pulling her off her feet. Rebecca clutched her skirts, heart pounding.

Allie jogged a few steps behind. "Rebecca, what should I do?"

"I don't know," Rebecca shouted as Allie drifted farther away. "Find Nicholas and send him this way."

Sam Mooney flung open the door of the mercantile, hurrying to Allie's side. "What's happening?"

"Trouble with those Drake boys." Tommy tugged Rebecca.

"I'll find Simon." Mr. Mooney waved, rushing in one direction while Allie went the other way.

Tommy slowed, and Rebecca tried to catch her breath. She barely managed to inhale when he tossed her over his shoulder like a hay bale. An angular shoulder jabbed her midsection with each galloping step, forcing air from her lungs.

"Tommy Weston!" The syllables bounced from her throat as her basket swung haphazardly. "Put me down this instant."

"No time, Miss Hogue. It's bad."

As Tommy shouldered his way through the gathered crowd,

Rebecca tried to make sense of her upside-down view of the world. She offered a faint smile and a diplomatic, "Pardon me. Excuse us. We're here to help," as they jostled a few bystanders.

Finally, Tommy planted her next to a motionless figure in the street and Rebecca dropped to her knees beside the unconscious man, gently stroking his well-whiskered cheek. Placing two fingers on the man's neck, she checked for a pulse. Elevated. She nudged his shoulder. "Mr. Fremont, can you hear me?"

A torn left pant leg revealed a disturbing injury, and she fought a wave of nausea. "Tommy, did you see what happened? Was he knocked out right away?"

"I saw the whole thing." Tommy wrung his hands. "The Drake twins tore through town on their little green-broke horse, spooking Mr. Fremont's mare, and she kicked. He was talking before I ran for you. I cut his pant leg."

Rebecca checked Mr. Fremont's head for injuries. "Did he hit his head when he fell?"

"No, ma'am. His elbows hit first. He passed out when I opened his pant leg, and he saw his injury."

"Nicholas." She searched the crowd. "Anyone see Nicholas Franks?"

No response.

"Tommy, see if you can spot him. Allie must have found him by now." She scanned the crowd again and pointed to two young boys. "Go get the barber."

The boys ran off. A man pointed toward Cane Hill. "Boys, not the barber. Get the doctor."

"The barber." Rebecca shook her head. "The doctors are out of town."

But the boys were already gone. Hopefully, Nicholas would be help enough. She wiped her brow before examining Mr. Fremont further.

Tommy and Nicholas appeared, maneuvering through the

crowd. Nicholas muscled past a few stubborn onlookers with Tommy pressing close at his back.

"Scram, or you'll have to deal with me." Nicholas's words took immediate effect, prompting a faint smile from Rebecca. He knelt beside her. "Someone causing trouble, Rebecca?'

"No. I need a strong pair of hands to assist." She patted Nicholas's broad shoulder before turning to Tommy. "I'll need splints for this leg. Can you find some wood planks?"

Tommy was already in motion.

"Let's make this quick." Nicholas rubbed his hands. "I've got saddles to make. It'd be nice if doctors would stop riding outta this town."

"I agree." Rebecca smiled at his usual impatience. Nicholas had always been there when she needed to treat injuries or illnesses in Ben Ewing's absence. Sometimes, she summoned the well-built saddler, while other times, he simply appeared.

"What do you want me to do?" Nicholas spread his hands.

She handed him a handkerchief-wrapped dogwood crochet hook. When he had gifted it to her, she hadn't known it would help mend limbs as well as socks. "Keep this in your shirt pocket. Hold him steady while I set the leg. If he wakes, he may bite the hook. Please keep it wrapped. I prefer no teeth marks on my new crochet hook."

"Not a mark." Nicholas flashed a toothy grin. "Took me forever to carve those hooks."

"I thought you'd ask Mr. Styles to make them since you're so busy." She appreciated Nicholas's light, easy banter in these situations. It put her at ease, distracting her from the fact she had never apprenticed, much less attended medical school. Though he frequently pointed out anyone could claim to be a doctor, she refrained from using the title.

"I wanted to make something special for you. But don't expect it every birthday."

"Miss Hogue! We've got the Doc!" Two boys skidded to a halt.

Doc? But how? Who?

She squinted into the sun. Her breath caught when she saw her brother, Simon, followed by the last person she ever expected to see again.

Ben Ewing.

Chapter Three

Rebecca stood, hands flat against her skirt. Her thoughts swirled like a river-valley whirlwind. A few deep breaths did little to relieve the tightness in her chest. She narrowed her eyes at Simon, who barely raised a shoulder.

Dr. Benjamin Ewing.

She swallowed hard, gesturing toward Mr. Fremont. "I imagine you remember Monroe Fremont." She fisted her hand on her hip. "He has a fracture in his left lower leg. I haven't found any other injuries, but you'll want to check."

Ben stood, unmoving, his gaze shifting from Simon to the patient. He approached Mr. Fremont, and a low groan escaped the man's lips. He halted, running a hand through his unruly curls. "I, uh—"

Tommy Weston arrived with two wooden planks. "Will this work?"

"What do you think, Dr. Ewing?" Rebecca glanced at Ben. "Do these splints meet your approval?"

Tommy noticed Ben for the first time and whistled low. "Dr.

Ewing? I hardly recognized you with all that dust and road on you."

Ben offered a barely perceptible nod, the only response as though some invisible force weighed on him. Rebecca pressed her lips together as she accepted the boards from Tommy and placed them beside Mr. Fremont.

"You okay, Miss Hogue?" Tommy wiped his mouth with the back of his hand. "Someone serve you vinegar pie?"

"I'll be fine, Tommy." She squeezed his shoulder. She hadn't expected to see Ben again. Not like this. Not when she was already stretched thin.

"Listen, Becks." Simon stepped toward her. "Sam said the Drake boys caused this. Have you seen them since it happened?"

"I don't know. We've been a little busy." She glanced at Ben. "We could use some help."

Ben stared at his shoes.

"We came as fast as we could." Simon placed his hand on Ben's shoulder. "And we'll do what we can."

We'll do what we can. Why didn't that work for her? How often did the town call upon her to do *more* than she had trained to do? Some days she wished she could simply be a boardinghouse proprietress instead of tending to the whole town.

Rebecca folded her arms. "Nicholas, are you okay with Tommy fetching a wagon from the livery? We must get Mr. Fremont home as soon as we tend his leg."

"Fine. Off you go, kid." Nicholas nodded.

Rebecca turned to Ben. "Examine him or set his leg." She held eye contact for a moment until he glanced away. "Nicholas has other work to do."

Mr. Fremont's eyes fluttered open. "Miss Hogue?"

Rebecca returned to her position kneeling beside the man, her voice calm against the *thump-thump-thump* in her chest. Perhaps he wouldn't notice her uncertainty.

"Mr. Fremont, it's your lucky day." She cut her eyes toward Ben. "You're in good hands. Dr. Ewing is here to treat you. You're his first patient since returning."

"No." Mr. Fremont's voice croaked. "I trust you, Miss Hogue."

Rebecca raised an eyebrow at Ben, who remained silent.

"You should trust Dr. Ewing." She gave him an encouraging smile, rubbing his arm. "He has much more experience than I do."

"Rebecca—"

She shot Ben a glare. How could he address her so casually after all this time, especially when he'd failed to tell her of his return?

Ben cleared his throat. "Miss Hogue, patients respond best to treatment when there's trust."

Trust. *Humph.* Heat crept up her neck. Why didn't he take charge of the patient? He knew she was underqualified? She nibbled her lower lip.

"Rebecca." Nicholas's deep voice refocused her. "I'd like to get back to my saddles. Mr. Fremont trusts *you.* I trust you. Let's get to it."

Shifting to get a better grip on the injured limb, she set her chin and squared her shoulders. She needed to execute a single, swift motion. It was a challenging task with her slight stature, tending to such a sturdy man. Taking a deep breath, she whispered a quick prayer.

Rebecca nodded at Nicholas, who pulled the fabric-wrapped hook from his pocket. She locked eyes with Mr. Freemont, maintaining her steady gaze. "This will be swift but painful. No way around it. Take a deep breath and bite the hook."

Mr. Fremont took the hook as Nicholas steadied him. His knuckles whitened as he gripped Simon's and Ben's hands. He nodded to Rebecca, inhaled deeply, and pressed his eyes shut.

A swift tug scraped bone against bone. Mr. Fremont released

a guttural moan. Rebecca's breath caught at the faint vibration. The bone wasn't aligned completely. She swallowed hard. He had trusted her, and she had fallen short.

"Mr. Fremont, it's not quite right. It needs another adjustment. Do you need a moment?"

The pleading in his soft gray eyes tugged at her heart. "Go ahead."

Rebecca exhaled. With a second, successful adjustment, the bone aligned, and Mr. Fremont's hands relaxed. His head rolled to the side. He went silent.

Rebecca sighed with relief. "Mr. Fremont?"

Ben placed two fingers on the patient's neck. "Pulse is strong. He likely passed out from pain and shock. You did well."

"A better job would have been setting it in one motion instead of two." She picked up the wood scraps.

"Setting a break like this isn't easy." Ben rubbed his hands together. "You did great."

Rebecca arranged the wood around Mr. Fremont's leg. She extended her hand to Ben. "Your belt."

Ben raised his eyebrows. "Excuse me?"

"You act as if you've never done this before." She sighed. "Your belt, so I can secure the boards."

"Aw, Rebecca, don't be like that." Nicholas chuckled, rummaging through his pouch. "I have leather scraps and buckles right here."

"I can always rely on you, Nicholas." She took a long piece of leather. "Can we cut this?"

"I don't have a knife with me." Nicholas rested his hands on his knees.

Simon withdrew a knife from the back of his waistband. "Hand it over."

"My goodness, Simon." Rebecca leaned back. "It's practically a sword."

"Nah. Just a little Arkansas toothpick." He grinned, cutting the leather.

Tommy arrived with the buckboard, stopping near the intersection. Nicholas waved at him. "Should be a canvas litter in the back. Bring it over."

"Before we move him, Dr. Ewing, how's his breathing?" Rebecca positioned the boards on either side of Mr. Fremont's leg.

"Seems fine."

Rebecca tilted her head. *Seems fine.* She pulled a pocket watch from her basket, dislodging the spyglass. It tumbled out with a clink and rolled across the ground.

Ben picked it up. "What's this?"

"Nothing." Rebecca's pulse quickened. The spyglass in his hands was worse than Allie or Eliza Dawn getting attached to it. She swapped it for the pocket watch, quickly hiding it under the fabric. Eliza Dawn's reminder about items not staying put came to mind. "Check his breathing. I want to know his respirations before we load him."

Ben flicked open the timepiece, counting breaths. "Have you been to Indian Territory? Have you ventured so far west to help patients?"

"Of course not."

"Then why the spyglass?"

"It's from the lost and found."

"So you're searching for the owner?"

"No." Rebecca fastened the first strap. "Respirations?"

"Normal." Ben snapped the watch closed and handed it back. "Why do you have it?"

"Long story." Rebecca sighed. "Short version, Edie."

Ben laughed softly, a smile lighting his face. "Edie. My goodness, she must be half-grown by now. I doubt she'll remember me."

"Not likely." Rebecca finished splinting Mr. Fremont's leg. "She was barely three when you left."

Ben grimaced.

Had she been overly harsh? Perhaps she ought to soften her approach, select her words more thoughtfully. She sighed, more exasperated with herself than with him. Hadn't she forgiven him? Hadn't she laid this at the Lord's feet? Or had she only said the words?

"How old is she now? Seven? Eight?" Ben rubbed the back of his neck.

"She turned eight a few months ago." Rebecca stood, dusting off her skirt. "Let's focus on the task at hand."

She pressed her eyes shut. After a moment, she fixed her gaze on Ben. "I apologize. I've been short with you, perhaps unfairly so."

"No." His gaze stayed on his shoes. "No less than I deserve."

"Nicholas, let's take Mr. Fremont home." She stepped aside as Simon and Nicholas loaded the patient into the wagon.

"I'll ride the mare for him." Tommy approached Mr. Fremont's horse with a gentle shushing. "She's a fine horse, just got spooked."

Rebecca faced Simon. "I imagine you'd rather walk home, Simon, since it's not far." Then she turned to Ben. "We can save some wear on your shoes. Where are you staying?"

"Justin didn't tell you?" Ben rubbed the back of his neck. "He settled me in my old room at Hogue House."

Chapter Four

"Sorry. I thought Justin told you." Ben's throat tightened as he repeatedly brushed his thumb over his fingertips.

"Must've slipped his mind." Rebecca avoided his gaze, gripping the edge of the wagon bed. Simon offered his hand, but she brushed it aside and hoisted herself up. She climbed to the front and settled next to Mr. Fremont.

"I've done a lot of walking today." Simon stretched. "How about I join you two for the ride?"

Ben waited as Simon climbed in and sat across from Rebecca. A dull ache pulsed in Ben's chest as he settled beside Simon.

Rebecca's hand rested on Mr. Fremont's chest, her other clutching a pocket watch. After studying it, she snapped it shut and adjusted his shirt collar, briefly meeting Ben's gaze.

A sinking sensation settled in his gut. He stared into the distance. After three years of her support during medical situations, why wouldn't she expect him to step up? But he couldn't. Not after California.

The buckboard hit a rut, jostling them. Mr. Fremont moaned, and Nicholas mumbled an apology. Rebecca slid her hand along the patient's arm, gently squeezing his elbow.

"Hold tight, Mr. Fremont." Her voice warmed Ben's heart, though it wasn't meant to comfort him. "You'll be home soon enough."

Home.

The word echoed in Ben's mind. He journeyed almost eighteen hundred miles, chasing the memory of home. Van Buren, Hogue House, Rebecca's side. When would he find the peace he craved?

Tommy slowed, keeping Mr. Fremont's mare steady beside the wagon. "Almost there. We'll turn onto Chestnut, then a short stretch to Moore."

"Good of you to bring Mr. Fremont's mare." Ben nodded at the gray horse.

"Ah, it's nothing." Tommy stroked the mare's neck. "She's a good one. Not her fault she spooked. Those new Drake boys are a handful. Don't see their pa much."

Rebecca tucked the pocket watch away. "Town is different lately with all these newcomers."

Ben inhaled slowly, trying to ease the dull ache threading through his muscles. Arkansas's wild reputation rivaled the West. He never understood why families uprooted themselves to live so far from protection. Why move to the edge of civilization? Didn't they know the risks?

The West was a hard place for grown men. Harder still for children. Illness, injury, and violence could devastate a family. A fifteen-year-old boy flashed through his memory. First running, then crumpling.

Ben's hands quivered at the memory of blood staining his palms. The boy's last rattling breaths. He rubbed his hands together. The blood had long since faded. But his hands would never be clean.

He closed his eyes, focusing on the wagon's sway. Just one more stop. Then he could retreat to Hogue House. His old room.

Safety.

Ben opened his eyes. Scattered structures dotted the horizon. Soon, the buckboard halted in front of a small white house. A sagging porch separated the house from the yard by a single step. Ben rubbed his knees.

Rebecca stood and moved to the back of the wagon. She turned toward him, her lips pressed tight. "Aren't you coming?"

"Mr. Fremont voiced his discomfort with me." Ben rubbed the back of his neck. "I wouldn't want to overstep."

Rebecca exhaled, her eyes closing. "You could help me down from the wagon since I *am* going inside. I'd think you would want to settle him, since you—"

Color flushed her cheeks. She turned away. Simon jumped from the wagon and offered his hand. She waved it away, tucked her skirt beneath her, and hopped down.

"I've got it." She brushed a strand of hair from her face. "Are you coming, Simon?"

"No. I'll stay to help settle Missus in a stall."

Tommy unhitched the mare while Nicholas and Ben got out of the wagon.

"What do you plan to do?" Ben rubbed his hands together. "Other than making him comfortable?"

"I'll elevate his leg until I can get a fracture box. Maybe folded blankets and a pillow will suffice." Rebecca tilted her head. "Isn't that what you'd do?"

Ben massaged his hands, easing the stiffness. Would she notice the tremor?

"I, uh—" He met her eyes. "If you have lumber, I can make one. Then you'll have it on hand whenever you need it."

"I don't want one on hand. I never intended to need one."

Ben flinched. Rebecca knew how to make her point, even if it lay between the lines.

"Will you get supplies from a doctor in town? I've heard

there are two. Maybe one of them can check on Mr. Fremont soon."

"We'll discuss logistics later. I need to get Mr. Fremont settled."

Nicholas nodded, prompting Tommy to dart into the wagon. Together, they lifted the stretcher. Mr. Fremont groaned as Tommy cautiously descended, cradling the head of the stretcher. They followed Rebecca into the house.

Ben lingered near the wagon, staring at his trembling hands. He massaged them, then shook them lightly. Sweat trickled down his back. He took a long breath, leaning against a nearby tree and patting his knees.

"Care to help with the mare?" Simon's voice startled him.

Ben followed him to the barn. Uplifted by its shade, Ben inhaled its warm, earthy scent.

Simon loosened the cinches, lifted the saddle, and nodded to the nearest stall. "Mind leading her in?"

Ben led the mare into a stall, scratching her behind the ears. She fluttered her lips and flicked her tail before softly nuzzling his shoulder. He slipped out, grabbed oats, and returned, offering the treat. Her soft lips brushed his palm.

"Not sure what those boys did to upset her." Simon joined him with a water bucket and a brush. "She's as sweet as summer hay."

Ben rested his forehead against hers. "Yes, she is."

"Doc, you okay?" Simon poured the water into the trough.

Ben blinked. "Hmmm?"

"Your hands. I noticed it when you asked Rebecca about Mr. Fremont's treatment, and she practically dared you to go inside." Simon picked up the brush.

Ben swallowed. "I'd hoped it wouldn't be noticeable."

"I'm probably the only one who noticed, maybe Nicholas saw." Simon shifted to the other side of the mare. "Rebecca is too taken aback by your presence, and Tommy, well, he's young enough to be oblivious. What happened? You get hurt in California?"

Ben hesitated. How could he answer? His body had survived. His soul hadn't. But how could he explain a wound no one could see? How could he heal a fracture a medical examination would never reveal?

"I need a respite. That's all." He shoved his hands deeper into his pockets. "California was difficult. I want to leave it behind. Could we keep this between us?"

"Of course, Doc." Simon slapped the brush against his palm. "I've faced my own troubles since you've been gone. I'm here if you want to talk."

"I'll keep it in mind."

"Justin mentioned you don't want to practice medicine anymore."

"It's true. I'm angling for a fresh start."

"I'm heading inside to see if the others need help." Simon opened the barn door. "You're welcome to join me."

"I'll stay by the wagon."

Ben followed him out. He paced beside the wagon, eyes straying toward the porch.

Five years.

Five long years since he left Van Buren.

Would anyone welcome him back? Would they all resent him?

Especially her.

He'd disappointed Rebecca once. Would she forgive him again? Or would she be newly disappointed when she learned of his plans to leave medicine?

"Lord, I don't even know what to say anymore." His voice rasped as he bowed. It had been ages since he last prayed. Longer since he believed it made a difference. Catching sight of the spyglass in Rebecca's basket, he reached for it, then pulled back.

Sweat beaded down his back. He crossed the yard, every step heavier than the last. At the door, he hesitated.

Inside, Rebecca waved him over. "Dr. Ewing, nice of you to join us."

"Thought I'd help Simon." He hedged.

"Come in. You're welcome to stay." Rebecca gestured. "I've asked Mrs. Fremont to give him willow bark tea until Dr. Dibrell or Dr. Pernot return. We've elevated his leg with quilts until a fracture box is available. Any other suggestions?"

Mrs. Fremont's gray eyes fixed on him.

"Um." Ben licked his lips. "Did you mention dietary needs?"

Rebecca smiled faintly. "Why don't you tell her?"

"Fluids and prunes."

Rebecca angled her chin at him before turning to Mrs. Fremont. "Have him drink plenty of fluids, especially water." She lowered her voice. "And prunes for regularity. If he doesn't like them, chop them up with apples." Rebecca redirected her attention to Ben. "Anything else?"

He shifted. "Exercise?"

"Of course. I'll demonstrate exercises for his good limbs."

"I'm going to …" Ben backed toward the door, heart hammering.

Slipping outside, he leaned against the front door. He rubbed his face, exhaling a trembling breath. His hands would not stop shaking.

Chapter Five

Rebecca pressed her palms against the dining room table, her gaze locked on Justin. "What were you thinking? Inviting him to stay here?"

"Rebecca, you didn't see him." He leaned back, arms crossed, as he glanced at Simon before meeting her eyes. "He looked awful when Dawn and I saw him in California."

"I can't believe you didn't tell me when you returned." Her pulse quickened as she planted her hands on her hips. "And you asked Dawn to hide it from me. Why?"

"I never imagined he'd return. Honestly, I'm surprised he survived California." Justin lowered his eyes. "He asked me not to say anything. He didn't want you to worry."

"Did you mention I've worried every day since he left?" She sank into a chair.

"He didn't want to hurt you more than he already had." Justin grasped her hand. "If you knew we'd seen him and he had no intention of coming home, it would've opened an old wound. It seemed wiser to stay silent and allow you to continue your life as usual."

"Life as usual." Rebecca exhaled sharply. "Except now I

couldn't find 'usual' if it were painted on the back of my hand." She faced Simon. "And you knew?"

"I didn't know about California. Honest, Becks." Simon leaned near, tapping the table. "I didn't know anything until a few days ago when Justin asked my thoughts on him staying here."

"Don't call me Becks." She gritted her teeth. "So, you had this planned before your conversation with Simon?" Rebecca glared at Justin, heat edging her neck.

Justin pulled back, studying his hands.

She faced Simon. "But if you had known, would you have gone along with Justin?"

"I voiced my concerns." Simon drummed his fingers. "But I agree with Justin. Ma would have welcomed Ben. She'd have ministered to him, and we should do likewise. He needs help getting back on his feet."

Rebecca folded her arms. "What do you mean he needs help getting back on his feet?"

"I can't go into details." Justin leaned closer, rubbing his knees. "I've invited him to stay in his old room with Mr. Perry, at no cost, for as long as he needs. I know things will be a little tight, but it's what Ma would do. He's welcome to help around here, or not. It's his choice. He needs time."

A little tight? Justin had no idea, and she wasn't about to tell him since he couldn't do anything about it. He struggled enough to get his horse ranch going.

"Time for what?"

"He needs time." Simon spread his hands on the table. "That's all."

"You're not making this easy." Rebecca sighed, going to the window. The golden twilight spilled across the landscape. Her fingers ghosted across the glass, chasing the light without catching it. "I don't like being in the dark. Justin, I know you were trying to help a friend, and I know you're the oldest, but you don't run the boardinghouse anymore. Not since you and Dawn moved out. You have to at least run these things by me." She turned to face him. "Ivajohn does. She occasionally invites missionaries to stay here, but she asks me first. You two are living your own lives, I get that. But if I must hold down the house, I need to know what's going on."

Justin's eyes stayed fixed on her for a long moment. Was he truly hearing her? Or thinking about his trip? She couldn't tell.

He folded his hands, tapping his thumbs together. "I know."

"Do you? It's unfair to leave me in the dark." She slumped against the wall. "I'm trying to manage a family and a business, constantly handling medical needs I'm underqualified for. And now this."

"I know. I'm sorry." Justin drew near, wrapping his arms around her. She resisted at first, but then leaned into his chest.

"Justin."

"Hmm?"

"Nothing about this day has been usual." She sighed as he rubbed her shoulders. "A bridal tea without Mama. Edie's unexpected gift. Mr. Fremont's mishap. And him. What am I supposed to do?"

"Do you recall when we took in Dawn?" Justin tilted her chin. "When Pa challenged the decision?"

"No."

"You reminded us Ma would have welcomed and ministered to her." He gently pinched her chin. "So we offered her a haven. We should extend the same support to Ben. Even if it's complicated."

"Fine." She leaned her head against his chest with a thud.

"Are we done arguing?" Simon knocked on the table.

Rebecca pulled away and, glancing at Simon, rolled her eyes. "We were never arguing."

"Could've fooled me." Simon rose, patting his belly. "I'm gonna grab a leftover biscuit."

"I'll get it. I've already straightened everything."

She skirted the kitchen table. A glimmer of brass peeked from the basket she had left there. Pausing, she pushed it back and handed Simon the plate of biscuits. She took a towel and a knife from a drawer, then grabbed the jelly jar and butter dish.

"Butter, no jelly." Simon settled at the table.

Rebecca's lips pressed into a line as she returned the jelly jar to the counter.

"I want jelly." Justin waved in a circular motion.

"I'm heading to the oak grove." She sighed. Lately, her nerves frayed quicker than usual. Too many plates spinning, too few hands to help. She grabbed the jar and carried the items to the table. "Please tidy up when you're finished. I'd like time to read before bed."

"Yes, ma'am." Her brothers grinned as they scrambled for the fixings.

Her mouth quirked. They were trying, in their own well-meaning way.

She closed the back door, inhaling deeply as she stretched. The sweltering September heat faded as the sun lowered, replaced by a light coolness brushing against her skin. The scent of earth and wood settled around her, soft and steady, like a quilt laid over tired shoulders.

A dusky grey-green light enveloped the oak grove beyond the yard. Flickers of light lured her nearer. Lifting her skirt, she tiptoed toward the cluster of trees. A handful of fireflies flitted, pairing two by two until a lone firefly remained. It beckoned to her.

And she followed.

~

AMBROSE BAAS CROUCHED in the shadows, observing the Hogue property. The final piece of his plan set in place. Bradley

House would be his by week's end, and Caine would see to the eviction. Contracts for properties between Bradley House and Hogue House were already signed. Yet an unfamiliar tightness lingered in his chest when he thought of the house and Rebecca.

A creak broke the hush. The boardinghouse's back door. Baas stepped deeper into the shade of a towering tree, disappearing into its darkness. The faint moonlight illuminated Rebecca Hogue's delicate features. He dragged a hand along his jaw, licking his lips as the breeze played with her hair.

The young proprietress was unlikely to yield. Women were always the hardest to corner in business. Nevertheless, he had a history of convincing even the most discerning women to part with their properties. This situation was different.

Hogue House was indeed a gem. But Rebecca Hogue? She was the darling of Van Buren. The real prize.

Chapter Six

Ben paused at the sound of murmuring voices as he descended the kitchen stairs. Justin's mellow baritone and Simon's smooth bass drifted up, but where was Rebecca?

He edged down the steps, surveying the room as he neared. Perhaps accepting Justin's offer to stay hadn't been the best idea. He and Rebecca were bound to cross paths. Maybe he could keep out of her way if he stayed busy with outdoor chores or found new work. But if his absence piqued her curiosity, what would he say?

It didn't matter. He could no longer treat patients, not after what he had done.

With one more peek, he took a deep breath and joined the brothers in the kitchen. "Justin, could I have a moment?"

"I'm heading home, but I can spare a few minutes." Justin raised the plate of biscuits. "Need a snack?"

"No, thank you." Ben sat near Rebecca's basket.

Justin handed the plate to Simon as he cleared the table. "What can I do for you, Doc?"

"I'd like to discuss my lodging." Ben picked up the telescope from the basket and fiddled with it.

"No can do." Justin patted Ben's back. "It's all settled. We spoke to Rebecca."

"She seems ill at ease with my presence here." He put the telescope back in the basket. "I don't want to impose."

"I'll admit, we ought to have involved Rebecca sooner." Justin swept crumbs off the table into his hand. "Given her time to adjust to the idea. That's on us."

"That's on you." Simon grabbed the butter and jelly. "The first I heard of it was three days ago."

"All right. That's on me." He popped Simon with the towel. "But it'll work out."

"Easy for you to say." Simon bit his lip. "You're leaving tomorrow. We're the ones who'll have to handle the fallout." He wagged his finger between himself and Ben.

"Maybe I should make other accommodations." Ben pressed his thumb to his nose. "Give her some space and not disrupt her routine."

"Nonsense. Your room at the end of the hall is distant enough." Justin grabbed his hat from the hook by the back door. "C'mon. Let's head to the stable. Simon can finish Pa's chores, and you can help."

Ben flexed his hands. Sleep did come easier and proved less fitful after physical activity, but was he ready to face Mr. Hogue again? He kneaded his shoulder, tension prickling beneath his skin. "Does Mr. Hogue know I'm here?"

"Pa was the first to know." Justin scratched his stubbly chin. "Part of me hoped he'd tell Rebecca. We're still working on our communication."

Ben followed the brothers out. The two-story house cast a long shadow as the sun dipped lower behind it.

"What time is it?" Ben rolled up his sleeves as they crossed the yard.

"Close to eight." Simon scanned the sky. "Where's your timepiece, Doc?"

"I misplaced it." Ben flicked his thumb nervously across his fingers. Admitting he'd sold it was unthinkable. "I forgot how warm the evenings are here. I've grown accustomed to it cooling off quickly at the end of a day."

"Might not get relief for a while around here." Simon held the stable door open.

Ollie straightened hay bales as Mr. Hogue stepped out of the tack closet.

"What are you boys doing out here?" Mr. Hogue lifted his hat and wiped his brow.

"Better call it a night, Pa. I'll collect you bright and early." Justin wrapped his arm around Ollie's neck, rubbing his knuckles over the teen's head. "See ya later, little brother."

Ollie's face twisted in annoyance. "Not if I see you first."

"Right." Justin patted Ollie on the back before leaving.

"You should go to bed, too, squirt. Ben and I will finish here." Simon took the bucket from Pa and ruffled Ollie's hair.

"Why can't y'all keep your hands to yourselves?" Ollie dragged his fingers through his hair. "I'll let it slide since you're doing my chores."

"Sleep tight." Simon grinned.

Clayburn Hogue paused in front of Ben. "Welcome home, son. Don't linger out here too long. Never underestimate the power of a good night's sleep."

Ben nodded. "Thank you, Mr. Hogue."

"Night, Doc." Ollie offered a firm handshake.

"I'll start seeking work tomorrow." Ben followed Simon to the well, and they filled the buckets.

"No rush, Doc." Simon held the stable door open. "It's okay to relax a bit."

"I appreciate it." Ben raised the bucket. "Which stall?"

"The one at the end." Simon pointed. "Rebecca's horse, Truly."

"Lovely name." Ben stepped inside and poured water into the trough. "Beautiful silvery-cream mare."

"I reckon Rebecca has had Truly three or four years now."

He rubbed Truly's belly. Her earthy, sweet scent soothed his senses. "Is Rebecca ever called to help with medical issues outside of town? When I lived here before, she didn't have a horse."

"Mr. Fremont's is about as far as I've known her to go." Simon swapped buckets with Ben. "What makes you ask?"

"Did you see the spyglass fall from her basket today?"

"Mm. Noticed it."

"Have you seen it before?" Ben poured the second bucket, and Truly nudged him aside.

"Can't say as I have."

"When I saw it, I feared she practiced medicine in outlying communities." Ben fastened the stall door behind him. "Or even worse, in Indian Territory."

"Doc, I was fifteen when you left and didn't fully grasp the situation. I don't understand much about how Rebecca came to do what she does." Simon peeked over the door of the seal-brown stallion's stall. "But she's never treated a patient without Nicholas Franks by her side. He's more impatient than anyone I've met, always eager to return to his saddlery. Yet, he never leaves her. It's strange."

"Strange?"

"For a while, I thought he had cottoned to her. What man sacrifices hours of work to follow a woman tending to others' injuries and ailments?" Simon scratched his head. "Yet he's never attempted to pursue her. Doesn't set foot in our home except to bring a patient. But he never allows her to go beyond town unless it's for the Snow family. She's unstoppable if they need her. They're family."

So Nicholas had honored his promise. When Ben requested the saddler watch over Rebecca before he left, he wasn't confident he had chosen the right person. Even then, Nicholas was single-minded about his craft. Did this fulfilled commitment strengthen the bond between Nicholas and Rebecca? They shared a playful shorthand, a rapport transcending mere professionalism. It was a glaring reminder of one simple truth. He had kept his distance. Nicholas had not.

How had Nicholas become her anchor, while he'd drifted with the current?

Because you let go, a whisper accused.

"Do you think ..." Ben swallowed. "Do you think Rebecca has feelings for him?"

"My sister's a hard read." Simon turned the buckets upside down. "If she had feelings for someone, you'd never know it. Listen, Doc, take a break. There's not much left to do unless you want to make a fracture box."

"Rebecca didn't seem keen on the idea, but it might be the best option. Never know when doctors might be delayed." Ben stretched. "Where can I find supplies?"

"Should be lumber and tools in the old forge. I'll sand it in the morning."

Ben stroked his stubbled jaw. "Do you know where Rebecca is?"

"She took a walk in the oak grove out back." Simon hoisted a bale of hay from the corner. "It's one luxury she occasionally allows herself."

Ben nodded. "I can't thank you enough for today."

"Aw, it was nothing." Simon waved him off.

Ben made quick work of the fracture box and then stepped into the humid evening air, rubbing the knotted muscles in his shoulder. Then he strode toward the back of the house. As he rounded the corner, he froze.

A figure stood near the grove. Stocky, motionless, half-hidden behind the oak.

Ben blinked.

Gone.

His chest constricted.

Thump. Thump. Thump.

He pressed his hand to his chest, willing himself to remain calm.

Don't do this, Ben. Don't conjure ghosts from the West.

Chapter Seven

Rebecca wandered through the trees, drawn to the lone firefly hovering near a gnarled old oak. Flickering ever brighter, it beckoned her, and she followed its warm glow as it flitted among the branches. Her spirits lifted, and a sense of calm washed over her. The fresh air filled her lungs as she stepped into a clearing awash in the muted light of the half-moon.

The little firefly danced around her before drifting to a nearby log. Rebecca took a seat, soaking in the tranquil beauty around her. Dappled light filtered through the leaves as crickets played their rhythmic tune. She shut her eyes, breathing in the sweet, lingering aroma of blackberries.

A light touch on her hand drew her attention. The firefly rested there. "Are you a still, small voice, my little friend? A reminder to seek light in the darkness? Why tonight?"

Leaves rustled behind her, and the firefly darted into the night sky. She whirled, a sharp breath catching in her throat. A shadow loomed beyond the pools of light.

"Didn't mean to startle you."

"Ben." Her voice trembled as her heart beat a new rhythm.

"I thought I saw—" He moved closer. "I wanted to check on you. Simon said you came out some time ago."

"I wanted some solitude." She hugged herself, rubbing her arms. "It's been a while since I've visited Lee Creek or gone on a ramble."

"I remember how you loved to connect with nature." Ben smiled.

"You didn't have to worry about me. Justin and Simon mentioned you needed to rest. You should have gone to bed."

"I owe you an apology."

An apology? It was a bit late. Where would he even begin? Had he kept a mental checklist of his wrongdoings like she had? Her jaw tightened. Perhaps she should dedicate journal entries to the intricacies of forgiving Benjamin Ewing.

"For what?"

"I should have written you about my return instead of relying on Justin to tell you." He toed the dirt. "It didn't cross my mind he'd move after he married. I meant my letter to be family news."

"Ah, I see." Rebecca pressed her lips together. Though it made sense, it seemed like an easy out. Shouldn't their past connection warrant a personal letter? "Justin and Simon weren't clear about your plans. Care to share?"

He cleared his throat. "I'm a little fuzzy myself."

"You should consider registering with the court clerk."

"Registering?"

"It's not required, but it's a good way to announce your intent to resume your medical practice. The clerk will publish it in the newspaper, free of charge." She rubbed her knees. "Another doctor in the community would be extremely beneficial."

"Are you registered?"

"I'm not a qualified doctor, am I?" She smiled, though her

throat tightened. "However, the whole of Van Buren chooses to ignore that fact because of you."

Ben grimaced. "Rebecca, it wasn't my intention—"

"I know." Her tone softened. "Still, your presence might ease my burdens."

"I planned to step back from medicine for a while." Ben sat at the other end of the log.

"Are you sure?" She cast a sidelong glance. "You might want to consider placing an ad to drum up business."

"I understand the local doctors are out of town. I don't want to seem like I'm trying to steal patients while they're away."

"Of course. When you're ready, check with Conrad Hildesheim. He's added rooms above the bakery." She paused, gauging his reaction. "He might rent space for an office."

"I promise I won't be in the way." Ben shifted uneasily. "If you prefer, I can move to the bunkhouse."

"Ben, I wasn't trying to get rid of you." Rebecca frowned. "I thought some suggestions might be helpful."

"Well, I'm not returning to medicine. Not soon, anyway." He rubbed his shoulder. "Though I made a fracture box at Simon's request. I hope you don't mind."

"Likely for the best. It's not unusual for the doctors to be delayed."

"I noticed the spyglass sitting in your basket." Ben cleared his throat. "Tell me about it."

"Not much to say. Edie grabbed it from the lost and found because she wanted a gift to present at the bridal tea. Simple as that."

"Ah, right." He rubbed his face wearily. "You should find the owner. It's a vital piece of equipment."

"We don't know how long it's been there." She kneaded her earlobe. "The owner's likely long gone. I don't have time to deal with it. Back it goes into the lost and found."

"I'll take up the search."

"That's nonsense. It's likely been here too long."

"Is it?" He arched an eyebrow. "You want me to resume my practice, but how can I gain patients if they think of me like Mr. Fremont? Maybe the spyglass could help me reconnect."

"Perhaps."

His mouth quirked. "So, you won't send the poor little spyglass to its room? Someone might need it someday."

She sighed. "Keep it to your end of the hall. Both of you can stay, the spyglass and its guardian."

Ben grew quiet, eyes distant. "It's strange being back in my old room. So much has changed. I used to know each of you so well. Now it's like meeting strangers with familiar faces. Catch me up?"

Rebecca hesitated. How much should she offer? A small kindness might remind them both where they came from.

"Justin, steady as ever. Oldest, most predictable, though ranch life keeps him out of touch with the day-to-day operations here."

Ben smiled faintly. "Then Ivajohn?"

"She continues to be involved in missionary journeys, but she stayed behind this trip. She's preparing the parsonage for married life."

He held her gaze a long moment. "And you?"

Rebecca smoothed her skirt as if the fabric might shield her. "Then me." She cleared her throat. "After me, there's Cordelia, forever dripping in drama and filled with mostly good intentions. Simon. Well, Simon envisions himself Champion of Van Buren. I'm not sure he's wrong. Wants to be a lawman. But I don't know if I'm ready for him to be so grown."

"A dangerous calling."

"He's twenty-one. I know he'll go his own direction eventually." Rebecca sighed. "Martie's sharp as ever, though her taste in boys is questionable. She fancies Tommy Weston."

"Tommy?" Smile lines pulled at the corners of his eyes. "'Didn't recognize you with all that road on you' Tommy?"

"Mm-hmm." She giggled.

His gaze lingered. "It's good to hear your laugh."

Her heart fluttered and she drew her chin in, stiffening. "Then the twins, Ollie and Nellie. Fourteen. Not quite as inseparable as they once were." She paused. "And finally, Edie. Newly eight. Tree climber. Gifter of mysterious spyglasses."

Ben gave a soft chuckle. "Thank you."

"For what?" Rebecca tilted her head.

"For reminding me what home sounds like."

She studied him. Was this how forgiveness entered the world? Quietly. Side by side with the one who had fractured her trust. Unsure how to piece things back together.

Ben stood, stepping into the dim light. Hadn't he been taller? With hunched shoulders, soul-weary green eyes, hollow cheeks, and stubbled features, the figure before her resembled more a shadow of the man than the man himself. The ache in her chest surprised her. It was easier when he stayed a memory.

Ben offered his hand. "Shall I escort you back?"

"Oh, no. I'll stay a bit longer."

"It's getting late. You ought to come inside." His gaze swept the tree line behind her. "I don't even have a cane to defend myself against wild animals. I'd feel safer if you accompanied me. There's safety in numbers."

Rebecca smiled, resting her hand lightly in his. His fingers enveloped hers in a tender caress, and a subtle warmth spread through her chest. His nearness stirred something painfully familiar, something she had long since laid to rest. As she stood, she stumbled and brushed against him. Her breath hitched, and she drew back.

Grasping her skirt, she trudged forward. "Perhaps it *would* be wise to head back."

Chapter Eight

Darkness surrounded Ben, underbrush lashing his legs. The need to hurry battled against the need for silence. In the clearing, the dim red sun disappeared on the horizon.

Plain Trousers. Fiery hair. Gold nugget. Sean.

Though Ben's feet moved forward, he drifted further away. A dark form, Wellington hat, blue steel, inched closer to Sean. A thunderous crack shattered the silence. His silhouette jolted.

In an instant, Ben caught the boy. The red sun bled into Sean's shirt, seeping into the earth as his life diminished. A scream echoed inside Ben, yet it wasn't his own.

The dark form advanced, casting a long shadow. Three figures reflected in blue steel. Sean's brothers and sister.

Red fury. Blue steel. Ben's vision blurred. He lunged at the dark form. Twisted shadows merged as they struggled for the revolver. Colt Dragoon. Grappling. Clawing. Blue steel. Red palm. Ben rolled and fired.

He jolted awake. Sweat soaked his skin, and his hands trembled. He squeezed his eyes shut and forced himself to steady his breathing. As the images of California dissolved, he opened his eyes to his new room.

The bed opposite his was unmade, the pillow askew. An oak dresser stood against the wall. He sat up, rubbing his face, the weight of the dream lingering. California come to life again.

A dappled sunlight filtered through the window, and he fell back with a groan.

"What time is it?" he muttered, breath uneven.

He studied the ceiling. How long since he'd enjoyed a solid roof over his head? Wiping sleep from his eyes, he sat up and stretched. He glanced around the room, his eyes landing on the bedside table. The spyglass sat there, its presence commanding his attention.

He picked it up, searching for anything distinctive. An engraving on the barrel read *H.v.Laun fecit Amsterd.*

He tugged at the ends, but the device refused to extend. When fully extended, it should measure about four inches, six if a hidden third section was included. Thumbing the eyepiece shutter open, he raised the instrument and peered through the lens. Dark. He examined the wider end. Ah, the lens cap. He ran his finger over the letters *MET* engraved on the cap. After removing it, he raised the telescope to his eye again. Still dark.

He rubbed his fingers along the polished barrel, regret gnawing at him. What he wouldn't give to have his telescope back. Telescope, pocket watch, horse, medical bag. What the gold rush hadn't taken, he'd given up or lost. Including Rebecca.

He sighed. When Rebecca first saw him, her shock swiftly turned to disdain. If only he had known how to share of his return. But he feared she would have told him not to come, and she had every right to do so.

Ben shook his head, half-smiling. Despite her attempt to relinquish Mr. Fremont's care, she had managed the situation with dignity and grace. He had always admired her quick mastery over her emotions and ability to act when necessary.

Ben rose, straightening the blanket on his bed, and went to the window. Warm sunlight brushed the tops of the oak trees, hinting at a coming transformation. He shut his eyes, recalling the scene in the grove. The graceful curve of Rebecca's neck, the honeyed strands framing her face, her striking blue eyes. She was even more breathtaking than he remembered. His hand instinctively reached for hers. Warmth radiated from his fingertips through his arm and beyond, igniting every cell of his being with the memory of her touch. What had compelled him to extend his hand? Suddenly, a haunting shadow from the past clouded the enchantment of the grove.

Thunk. Ben's eyes snapped open, quickly scanning the area around the window.

"Apologies, Dr. Ewing," Ollie called from below. Nellie and Edie hurried by, stopping to wave before they all sprinted away.

Ben raked his fingers through his hair, surveying the room. No mirror. He released a weary breath. The trunk at the foot of Coleman Perry's bed was open. He peeked inside. Empty.

Was it laundry day? Pulling on suspenders, he straightened his wrinkled shirt and grabbed the spyglass before stepping into the hall.

As Ben shuffled down the stairs, the back door burst open. Edie rushed in like a whirlwind, stopping when she spotted him.

"Oh, hi." Her wild blond hair swayed in all directions even after she had stopped.

"Hello. Edie? Am I correct?"

"That's me." She grinned, showing gaps on either side of her front teeth.

"I see you've lost a couple of teeth recently."

"Only I don't mind 'cause big teeth are coming in. That means I'll be grown up soon, and folks will have to take me serious." She scrunched her freckled nose.

"Naturally." Ben descended the last few steps. "What are you up to today?"

"I'm gettin' a drink right now 'cause it's so hot today." She wiped her forearm across her mouth. "You slept all day. I thought we should wake you up to eat, but Becca said to let you sleep. She never lets me sleep. I gotta get up and do chores. Then I gotta do more chores. And then I gotta do more chores. But after that, I get to play 'cause it's Saturday. Are you hungry?"

Ben's stomach grumbled at the mention of food, causing Edie's eyes to widen.

"See there? I was right." The little girl placed her hands on her hips. "Becca never listens to me 'cause she thinks I'm just a kid, but I know things."

"I'm sure you do."

She grabbed Ben by the hand, dragging him to the kitchen table. After pulling out a chair, she shoved him into it. "You sit right here. I know where everything is. We gotta tidy up after 'cause nothing makes Becca more fustrated than a messy kitchen."

"You mean frustrated."

"No, sir. I meant *fuss*-trated." Edie stretched to the back of the counter, her feet scarcely touching the floor. "You ain't never seen no one fuss like her over a dirty kitchen. Oh, by the way, don't tell her I said 'ain't.' She don't like it. But that's what all the boys at school say, and I'd rather play with them than those prissy ol' girls. I like to climb trees, too, but that's on Becca's 'Can't Do' list. Somethin' about it's not proper for girls. I don't know why boys get to have all the fun. Don't seem fair."

Edie set the plate in front of Ben and took a full-body breath. "Oh, you'll need a fork. And it's best to get a napkin. Don't leave any crumbs, okay?"

"Yes, ma'am." Ben grinned. He took the spyglass from his pocket and placed it on the table, waiting for Edie's reaction.

She pulled a fork from one drawer and a cloth square from

another. Pivoting on her heels, she glanced at the table, halted, and gasped in astonishment.

"What's that?" She pointed.

"I was hoping you might tell me." He gestured to the seat next to him. "It's lovely, isn't it?"

"And it's useful." Edie's voice softened, along with her energy.

"What do you know about telescopes?"

"Oh, I know you can see a long way with a spyglass, even if you ain't spying." She pointed at Ben's plate. "I'd eat that chicken first. It's the best. I wanted to give it to Ivajohn for her upcoming nuptials. The spyglass, not the chicken."

"It's a very thoughtful gift." Ben picked up the chicken leg and took a bite, the salty crunch causing his stomach to growl again.

"It was the thoughtful-est." Edie pulled her fingernail through her hair, separating the strands. "Ivajohn needs a good telescope because she's going on a long journey."

Ben covered his mouth with the napkin. "For her missionary work with the pastor?"

"Yes. They carry missionaries into Indian Territory and bring some back. Sometimes they stay awhile." Edie picked at the hem of her dress. "But they're starting a whole new journey. It's gonna last the rest of their lives. I don't know if I'll ever see her again." She lowered her head, took a deep breath, and squared her shoulders. She eyed the telescope, then him. "I reckon there's no better time for a good telescope than a journey like that. Seems like it'd be absolutely necessary."

"Unquestionably." He set down the chicken leg, wiped his hands with the napkin, and picked up the telescope. "You must have had quite the time saving for this. Did you do odd jobs? Help some church ladies with their laundry or something like that?"

"No, sir." Edie's head dipped low as she folded her hands in her lap. "I expect that's why Becca was so upset with me at the party." Her eyes popped up. "They call it a tea, but it's a party. They don't want it to sound like we're having too much fun."

"Hmm." Ben rubbed his chin. "If you didn't save up for it, how did you come by it?"

"Ollie." She sighed heavily. "He didn't give it to me. I saw him putting it in the lost and found, and the moment I saw it, I knew Ivajohn had to have it." Her shoulders drooped. "But now she doesn't have it. She's going on this long journey and has nothing to remember me by."

"Why wouldn't she remember you? You're her sister. She wouldn't forget you."

"People forget when they've been apart a long time." Edie barely whispered, wrapping her arms around her middle. "Mama's been gone a long time. I try real hard to hold her in here and here." She pointed to her forehead, then her chest, shutting her eyes tightly. "But she's slipping away. I can't see her like I used to."

Ben's throat constricted, and he swallowed hard, a heavy sense of foreboding rising from his stomach. He drew her into his arms, her little frame trembling against his chest. Grief and hope braided together in the hollow places between their hearts.

Lord ... The rest of the prayer caught in his throat, swallowed by guilt, grief, and something too sacred to name.

"Do you have anyone you've forgotten?" she whispered.

He closed his eyes, resting his cheek on her head. An image of the fifteen-year-old boy with wild red hair, lively blue eyes, and a winsome smile filled his thoughts. His chest tightened. Would he ever forget?

"No, not yet." He brushed Edie's hair, then leaned back. "Edie, I know it's too late for Ivajohn's bridal tea, but what if I helped you with a new gift?"

"Would you, Dr. Ewing?"

"Please, call me Ben." He patted her head.

"Ollie says we can't call you Ben if you ask us to."

"Oh? Why's that?"

"'Cause he says we don't know if you're gonna hurt Becca." She tilted her head, studying him up and down. "I told him that's a silly idea since you're a doctor and doctors don't hurt people. They help. He says I don't understand 'cause I'm just a kid." She wrinkled her nose. "Anyway, Ollie says he'll fight you if you hurt Becca. I'll fight you too. Only I don't think it will come to that with you being a doctor and all."

"I'll try not to disappoint you, Edie."

The floorboards in the front room creaked, causing Edie to jump up.

"That's Becca!" She took the spyglass and thrust it into Ben's hands. "Put it in your pocket. Don't leave a mess. I'll get my drink from the well."

And like that, she was gone, before he knew he needed her to stay.

Chapter Nine

Rebecca retrieved the boardinghouse register from the china cabinet in the dining room and went to the kitchen, stopping when she spotted Ben.

"You're awake."

"Yes, I am." His hand disappeared into his pocket.

"Telescope?"

"It doesn't wish to be expelled." His lopsided smile sent a warm sensation spiraling through her. "Nor do I."

She stiffened, trying to ignore the flutter his grin caused. Five years apart. How could a mere crooked smile stir such emotions? She placed the book on the table with a thud. "I see you've discovered the dinner plate. Sit. Eat."

She sat across from him, opened the register, and scribbled in the columns, closing Mr. Perry's account. After a deep breath, she tucked the pencil behind her ear and forcefully shut the book. Sighing, she massaged the stiffness in her neck and shoulders.

"Well, that's that." She patted the book.

"Were you adding me to the register?"

"No, Justin handled that yesterday." She crossed her arms over the book. "I removed Mr. Perry."

"I saw his trunk was empty." Ben ran a hand through unruly curls. "So, he's moved?"

"Mm." Rebecca pursed her lips. "He left for a job in Missouri. It was 'un-turn-down-able.' You now have the rare treat of a private room."

"I'm not sure how I feel about that."

"I know how I feel." She stood, glancing at him. "Your clothes are mussed as if you slept in them."

"I did."

"Were you so exhausted?" She grabbed a towel to busy herself. "I guess it's a good thing I let you sleep late."

"I was tired." He cut a bite-sized piece from a potato. "But also, this is all I have."

Rebecca chuckled softly. His silence prompted a sidelong glimpse. Threadbare socks, frayed hems, grimy collar. How had she missed this yesterday?

"Ben, what happened to your clothes?"

He cleared his throat. "I lost a few things during my journey."

He carried himself like a man who hadn't just lost his belongings, but his footing. His roots.

"How?"

He pushed his fork around his plate. "I can't say exactly. It didn't happen all at once."

"Lost your belongings?" She frowned. "What exactly did you arrive with?"

"This." His jaw flexed as he motioned to himself with his fork and then toward his room. "And my shoes."

Rebecca exhaled sharply. Joining him, she perched on the edge of her chair with the rumpled dish towel in her lap. She reached for his hand, but he recoiled, his eyes widened.

"Why didn't you speak up? Did you tell Justin?" She tilted her head. "Is that why he permitted you to stay free of charge?"

"I won't be a burden to you." He set down his fork and carefully folded his napkin. "I'm broke, but I can chop wood, clean stalls, or handle repairs. Just let me know what you need."

"Ben."

"I'll tidy up, head to the mercantile, and post a notice. Does Mr. Mooney keep a notice board?"

"Ben."

"I won't be a burden to you, Rebecca." He locked eyes with her. "I won't. I promise I won't."

"I know you won't." Her voice faltered, a lump rising in her throat.

What had become of him? Where was the man she once knew? Hugging herself and rubbing her shoulders, she moved to the pantry. She filled a tin with biscuits, jerky, nuts, and an apple. Returning, she set it before him.

"What's this?"

"Something to eat for later. You can carry it with us." She tapped the lid. "I'm heading to the mercantile. We'll go together. You can post your notice, and we'll visit Nicholas. Maybe he'll have something you can help with. Then, we'll stop by Levi and Allie's."

"What time is it?"

"Shortly after noon."

"Oh, I thought I'd slept all day."

"There's time enough for business." She patted the table lightly. "I'll put Cordelia and Martie in charge of the evening meal. It may not be gourmet, but it'll be edible."

"I'm thankful for every meal set before me." He lifted the tin. "I can walk back if you want to visit Allie. I don't want to be in the way."

"Of course I'll visit Allie, but you'll talk to Levi about a horse. He's helping with Justin's stock while he's away." She rose, squeezing his shoulder. "But first, I'll speak with Simon. You need something suitable to wear."

Rebecca stepped outside. Two men lingered beyond the front fence. Ambrose Baas, the new hotel owner, clothed in ambition and a fine suit. The other, a disheveled figure, presenting a disconcerting contrast to Mr. Baas. She bristled. What could have brought them here?

Baas tipped his hat before they turned and headed down Cane Hill toward Main Street. Their silence only deepened her suspicion.

She peeked into the stable. "Simon? You here?"

"Over here." He waved from a back stall.

"Did you notice those two men across the road?"

"Haven't been in the yard much today." He patted Noble's rump. "I've mucked Mr. Perry's stall and cleaned Noble's hooves."

"He smiles when you call him Noble."

"Never warranted the name Devil." Simon applied pressure at the stallion's fetlock, and Noble raised his hoof. "Now, what about these men?"

"Could be nothing. They stopped in front of the house." She lifted a hand and let it fall. "One of them was Ambrose Baas, the new hotel owner."

"Baas? I've heard mixed opinions about him. Some say he's a charmer initially, but things turn sour." Simon patted his knees. "I'll keep an eye out. Is that all you needed?"

"No. It's not why I came out here at all." She traced a circle in the dirt with her toe. "Did you know Ben returned empty-handed? He only has the clothes on his back."

"Are you certain?" Simon stood, wiping his hands. "Justin mentioned he was down to the blanket, but I thought he at least had a saddlebag with extra clothes."

"He's not *just almost* broke, Simon. He has nothing at all. He slept in the same clothes he wore yesterday." Rebecca shook her head. "He can't stroll Main Street in that outfit. People won't trust him as a doctor. Do you have anything he could borrow?"

"Becks, you're not listening." Simon stepped into the doorway, his presence commanding yet gentle, eyes steady with concern. "Ben needs a break. He's searching for a different type of work."

"Until he can get back on his feet. I understand it'll take time."

"I know you're accustomed to mothering everyone." Simon tilted her chin, his gaze unwavering. "But you've got to allow us to chart our own paths. Don't pressure him."

"You said, 'chart *our* own paths.' Am I holding *you* back?" Rebecca furrowed her brow.

"It's not just you." His voice softened. "I've wanted to be a lawman since Ma was shot."

Rebecca blinked, the weight of that day settling between them.

"Billy Kinder has never faced justice." His voice shook slightly, but he held her gaze, steady and sure. "The Sheriff asks me weekly when I want to be sworn in. But I won't do it without my family's blessing."

"Oh, Simon, we couldn't bear the thought of—"

"I know." His jaw tightened as he strode past her. "Thanks for telling me about Ben. I'll bring him some clothes." He paused at the door. His chin tilted slightly toward her, but his eyes didn't follow. "If you're heading to town, take Noble. Don't ride Truly double. She's too small."

Simon strode down the aisle and out the door. Rebecca sighed as she closed Noble's stall. She entered Truly's, wrapping her arms around the mare's neck. "Not listening. That's what Edie says about me. What do you think, girl?"

Truly fluttered her lips and nodded.

"Tell me what you really think." Rebecca laughed, patting the mare's neck.

"How did Mama manage it all?" She pressed her cheek to Truly's. "Why did you take her from us, Lord? We still need her." Rebecca swallowed hard, her arms looped around the mare's neck. "I don't want to lead every battle, Lord. Sometimes I just want to be the sister. Not the one holding everyone together."

She threaded her fingers in Truly's mane. "I can't do what Mama did. She always said, 'Tend the roots, and the tree will stand.' But what if I don't even know where the roots are anymore?"

The mare pressed against her, comforting her. If the Lord sent comfort through creatures, He'd surely chosen this mare. "Sweet girl. You're always here when I need a hug. I'm not keen to ride another horse."

Truly whinnied.

As she scratched Truly behind the ears, she kissed her nose. "Guess I better see what I can do to help Ben."

Maybe tending to his roots would help them both stand.

Chapter Ten

The front door creaked, alerting Rebecca to Ben's presence and drawing her attention from bridling Noble. Ben approached wearing a russet and tan plaid shirt that hugged his broad shoulders and complemented his eyes. She had forgotten how well the color suited him. Gone was the tweed coat and tie she remembered, replaced by an open collar and ease in his movements.

He stretched his arms and grinned. "So, what do you think?"

"It'll do." She nodded, gripping the saddle horn as she climbed on. Removing her foot from the stirrup, she leaned to offer her hand. "Let's go."

Ben grasped the rear of the saddle and took her hand. She leaned to the opposite side to counterbalance him as he hoisted himself behind her. After steadying himself, his arms moved awkwardly. In, out, up, down.

"What are you doing back there?" She shifted in the saddle.

"I'm trying to figure out what to do with my hands." He raised them. "When we used to ride together, I held the reins."

"Oh." Heat rose in her cheeks. She couldn't risk his arms

around her stirring up past emotions. The safest option for riding double was him gripping the saddle's cantle, but that didn't sit well either. Her expression tightened. "Hold onto my waist and be still. We need to find you a horse soon."

His light touch at her waist sparked a warmth she tried to ignore. She straightened in the saddle, eyes focused ahead. Safeguarding her heart proved to be trickier than expected. She urged Noble into a trot with a squeeze of her legs. Ben inched closer, and she caught a trace of citrus and rosemary. Had Simon shared more than fresh garments?

Ben's nearness evoked memories of past rides together. Country house calls—intense journeys and, at times, harrowing. But the return? She sighed. Riding home, she rested in the safety of his strong arms as he held the reins. Occasionally, he indulged her thirst for knowledge, responding to countless questions about their cases. He praised her instincts and creative problem-solving. Yet the moments his breath grazed her ear while he pointed out a fox or rabbit left her breathless. As the bustle of Main Street came into view, she guided Noble to the hitching post.

"Well, here we are." Rebecca patted the horse.

Ben dismounted and extended his hand. She hesitated but accepted it, allowing him to help her down.

"I'll head inside." She swept a wavy strand from her face. "Post your notice, talk to Nicholas, and I'll find you later."

His smile was a little crooked. "Yes, ma'am."

As Ben walked to the notice board, Rebecca entered Mooney's Mercantile. Mr. Mooney greeted her at the counter, glancing at the list she slid toward him.

"Interesting turn of events when Doc showed up unexpectedly." He thumped the paper.

"Mm." Her eyes followed Ben across the street.

"Where is he staying?"

"Mm?" She rested her hands on the counter.

"Doc Ewing?" Mr. Mooney patted her hands. "Where is he staying?"

"Oh." She blinked, shaking off the haze. "Justin provided him a room at the boardinghouse."

"Justin?" Mr. Mooney tilted his head. "When did he start signing on new boarders? I thought he intended to leave this morning."

"He certainly did." Rebecca sighed, withdrawing her hands.

The bell above the door chimed, and a ragtag boy entered, nodded, and slipped down the aisle. Mr. Mooney nodded in return.

"When did Justin find time to make these boardinghouse arrangements?" Mr. Mooney grabbed an empty box.

"I'm not sure." Rebecca tucked a loose strand of hair behind her ear. "But you know Justin. He always finds time for a friend in need."

Mr. Mooney leaned in, nodding in Ben's direction. "So, he's a friend?"

Rebecca's jaw tightened, then relaxed. "What else would he be?"

"Well, I don't know." Mr. Mooney cleared his throat. "But rest assured, I'm on your side. What sort of help does he need?"

"There are no *sides*, Mr. Mooney." She glanced out the window. Justin and Simon had emphasized Ben's need for rest, but surely there was more he needed. "I believe what Ben—Doctor Ewing—needs most is friendship and community."

"Friendship. Mm-hmm. That's what every man needs."

"Oh, stop." Rebecca rolled her eyes. "Don't try to be a matchmaker here. Better yet, focus on yourself."

"What do you mean?" Mr. Mooney stepped around the counter, holding the box and her list.

"Don't tell me you haven't noticed how Caroline Brandt

brushes your hand when she comes to your counter." She grinned in satisfaction as his cheeks reddened. "And don't think I haven't noticed the butterscotch you add to her orders. Three pieces."

"Well, now …" Mr. Mooney stammered, fumbling with items on the shelves. "She's been a mighty fine customer."

"So has my family, but we never get complimentary butterscotch." She plucked a piece from the candy jar, amused by his mild flusteration. "I doubt it was in her orders until that cross-stitch appeared above your counter." Rebecca gestured to the artwork, appreciating the understated beauty. "Faith. Hope. Love. Three significant words. Three delightful little treats."

A crimson blush spread from his cheeks to the tips of his ears. He returned the box to the counter, nodded toward the boy in the aisle, and mouthed a *shush*.

"It appears butterscotch is complimentary for you today as well." Mr. Mooney recorded the items in his ledger. "By the way, did your father and Justin get started all right this morning?"

"They did." Rebecca popped the candy into her mouth, savoring its buttery sweetness. "I hope they're back in time for Ivajohn's wedding."

"Ah, now. A quick trip to Missouri. He never encountered any issues before." Mr. Mooney tapped the ledger page. "Putting this on your tab?"

"Yes. I hope it isn't too much trouble."

"Not at all. I'll have it delivered in a few hours."

Rebecca hesitated. "Mr. Mooney, I know we usually settle our account at the end of the month, but could we have a two-week extension?"

"I'm afraid I can only extend for one week right now."

"That will do." She patted the counter. "Thank you. Ben and I are going to Levi's, but Simon and Cordelia will accept delivery."

"Oh, that reminds me, I have something for Martie."

The boy approached the counter, his copper hair askew. "Mister, I got a question."

"What can I help you with, young man?"

The boy jingled some coins, setting them on the counter. "How much beans and rice can I buy with this? I wanted apples and peaches, but it ain't enough."

"Why, this is enough for three apples."

"I got three brothers I gotta feed for days. Best stick to beans and rice." He pushed the coins to Mr. Mooney. "How much can I get?"

"This is good for a pound each of rice and beans." Mr. Mooney rubbed his short, white beard. Rounding the counter, he selected three gleaming red apples and three ripe peaches. Returning, he placed all the items into a burlap sack. "Tell you what, I'll throw in the apples and peaches."

"Thanks, Mister." A broad smile lifted the boy's rosy cheeks. "I'll sweep your floor every day for a week."

"Oh, no need."

"No, sir. Drake boys don't take no charity." Grabbing the bag, he darted out, shouting, "I'll be back."

Rebecca sprang through the door after him. A covered wagon rattled by, blocking her way. When the wagon passed, only a cloud of dust remained. She sighed. The dust settled like a weight in her chest. So many boys too young to carry so much.

"Drake boys?" Mr. Mooney joined her. "Do you see any more?"

"No. I imagine the rest are hiding." She followed Mr. Mooney back inside. "Do you think he is one of the twins?"

"Don't know. I've seen them a time or two from a distance. Three of the four are redheads." He disappeared behind the curtain and returned with a book.

"He appeared small to be in charge of three brothers. Surely, he's not the oldest?"

"Can't say for certain." Mr. Mooney placed a copy of *Jane Eyre* on the counter. "Caroline left this for Martie. Tell her I said 'hello.'"

"I'll see she gets it." Rebecca took the book. "Oh, one more thing. Do you know anyone missing a spyglass? Nothing fancy, simple brass. Maybe a customer has mentioned it?"

"Newly arrived at the lost and found?"

Rebecca raised her eyebrows in surprise.

"Allie mentioned it. She stayed to chat instead of returning to the homestead before the sleepover." Mr. Mooney chuckled. "Said you want to lock the charming little thing in the lost and found."

"It's not charming." Rebecca rolled her eyes. "Probably thrown away because it's broken. The sections don't extend."

"That's no reason to get rid of it. Needs a good cleaning." Mr. Mooney extended his hand. "Do you have it? I can show you."

Rebecca shook her head. "I was only inquiring."

"Right, then. I guess it's back in the lost and found."

"Well, no." She fidgeted with a bent nail puzzle, likely one of Levi's creations. "I intended to return it to the lost and found."

"Does that mean Ben has it? Is that why you came to town together?" Mr. Mooney raked his hand through his beard. "Doubling your efforts. Good idea."

"Oh, we're not—" Rebecca lifted the book higher, as if it could shield her. "I'll deliver this to Martie."

"Let Simon know he might find the Drake boy sweeping my floors this week."

"Why should I tell Simon? Isn't the sheriff back?"

"No, he's still with the posse, tracking the Cutter-Doyle gang. Rumor has it Billy Kinder is among them."

Rebecca froze. "Billy Kinder? With a gang?"

"Life on the run changes a man." Mr. Mooney squeezed her hand. "The sheriff asked Simon and Nicholas to handle things while he's gone. Given his many siblings, Simon's more comfortable with children."

A hollow flutter rose in her chest. How fragile the town seemed without the sheriff's steady hand.

"I'll let Simon know." Rebecca left, her thoughts lingering on Billy Kinder, the boy she had once known, and what he had become.

Chapter Eleven

The unyielding sun blazed overhead as Rebecca tucked the book into her saddlebag. Three riders went by, stirring the dust, and she retrieved a handkerchief to wipe the sweat and grit from her neck. Placing the cloth back into the bag, she glided her hand down Noble's almost black neck. He whinnied, tossing his head.

"I understand. You don't like staying still for long. Me either. But no hard rides today. We'll take it easy with Ben for now." She scratched behind Noble's ears. "Simon will get a good run with you once it rains."

Noble nickered.

"Miss Hogue?"

Rebecca turned, a slight frown pulling at her lips as she saw Ambrose Baas standing before her. His dark gray bowler hat tipped low, adorned with a black-speckled feather. His figure imposing, yet composed.

"Mr. Baz."

"Pronounced Boss." His smile barely softened his features, and for a moment, Rebecca thought she saw something unreadable flicker in his eyes. "Though close friends call me Baz, short for Sebastian. My middle name."

"Boss. Interesting name. Where's it from?"

"It's Dutch. *B-a-a-s*." He removed his hat and gave a half-bow. "Would you join me for pie at Gray's Café? I want to discuss the business proposal I mentioned yesterday."

"I saw you earlier today." Rebecca hesitated, unease niggling at her. "Across from the boardinghouse with a taller man?"

Noble rested his muzzle on her shoulder, pulling her closer, and she stroked the bridge of his nose.

Baas nodded, his face darkening as a shadow swept across his sharp features. "Yes, I do apologize for our presence. A pleasant afternoon admiring the local properties led to a stroll. A rare delight, since I'm usually so occupied with business." His gaze lingered longer than necessary, and Rebecca caught a glimpse of something behind his eyes. Perhaps weariness, perhaps regret.

Rebecca studied him, a slight pull of curiosity tugging at her despite her resistance. "I understand. It's a challenge for me as well." She relaxed a little, but her caution remained. "You should speak with my father regarding business proposals."

His eyes drifted to the ground, then met hers again. "I thought you were the proprietress of the boardinghouse. My apologies."

Rebecca crossed her arms, spine rigid. "I oversee the business for my father. He's the primary decision-maker."

"I see." His voice softened, though it quickly hardened again. "Perhaps I should meet with you both."

"My father is away for at least a week." She searched for Ben's familiar face. "I'm due to meet someone at the saddlery."

"Surely your meeting can wait for a bit." Baas smiled, this time with a touch more warmth. "We could discuss this over pie today and involve your father upon his return."

Rebecca glanced toward the saddlery. No sign of Ben yet. She pursed her lips, then sighed, stepping back a little. "I'll spare fifteen minutes. That's it."

His smile widened, but a fleeting softness in his eyes made her hesitate. "You'll be glad you did."

"I'll be back soon, boy." She patted Noble, who showed his disapproval by pawing the ground repeatedly. "I'll be fine."

At the café, Baas held the door for her with a slight bow, a faint tension marking his posture as Rebecca passed him. His hands betrayed a stillness that seemed out of place in such a bustling café.

"Rebecca, dearie. What brings you today? I wasn't expecting you until mid-December. When the weather is cooler." Mrs. Gray beamed, then paused at the sight of Baas. "Who's this?"

"Mr. Baas, the new owner of the hotel." Rebecca patted the tabletop. "We're having a brief business meeting over pie before I go to the saddlery."

"I see." Mrs. Gray's usual jovial expression faded a touch. "What kind of pie would you prefer? I have apple and peach pie. Or my famous blackberry cobbler."

"Two slices of apple." Baas's gaze flicked to Mrs. Gray, his wariness palpable. "And tea."

"It's thoughtful of you to order for me." Rebecca smiled politely. "But I'll have the cobbler."

"A touch of cream, darling?"

"Of course." Rebecca beamed. "Thank you, Mrs. Gray."

Mrs. Gray leaned in, whispering behind her hand, "Watch him closely, dearie."

"Right you are." Rebecca raised an eyebrow but gave a quiet nod. "I shan't have sweet tea if I'm having cream on my cobbler. Watching my waistline. Water will be fine."

She gently squeezed Mrs. Gray's hand, thankful for her discretion.

"So, what's this business proposition you have in mind?"

Rebecca folded her hands, her curiosity piqued despite herself. "Perhaps rooms on reserve for when the hotel is full?"

He frowned, stroked his jaw, then leaned in slightly. "I'd like to buy the boardinghouse outright."

Rebecca's eyebrows shot up. "Buy our home?" She shook her head slowly. "That's not possible. Hogue House isn't for sale."

"I'm prepared to make a handsome offer." His voice dropped an octave, the warmth there, but with an edge.

"Any offer would fall short. This home has been in our family for fifteen years." Rebecca tugged at her collar, glancing at the cold fireplace. Why was it so hot in here? "Hogue House has been our only home since my father left the steamboat business."

"I understand the sentimental attachment." Baas folded his hands in front of him. "You might find it interesting that I started in the steamboat business and retain a stake in it. I've recently become the owner of *The Valiant*."

"Captain Sterling Reed's vessel?"

"The very one. I started long ago as a deckhand and worked my way up." He glanced away for a beat. "Care to guess who first employed and mentored me?"

She stiffened, her mind already bracing for the name. "Who?"

"A certain Clayburn Hogue."

"My father?" Rebecca suppressed her surprise.

"Indeed. He taught me everything I know about the business. I hoped to return the favor." He offered a small, almost apologetic smile, but it quickly turned back into business proper. "I've prepared another offer, but we should wait until your father returns to discuss it. Although time is of the essence." The corner of his mouth twitched, and his eyes narrowed slightly. "Since Hogue House has outstanding expenses."

Rebecca stared out the window, drumming her fingers on her water glass. They owed the feed store, the mercantile, and other shops. Mr. Mooney had only given her a one-week extension. How did he know? With Mr. Perry's departure and another mouth to feed, she had to explore all options. She cleared her throat and returned her attention to him. "I'll hear your proposal in my father's absence."

"I appreciate your consideration." Baas smiled, a sharpness in his gaze as though trying to read her every reaction.

She swallowed hard, forcing a smile.

"While this may seem unusual, we could join our businesses through a more permanent union."

She nearly choked as her water went the wrong way. She coughed, struggling to swallow. The walls of the café seemed to tilt. Surely, she had misunderstood.

Of course. That's what this had been about all along. Not just her family home, but her hand.

"Oh, sweetie, are you all right?" Mrs. Gray hurried over with the pie.

"I'm fine." Rebecca waved her hand. "Went down—the wrong way."

"You should be more careful, dearie." Mrs. Gray patted her back. "Here's your cobbler." She set it down like a lifeline.

Rebecca stood, wiping her mouth. "I've completely lost track of the time. I need to get to the saddlery." She pulled coins from her pocket, handing them to Mrs. Gray. "Please deliver the cobbler to Mrs. Brandt. Tell her it's from Sam Mooney."

"Happy to." Mrs. Gray grinned from ear to ear.

"Miss Hogue, can we resume our discussion at another time?" Baas pressed.

"I am rather busy as of late." Rebecca swallowed hard. "I apologize and wish you a pleasant afternoon."

She dared not turn around until safely through the café door.

To think he'd spoken of marriage and property in the same breath as if she could be bought and sold. Her legs moved faster as her heart tried to catch up.

Chapter Twelve

Ben cracked the saddlery door, inhaling the rich, earthy aroma of oiled leather. "Good afternoon, Nicholas. May I come in?"

"I'm open for business." Nicholas remained focused, cutting designs into a piece of leather. "Do as you want."

Ben stepped inside, closing the door. "I wanted to express my gratitude for all you've done for Rebecca while I've been away."

Nicholas set down the swivel knife, his frown deepening. "Shouldn't have done her that way, Doc. Showing up with no notice."

"I—I didn't know how to tell her." Ben sniffed uncomfortably. "I had to come home. I won't take much of your time. Just wanted to thank you, that's all." He turned toward the door.

"Sit down, Doc." Nicholas pointed to a barrel. "We need to catch up."

"I don't want to impose."

"Impose? If you were an imposition, I wouldn't have asked

you to stay." Nicholas's tone evened. "I don't mind telling people to get out when I'm done talking.

"True enough." Ben grimaced. "You're nothing if not direct."

"Saves on miscommunication." Nicholas continued his work, gesturing for Ben to speak. "Ask what you came here to ask."

Ben cleared his throat. "How is she?"

"She's hurt." Nicholas locked eyes with him. "She has more grit than any woman I've known. Thought she might break after her mother died, but she carried on. You were a fool to leave her."

"I can see you're close." Ben's shoulders slumped as he rose. "I won't stand in your way."

"Sit down." Nicholas slammed the swivel knife on the table. "We're not close the way you think. Rebecca hasn't had room in her heart for anyone since you. The only reason I didn't whip you in the street yesterday is because I owe you my life. But my loyalty lies with her. So, if you're not staying, leave now."

"I'm not leaving again." He swallowed past the knot in his throat. "But the townsfolk might run me out if they share Mr. Fremont's opinion of me."

"Doc, I'm glad you're back despite my warning. We could use another doctor." Nicholas paused. "Rebecca shouldn't have to carry that burden. It'll help me with my work here too."

"I'm not the doctor I was. Need a fresh start doing something different." Ben crossed his arms. "Thought you might take me on as an apprentice."

Nicholas eyed him, picking up the swivel knife. "I don't have much patience with apprentices. Took on that boy several years ago. It was a real test. Nearly tied a knot in him."

"I remember him, young and somewhat scattered." Ben chuckled. "I'm sure I'm more focused. Older, at least."

"My sister wants me to teach her son. If they stay, I'll have my hands full." Nicholas sighed. "Levi Snow's better with apprentices. Get on with him, and you'll be in fine shape."

"We'll ride out to the Snow place later today."

"You and Rebecca?"

Ben nodded.

"Better get your own horse, Doc."

"Rebecca agrees. She suggested Levi could help."

"Seems you're all set." Nicholas paused. "Anything else?"

"One more thing." He pulled the telescope from his pocket. "You see a fair number of customers each day. Anyone mention missing a spyglass like this?"

"If I had a penny for every fella thinks he's an explorer, I'd be rich."

"If anyone mentions it, I'm interested in finding the owner."

At that moment, Rebecca burst through the door with enough force to jolt a leather punch off its hook. She patted her chest, closed her eyes briefly, and straightened as she saw the two men. Ben and Nicholas exchanged worried glances.

"Are you all right?" Ben approached.

"I'm fine. Close call with a wagon." She waved him off, then spotted the telescope. "So much for talking about work."

"Careful, Rebecca." Nicholas gave a sly glance. "You might offend me. Why ask the doctor's help locating this telescope's owner before you asked me? After all, these lost trinkets seem to lead to marital bliss."

Rebecca flushed, snatching the brass instrument from Nicholas. She waved it in Ben's face. "This thing's trouble. I tried to tell you. It's going back to the lost and found room."

Maybe it was trouble. Perhaps it was a second chance too.

"But ..." Ben stepped back, his chest tight with embarrassment. He stumbled into a rack of stretched leather, the supple material yielded easily, and he fell.

Heat flared up his neck as Nicholas's laughter rang out. Nicholas doubled over, clutching his stomach as Ben scrambled to his feet.

"Oh, oh. You should have seen your face." Nicholas wiped

tears from his eyes. "Oh, how I love getting you riled, though it's nearly impossible."

"Nicholas Theodore Franks." Rebecca stiffened.

"You used my full name." His eyes went wide. "Only Ma calls me that."

"Well, what would she say if she heard you making a joke of marriage and intentionally trying to 'rile' a woman?" She tilted her head, fixing him with a pointed glare.

He straightened his shirt. "She'd have used my full name."

"Mm."

"Aw, I was only kidding. Give him his toy." He pouted. "See, Doc? This is why I stick to work. I get into trouble when I'm not busy."

"Sometimes, I think men are just a bunch of boys at heart." Rebecca returned the telescope to Ben. "I'm not amused."

"Obviously," Nicholas muttered under his breath.

Rebecca leveled a stern expression at him before turning to Ben. "You've had your fun. We should get to the Snow place before the day gets away from us."

Ben tucked the telescope into his pocket, exhaling a long breath. Typical Nicholas. Always stirring the pot. Ben followed Rebecca out the door, hurrying to keep pace with her.

"Are you sure you're all right?" He touched her shoulder.

She jumped. "It was a very close call with a wagon." At Noble's side, she inspected the saddlebags. "I hope I don't encounter him—it—again."

"Did the wagon driver threaten you? Did you go to the café?"

"Yes, I was there," she admitted, voice low. "But it wasn't the café that rattled me. Let's go."

"Is there something you're not telling me?" His muscles tensed as he mounted behind her.

"There's much I'm not telling you." Her tone was even, the bitterness tucked neatly within it, measured and precise.

"You've only just returned after a five-year absence, and I had no say in the matter." She leaned forward, increasing the space between them. "While I am concerned about you and your situation, I'm not ready to open my heart to you again. So, yes, there's plenty I'm keeping to myself."

"I should have—"

"To make matters worse, everyone close to me knew of your return, but didn't tell me." She glanced at him. "So let's keep quiet for the remainder of this ride. I need time alone with my thoughts."

Ben's heart sank. He'd had more than enough time alone with his thoughts. It was the last thing he needed. The silence between them was so weighted he could barely breathe. Why hadn't he found a way to tell her of his return?

She sat inches away, shoulders squared and back rigid. Mere inches might as well have been an insurmountable chasm. He was foolish to think he could return home. Naive to believe he could rekindle their old friendship, let alone something more.

He sat back, his hands resting loosely at her waist, letting the silence stretch like penance. If he could pray, he would ask for one more chance—not to make her love him again but to make something right for once.

Chapter Thirteen

The rhythmic clip-clop of Noble's hooves slowed as they neared the Snow homestead. Ben pressed his eyes shut, tapping his knee in rhythm, grounding himself. When Noble stopped, Ben dismounted, stretched, and offered his hand to Rebecca. When she didn't accept Ben's hand, Levi offered his, and she dismounted. Ben's heart pricked at the rejection.

"Good afternoon, Levi." Rebecca motioned to Ben. "Look who's back in town."

"We crossed paths yesterday." Levi patted Ben's shoulder. "Good to see you again, Ben."

"You too."

"See there? I am the only one who didn't know you returned." Rebecca grimaced, then turned to Levi. "I thought I'd visit with Allie while you two catch up."

"Allie and Dawn are eager to visit with you. I'll take care of Noble." Levi took the reins, guiding Noble to the round pen before filling a trough with water. "So, Ben, how've you been?"

"I'm not sure." He propped his foot on the rail as Noble ran circles. "I'm questioning if returning to Van Buren was wise."

"What brought you back?"

"I couldn't stay in California any longer. Didn't know where else to go. Van Buren's the last place I felt at home."

"Then stay. Be prepared to do some hard work." Levi folded his arms. "A place to call home is worth fighting for."

"Becoming a doctor has proven harder than I expected. Maybe I should work with my hands. Smithing, perhaps?"

"You miss my meaning." Levi turned, resting his hand on Ben's back. "I'm talking about spiritual labor. Do you know how to invite the Lord into the hard places?"

Ben hesitated. "I thought I did. I once had a fire in my soul, but it's gone. My faith's barely holding on. I'm stuck in a dark place and can't see my way out."

Levi gestured toward the forge. "Come with me."

He unlatched the oversized doors of the forge, opening one side and gesturing for Ben to follow suit. Inside, the air smelled of ash and iron. One corner featured a sitting area with a makeshift stool and an open Bible resting on the table.

The remaining area was a dedicated workspace. Two anvils on hefty tree stumps, tools suspended from metal racks. The walls displayed wagon wheel hubs, fireplace tools and grates, ornamental wrought iron pieces, and objects Ben didn't recognize.

"You need to learn to draw out." Levi pulled a rod from a scrap metal bin and handed it to Ben.

"Draw out?" He raised an eyebrow.

"It's the first thing every blacksmith learns. Put on this apron and gloves." Levi tossed them to Ben. "You'll work there."

"So, you're going to teach me to be a blacksmith?"

"I'll teach you to draw out what's buried deep inside." Levi secured his apron. "But first we'll get your hands busy and your mind at rest."

"Something is hidden inside the metal?" Ben joined Levi at the forge, placing the rod in the fire.

"Something is hidden within you, something holding you back."

Ben heated the rod in the fire, then followed Levi's instructions, tapping it on the anvil. He developed a swift rhythm. Tap, tap, tap, turn.

"Close your eyes."

Ben stopped. "Why?"

"Just trust me. Keep tapping."

He obeyed.

"Picture the place where you feel trapped. What do you see?"

Ben lowered his head, waiting for an image to take shape. "I'm in a cave. Dark. Cold. Something is blocking the light. A boulder."

"You're doing fine." Levi kept his voice low and steady. "Is the Lord there with you?"

"No." His breathing matched Levi's. "I'm alone."

"Look around. Is He anywhere nearby?"

Ben's breath caught. "Yes. He's outside, resting beneath a tree. But the boulder is in the way." Loneliness seeped deeper, a cold weight pressing against his ribs. He stopped tapping and opened his eyes. "Why doesn't He move it? Why doesn't He free me?"

"Let's find out. Close your eyes. Keep tapping." Levi's voice ranged low. "Who put the boulder there?"

Ben paused, then whispered, "I did. I shut Him out." He opened his eyes, his hands frozen. "I built the wall to keep the pain away. To keep everyone out. Somehow, I've put Him on the wrong side of it."

"The Lord won't force His way past a barrier you've built." Levi turned and patted Ben on the back. "But He'll wait. All you need to do is ask Him to sit with you in that dark place. That's where the healing begins."

Ben swallowed hard. "I don't know how to thank you."

"I've been there." Levi smiled. "Do you say your prayers before bed?"

"I've fallen out of the habit."

"Get back to it. When you pray, picture the cave and invite Him in. Don't do all the talking. Listen. And when trouble rises, call on Him then too. That's how you draw out what's hidden. One prayer, one blow at a time."

Levi hitched his thumb toward the barn. "Let's get Noble some oats. Anything else I can help you with?"

"Rebecca suggested I inquire about a horse, but I can't afford one. What I need is a job."

"I know doctoring is tough, but you're good at it. Be patient. People will come around."

Ben rubbed his neck. "It's not that. Something happened in California." His hands trembled. "A boy died under my care. Every time I'm confronted with a patient, my hands shake. I can't handle it."

Levi nodded as they entered the barn. "You've lost patients before."

Ben's hands shook slightly, and he massaged them. "This was different."

"Want to talk about it?"

"I don't think I'm ready."

Levi placed a hand on his shoulder. "It's all right. I'm here when you're ready." He grabbed a bucket of oats, handing it to Ben. "What would you rather do, if not doctoring?"

"Anything. I'd happily apprentice under you or help with maintenance around your place."

"Sorry, Doc. I can't pay you."

"For the experience, then."

Ben climbed the pen rail, setting the oats over the side. Noble sauntered up to him, nuzzling his hand before eating.

"I don't want to take advantage of your situation. But if you need to talk or apply your hand to something productive, I'll be glad for the extra help." Levi stretched. "Since Justin moved to the next property, we've been helping each other a lot. I'll miss him nearly as much as Dawn will."

Ben hopped off the rail. The telescope slipped from his pocket and rolled across the ground. Levi picked it up, gave it a good once-over, and smiled.

"Is this the spyglass that caused such a stir at the bridal tea?"

Ben's face flushed. "Yes, that would be it."

"I heard Ivajohn held it like a dead rat." Levi laughed. "It's certainly not the charming nativity that brought Allie and me together, but it's not as bad as a dead rat either."

Ben managed a genuine smile, the first in a long time.

"Rebecca wouldn't approve." He hid the telescope in his pocket. "She'll expel both of us from the boardinghouse if she sees you waving it around."

Levi raised an eyebrow. "How'd you get her to agree to keep it?"

"I convinced her the telescope would help me reconnect with the people here. She agreed, provided I keep it out of sight."

"So you don't intend to find the owner?"

"Oh, I do. I'll use it to reconnect with Van Buren's residents, but I also want to find other opportunities." Ben patted his pocket. "I can't go back to being a doctor."

Ben glanced at the cabin's closed curtains. He withdrew the telescope, shielding it from the window's view in case Rebecca checked on them. "Know anyone who might carry one like this?"

Levi studied it. "I can think of a few people who might have one. The doctors, the sheriff, or a steamboat captain. Start with the captains. The sheriff and both doctors are out of town."

"Great. In the meantime, I'll find out what Ollie knows. He put it in the lost and found."

"Tomorrow's Sunday. You should go to church with the Hogues."

"I'm not sure I'm welcome. I haven't had the warmest reception so far."

"I'm giving the sermon. If needed, I'll remind them how we welcome returning guests." Levi raked his fingers through his short, dark beard.

Ben wasn't sure a welcome was his to claim.

"I'll think about it."

"Wonderful. Now, let's get you a mount."

"Only if we work out a way for me to pay." Ben pressed his palms together.

"Not necessary. You'll borrow the horse." Levi gripped his shoulder. "Besides, you've rendered aid to me in the past without payment."

"You've rarely needed my services, and you've always paid. Eventually." He wiped the sweat from his cheek. "They're Justin's horses anyway."

"Even better. I know you've cared for the Hogue children at times when Clayburn and Mahala couldn't pay, and that includes Justin. So borrowed it is."

Ben pressed his lips flat. "I'll pay as I'm able. Even for a borrowed horse."

"Suit yourself. Consider today's work in the forge a week's payment." Levi patted his back.

"I didn't make anything at all. How was it worth wages?"

"It might have been a different kind of work, Ben, but it kept the forge fire lit." Levi propped his hands on his hips. "Keeping it lit is more difficult than it appears."

Chapter Fourteen

"I hear you expected me." Rebecca glanced from Allie to Eliza Dawn. "Funny. I never said I was coming."

Allie glanced at Eliza Dawn, who became unusually committed to her crochet project. Allie set aside her partially finished shawl, gesturing for Rebecca to sit. She then retrieved a set of Jane Austen books from the shelf.

"Do you have room in your saddlebags for these?" She handed them to Rebecca. "They're for Martie."

"So, you won't tell me how you knew I was coming?" Rebecca set the stack beside her chair. "How long have you known?"

Allie resumed her seat, picking up her shawl. "I learned about Ben's arrival this morning. Levi mentioned seeing him at the boardinghouse before Mr. Fremont's accident."

"Levi saw him at the boardinghouse? I thought he only saw Ben in passing." Rebecca crossed her arms.

"He went to the mercantile yesterday, stopping by the boardinghouse as usual." Allie turned another row. "Ben was there, but he left to assist with Mr. Fremont before they could speak. So, yes, he saw Ben at the boardinghouse, but also in passing."

Rebecca turned to Eliza Dawn. "And you? You saw him in California and never said a word?"

"I'm sorry, Rebecca. Justin asked me not to mention it. I only found out this morning he'd returned, and that you were upset."

"We wanted to check on you right away, but we knew you had other things to handle first." Allie dropped her hands to her lap. "So we prayed and waited."

"When did you run into him? How are you feeling?" Eliza Dawn scooted forward, leaning closer.

"I was called to assist Mr. Fremont with a horse injury and saw Simon bringing Ben along."

"Tommy Weston picked her up, tossed her over his shoulder, and galloped off." Allie shook her head. "Quite the spectacle."

Rebecca stood, pacing. "The lengths this town will go to for my services. It's ridiculous, especially when I'm not even trained."

"Did you get to speak with Ben?"

"I haven't had time to think. It's been a whirlwind." She propped her hands on her hips. "And Mr. Perry left this morning."

"What do you mean he left?" Allie's attention shifted.

"After Pa set out, Mr. Perry said he'd accepted a job in Missouri and no longer needs lodging. He waited until Pa and Justin were gone. Probably because Mr. Perry has such great respect for Pa and would have a harder time telling him."

"What does it mean for the boardinghouse?" Eliza Dawn scrunched her nose at her inconsistent practice stitches.

"It means we have nine mouths to feed, but no paying boarders. Cordelia, Martie, and I will seek work beyond our doorstep." Rebecca slumped into the chair. She wasn't ready to consider or share Baas's unreasonable proposition with anyone. She couldn't shake the thought of his offer, though, and how he had smiled when she rejected it—how his smile lingered like a challenge.

"I'd stay in my old room while Justin is gone. I'd have no trouble paying and would be closer to the newspaper office." Eliza Dawn pulled out several stitches. "But with reports of lurkers around homes in town and outlying homesteads, I'd better stay and keep an eye on the ranch."

"That's sweet, but you're family now. We'd never ask you to pay for a room. Besides, Mama used to say God will always provide, even when you're shaken to your roots." Rebecca folded the memory close to her chest, needing it more than she wanted to admit. She presented an upturned palm, and Eliza Dawn handed her the hook, yarn, and stitches. "Should you stay at the ranch alone, though?"

"I'm not alone." Eliza Dawn crossed the room to the bookshelf. "Amos and his daughter Hattie are staying in the bunkhouse until they build their home. Amos is strong, and Hattie is gentle and wise. I'm thankful they came."

"Dawn's close by. Levi could be there in no time if needed." Allie finished the shawl, holding it up to show the others. "What do you think?"

"I think I'll never get the hang of crochet." Eliza Dawn rubbed her forehead.

"Is this suspicious activity what you planned to investigate while Justin is away?" Rebecca modeled a few stitches and handed the piece back to Eliza Dawn. "Perhaps you shouldn't without Justin around for protection. Didn't you have enough close calls covering the gold rush?"

"I can't help it. I find it curious reports of lurkers increased when the railroad talk started." Eliza Dawn pulled a book from the shelf, returned to her seat, and stashed her crochet project in her satchel.

Allie drew the shawl close. "There's been a lot of talk about who owns what with the railroad coming. Uncle Shadow's had three offers on the mercantile this month."

"Railroad fever." Rebecca tapped her chin, gears turning. She didn't voice her thoughts aloud, but a whisper of Baas's words echoed in her mind. *We could join our businesses through a more permanent union.* A ridiculous offer, but he'd said it like it had weight, and it stirred an unease in her.

Her thoughts drifted to the railroad. Baas owned a hotel now, but he had started on the steamboats. Was he aiming higher? Had he set his sights on the railroad? It didn't make sense. Not yet anyway. The proposed railroad route didn't touch Hogue House directly. Yet, she couldn't shake the feeling that his sudden interest in her family's business wasn't as straightforward as it seemed.

Allie sighed, stretching. "Every time progress rears its head, so does a new batch of problems. It's all very taxing to think about."

Eliza Dawn fanned herself with the book. "Is it warmer than usual in here? I've been breaking into gooseflesh and sweat at the same time."

"Are you writing late into the night?" Rebecca arched her brow. "You need more rest."

"Perhaps it's nerves or a change in the weather. Or maybe it's all the crocheting. You always get worked up when your stitches go lopsided." Allie tossed a loose ball of yarn her way.

"Maybe. Came over me suddenly." Eliza Dawn laughed softly, tucking the yarn into her lap. "By the way, is the telescope in the lost and found room? Is it abiding by your rules?"

Rebecca grimaced. "It's getting late. Ben and I should head back soon."

"It's here, isn't it?"

"I wish Edie had let it be. I don't know what to do about her."

Allie scooted to the edge of her seat. "I understand why you don't talk to Cordelia. She does get wrapped up in herself. But why don't you ask Simon his thoughts on the matter? Or even Martie? I know she's only seventeen, but she has a good head on her shoulders. She might surprise you."

"I just don't want to put the burden on them." Rebecca swiveled toward the window. "I couldn't save Mama, so I owe it to them to try to fill the hole she left in our lives. I owe it to her."

"Oh, honey." Eliza Dawn joined her, embracing her in a side-armed hug. "I know they probably needed that from you in the beginning, especially the way your pa grieved. There's no way anyone can truly fill the hole. I'm sure they don't expect you to."

"It's time to share the burden with them." Allie joined them, taking Rebecca's hands in hers. "Time to carry the weight together. It'll make you stronger as a family."

"What if I can't? What if I don't know how?" Rebecca's eyes met Allie's.

"Pray. And we'll pray too." Allie wrapped her in a hug. "We'll be here anytime you need us."

The three remained locked in a hug for a long while before Eliza Dawn pulled away, her eyes shining. "So, this spyglass, is it in your possession or Ben's?"

"Ben's asking to borrow a horse." Rebecca grinned, shaking her head. "Since they're Justin's, should you approve it, or let Levi?"

"Oh, Ben can borrow any horse he likes." Eliza Dawn clapped, grinning. "I warned you. Those lost trinkets have a will of their own. Since you're not offering any information, my guess is it's in his pocket right now. Try as you might to avoid it, you'll be pulled in eventually. Mark my words."

Rebecca pressed her lips together. She wasn't sure if the spyglass or Ben posed more danger to her peace of mind—but she was unwilling to give either more ground than she already had.

Chapter Fifteen

"Levi's story about this horse doesn't exactly inspire confidence." Ben kept the blanket Appaloosa reined in as they trotted along Poplar Street. The animal pushed against Ben's legs with palpable energy. "He's eager to run."

"We're almost to the boardinghouse, and he's done fine." Rebecca sat relaxed in the saddle, a more accomplished rider than Ben remembered. "He doesn't want to run *off*. Loosen the reins. Let him have a little fun."

"I don't know. The original owner called him Pickle because he spooked easily, leaving the rider in a *pickle*." The gelding's ears turned toward Ben as if listening. He shifted in the seat, all too aware of the gelding's strong forward pull, indicating his desire to run. "The last thing I want right now is to be in a tight fix with an unpredictable horse."

"If you're serious about finding the telescope's owner, you'll need a horse. Without one, expect to do a lot of walking. Your shoes wouldn't hold up. Trust him." Rebecca lifted her reins to show the slack she had given Noble. "A little slack won't hurt."

"I'm grateful for the horse, but it's been a while since I've ridden regularly." Ben shifted his weight downward, settling deeper into the saddle. He laid the reins to one side, then the other. Pickle responded by slowing and trotting a wavy line. Ben breathed easier as the tension lifted from the gelding's neck.

"Justin keeps two types of horse stock. He breeds Missouri Fox Trotters but rescues and retrains those considered problematic. He finds the owners to be the issue in most cases." She rubbed Noble's neck. "Noble and Pickle are rescues. Only Justin, Simon, or Levi can ride a rescue until it proves steady. Justin's horses are the finest in town, full-bred or not."

A buttery ribbon painted the sky, melting into pink, lavender, and blue hues as they rode toward Cane Hill. Ben's gelding trotted steadily, its light copper coat shining in the sun. He inhaled deeply, allowing his body to rise and fall in unison with the gelding.

"Better?" Rebecca raised her eyebrows.

"Too soon to say, but Pickle might be the right fit after all." He relaxed his shoulders and slid his hand down the reins.

"You seem more comfortable with each other than when we left the Snow homestead." A subtle smile curved her lips.

"Speaking of comfort …" Ben massaged his neck. "I haven't thanked you for letting me sleep in this morning."

"My brothers insisted you needed rest, so I sent the younger siblings to play. With no other boarders, the house was quite peaceful. I can't guarantee it will be like that every morning."

"Any news on Mr. Fremont?"

"He appears to be doing well, all things considered. Simon and I checked on him early this morning and brought the fracture box. Swelling was minimal. However, I decided to wait another day before confining his leg."

"Good call." Ben yawned. "Pardon me. Even with the extra rest, I could easily drift off."

"Maybe I'll let you sleep in again tomorrow."

"I appreciate it, but I must return to a routine." He rolled his neck from side to side. "Sleeping and eating are a good place to start."

"Then I'll have Edie ring a bell at your door in the morning." Rebecca's eyes twinkled with mischief. "She was quite concerned when I didn't wake you for breakfast today."

Ben chuckled. "She voiced her concerns when I came downstairs after missing the noon meal."

"Oh, I didn't realize she'd come in. She didn't bother you, did she?"

"Not at all. She was rather helpful. Brought the plate you set aside for me and reminded me to keep things tidy." He chuckled. "We had an interesting chat about the—" He patted his pocket. "She's concerned about Ivajohn's lifelong journey with Pastor Turner. She believes the spyglass is a crucial gift for Ivajohn's travels."

Rebecca's face softened, and she shook her head. "Poor girl. She must've misunderstood. She's heard us talk about marriage as a lifelong journey. She probably took it literally."

"She thinks Ivajohn will be gone for a long time and may forget her." His smile dimmed. "She hoped the spyglass could remind Ivajohn of her."

Rebecca released a heavy sigh. "I had no idea. I'll talk to her and clear things up."

Ben's smile returned. "I offered to help her make a new gift."

"That's thoughtful." Her gaze brightened. "What did you have in mind?"

"I'm not sure." He stroked his stubbled chin. "But I did find out how she got the spyglass."

"Oh?"

"She saw Ollie put it in the lost and found room. She thought it would be perfect for Ivajohn's wedding gift." He rested a hand on his knee, yawning. "I'd like to ask Ollie about the spyglass if it's all right with you."

"Permission granted." Rebecca nodded. "I'll talk to Nellie.

The twins stick together like pulled taffy. She might know something."

Suddenly, a boy rushed at them from the trees north of Poplar Street, flailing his arms. Pickle sidestepped but didn't bolt. Rebecca guided Noble around Ben and paused to let them regain their composure.

"Whoa, whoa, easy now." She took a firm hold on her reins. "Are you all right? What happened?"

"I need help. Oscar has been snake bitten." The boy collapsed to his knees, gasping. "A big rattler."

"You follow the boy." Rebecca glanced at Ben. "I'll go to the boardinghouse for supplies and catch up. Tell us where Oscar is."

"He's in the middle of that stand of trees." The boy pointed toward the woods.

Ben's heart pounded. He whispered to Rebecca, "This will require an incision. I can't do it."

"Trust me, Ben. All you need to do is keep the boy and Oscar calm." She reached over to squeeze his hand, her touch brief but steady. Ben clung to it longer than he should, anchoring himself to her certainty. "I'll be there soon. I have a plan."

She galloped toward Cane Hill, leaving Ben to stare at the boy. Taking a deep breath, he extended his hand, and the child swung up behind him.

"What's your name?"

"Jace."

"Nice to meet you, Jace. I'm Ben." He guided Pickle through the trees, avoiding low branches. "What were you and Oscar up to?"

"Hunting."

"Did you get the snake?"

"I tried but missed. All I got for hunting is rocks." Frustration tinged his voice.

When the trees grew too thick, they dismounted. Ben tied Pickle to a tree and followed Jace through the dense underbrush. He stopped as a yelp rang out, fading to a whimper. Stretching his arm across Jace's chest, he protected the child from the unseen.

"That's him," Jace whispered. "Oscar. Let's go."

"Wait." Ben held Jace back. "How do you know Oscar? Is he your friend?"

"He's my best friend." Jace tugged Ben's arm. "The best dog ever. You gotta help him."

Ben's heart settled. Oscar, the dog. Not a patient. Relief hit him so hard his knees weakened. Shame followed close behind. He hadn't even asked. He'd only feared.

His pulse slowed as Jace urged him forward. Kneeling beside the yellow dog, Ben reached out. The dog lifted its head, and Ben paused. Some unspoken understanding passed between them, and the dog lowered its head. Ben's hand trembled as he touched the wound.

"An incision should be made here." He pointed to the spot, recoiling at the thought. "And then we extract the venom."

"Do it, mister." Tears welled in Jace's eyes. "I can't lose him. He's my best friend."

Ben swallowed hard. "I don't have a scalpel."

"A what?"

"A knife."

Jace pulled a folding knife from his pocket. Ben raised an eyebrow. "I thought you only had rocks."

"Can't be throwing my knife. Might never find it."

Ben extended the blade, his hands trembling despite his firm grip. The boy grew wide-eyed and fixed. Ben closed his eyes and steadied his breath. Opening his eyes, he inched the blade closer to the dog's wound. Then, he froze.

"Ben, stop!" Rebecca burst through the trees, breathless.

Ben dropped the knife and ran his hands through his hair,

nausea harassing his stomach. "Rebecca, we need to make the incision. We're running out of time."

"There is another way." She handed Ben an egg, then pulled a salt cellar from the pocket under her skirts. She cracked the egg, emptying its contents into her palm. "Add the salt. A lot of it."

He shook salt onto the yolk. "I don't understand. What are you doing?"

"I'm preparing a poultice." She mixed it. "The salt should draw the venom from the wound." She smiled reassuringly at the boy. "You didn't mention Oscar was a dog."

"Will it work?" Jace's eyes sparkled with hope.

"It's worked before. But if too much time has passed, it might not." Rebecca applied the poultice to the wound. "We'll leave it for twenty minutes. If it turns green, it's working."

"What now?" Jace rubbed Oscar's head.

"We apply a fresh poultice every twenty minutes until the egg stops turning green." Rebecca touched Ben's arm. "We'll take him to the boardinghouse and make a bed for him in the old forge."

"Jace can ride with you, and I'll carry Oscar on Pickle. He's itching to run anyway." Ben hoisted the dog onto Pickle's back and mounted.

Jace stepped toward Pickle and stroked Oscar's paw. "Can I stay with Oscar?"

"We have rooms at our house. I think you should stay." Rebecca helped Jace onto Noble, her arms wrapping around him. So small. And yet he fiercely clung to her. Rebecca held him like someone who knew the cost of letting go. She glanced at Ben. "But first, we need to contact your parents."

"I ain't got no ma. And Pa is gone right now." The boy bobbed up and down in front of her. "I want to sleep with Oscar."

Rebecca brushed his copper hair. "Wouldn't you prefer to sleep in a cozy bed?"

"No, ma'am. I'd rather be with my dog."

"He can sleep in the forge. I'll stay with them." Ben rested his hand on Oscar's chest. Pickle's gentle trot almost masked the shallow rise and fall of the dog's breath.

"Are you sure?" Rebecca glanced at him.

He nodded.

"All right then. You can stay with him." She patted Jace's leg. "But first you'll have supper in the house."

"Uh-uh. You got biscuits?" Jace shook his head, red hair swaying back and forth. "I'll eat in the forge by Oscar."

"You need to keep your strength up because Oscar needs you." Rebecca set her chin. "Come in for dinner, or you won't be permitted in the forge."

"But—"

"No buts." Ben dismounted, leading Pickle through the gate. "Miss Hogue is correct. You won't be able to help Oscar if you're not well-rested and nourished. So, what do you say to her?"

"Yes, ma'am." Jace's voice was small but sure.

Chapter Sixteen

As Ben tied Pickle to the post by the stable, he couldn't help but grin. When had Rebecca become so accomplished? He'd always believed she would thrive in medicine. She had ingenuity and courage, but her progress without a formal apprenticeship surprised him. His gaze lingered as she dismounted, secured Noble to a post, and embraced their young friend. She was strong, tender, commanding, and compassionate all at once.

Rebecca turned to face him, and he averted his eyes, a slow heat unfurling within him. He cleared his throat, tugging Oscar into his arms. "Could you get the door?"

Rebecca opened it, and he slipped inside the forge. It was dim and hollow compared to his memories at Hogue House. Only a few tools and one anvil remained, and two leather aprons hung on the back wall. A box of matches rested beside a candle holder on a table next to the wood stove. On the stove, neatly stacked tin cups sat beside a coffee pot. At the back, ornate candles stood on a shelf.

As Jace stepped through the doorway, Rebecca grabbed his shirt collar. "Not so fast, sir. You've got to eat first, or I'll have to keep you from Oscar for fifteen whole minutes." She winked. "No way around it."

Ben marveled at how effortlessly she wielded both compassion and authority.

Jace pouted. "Yes, ma'am."

Ben placed Oscar on the worktable by the forge. The dog lay unnaturally motionless, and only his chest's faint rise and fall gave any sign of life.

Ben wedged the door open with a wooden block and entered the stable at the opposite end of the structure. After grabbing some rags from the tack closet, he picked up a hay bale, then went back for two more. When he finished, he met Rebecca and Jace at the forge door.

"Can we help?" She tousled the boy's copper hair.

Ben used snippers to cut the twine from the hay bales. "Could you get a pail of water?"

"Is it needed for drinking or washing?"

"Both." He broke up one bale, fashioning it into a nest.

Striking a match, he lit the candle. A slight tremor persisted as he grasped the candleholder.

It's a dog, Ben. Relax.

He returned to the worktable, holding the candle near Oscar's wound. Rebecca and Jace appeared with two buckets of water and joined him.

Rebecca inched closer. "So?"

Her breath on his ear sent a shiver down his spine. "It's green. I think it's working."

"Wonderful." Rebecca scooped the poultice away and dropped it into an empty coal pail. "We'll bury it later. If we throw it out, other animals could get into it. I don't know if the venom would lose potency."

Jace whooped. "Oscar's gonna be okay. I know it."

"Don't get too excited." Rebecca took his arm and pulled

him aside. "This is good, but we don't know if we reached him in time. It's too early to tell."

"He's got to make it." Jace's grin faltered. "He's my only friend."

She wrapped her arms around him, squeezing him tightly. "I'll bring a bowl of eggs and the salt cellar. When I come back, we'll say a prayer. Sound good?"

Jace nodded, and Rebecca disappeared through the door.

"Jace, how about helping me with our pallets?" Ben moved the candle to the table by the stove. "Afterward, I'll show you how we'll give Oscar something to drink."

They spread the hay for two makeshift beds. Then, Ben moved Oscar to the hay nested by the door. Next, he placed one bucket on the stove and the other on the worktable. He set a rag on the unlit stove and put two more on the worktable.

"This bucket is drinking water." He patted the one on the stove. "The other is meant for washing." He soaked a rag in the drinking water, wringing it to a slow drip. "We'll give Oscar small amounts at a time, so he doesn't choke. Hold the cloth above his mouth, open his lips, and squeeze."

Water drizzled over Oscar's teeth, and his tongue wiggled slightly. Ben rubbed the dog's throat, the neck muscles undulating as the dog swallowed.

"This is a good sign." He handed the rag to the boy. "Give it a try. Don't overdo it."

Jace beamed, carefully squeezing the rag before handing it back. "I did good, right?"

"You did great." Ben patted Jace on the back.

Jace rested his head on Oscar's side and wrapped his arms around the dog. Petting in all directions, he released a quiet hum.

"All right, young man. Time to rest." Ben gestured to the pallets. "I'll wake you when it's time to water him again."

Rebecca entered with Martie behind her. "I brought the eggs and salt. Martie has bedding and your dinner, Ben."

"You've been here barely a day, and already you're caught in one of Becca's adventures." Martie chuckled as she set the plate on the table. "The boardinghouse may not be ideal for rest. The chicken is a bit dry, Doc. I apologize."

Ben accepted an egg from Rebecca. Cracking it, he mixed in the salt and formed a paste. As his hands steadied, he sighed in relief, then knelt beside Oscar to apply the poultice.

"Are we gonna pray?" Jace grabbed Rebecca's hand. "You promised."

"Of course. Let's hold hands." She waited for Ben and Martie to join them. "Ben, could you lead us?"

He cleared his throat. "Maybe it's best if you do."

"Okay. Let's bow our heads." She took a deep breath, eyes fluttering shut. "Lord, thank you for the chance to minister to this boy and his dog. Please continue to guide our hands. Strengthen us and Oscar as only you can. Sustain us throughout this long night. Amen."

"I'm heading in now. Y'all take care." Martie squeezed Jace and nodded to Ben as she left.

"I'll be in shortly. I'm going to stay while Ben eats."

Ben raised an eyebrow. "You don't have to."

"I'm not coming back for your plate," she teased. "And I want to ensure a certain young man uses his pallet."

Ben dipped a cup of water and sat at the table with his food.

Rebecca helped Jace spread sheets and blankets over the hay. "How's that? Comfortable enough?"

Jace wiggled around, shaping the hay to his liking. "Way better than where I sleep with my brothers. Plus, no elbows in my side tonight."

"You have brothers?" Ben paused, setting his fork down. "You didn't mention them when Miss Hogue asked if we could contact someone on your behalf."

"Well, they wouldn't care." He scrunched his nose. "They're always shoving me out of the bed."

Ben exchanged a glance with Rebecca. "How many brothers do you have?"

"Three. My oldest brother and twins."

Their eyes widened.

"Jace," Rebecca said carefully, "what's your last name?"

"Drake." The boy beamed. "Pa named me Jace Cooter Drake. Cooter on account of he says I came into this world with strong legs, just like the river turtles called Cooters."

"Jace, you get some rest. Remember, Oscar needs you." Ben rose, helping Rebecca to her feet. "Miss Hogue and I will stable the horses."

They stepped into the thick night air.

"Well, if that isn't a curious bit of happenstance." Ben chuckled.

"I don't believe in happenstance." Rebecca smiled brightly. "Divine intervention, that's what it is."

"Divine intervention?" Simon appeared at the gate.

"Rebecca and I happened upon the brother of those Drake twins." Ben wiped his forehead. "Can you believe it?"

"Where is he?"

"In the forge."

"I need to speak with him." Simon moved toward the forge, but Rebecca blocked him.

"He's not going anywhere. We're caring for his dog. Talk to him tomorrow." She rested her hand on Simon's chest. "Could you assist Ben with the horses? I need to help the girls." She turned to Ben. "I've kept some of Ollie's old clothes for Edie to play in. I'll find something nicer for Jace to wear to church tomorrow."

"I thought Jace and I would stay here with Oscar."

"It might do you both good to go." She gave Ben's arm a reassuring pat. "It refreshes the spirit."

"Levi urged me to attend also. I'd hate to disappoint him. Maybe we *should* go." He rubbed his neck. "If we're fortunate, the boy may lead us to his brothers."

"Wonderful." Rebecca turned to Simon. "So, you'll help with the horses?"

"Sure, but I want to know more about this boy." Simon pursed his lips.

"Tea in the dining room when I'm finished?"

Simon nodded, and Rebecca faced Ben.

"Well done today." She squeezed his arm as she passed. "Almost like old times."

Almost like old times. Almost. But not yet.

Rebecca disappeared inside. Almost like old times. The sentiment lingered with Ben as he followed Simon to the horses.

Chapter Seventeen

"Thank you both for preparing the evening meal. It was quite good." Rebecca handed Martie one end of a bedsheet. "Who thought of folding the laundry for me?"

Martie smiled, bouncing her eyebrows. "I'm sorry the chicken was dry. We lost track of time."

"Do you remember all the overcooked chicken we ate when Mama taught me to cook? With time and practice, you'll get it." Rebecca folded two corners of the sheet together and joined Martie in the middle to grasp the opposite corners. "I'm sorry I haven't had as much time to teach you as Mama took with me."

"I don't plan on giving it much practice." Cordelia sat at the end of the dining table, continuously pairing the same set of socks. "I plan to marry into wealth and have a servant to handle the cooking. I'll host extravagant parties and entertain everyone around the piano."

"I want to learn to cook over an open fire in the yard." Martie swayed as she folded a towel. "Tommy and I intend to marry one day. We'll head west, and I'll be a trail cook until we settle somewhere."

Rebecca sighed, rubbing her chest to soothe the dull ache. To be seventeen and in love with grand dreams and abounding hope. If only Martie understood how life could disrupt even the most carefully crafted plans. Rebecca bit her lip, acutely aware of how swiftly life could box a person in. Sadly, she had no clever solutions for shielding her sisters from derailed lives. Aspirations of securing a prosperous marriage or seeking adventure in the West were unrealistic and foolish.

"I have news." Rebecca placed the bed sheet on a stack of linens. "Mr. Perry won't be staying with us any longer. He left for a job in Missouri about an hour after Pa and Justin left this morning."

"Mr. Perry's been with us for a decade. He didn't even bid us all farewell?" Martie's brow furrowed as she picked a shirt from the dining table.

"I think it was a tough choice for him. He promised to write."

The ticking of the parlor clock punctuated the silence. Martie stared at the shirt she folded while Cordelia feigned rummaging for socks. The uneasy quiet stretched on like the Arkansas River. Rebecca sorted kitchen towels.

"I have something else to tell you." She sighed and tossed the freshly folded towel on the table. "We have no boarders."

"That's not true. Ben Ewing is in his old room." Cordelia paired the same socks for the third time. "He may be in the forge tonight, but you know what I mean."

"We have no *paying* boarders." Rebecca squeezed her eyes shut and sighed.

"Pardon?" Cordelia matched the socks yet again before adding them to the first pair.

"I trust this stays between us. Justin is allowing Ben to stay free of charge." Rebecca clutched the towel to her chest. "He needs time to rest."

Martie shifted her gaze between Cordelia and Rebecca. "What does that mean?"

"It means the three of us must figure out how to make some money." Rebecca tensed, placing her hands on her hips. "It won't be easy, but if we pull together, we'll be all right."

"What about Simon?" Cordelia fiddled with a different pair of socks.

"Simon is busy stepping in for Justin and the sheriff while they're away."

Cordelia's face pinched. "Seems like he could do more to help out here."

"Let's be honest, shall we, Cordelia?" Rebecca jabbed the air with her finger. "You put more effort into avoiding work than contributing here. You're constantly on the prowl for a well-to-do suitor. It's frivolous and irresponsible, and it's gone on long enough."

"Well, I—"

"Not another word." Rebecca raised a flat palm. Clenching a nearby towel, she reminded herself she had held her tongue long enough. "Pa has coddled you, but I will not. You ought to be a proficient cook by now. You are not. You should excel at sewing and darning. You do not. I suggest you first inquire with Mrs. Gray at the café or Mrs. Brandt at the tailor shop. It would be a valuable experience for you."

"Oh, I would be thrilled to work with either of them." Martie folded her hands under her chin, bouncing on her heels. "Mrs. Gray is delightfully entertaining, while Mrs. Brandt is utterly fascinating. Cordelia, who will you ask first?"

"I cannot be seen working in a local establishment. Think of the impact on my prospects." Her face contorted as her hand flew to her chest. "Men of means would never consider pursuing a woman who works outside the home."

"Honestly, Cordelia, Mama should never have let you spend

six months with Aunt Lucinda in St. Louis when you were fourteen. She filled your head with such nonsense." Rebecca pursed her lips. "Where will you look for work?"

"Where will *you* look for work?" Cordelia straightened, eyes sharp and incredulous.

"I don't know." Rebecca sighed. "It's more challenging for me. I'll need time to drum up boarders and manage the household. Unless you'd prefer to handle it?"

"I won't be wrangled into herding this wild bunch. Tomorrow, after church, I'll meet Caroline Brandt at the picnic in the square." Cordelia shoved the socks back into the pile and stormed out.

"I suppose I'll be visiting Mrs. Gray then." Martie's shoulders drooped. "I hoped to work with Mrs. Brandt. Her hats are simply delicious." She beamed. "But Mrs. Gray is the most jovial woman I know. Maybe I'll improve my cooking."

Rebecca rounded the table and embraced Martie. "You've always had such an endearing optimism."

"Becca, have you had a chance to think about my request since Ivajohn moved to the parsonage?" Martie paused. "About me moving into the older girls' room with you and Cordelia?"

"Are you sure you want to be in such close quarters with her?"

"I can't blame her. I try to imagine what it must have been like to be the baby girl in the family for five years." Martie tapped her lips thoughtfully. "Then I arrived, and suddenly, she wasn't the baby anymore. That must have been tough for a five-year-old."

"Well, she's twenty-two. She should have worked it out by now." Rebecca pinched Martie's chin.

The front door groaned open and shut. Rebecca stretched her neck to glimpse into the parlor. "Simon, is that you?"

Simon entered, hat in hand. Fine lines deepened around his blue eyes as his gaze met Rebecca's. He slumped into the chair at the end of the table, resting his hat on his midsection, elbows drooping over the arms.

"I want to hear about this boy."

"He approached us on Poplar Street from the large stand of trees near the McPherson place, seeking help for an injured friend named Oscar, who turned out to be a dog." Rebecca pulled out a chair. "We brought them into the forge. Turns out his last name is Drake."

"Are you serious? I've been searching for these Drake boys all day, and one is right here in the forge." Simon wiped his brow with his sleeve. "How long?"

"A couple of hours, maybe." She patted his knee. "But there's more."

"Please." Simon yawned, slumping in his seat. "Tell me."

"I was at the mercantile earlier when another redheaded boy came in for beans and rice." She grinned. "Sam gave him a few apples and peaches, no charge. He said Drake boys don't take charity, and he promised to return to sweep floors."

Simon sat up. "You've stumbled upon two of them in a single day? I've found nothing."

"Mm-hmm. The boy from Mooney's didn't say when he'd return, but he was there before two o'clock today. Of course, the mercantile is closed tomorrow, but maybe he'll return Monday."

"I'll visit Sam tomorrow to see if he remembers seeing the boy before today. First, I'll talk to your friend in the barn." He traced his finger along the hat brim. "I'll take Noble tomorrow. If I find the other Drake boys, they may give chase."

"Must you track these boys? They haven't violated any laws and likely meant no harm." Rebecca hesitated. "Though riding a green-broke horse through town was unwise."

"I don't intend to punish them." Simon set his hat on the table. "But they need to learn responsibility. They should help around Mr. Fremont's place. Better I catch up to them than

Nicholas. I'll ask where they're staying, how they're getting food, and so forth. Nicholas would only frighten them."

"You should bring them here for a meal when you find them."

"That's a great idea." He rubbed his face. "I visited the Fremonts before heading home. They're doing well, but will need help soon. It's essential to find the rest of those Drake boys."

"I'm sure we'll track them down now that we've found Jace."

"Listen." Simon lowered his voice. "More folks are reporting unfamiliar faces at night. Don't go wandering too far into the grove."

Rebecca pressed her lips together, resisting the urge to bristle. She was capable. Careful. She'd always found clarity among the trees, but now even the grove was off-limits?

Simon thumped his hat. "Another busy day tomorrow."

"Not too busy. Tomorrow is Sunday, remember?" Martie picked up the towels and went to the kitchen.

"Simon, maybe you could wait until after church to speak with our young friend?" Rebecca propped her chin on her hand. "Give him some time to see we care. Build trust."

"After church, then. But not a moment longer."

Rebecca patted him on the back. "Tomorrow will be an easy day for you. Enjoy it. Why not ask someone to share a picnic blanket with you?"

"Nah. I'm beat. I was called to the saloon to bust up a disturbance." He rubbed his hand over his short blond hair. "I'll rest if I don't find those Drake boys."

"Perfect Sunday plan." Rebecca sighed. "What I wouldn't give for such an afternoon."

"Go ahead." Simon tapped her shoulder with his hat. "You deserve it more than I do."

"I can't. I'll put up a vacancy notice at the mercantile while at the picnic and ask Mr. Mooney for suggestions on increasing revenue since Mr. Perry's departure." She yawned. "And you should tell folks to call for Nicholas whenever there's a problem. It's best if you stay out of it. He's closer anyway."

"No need for Nicholas to get caught up in it either, especially since everyone knows he dislikes leaving his work at the saddlery." Simon squeezed her shoulder and whispered, "Besides, I *enjoy* the work." He laid his hat against his chest, his volume returning to normal. "I'm good at diffusing these situations, extinguishing the flames of conflict between people. I only wish my family could see and accept it."

She studied his face. For all his bravado, Simon carried the ache of needing to be seen. How had she never noticed they had that in common?

"One day you might get hurt ..." Rebecca tightened against a twinge of nausea. "Or worse."

"I agree." Martie's bright eyes dimmed. "I couldn't bear losing you like we lost Mama."

"Well, you don't need to worry about it this evening." Simon put his hat on. He hugged Martie and then Rebecca. "I'll be sleeping in the bunkhouse. It'll keep me from waking the rest of you when I pop in and out to check on Ben and his young friend during the night." He ambled through the parlor to the front door. "Get some rest, Becks."

She pressed a smile, shook her head, and muttered, "Don't call me Becks."

Martie giggled. "He thinks the world of you. I doubt there's anyone he admires more."

"Funny way of showing it."

"That's the way of siblings, isn't it?"

"I suppose so." She patted the table. "Could you please finish this last little bit without me? I need to talk to Edie if she's awake."

"You know she will be. Little Miss Night Owl is likely talking Nellie's ear off." Martie tossed a few pairs of socks into the basket. "It's another reason I'm eager for a room change. I'd enjoy a bit more quiet."

"Good luck finding it in this house. Miss Prim and Proper snores." With a wink, Rebecca exited the dining room through the kitchen and went up the back staircase.

At the top of the stairs, she rounded the banister toward the family rooms and paused. She turned toward Ben's room. Her breath stalled, and she pressed her eyes shut. A deep inhale set her in motion. Her heart kicked hard against her ribs. With her hand on the doorknob, she hovered a moment longer before stepping inside.

The blankets were pushed aside, and the pillow sat askew on Coleman Perry's bed. The chest at the foot of the bed stood open. Ben's bed was neatly made. A copper-colored striped shirt and tan pants lay at the foot of the bed. They were Simon's, refolded with Ben's signature mark of square precision. Even broken men clung to order. Maybe especially them. She smiled.

A solitary oil lamp occupied the bedside table. Perhaps she should ask Levi if he could procure a Bible for Ben. Against the far wall, a wash rag hung over the rod of the washstand, and a small, curved bottle rested beside the basin. She went and picked it up. Uncapping it, she held it to her nose and inhaled deeply. Citrus and rosemary.

A flicker of movement outside the window drew her closer. Ben stood in the yard, stretching his arms skyward, swaying from side to side, and flapping his arms around his shoulders before rubbing his eyes. So small against the vastness of the yard. She wanted to call him back inside, but she stayed silent.

Her heart softened. *He needs rest.* Her brothers' words echoed in her ears. Today had not given him much chance to relax. She frowned. The idea of performing the traditional snakebite procedure had unsettled him. Maybe a break from practicing medicine *was* in order. Despite this, he had volunteered to spend the night in the forge with the boy and the dog.

Ben yawned and stretched, then glanced toward the window. Rebecca stepped back, sipping air. She waited, then leaned closer as he entered the forge. Pivoting, she leaned against the window with a sigh and half-wished she could lay down her burdens, but was afraid of who might pick them up if she did. She took another sniff from the fragrance bottle, capped it, returned it to its place, and left the room.

Chapter Eighteen

Rebecca quietly pushed open the door to the younger girls' room. She glanced at Nellie, who rolled her eyes as Edie prattled on in a less-than-quiet whisper. She crossed the room and slid into bed beside her youngest sister, wrapping her arm around the child.

"Edie, why are you still awake?"

"I lay down, and my brain keeps going." Edie's wide blue eyes went all puppy dog. She propped on her elbow and faced Rebecca. "Becca, check my nose. Do you think I have more freckles than I did this morning? There are more, I know it."

Nellie huffed. "I'm going downstairs for a glass of water."

Rebecca waved in acknowledgment. "Edie, there are no more freckles than you had when the day began." She tapped Edie's nose and drew her into a hug. "Now, lie down here, and let's talk."

"What about?"

"The spyglass."

Edie's petite frame tensed. "I said I was sorry."

"Honey, I spoke with Ben. He mentioned the two of you had a fascinating discussion about it."

Edie sat up with a frown. "He's a doctor. I thought doctors couldn't share information with people. They're supposed to be confident."

Rebecca chuckled. "The term you want is confidential. Doctors must uphold confidentiality, but it only pertains to their patients." As Rebecca gently brushed Edie's hair and rested her hand on the child's cheek, Edie settled back down. Rebecca drew her close again. "Were you Dr. Ewing's patient when you talked to him?"

"No."

"Then he broke no confidence with you. He's trying to help."

"He'd be more helpful if he knew how to be quiet."

"Is the pot calling the kettle black?" She smiled. "Is it true you think Ivajohn is leaving on a long journey? Away from us?"

"No, ma'am. Not a long journey. She's going on a *lifelong* journey." The liquid shimmer in Edie's eyes pierced Rebecca's heart. "That's the longest journey I ever heard of."

"Oh, Edie." Rebecca squeezed her extra tight. "You misunderstood our meaning. Ivajohn isn't planning to leave town, sweetie. Her only trips will be the brief missionary journeys we've grown accustomed to her taking with Pastor Turner. The term 'journey' isn't limited to travel. It can also describe life experiences or personal growth through different stages. Ivajohn and Pastor Turner will grow together through all their shared experiences for the rest of their lives."

"So she's not leaving Van Buren forever?"

"No, honey. They'll live at the parsonage." Rebecca tousled Edie's hair. "We'll see them at church. They'll ask us to tea. We'll have suppers together from time to time. You'll see her often enough."

"So," Edie's voice faltered, "it won't be the same as when Mama left?"

"No, sweetheart." Holding back tears, Rebecca kissed the top of her sister's head. "Mama was a special case. I doubt any of us will depart like she did. So don't worry about losing us, all right?"

"I can't remember." Edie sniffled, burying her head in Rebecca's shoulder. "I can't picture Mama's face." Edie stroked Rebecca's hair. "But I remember how soft her hair was, like yours."

Rebecca's chest ached. *Oh, Lord, why did Mama have to leave us? How will we survive without her?*

She raised Edie's chin. "Mama's portrait hangs above the mantle in the parlor."

Edie nodded.

"You can look at it whenever you're unable to hold on to her image here." She tapped Edie's forehead.

"But someday, we will all grow up. We'll all live in different homes." Edie rubbed her nose. "Who gets Mama's picture then?"

"Hmm." Rebecca gazed at the ceiling. "I hadn't considered it. There must be a way for all of us to have a picture of her. I'll think about it a bit more, okay?"

"I'd like that." Edie nodded, her eyelids drooping. She yawned and rolled over, quickly falling asleep.

The bedroom door creaked open, and Nellie peeked in. She mouthed, "Is she asleep?"

Rebecca nodded, got out of Edie's bed, and went to Nellie's. She smoothed the blanket. Nellie climbed in, sitting cross-legged on top of the blanket.

"Listen, I wanted to ask about the spyglass." Rebecca placed her hand on Nellie's knee and nodded toward Edie. "It's my understanding she saw Ollie put it in the lost-and-found room. Do you have any idea where he might have found it?"

"I know he didn't give it to her."

"Oh, no. Ollie's not in trouble. I'm certain he didn't give it to her." Rebecca pressed her lips together. "She watched him put it in there and went in after he left. I'm curious about where he got it. You twins spend so much time together, I thought you might know."

"I don't want to get Ollie in trouble."

"Has he done something he shouldn't have?"

"You won't like it." Nellie folded her knees up to her chest.

"Nellie, if you confide in me, I will manage the situation with as much grace as possible."

"Instead of coming straight home from school, he's been slipping away to the riverfront with the other boys." Nellie picked at her fingernails. "I stay with the girls after school to clean the blackboard. Then we take turns swinging and chatting about boys. Anyway, I suppose he discovered it while wandering along the riverbank."

"I understand."

"I urged him to stay at school or go home. I knew you wouldn't be happy with him hanging around the riverfront." She sighed. "But he didn't listen. Is he going to be in a lot of trouble?"

Rebecca bowed her head in thought.

"Becca?"

"I've never been a fourteen-year-old boy, so I may not have the best perspective." She took Nellie's hand. "Perhaps I'll seek advice from someone who knows what it's like to be a teenage boy before deciding. Sound good?"

"Fair enough."

"Sleep well, Nellie." Rebecca kissed her on the forehead. Then she walked to the door.

"Becca?"

"Yes?" She poked her head back in.

"I appreciate you not pulling Ollie out of bed to talk to him." She offered a faint smile. "Although he probably needs a talking-to."

Rebecca padded down the hallway to her room and nudged the door open. Cordelia slept in the bed nearest to the door. She grabbed her journal from the bedside table and tiptoed down the back stairs. As she crossed the kitchen, she glanced into the dining room.

"Martie, I expected you would have gone to bed by now. Is everything all right?"

"Waiting for Nelli and Edie to fall asleep. I noticed a stack of books on the parlor table and thought I'd read for a while." She closed the novel, keeping her place with her finger. "I hope that's all right."

"Of course. Caroline Brandt sent over *Jane Eyre*. The others are from Allie." Rebecca furrowed her brows. "What's the deal with all these books?"

"I thought reading might help me fall asleep despite Edie's talking. I'll read in bed tomorrow night and see if it works." Martie smiled.

Rebecca tapped her journal. "I'll sit outside and write in my journal."

"In the dark?"

"In the fading moonlight. It will be the most time I've had to myself all day. The sliver of moonlight will vanish in a few days, and I'll lose these solitary moments for a bit." Rebecca wiggled her fingers. "Back soon."

She strolled through the kitchen and stepped out the back door to a small circle of stumps. Wood shavings dotted the center of the fire ring, a remnant of Pa and Simon's whittling sessions. She glanced to the north. How far had Pa and Justin traveled before setting up camp? Were they making good time? Would they arrive home in time for the wedding?

She opened her journal, removed the pencil, and scanned the back side of the Hogue property. Licking the tip, she made gentle strokes on the page, planning to darken the fine lines later. Her heart lifted as nature's nightly lullaby unfolded—the crickets' tenor chirps harmonizing with the frogs' low, guttural croaks. The fire ring, the moon, and the oak grove emerged in her sketch as her hand flowed freely across the page.

If only she could fill the boardinghouse as swiftly. Then her sisters might avoid seeking jobs beyond their usual chores. She sighed.

"Lord, I have countless concerns demanding my attention. Justin and Pa, Ivajohn's wedding, Ollie's adventures, Mr. Fremont and the Drake boys, the issues with the boardinghouse. And Ben. So much more. I try not to worry, yet figuring out how to address everything is overwhelming. I'm not sure I can manage like Mama did."

A twig snapped in the distance. Rebecca's head lifted, her eyes scanning the tree line. Nothing moved. Probably a possum or raccoon. Even so, her hand hovered above her journal a beat longer as she held her breath.

A cat skittered across the yard, and she dropped the pencil into the journal's crease, resting her hand on her chest. Her lungs expanded and contracted. Filled and emptied. A faint, flickering light caught her attention. A tiny firefly drew nearer and nearer until it landed on the end of the pencil.

"Why are you out here so late all by yourself, little one?" She raised the journal, drawing the firefly closer.

Another small light sparkled in the grove. The firefly on her journal darted uncomfortably close to her face before veering back to the trees. Soon, two glimmering lights danced through the oak grove, finally disappearing from view.

Rebecca jotted a note in the journal and closed it. "Perhaps you aren't alone in the dark after all."

A soft breeze stirred her skirts, and an unexpected chill tiptoed down her spine. She glanced again toward the grove, hushed and empty, but the sensation lingered. Odd, that. Nothing visible, yet her senses refused to settle.

She shook it off. The fireflies had stirred something more

profound than usual tonight. Yet, the feeling of being watched clung to her like mist.

～

As Rebecca stepped out of the boardinghouse, Ambrose Baas melted into the shadows of the old oak. Her hair shimmered like golden honey under the soft moonlight as she opened a book. Or a journal? Grasping a pencil, she surveyed her surroundings. Was she aware of his presence?

He edged deeper into the old tree's shadow, pulling his bowler low on his brow. Her delicate porcelain hand glided quickly across the page, first one way, then the other. Sketching, perhaps?

His eyes followed the graceful line of her bowed neck down to the soft curve of her waist. Pressing himself against the oak, he yearned to bridge the gap between them. Soon, she would be his.

"Isn't she a lovely little thing?" Caine's raspy whisper grated on him.

Baas's hand shot out, gripping Caine's shirt and thrusting him back against the tree. His forearm pressed firmly against the man's collarbone. His jaw tightened.

"Why are you here?"

Caine ran a hand through his dark hair and let out a low, careless chuckle. "If I'm risking my neck, I want to see what makes her worth it." He wiped his lip, the scent of whiskey lingering on his breath. "And I want to get paid."

"You'll get paid when the job is finished." Baas's voice was cold, but his eyes flickered toward Rebecca as she sat, focused on her work.

"Perry left for Missouri this morning. The job is done." Caine's grin widened, but a gleam in his eyes hinted at something far more sinister. "He'll not be coming back."

Baas stiffened, his pulse quickening. He didn't want to think about what *exactly* that meant. It was a transaction, business. Nothing personal. Yet his fingers tightened in his coat pocket, itching to do something, anything, but push it all away. He needed this. It had to be done.

"You're sure?" Baas kept his eyes on Rebecca. "Did he ride out alone? Any chance he'll return?"

"With the money you offered, he'd ride to Canada." Caine sucked air through his teeth. "But he rode out with the boys. They'll make sure he makes it to Missouri or doesn't come back."

The stench of sweet corn whiskey burned Baas's nostrils, but he pushed the discomfort aside, focusing on the task at hand. Baas pushed his arm forward, transferring pressure from Caine's collarbone to the lower section of his throat.

"No drinking while working for me. Stay clear-headed."

"I finished the job." Caine offered a lazy smirk.

"Perry was only one part of the job." Baas glanced back at Rebecca, her hand continuing its journey across the page. "Have you visited Paulette Bradley?"

"I issued marching orders to those hens today. Two days to vacate." Caine sniffed with satisfaction. "The Bradley woman sure was shocked to see her husband's signature on the deed. She hasn't seen him in two years."

"Finding people is one of my unique skills." Baas narrowed his eyes. "He was eager to sell. These transactions are much easier when the woman is married, and the man is in the bottle."

Caine grunted and shoved Baas's arm away. "My money."

"You'll receive payment once those women leave town."

"You didn't mention anything about running them out of town." Caine dragged his hand down his chin. "You wanted 'em out of the boardinghouse."

"I don't want those women lodging within fifty miles of this town." His voice was sharp, though a flicker of discomfort lingered in his chest. "Their plight shouldn't create an additional source of income for anyone willing to house them."

"What about this? This is about more than securing property." Caine's gaze flickered as he sized Baas up. "What's the plan for Little Miss?"

Baas flinched at the tone but covered it quickly. "I worked on her father's steamboat in St. Louis, gradually advancing. My goal was to buy my own vessel. Clayburn Hogue chose Hale Cobb as his second in command instead of me, causing my financial backer to withdraw support." His lips pressed together, a hint of something raw below the surface. "Soon after, Hogue let me go. It took years to claw my way back to success."

"Put you in your place, did he?"

Baas pinned Caine again, pressing hard at the base of Caine's neck until the man clawed at his arm. "My stepfather was to be the financial backer. Now I own a steamboat company and hotels in several cities. If I can secure a railroad deal, I'll outshine my stepfather. I'll prove to him, and Clayburn Hogue, what a mistake they made."

Caine's eyes glinted. "She's more than property to you, isn't she?"

Baas clenched his jaw. "She's a means to an end, Caine. Nothing more." Even as the words left his mouth, a hollow ache gnawed at his chest. "But there's more at stake than land. It's about showing them all who I really am."

The words hung between them, but something in Baas's chest tightened when he glanced back toward Rebecca.

Caine smiled slyly. "Won't Clayburn Hogue be surprised when he returns to a new son-in-law?"

Chapter Nineteen

Ben shuffled toward the door of the church at the end of the service, holding Jace's hand. A murmur of conversation hummed around them. Though few people spoke to Ben, several regarded him with curiosity. Or were they staring at the young Drake boy?

"I'm glad to see you made it." Levi offered a solid handshake and a comforting pat on the shoulder. "And you brought a friend along."

"This young fella is Jace." Ben patted Jace's head. "He sought Rebecca's help for his wounded dog."

"You helped, too, Mr. Ewing." Jace's vibrant blue eyes sparkled beneath a tangle of red hair.

"It was nothing." Ben forced a smile. He had never been called *Mister* Ewing. It was always Dr. Ewing or Doc. He rubbed his jaw, unsure of how it set with him. Would he grow accustomed to a new moniker if he left medicine for good? He didn't *feel* like Mr. Ewing. Then again, Dr. Ewing didn't fit well either.

"Mr. Ewing taught me how to apply a poultry."

Ben chuckled at the error. "A poultice."

"Jace, can I have a moment alone with *Mr.* Ewing?" Levi beckoned to Ollie with a wave. "Ollie, could you keep an eye on Jace? Maybe take him to play with the other kids in the churchyard?"

"I'd like that. Let's race." Jace took Ollie's hand. "Bet I can beat you."

"We don't bet." Ollie frowned.

"Then I dare you."

"We don't dare." Ollie's frown lifted as he jogged with the boy a few steps from the door. "But I'll race you."

"So, you've done some doctoring?" Levi grinned.

"Not exactly. It was primarily Rebecca." Ben hooked his thumbs in his pockets while searching for her face among the churchgoers. "She had an excellent command of the situation. And her compassion. I'm not sure my bedside manner ever matched hers."

"She had a lot of practice in your absence. It's impressive how much she's learned from the medical books you left." Levi's expression warmed, admiration flickering in his eyes as he nodded toward Rebecca. "All the same, she's hard on herself when the outcome isn't what she hoped. She compares herself to you."

"Me? I don't see myself as someone to be compared to. Certainly not in terms of medicine." He observed Rebecca talking to a woman with two small girls. The taller girl showed her bandaged hand, and Rebecca lifted the dressing, smiling and nodding. "She has more strength than I'll ever possess."

"Come with me." Levi gestured to Allie, who took his position by the door. He led Ben to a pavilion located behind the church.

"This is new." Ben patted a corner post.

"Allie's idea. She decided the church should have outdoor space for song services so the elderly could sit in the shade."

Levi motioned to the pavilion's roof. "How was it? Helping the boy's dog?"

"We didn't know the patient was a dog. I assumed we were summoned to treat a man or boy suffering from a snake bite." Ben swallowed hard. "The idea of having to perform an incision unsettled me."

"Did you ask the Lord into your difficult moment?"

"I didn't think of it." He hung his head. "It's been ages since I've sensed God's presence. I'm not sure He would abide with me even if I invited Him."

"God's Word assures us that even if the mountains walk away and hills crumble, God's love will remain with you, my friend." Levi squeezed Ben's shoulder. "God has compassion for you and cares for you. This doesn't mean adversity won't find you. Rather, you can rest knowing He will be with you during difficult times."

"What if I'm too shaken to remember to let Him in?"

"It's okay. Remembering a new habit can be tough when you're overwhelmed." Levi pulled a piece of metal from his pocket. "I thought about your hands shaking. In those moments, I'm sure your focus shifts to them. I fashioned this nail into a ring. When your hands tremble, you'll see it and remember."

"I appreciate it, Levi." He slid the ring onto his finger. "More than you know."

"Tell me more about young Jace."

"We don't know much, but there is reason to believe his family may be at risk. We aim to be of further assistance to them. However, Simon and I need to gather more information first. We're going to talk with him before the picnic."

"I won't keep you, then." Levi smiled. "You're welcome to use the pavilion. I'll send them this way. See you on the square."

Levi took a few steps and paused. "Mind if I make an observation?"

Ben raised an upturned palm.

"You bristled when Jace referred to you as Mr. Ewing." Levi arched his brows. "It was barely perceptible, but it was there. A hint of displeasure."

"It was my first time hearing it." Ben ran his thumbs across his fingernails. "My father and grandfather were both doctors. I've never heard them called mister. I've never been called mister either. Getting used to this might be harder than I anticipated."

"It's something to think about." Levi winked and continued to the corner of the building, where Ollie and Jace almost toppled him as they rounded the corner. Ben laughed. Levi directed them in Ben's direction, and the two boys skidded to a stop at the pavilion's edge.

Ollie ruffled Jace's hair. "Okay, kiddo, you got me."

"Ollie." Simon rounded the corner. "Could you help Becks carry the picnic baskets to the square? We'll meet you there a little later."

"Sure thing, if it means I get to eat before you." Ollie laughed and launched into a sprint.

Jace leaped up to chase after him, but Ben caught his arm. "Wait a moment, little buddy. Simon and I need to talk to you before the picnic."

"But I'm starving."

Simon pulled a small bundle from behind his back and sat on the bench, making room for Jace in the middle. "I brought a little snack to hold you over. I've got biscuits, a few bacon pieces, and some lemon drops from Mr. Mooney."

Ben lifted Jace onto the bench between them. "You took excellent care of Oscar last night. We've extracted as much venom as possible, but Oscar will be extremely weak for a long time. Possibly days, weeks, or even months. There's no way to tell. We must keep Oscar at the forge to get the care and rest he needs."

"I'm sorry, Mr. Ewing." Jace shook his head vigorously. "Oscar's got to stay with me."

Simon rested his hand on the young boy's back. "It's truly best for Oscar to stay at Hogue House, but we have more than enough space. You're welcome to stay too."

"Umm-umm. No, sir. We gotta stay together 'cause we may need to leave quick when Pa returns. If I don't get back to my brothers today, I might get left behind when Pa comes."

"Where is your pa?" Ben exchanged a glance with Simon.

"We don't know. He does secret work for a man he met back east."

Simon opened his handkerchief to reveal the treats inside. He handed the boy a biscuit and a slice of bacon. "Your pa just leaves you alone while he goes off to do this work?"

"He doesn't leave us alone. He leaves us with each other." The boy shoved half a biscuit into his mouth and bit into the bacon.

"Slow down there, buddy. You might choke." Ben patted his back. "Who's watching you boys while your pa is gone?"

"Pa says Hayden is in charge since he's the oldest." Crumbs tumbled from Jace's mouth as he talked. "But the twins think they ought to be in charge. While they're fighting about who's in charge, I do what I want."

"I see." Simon lifted his eyebrows, eyes sliding from the boy to Ben. "Were you with the twins when they rode their horse through town on Friday?"

"No, but I heard how some fella's horse went crazy and kicked him. He let out a holler that almost made the twins wet their pants. So they got out of there quick."

Ben picked a piece of bacon from Simon's handkerchief and passed it to Jace. "Listen, Jace. Could you show us where you and your brothers stay when your pa is gone?"

"No, sir. Not on your life. Pa says we gotta keep our place hidden." Jace took another slice of bacon from Simon and stuffed the entire piece into his mouth. "I don't care about being in trouble with my brothers, but I don't want to get in trouble with Pa."

Simon shifted on the bench, crossing his arms and resting one elbow on the backrest. "Jace, do you mean to say that your father is a harsh man?"

"No, sir. Pa never hurt us." The boy gobbled the last bite of biscuit. "I just don't wanna make him unhappy. He works hard taking care of us since we ain't got no ma."

Ben turned to Jace. "Why do you keep your place a secret while your pa is away?"

"He doesn't want the bad man to find us."

Ben's chest tightened. "What bad man? Do you know his name? Can you describe him?"

"Don't know his name. Never seen him. My brothers think Pa made him up to scare us into being good while he's gone."

"How about this?" Simon rubbed his hands together. "Can you find your brothers and persuade them to stay at Hogue House? You'd all be together. You'd be safe. You'd have a comfortable place to sleep and eat, plus someone to protect you while your pa is away."

"So, can I stay with Oscar?"

"Miss Rebecca might like you to share a bedroom with your brothers in the house. But you could check on him whenever you wish. What do you think?" Simon patted his knee as the boy pondered this. "Plus we have a stall in the stable for their horse."

"I'd like that."

"Fantastic." Ben rose, extending his hand. "Shall we go join the others at the picnic?"

"My sister made some tasty potato salad." Simon stood.

"Mm-mmm. Can't remember when I had potato salad." Jace rubbed his belly. "Chicken jerky last night and potato salad today. My brothers are sick of beans and rice. They might come for the food."

The men chuckled as they each took one of Jace's hands. As they strolled toward the square, Jace pulled back a little, his grip tightening, before sprinting forward between them. With practiced timing, the men swung him into the air. The young boy's laughter rang out as his feet touched the ground and he did it again. A rush of bittersweet joy washed over Ben, his memory flashing to fifteen-year-old Sean swinging his youngest brother. When Jace's hand slipped, Ben's hold ratcheted.

"*Ow!*" Jace squirmed. "Too tight."

Ben slowed the swinging motion while Simon caught the boy around his waist. They lowered him to the ground, and he sprinted across the courthouse lawn to Ollie with peals of laughter.

"You all right, Doc?" Simon tipped his hat and wiped his forehead.

"Fine. Fine." Ben glanced at the sky. "Haunted by memories of the past."

"Take a look, Doc. This isn't California. You're back home." Simon patted him on the back. "Take a breath and step into the present with me?"

Ben buried his hands in his pockets. The polished brass telescope pressed against his left hand, and he smiled faintly. "I think I will. Could you watch Jace while I have a word with Ollie?"

"Sure. The shorter, the better, though. I won't be here long. I'm heading home to get some rest."

"I'll be quick." Ben waved to Ollie. "Ollie, a word?"

Ollie and Jace raced each other, carving a tight circle around Ben and Simon before speeding off. Ollie's gaze met Ben's briefly. Or did it? Wariness clouded the boy's eyes on the first night Ben was reintroduced to him in the stable. Then, there was Edie's mention of Ollie's desire to fight him if he hurt

Rebecca. As the boys darted by again, Ollie gave Ben a piercing glare.

"Ollie." Rebecca joined them, standing at Ben's elbow. "Dr. Ewing called you. Come on over."

He joined them, irritation etched on his face. Rebecca drew him to her side, wrapping her arm around his shoulders.

"Ollie, Dr. Ewing is curious about the spyglass Edie brought to the bridal tea."

Ollie opened his mouth, but Rebecca placed her finger on his lips.

"I know you didn't give it to Edie. She acted alone, so you aren't to blame for it being at the tea." She squeezed his shoulders in a side-arm hug. "However, you and I need to discuss later how you acquired it. Agreed?"

"Yes." He nodded.

"All right, go for a stroll with Dr. Ewing." She tousled his hair, and he recoiled. "Ben, if you'd like, I'll save you a spot on the blanket for lunch."

"Of course. Ollie, shall we?"

They strolled along the white split rail fence surrounding the courthouse square. Wavy branches adorned with yellow-tipped leaves cascaded above, softening the stoic appearance of the red brick building at the center of the square. A distant, moaning steamboat whistle pierced the thick air.

Ben cast a sidelong glance at Ollie. "You've grown up quite a bit since I last saw you."

"Life throws challenges your way, and you must grow up." Ollie studied his feet, hands tucked in his pockets. "That's just the way of it."

"That's been my experience as well." Ben wiped his brow. "If I remember correctly, you were about nine when I left for California. You might not recall much about me."

"I remember enough. I saw how sad Rebecca was for weeks." Ollie grew quiet, his expression darkened. He pulled a pebble from his pocket, flicked it off his thumb, and caught it mid-air. "Then Ma died. Rebecca was never the same after that. None of us was the same."

"I'm sorry I wasn't here for your family when your mother died. I never meant to cause pain to Rebecca, and I had hoped to return to her sooner." Ben rubbed his neck. "Life doesn't often go according to plan. I had to wait until I had the means to return home. I hope, in time, your family and the town can forgive me."

"I thought you wanted to discuss the spyglass." Ollie flicked the rock again.

"I thought it best we cleared the air first."

"Okay, Dr. Ewing, let me be straight with you. I won't sit by while Becca gets hurt again." He paused to face Ben, the stone fisted in his hand. "Though I'm the youngest of the Hogue brothers, I'm man enough to take you down. If you hurt her again, you'll have to face me."

"I respect your position." Ben's jaw tightened as Ollie's words struck a chord of unease. He held Ollie's eyes squarely. "Rest assured. It is not my intention to hurt Rebecca." But good intentions weren't enough. Not here. Not with her. "Should there ever be a moment when you believe I've overstepped, I'll depart quietly and promptly."

"Good."

"Since we have come to an understanding, may I ask for your assistance with the spyglass?"

"My help? I don't know what I could do."

"Can you tell me who brought the spyglass to the lost and found?"

"I'm not at liberty to say. I can only tell you it was discovered at the waterfront near the steamboat dock."

"Are you sure there's nothing else you can share with me?"

Ollie rolled his lips together, his gaze flitting away before returning to Ben. "I'm sure." He rested his hand on his stomach. "If you don't mind, I'd like to grab a bite now."

"Of course, go ahead."

Ollie ran a short way when Ben shouted after him, "Hey, Ollie."

The young man turned. "Yes?"

"Thank you for your time."

Ollie nodded and sprinted to the front of the courthouse. Ben leaned against the fence, studying the building. The narrow-domed cupola rising prominently overhead accentuated its rigid exterior. At last, something remained unchanged. He smiled, aching for life to be so simple again.

Chapter Twenty

"Excuse me." A short, stocky man approached from the street. "Are you Dr. Ewing?"

"I am Ben Ewing. And you are?"

"I'm Ambrose Baas, the new hotel owner in town." He walked a few steps toward the fence opening to join Ben. As he rounded the fence, there was something oddly familiar about the man's build. "Am I to understand you're in need of work?"

"I am."

"I don't want to take much of your time on a Sunday, but could you visit the hotel tomorrow?" Baas removed his hat and fanned his face. "Say around two o'clock?"

"What kind of work did you have in mind?"

"Aren't you a doctor?"

"After several years in medicine, I'm considering a new direction."

"I have a few less skilled positions." Baas tucked his hand in his pocket, narrowing his eyes as if sizing Ben up. "But I would offer a higher salary to a doctor. Stop by tomorrow, and we can talk about it more."

"Ben, are you coming to eat?" Cordelia sashayed toward

them. "Rebecca sent me to fetch you. If you don't hurry, the boys will eat it all."

"I regret we haven't met." Baas tucked his hat under his arm, smiling. "And who might you be?"

The man was the picture of charm, at least on the surface. But Ben had seen men like him before. Slick, smooth-talking businessmen who could turn on the charm at a moment's notice, but it was always about money when their true motives came to light. It was the way they handled themselves with others, especially women. The false courtesy. The hidden agenda.

"I might be Cordelia Hogue." Her eyelashes fluttered. "And yourself?"

"Ah, one of the exquisite women of Hogue House. I should have known. Word of your beauty and charm precedes you." A corner of his mouth edged up, revealing a dimple. "I am Ambrose Baas. I own the hotel."

Ben caught the subtle way Baas ogled her up and down. It reminded him of Carraway, a business tycoon he knew in Angels Camp. That man had a talent for captivating both women and men. Women viewed him as a prince, while men saw him as a close ally. But his true nature eventually surfaced, revealing a ruthless underbelly beneath the charm. Ben didn't like the way Baas's eyes lingered on Cordelia.

"Oh, a successful businessman." Her eyes twinkled, accentuating a demure smile as she clasped her hands at her chest. "I'm sure you have many fascinating stories to share."

"I certainly do, but many of the best stories relate to my steamboat business. Some are better shared around a poker table than in polite company."

"I would love to hear them. The more modest ones, of course." She smiled coyly, twirling a strand of dark hair around her finger. Ben's stomach churned.

"Another time, perhaps. I must be on my way, but pleasure

meeting you, Miss Hogue." He donned his hat, took her hand, and kissed the back of it. He tipped his hat to Ben. "Dr. Ewing, until tomorrow."

"Well, he seems delightfully wealthy." Cordelia's gaze followed him until he disappeared. "What did he mean by 'until tomorrow'?"

"He could have some work for me." Ben took her by the elbow and guided her toward the front of the courthouse. "You'd be better off staying away from the likes of him. Men of his kind are ruthless and conniving. I don't know what game he is playing, but you don't want to be caught in it."

"Who are you to say where I want to be caught, Benjamin Ewing?" Her face pinched. "Thanks to you, I've been at the mercy of a dour and high-handed sister these last five years. She used to be convivial and carefree."

"Dour and high-handed? I can't imagine anyone would describe Rebecca in such terms."

"She changed when you left." Cordelia turned to face him. "Just never you mind. I will marry well and be out from under her. Don't even think of standing in my way."

With her dark coils bouncing, Cordelia marched across the lawn toward Caroline Brandt. Ben sighed. An uncomplicated life. It was a fool's dream. How could he rebuild Rebecca's trust if he couldn't reconcile with her siblings? Relations with Cordelia would never be smooth if she set her sights on Ambrose Baas. The man was trouble. He had to be. Ben would do whatever he could to keep her from the man's clutches. Regardless, he had managed to win over Justin, Simon, and Edie. Three out of eight wasn't a bad start.

Edie rushed over and took his hand. "Becca says you have goals. C'mon."

"Goals?" His eyebrows arched.

"Yes, siree. She says you aimed to eat and sleep reg'lar, so I made a ham sammich for you." She dragged him across the lawn to a blanket where Rebecca sat. "Sit and eat. We gotta get you strong."

"Strong?" He chuckled as Rebecca handed him a small plate of potato salad. "Is there a reason I need to be strong?"

"Because you'll want to do fun things like spin me around." Edie slapped the sandwich onto the plate. "I saw you and Simon swinging Jace, and you nearly dropped him. I'd hate for my fun to be spoiled just because you can't keep me in the air."

"Goodness, Edie, how presumptuous." Rebecca handed him a tin cup filled with lemonade.

Edie scrunched her nose. "What does zump-tus mean?"

"Pre-sump-tuous. It means rude, improper, and pushy."

"Becca, didn't anyone ever tell you it's okay to use small words that just mean one thing? You don't have to crowd all your meanings into one big word." Edie shook her head. "No wonder boys don't want to talk to you. They like simple words like 'ain't.'" Edie spoke to Ben behind her hand. "I'm making a good case for using ain't, don't you think?"

"I think it's best if I limit my opinions to the potato salad, which is outstanding." Ben pointed his fork at his plate. "I wouldn't want to come between such devoted sisters."

"Oh, that's called wisdom, I think." Edie's mouth pulled to one side. "I wish I knew how to get more of that."

"Sister, dear, it's time you go play."

"Play what?" Edie's smile took an immediate downturn. "You won't allow me to climb trees in public like the boys."

"Look, there are some girls over there playing with rag dolls. Why not join them?"

"Ugh. Not the Prissy Pollies." She groaned and slapped her palm to her forehead. "Did you bring any books? Something thrilling? I'll find a reading tree and sit at the bottom." She spoke behind her hand to Ben again. "A book is much better up a tree, though."

"Try this." Rebecca offered Edie a copy of *Masterman Ready, or the Wreck of the Pacific*.

"What's this?" Edie's eyes widened.

"This adventure is about surviving at sea, but I hesitate to recommend it. I doubt you'll understand many of the words." Rebecca flipped through the pages, pointing out the drawings. "However, it does include some pictures. You can use those to help decipher the words."

She leaped up, kissed Rebecca's cheek, and hurried away to seek a cozy reading spot.

"It seems you've thought of everything." Ben smiled.

"What can I say? It's always good to be prepared." Rebecca patted the picnic basket. "I noticed you and Cordelia didn't come back straight away."

"We had a quick conversation to catch up." He sipped his lemonade. "Is Simon keeping an eye on Jace?"

"Oh no. He wanted to get to Justin's and return early to have the house to himself. Jace is with Ollie." Rebecca pointed to the two boys chasing each other in the distance. "How did your talk with Ollie go?"

"I'm afraid I didn't learn much." Ben scooped potato salad onto his fork. "He couldn't disclose who brought the spyglass to Hogue House, but it was discovered at the waterfront."

"I'm not surprised he refused to reveal the name of the individual who delivered it to the boardinghouse."

"Oh?"

"I spoke with Nellie. She mentioned Ollie has been visiting the waterfront after school without permission." She handed him a napkin and took his plate. "Naturally, he wouldn't want to implicate himself for fear you might inform me."

"I see."

"I don't know what to do." She watched Ollie intently. "Perhaps I've been overly strict with everyone since Mama's passing." Her eyes met Ben's. "What do you think? Should a fourteen-year-old boy have greater freedom to explore?"

"Before I traveled west, I would have said yes. But now, I'm uncertain." He traced his fingers along his clean-shaven cheek.

"Ben, what happened?" Rebecca twisted the napkin in her lap. "I can't fathom what kind of experience could lead you to abandon medicine. You used to be so passionate about it."

"I planned to go out with the military and return as soon as their survey mission was complete. I did it for us." His eyes met hers. "I was promised good pay. It was a better start to our life together than the usual compensation of chickens, milk, and bushels of vegetables. It would have provided something extra to sustain us during lean times." Staring into his tin cup, he thumbed the handle. "However, when we arrived, the need for medical care was great, and doctors were few. I chose to stay for a while at Angels Camp."

"I appreciate what you were trying to do. I only wish we had made the decision together." She cleared her throat, fiddling with a loose napkin thread. "So, you stayed. Then what happened?"

"I became close with an Irish family, the Maguires, who had three sons and a daughter." Ben paused briefly. "During the cholera pandemic, both parents died, and suddenly, Sean was responsible for his younger sister and two brothers. He was only fifteen."

"Not much older than Ollie."

Ben's hands trembled as he placed the tin cup on the blanket. He squeezed his eyes shut. A tender caress enfolded his hand. He opened his eyes as Rebecca traced her fingertips across his palm.

"You don't have to continue."

"I didn't let you know about my desire to return." He met her gaze again. "Now I'm staying in your home, and you weren't included in that decision. You deserve to know." He stared into the distance. "But I don't think I can talk about it."

"Did something happen to the children?"

"Sean. He's gone." The words choked in his throat.

"Have you tried to talk to Levi or Simon about it?"

"No." He shook his head. "Not yet."

"What's this?" She tapped the nail encircling his finger.

"Something Levi made for me." He rotated the ring on his finger. "I didn't elaborate much, but I told him I faced some tough challenges. So, he gave me this as a reminder to invite the Lord to sit with me in the hard places."

"Oh, I never considered that idea." She clasped her hands in her lap. "I generally pray for His swift deliverance from them."

"I take the same approach to praying through challenges." Ben raked his thumb across his chin. "But Levi believes there is value in sitting in those places."

"Is it helpful?"

"I haven't tried it yet. Levi and I talked about it yesterday. The situation with Jace and Oscar would have been an ideal time to test it out, but I didn't think of it."

"Levi." Rebecca smiled, shaking her head. "He anticipated you'd forget, didn't he? So, he made the ring after we left, hoping to see you at church today."

"Levi is very different from the man I knew."

"I've often wondered how much time he spends smithing in the forge." She tilted her head, squinting against the sun. "Did you see his Bible? Justin says he keeps one in the forge. He keeps a second one in the cabin and carries it to church."

"I noticed it on the table in the forge's sitting area."

"I think he dedicates nearly as much time to Bible study as he does at the anvil." Her eyes met his in a lingering gaze. "I'm pleased you reached out to Justin about coming back. It took courage to return."

Courage. The word stuck in his throat. Fear had brought him home. Not courage. Fear, exhaustion, grief, a desperate flight from the darkness. Not courage. Not yet.

He tented his knees and wrapped his arms around them. *Lord, would you,* he swallowed, *join me?*

"Becca! Becca!" Edie rushed over, collapsed onto the blanket, and rolled onto her back, raising the open book above her. She gazed at the pages and sighed. "It's perfect. It has gales, thunder, fire, and a raging sea. How will they ever survive? Can I have some pie?"

Rebecca's laughter echoed through the dusty corners of Ben's heart. Maybe hope wasn't a blazing torch, but a tiny flame, flickering back to life. He smiled, smoothing his shirt. His mind drifted back to picnics overlooking the bluff on the same, brown-striped quilt adorned with blue gingham and flowers. The sun glimmered in Rebecca's eyes, as pure blue as ever, though now touched with a hint of uncertainty.

"Yes, you may. But don't cut it too thick." Rebecca winked at her sister.

"Oh, Doctor Ewing, don't you adore pie?" Edie sighed, picking a blade of grass to use as a bookmark. "Especially buttermilk pie."

"I haven't had your mother's buttermilk pie in years." Ben grinned as Edie positioned the butter knife over an ample slice. "That's quite a generous portion, wouldn't you agree?"

"If anyone needs a big slice of pie, it's you." Edie giggled. "Becca, can I bring my pie to my reading spot?"

"Sure, but I planned to invite Ben for a stroll. You can use the picnic blanket if you'd like. What do you say, Ben?"

"I could use a walk. Could you save my pie, Edie?"

"Of course I will." She grinned.

He smiled as Edie turned onto her stomach, holding a fork in one hand and a book in the other. Ben stood and helped Rebecca to her feet, offering her his elbow. She tucked her slender fingers into the crook of his arm. It was like a fresh breeze through the stuffy attic of his heart.

And it felt almost like … home.

Chapter Twenty-One

"How was your lunch?" Rebecca lightly squeezed Ben's elbow. "Did you get enough to eat?"

"It hit the spot. Just what I needed." He stroked her fingers in the familiar way he used to when they had meandered together, arm in arm. "Do you have a purpose for this stroll, or did you just want company?"

"I think we need to discuss a few things." She withdrew her hand from his arm. As she pressed her palms down her skirt front, she angled her steps to slightly increase the distance between them. Had she given him the wrong impression? "I've resolved the misunderstanding with Edie regarding Ivajohn's long journey. Have you thought about how you could help her with a new gift?"

"What about a silhouette portrait? Although Ivajohn isn't traveling as Edie expected, it could still be a lovely reminder of a sister she'll see less frequently in this new stage of life."

"Oh, what a charming idea. Edie will adore posing by candlelight."

"We'll have to make a white silhouette unless you have India ink. A handsome, patterned paper could make a great background. Any suggestions?"

"If Mr. Mooney has recently ordered wallpaper for someone, he may have some leftover scraps."

"Perhaps I should ask Mr. Styles to help me make a frame for it. I wonder if he'd be willing to take on an apprentice?"

"Carpentry? It's hard for me to imagine you as a carpenter."

"Unfortunately, my experience leans more toward carpentry than saddlery or blacksmithing." A pained expression passed over his face before vanishing like a cloud. "On the other hand, it may be easier for Levi or Simon to handle the frame."

The thought of using a saw for amputation made Rebecca's stomach twist. She had never faced such a situation. The fragility of life weighed on her. Her eyelids slid shut as she recalled images of the last healthy baby she had delivered. Reflecting on moments of strength, resilience, and vibrancy kept her afloat amidst the sorrow of life's vulnerability.

"Ollie may be able to help if Simon and Levi are too busy. I'm sure there's enough scrap wood in the old forge or the shed." She folded her arms. "The silhouette portrait is a brilliant idea. This leads me to why we needed a new gift in the first place. The spyglass."

"I've tried to keep it hidden." Ben rubbed his hands together. "I hope it hasn't caused too much trouble."

"That's not it at all." Rebecca clasped her hands together, gathering her thoughts. "I only discovered Ollie sneaking to the waterfront after talking to Nellie about the spyglass. It dawned on me that I'm not as in touch with him as I believed."

"Rebecca, you have four siblings young enough to require significant care and guidance. Three of them are teenagers eager to spread their wings." His green eyes softened under tented brows. "I can't fathom the effort it must take to manage their needs. You deserve some grace."

"I try not to be too hard on myself, but it got me thinking.

Perhaps I should venture out of the boardinghouse more often." She tucked a wavy lock behind her ear and sighed. "If I had been out and about once in a while, I might have seen Ollie around town and realized he was hanging out with his friends at the riverfront."

"Perhaps. Or he may have found ways to avoid you."

"I'm considering joining your quest to find the owner of the spyglass. If I shared their interest, it might strengthen my bond with Ollie and Edie."

"If that's the case, would you like to join me now? I intended to discuss it with the captains today."

"Oh, you want to get started right away." Her eyes widened.

"Imagine the joy of sharing news with Ollie and Edie when we get back to the courthouse. I can already picture Edie's reaction."

"Sure. Let's do it." She fanned herself with her hand as a bead of sweat rolled down her back. "It could be an enjoyable break from my regular duties."

They strolled to the waterfront, where Ben escorted her onto the wharf. Some dock workers and steamboat hands directed catcalls at Rebecca. She sensed their gaze lingering on her as Ben looped her arm through his, pulling her close.

"Maybe this was a mistake," she whispered.

A booming voice thundered across the dock. "I best not hear another cat call or whistle. The next man who disrespects this young lady will answer to me, and you'll wish your mother were here to wash your mouth out with soap." Hale Cobb drew her from Ben and looped her hand in the crook of his elbow. "My apologies, Miss Hogue. It won't happen again."

"Thank you, Captain." She peeked past him at the men who slighted her. "I believe you know Ben Ewing."

"Doc, it's good to see you again."

Ben shook Captain Cobb's hand. "It's good to be back."

"We've missed you and Nute at the boardinghouse lately." Rebecca lightly nudged him with her shoulder.

"Nute and I planned to attend church this morning but encountered some urgent, unexpected repairs." He gently squeezed her hand. "What brings you out here?"

"A spyglass turned up recently at the boardinghouse. We wondered whether it belonged to one of the steamboat captains. Do you know if anyone has reported one missing?"

"How long have you had it?"

"Edie presented it at Ivajohn's bridal tea on Friday." Rebecca noticed a dockworker lurking nearby out of the corner of her eye. "We think Ollie discovered it somewhere along the waterfront."

"Every captain is aware of the lost and found at Hogue House. If anything were missing, you would have already heard from them."

"Would you mind looking at it?" Ben tugged Captain Cobb farther down the wharf, and the shabby wharfman edged behind them.

"I would be glad to."

Ben took the telescope out of his pocket and handed it to Captain Cobb. "Do these markings mean anything to you?"

Rebecca eyed the wharfie warily. He moved crates at the end of a gangplank a few feet away. Before long, it became evident he was shifting the same crates repeatedly. Pitted cheeks, leathery skin, and a weak jawline—unsavory. Through a curtain of stringy blond hair, he cast furtive glances their direction.

"H.v. Laun fecit Amsterd." Captain Cobb traced the inscription with his fingertip. "This engraving indicates the maker and his place of origin. For instance, a telescope inscribed with Dollond London is crafted by John Dollond in London, England, while Ramsden London is associated with Jesse Ramsden, also in London. I am not acquainted with this maker."

"Amsterd. Amsterdam? In the Netherlands, isn't it?" Ben

folded his arms across his chest. "Can this information help us?"

"I doubt it." Captain Cobb shook his head while stroking his thick salt-and-pepper beard. "If you asked every captain in port right now, you'd likely discover each one has instruments made by different craftsmen in various countries. These tools were probably ordered from mercantile shops in different ports along our journeys. The inscription holds little value for your search."

"Any idea what the letters on this cap signify?" Ben took the spyglass and turned the end toward Captain Cobb.

"Those could be the initials of the owner. That'd be my guess."

The dockworker lost his grip on a crate, and it toppled to the ground. It landed with a thud, bumping against Ben's legs. As he muttered apologies, Rebecca was sure he'd stolen a glance at the spyglass. An unsettling sensation crept through her.

She placed her hand on Captain Cobb's arm and guided him to the other side of the wharf. "I know this could be a long shot, but did you see a passenger with a telescope by any chance?"

"You there, stop lollygagging and get those crates loaded." A sawed-off man with eyes of stone and skin like dark rawhide approached, pointing to the dockworker. Hands on his hips, he turned his attention to Captain Cobb. "What do you have there?"

"A fine pocket telescope. These two are attempting to locate the owner." Captain Cobb wagged his finger between Ben and Rebecca. "Robert Horn, this is Dr. Ben Ewing and Rebecca Hogue."

"Careful there. Hogue House is gaining a reputation for its wild goose chases." Horn chuckled. "Anything I can do to help?"

Rebecca cleared her throat. "I asked Captain Cobb if he noticed any passengers carrying a pocket telescope."

"There was a passenger, quite an irritating fellow. Kept attempting to direct us down the river with his antics. Blustery, ruddy-faced fellow. Can't believe I overlooked him." Captain Cobb propped his hands on his hips and laughed. "We docked on Wednesday, if that's of any help."

"Can you recall his name?" Ben tucked the telescope back into his pocket.

"Sorry." Captain Cobb shook his head. "And what about you, Robert?"

"There was a couple, around our age." Horn wagged his thumb between himself and Captain Cobb. "Husband used a telescope to point out interesting sights as we traveled. And before you ask, no, I don't know their names. We made port on Thursday."

"Captain Horn, can you provide us with a description of them?" Rebecca tilted her head.

"*Psh.* Do you have any idea how many passengers I carry around, miss? I try not to remember most of them." He scratched his head. "Uh, the man had a bulbous nose, much too big for his face. Woman talked a great deal. It's all I recall about them."

"Well, the prominent nose should be a helpful feature." Ben rocked on his toes. "I know Captain Cobb's vessel is the *Resilient*. Captain Horn, what is the name of your vessel?"

"The *Coffee No. 7*." Horn saluted casually before heading off again. "I've got to get back to it. Best of luck with your search and enjoy the wedding."

"How did he know about Ivajohn's wedding? I thought you were the only captain closely acquainted with our family beyond the lost and found."

Captain Cobb laughed heartily. "I highly doubt Robert even knows you have sisters. But everyone on the boats knows that the lost and found has sparked two searches that ultimately resulted in marriage." He pointed his finger back and forth between Ben and Rebecca. "He's referring to your wedding."

"Um, well …" Rebecca's cheeks warmed. "That's not …I mean …"

"What she means to say is this search is simply a search. Nothing more, nothing less." Ben cleared his throat.

"Is it now?" He chuckled. "Well, keep telling yourself that. I need to return to my boat too. You know where to find me until I set sail again if you need anything else. It was nice to see both of you."

Rebecca and Ben turned, lowering their heads as they moved along the wharf. Ben's cheeks were as flushed as hers felt. Holding her breath for a moment, she wondered if their partnership in the search would spark similar reactions wherever they went. Maybe becoming involved with Ben was a mistake. Not involved, but oh dear. People might think they were. She released an extended swoosh of air.

"Don't let Horn's remark unsettle you. I don't expect this search to lead to anything." Ben kept his head down as he spoke. "Except the telescope's owner, of course. There's no pressure for anything more. If you'd prefer to step back, I can carry on alone."

She remained silent as they wandered along Water Street to Main Street.

"Ben." Rebecca halted and placed a hand on his shoulder. "You're right. It's absurd to assume that every search initiated from the lost and found leads to, well, you know. Granted, it occurred with Levi and Allie and again with Justin and Dawn. But that doesn't mean it will happen to us." She withdrew her hand. "I genuinely think these objects connect people. Perhaps this time could be different, though. Maybe it will unite my family instead of a couple."

"I don't see why it couldn't." His eyes met hers.

"Of course." She resumed walking, and Ben fell in step. "It seems we've been so disjointed since Mama's passing. We all struggled to sort through our grief. Then Justin found Dawn, and they married. Ivajohn will tie the knot soon. Everything is changing so fast. I'm uncertain how to hold our family together." She let out a sigh. "Mama would have known what to do. She would have understood how to reach everyone and nurture the bonds among siblings. I feel lost."

Ben lowered his head, remaining silent as they moved past Columbus Street toward Thompson Street.

Rebecca stared at him. "Aren't you going to say something?"

"Rebecca, I don't need to say much." He cleared his throat. "What you need is someone to listen. You are among the most compassionate, resilient, and relational people I know. You've faced overwhelming challenges and significant changes. It's normal to lose touch with yourself and others. You will find your stride within your family relationships soon enough." He stopped her, taking her hands in his. "Grant yourself some grace. You might be surprised at how your siblings rise to the occasion by taking responsibility for their relationships when you're overwhelmed."

She blinked several times as her breathing slowed. His hands lingered for a breath before falling away, as if reluctant to release the moment. She continued toward Thompson Street. After a cleansing breath, she found her voice. "Thank you, Ben."

As they came into view of the courthouse square, Ben stopped. "Do you mind going the rest of the way without me? There is something else I need to discuss with Captain Cobb, but I wanted to ensure you got back to the square safely after the questionable behavior of the men on the dock."

"Of course. I can handle it from here." She smiled and turned toward the courthouse. Behind her, Ben's footsteps faded, but the warmth of his words stayed with her—more unsettling than the catcalls had ever been.

Chapter Twenty-Two

"Rebecca!" Mr. Mooney called out as he waved from across the lawn.

She smiled as she approached him. "Mr. Mooney, you're quite cheerful today."

"I missed the opportunity to chat with you at church. More folks attend on the day of the monthly town picnic." Mr. Mooney pointed to Ollie and Jace as they ran behind the courthouse. "I've been eager to ask about your new redheaded friend. Is he—"

"Yes, he is. His name is Jace Drake, the youngest of the Drake brothers." She placed her hand over her heart. "He rushed Ben and me as we returned from Levi's yesterday."

"Rushed you?"

"He burst out of the woods in a state of panic because a snake had bitten his dog." She patted her chest. "Ben and I didn't initially realize he was referring to a dog. He and the dog stayed with Ben in the forge at Hogue House last night."

"Sounds like you had quite the eventful day."

"Simon was plenty frustrated. He spent the entire day

searching for those Drake boys while I stumbled upon two of them in a matter of hours." She giggled.

"They sure are keeping things lively around town." Mr. Mooney chuckled. "No sign of the twins, though?"

"Not yet. Ben and Simon are trying to convince Jace to help them locate the other brothers. We have plenty of room at Hogue House and would love to have them stay with us while their father's whereabouts are unknown."

"That is a wise plan."

"Simon plans to hold them accountable for the accident by having them do some work on the Fremont property. Mrs. Fremont will need the help."

"Excellent idea." Mr. Mooney raked his fingers along his jaw. "Speaking of Mr. Fremont, has Dr. Pernot had a chance to see him yet?"

"Dr. Pernot is in Indian Territory, remember?"

"No, he got back late last night. Didn't he drop by this morning to update you?"

"It must have slipped his mind."

"He joined his wife for the picnic a bit ago. I think they're on the other side of the courthouse from where your blanket is spread." Mr. Mooney gestured across the square. He turned red when he made eye contact with Caroline Brandt, and she responded with a wave. He quickly returned his attention to Rebecca and cleared his throat. "I, uh, I thought news of his arrival might bring you some comfort."

"It would be a blessing if Dr. Pernot could assume his care today. I'll try to locate him before we head home." She couldn't help but flash a playful smile. "Mr. Mooney, did I mention how positively charming you look today? It seems I'm not the only one who holds that opinion."

Caroline waved a brisé fan, fluttering her eyelashes. Then, she spoke to Cordelia, concealing her face behind it. The shadow lifted from Cordelia's countenance, her eyes lighting as she gestured toward the tailor shop window. A quiet warmth stirred in Rebecca's chest. Perhaps Cordelia had taken their conversation to heart.

Caroline wiggled her fingers at Mr. Mooney once more. Rebecca shifted her gaze between Caroline and Mr. Mooney. Upon realizing Rebecca was watching him, Mr. Mooney averted his eyes, muttering.

"Mr. Mooney, Caroline Brandt is flirting with you." Rebecca clicked her tongue. "If you don't acknowledge her, all the butterscotch in the world won't save you."

He gave Rebecca a weak smile before nodding and waving at Caroline. Caroline leaned in to say something to Cordelia before standing up and sashaying across the lawn.

Mr. Mooney glanced nervously from Rebecca to Caroline. "She's approaching us. What do I do now? What should I say?"

"What topics do you discuss when she comes by the store?"

"We discuss apples, potatoes, fabric, and sewing notions."

"Is that all? There's nothing else you discuss?"

"I ask after her father-in-law when I haven't seen him for several days."

"You might consider asking to join her on the picnic blanket."

"What? No."

"What's stopping you?"

"Would it not be improper?"

"Five years have passed since her husband died. It has been quite some time since she last wore mourning clothes. I believe it's more than fitting you would ask."

"Good afternoon, Sam." Caroline lightly touched his wrist.

"Mrs. Brandt." Mr. Mooney's cheeks pinked, and Rebecca hid a smile.

"Sam Mooney, how often must I ask you to call me Caroline?" She fanned herself, steadying her gaze on Mr.

Mooney. "Thank you for the butterscotch included in my order this week."

"Oh, it's no trouble at all. It's just a small gesture I enjoy offering my most valued customers."

Rebecca clicked her tongue, as if deeply offended, then winked at Caroline. "He means 'most valued customer' without the *s*. We don't receive butterscotch with our order at Hogue House."

"Well, now ..." Mr. Mooney's eyes flashed wide in warning to Rebecca, and he cleared his throat. "Mrs. Brandt is not just a valued customer. Her handiwork has also added a touch of beauty to the shop."

Rebecca took Caroline's hand. "Oh, yes. The needlepoint over the counter adds a lovely charm to the store."

"Thank you, Rebecca. That empty spot has troubled me for years. It needed some warmth. There's no reason a business can't be filled with the warmth of home. After all, many of our unattached shop owners reside above their stores."

"Mr. Mooney's shop is certainly homey. I could stay and chat with him for hours."

"So could I." Caroline smiled warmly, her gaze fixed on Mr. Mooney. "What do the two of you chat about, dear?"

"Me?" Rebecca's eyes widened at the question. "Mostly business and family. However, at the moment, I'd seek Mr. Mooney's guidance about how I might bring in some extra money at the boardinghouse. His business ideas have greatly benefited my brother in the past."

Mr. Mooney blinked and then hesitantly turned his attention to Rebecca. "Is the boardinghouse having difficulties? Is that why you inquired about an extension?"

"Not exactly. Not yet anyhow." She shifted her weight and folded her arms across her chest. "However, I must soon fill our vacant rooms or figure out how to sustain us until I can bring in new tenants."

"Do you, by any chance, make anything I could sell at the store?"

"I doubt I create anything you don't already carry. I crafted some crochet and fabric potholders for Ivajohn's bridal tea." She rubbed behind her ear. "No one knows this, but I sometimes dip candles since Levi and Justin aren't around to use the forge. When I was twelve, Mama taught me how to add small decorative touches to them. She always seemed to be able to do anything."

"I bet the old forge doesn't see much action these days." Mr. Mooney scratched his cheek. "Since Justin lives next to Levi, he drops by Levi's forge whenever he needs to make horseshoes. I wonder if you might rent it out like Justin did with the Scots in '49."

"Sam, what a fabulous idea." Caroline's eyes sparkled.

"It's one of the best ideas I've come across." Rebecca folded her hands together in front of her chest. "However, I don't know who I would rent it to. I don't know anyone with the skills except Levi and Justin. But if you know someone, I'd happily consider it."

"Let me think on it. Meanwhile, bring any items you have. Don't worry about whether I already sell something similar. Your family has always supported me in my need, and I would gladly return the favor."

Rebecca spied Dr. Pernot across the lawn, picnicking with his wife. Glancing from Mr. Mooney to Caroline, she smiled as an idea took shape. "Mr. Mooney, have you eaten anything?"

"I mostly catch up with old friends at these town picnics. I'll have something to eat when I get home."

"Nonsense. Why not come join—" Rebecca glanced across the way as if noticing Dr. Pernot for the first time. She turned to Mr. Mooney. "Oh, there's Dr. Pernot. I should speak to him. Excuse me, Mr. Mooney."

"Sam, why not join me? I have more than enough food and

would love the company." Caroline took his hand as she guided him across the lawn.

When Mr. Mooney glanced back at Rebecca, she winked and mouthed, "You're welcome."

She strolled over to Dr. Pernot, glancing back at Mr. Mooney and Caroline as they enjoyed their picnic. They chatted, smiled, and laughed. Rebecca couldn't help but grin to herself. Maybe a little matchmaking could work out for good, even in a world shadowed by loss.

While Dr. Pernot gathered plates and utensils to help his wife repack their picnic basket, Rebecca knelt beside them on the blanket.

"May I help?" She took a cloth napkin, folded it, and handed it to Mrs. Pernot.

"Ah, Rebecca." Dr. Pernot shook his head. "I'm sorry I didn't stop by this morning to tell you I'm back. I was exhausted. I returned late last night, went straight home, and slept as long as possible before the picnic."

"I understand. I hope your trip went well."

"I usually have no issues when I visit Indian Territory." He raised an eyebrow and pressed a smile, casting a sidelong glance at his wife. Understanding the unspoken cue, Rebecca refrained from further probing about his experiences in Indian Territory. "What about here? How have things been?"

"Mr. Fremont suffered a broken leg due to a horse kick. I took a fracture box to his house yesterday, but thought the swelling should go down a little more."

"You have a fracture box?"

"No." Rebecca gathered tin cups. "Actually, I suppose I do now. Dr. Ben Ewing was a former resident of Hogue House. He returned Friday, right around the time of the incident, so he made the fracture box since we didn't anticipate your return until tomorrow."

"Ah, Mr. Fremont is under his care."

"Not exactly. Mr. Fremont has been in my care." She placed the cups atop the empty pie plate Dr. Pernot held. "Ben is back from California and no longer wants to practice medicine."

"How unfortunate. Having another doctor in town would be beneficial. If we had three doctors, one could stay in town while the other two could address needs in the surrounding areas and Indian Territory."

"It would be nice. And I could get back to my regular duties."

"Naturally. As a young lady, you may wish to find a husband, create your own home, and start a family. I expect it has been challenging to care for your siblings and attend to the town's medical needs while Dr. Dibrell and I were away. We truly appreciate your readiness to assist in any way possible."

"It always makes me somewhat anxious. My abilities fall short compared to yours and Dr. Dibrell's."

"Don't sell yourself short." He patted her hand. "You've always done quite well, even when we're not around."

"I suppose you want to take charge of Mr. Fremont's care?"

"Certainly. I'll head out to see him this evening."

"Thank you, Dr. Pernot." She acknowledged his wife with a nod. "Mrs. Pernot, it was lovely to see you. Enjoy the rest of your afternoon." She rose, then paused. "Oh, before I forget, did you happen to lose a spyglass?"

"No, mine is safely tucked away in my medical bag."

Rebecca smoothed her skirt before crossing the lawn. She waved at Ollie as she passed. He bent over, hands on his knees, breathless after racing Jace again. In another corner of the lawn, Martie and Nellie chatted with other teenage girls sitting on a blanket while Edie remained engrossed in her book. No sign of Ben or Cordelia.

Ben must still be catching up with Captain Cobb, but where was Cordelia? Rebecca sighed. That girl. She seemed to grow more restless each day. Rebecca had no idea how to help her.

She had seldom faced such restlessness herself, especially with the added medical duties from Ben's absence and the increased family obligations following their mother's death.

Her eyes turned back to Mr. Mooney and Caroline again, laughter woven through their chatter. It would suit Cordelia well to work with Mrs. Brandt. Not only was she the embodiment of elegance, but she also upheld strong values and was dedicated to her work. Caroline Brandt would have a positive influence on Cordelia. She suppressed an urge to speak to Mrs. Brandt about her sister. What had Ben said? *You might be surprised by how your siblings rise to the occasion.* Rebecca must trust Cordelia to find her way in this new relationship. She sighed.

As Edie kept reading, Rebecca opened the picnic basket. Edie's blonde hair splayed across the blanket, the book just inches from her face, and she barely noticed Rebecca's presence. Rebecca pulled a piece of paper from the basket.

"Edie."

"Hmm?"

"Edie."

The child sighed and turned the page. Time to simply sit and read like Edie would be nice. To be the little sister again, even if only for a moment.

"Edie."

She blinked hard and reluctantly turned to meet Rebecca's gaze.

"I'm going to Mooney's to post a notice on the board. When I return, we can pack everything up and prepare for home. Okay?"

"Do you want me to gather everyone together?" Edie scrunched her nose.

"No, I just wanted to let you know in case the others check in with you." She tilted her head. "Let them know we'll be leaving shortly. However, you don't need to round everyone up. Do you understand?"

"Got it. If I see anyone, I'll tell 'em to get ready." Edie flipped onto her stomach and resumed reading.

"I'll be back shortly."

Main Street was much quieter than during the week, with only a few ponies and wagons visible and many businesses closed for the day. She recalled the business owners who were family friends, Mr. Mooney, Conrad Hildesheim from the bakery, the Brandts, Nicholas, Mrs. Gray, and Levi at his blacksmith shop far beyond Main Street. She filled her lungs with a deep, contented breath. How she loved this town. She cherished Van Buren the way her mother had.

For years, she yearned to journey west and experience the stunning, untouched landscapes. She had imagined a life with Ben in a secluded mountain oasis. Yet, her aspirations of going west were crushed when he chose to go to California without her.

For five years, she dedicated herself to her community's needs, prioritizing their welfare over her desires. She was the closest thing they had to a doctor for a time. Her bond with these people had grown profoundly. She had welcomed their newborns and comforted them in moments of loss. She held their hands through the uncertainty of illness and injury. Countless faces flooded her mind.

Maybe Ben's departure was a blessing in disguise. She wouldn't have been with Mama if she had gone halfway across the continent with Ben. She rubbed her palm, the final hours of Mama's hand resting in hers clear in her mind. God had known exactly where she needed to be. She affixed the notice to the mercantile board and turned to survey the square. Sunlight danced across the grounds, enveloping her cherished community in a warm, nostalgic glow. Could she leave now, even if the opportunity arose?

"Miss Hogue, what a pleasure meeting you here."

A shiver crawled down her neck. The square seemed to

shrink into the distance as if seen through the wrong end of a telescope. In an instant, her community, her support, were alarmingly far away. She turned, her unease prickling as Ambrose Baas tipped his hat.

"Did you enjoy the picnic?"

Rebecca's jaw tightened. "The mercantile is closed, Mr. Baas."

"I do not need the mercantile." He stepped closer, his presence commanding in the empty street. "Have you had time to consider my proposal?" His lips curled slightly.

Her heart thudded in her chest. She scanned the empty street, the silence pressing in on her. Not a soul was nearby. She swallowed the knot in her throat. "Mr. Baas, my family has owned Hogue House independently for many years. We do not wish to partner through a business contract. Or marriage."

"I encourage you to reconsider. Perhaps take a little more time to think about it." His hands folded at his waist, his posture almost too relaxed for the tension between them. "I'm leaving on business later this week. I'll expect your answer before then."

Rebecca's chest tightened. She tried to quell the unease that bubbled beneath her ribs. "I don't need any more time. If you'll excuse me, I must return to the picnic."

She spun on her heel but halted as his voice called after her.

"Rebecca."

She glanced back at him, her skin prickling as his gaze lingered on her with unnerving interest.

"Tell Cordelia I enjoyed our chat." His smile revealed the edge of something colder below the surface. "She mentioned your mother's quilts. Said they added the perfect touch of comfort for a home. It made me wonder what kind of home she'll want for herself."

His eyes held hers for a moment too long before he made an about-face and strode away.

A cold, instinctive protectiveness flared in her chest, not just for Cordelia but all of them. Hogue House was their home, and Baas circled like a wolf. Rebecca stood frozen for a long beat, her heart pounding. A chill settled in her bones despite the driving sun. If she was a pawn on the board, Baas was playing the game to perfection.

Chapter Twenty-Three

Rebecca flexed her fingers, casting frequent glances over her shoulder. Where had Baas appeared from? And where had he disappeared to? Her jaw tightened. "Tell Cordelia I enjoyed our chat," he'd said. When had he spoken to her sister? He was precisely the sort to charm her. Handsome, self-assured—Rebecca grimaced—moneyed. Cordelia would see a man of position and means. She would not ask what lay beneath the finery.

Would Baas use Cordelia as a pawn to take control of Hogue House?

The thought twisted in Rebecca's gut. While not an extravagant inheritance, it was their home, the only place the family had lived under one roof. During much of Justin, Ivajohn, and Rebecca's childhood, their father was away on the steamboat. This was the only home Ollie, Nellie, and Edie knew, and the only one Martie could recall. It was the one constant where their family had ever been whole.

But Baas—he could tear it all apart. If he proposed, Cordelia would eagerly accept. Then she would sweet-talk Pa into nearly anything. She was his cherished baby doll, born on a steamboat and spoiled ever since. Could she persuade Pa to hand Hogue House over to her and Baas completely? The thought of Cordelia controlling Hogue House alongside Baas sent a shudder down Rebecca's spine. Justin and Ivajohn had their own homes now, but Rebecca was still here, still fighting to hold the family together. Could Cordelia convince Pa to rewrite the future and edge her out entirely?

And why did Baas want Hogue House in the first place? What drove his determination to acquire it?

Her chest tightened as she exhaled, trying to release the pressure building inside her.

"Becca! Becca!" Edie sprinted to her with wide eyes and disheveled hair. "Come quick. Jace is gone."

Oh, Lord, please help me. She lifted her skirt and hurried to meet Edie.

"What do you mean Jace is gone? What happened?"

"Ollie lost him. He's gonna be in big trouble, ain't he?"

"Edie." Rebecca paused to regain her breath.

"I know. Don't say 'ain't.'" Edie frowned.

"Well, yes, but where is Ollie now?"

"I don't know."

Upon reaching the courthouse lawn, Rebecca went straight to Mr. Mooney and Caroline. "Mr. Mooney, the Drake boy is missing. We also don't know Ollie's whereabouts."

"I'll gather some folks to search for them."

Nellie and Martie joined them and began chattering all at once.

"Girls, one at a time, please."

Martie gestured to Nellie. "Go ahead, Nellie."

"Ollie wandered off with those boys who hang out at the riverfront." Nellie shook her head. "I'm sorry, Becca. I should have found you when I saw him with them. I couldn't tell if Jace was with him or not."

"It's okay, Nellie. Jace likely followed Ollie to the riverfront or returned to his brothers." Rebecca embraced Nellie. "Don't worry. Oscar is still at the forge. Jace will show up for the dog. Eventually." She faced Martie. "What were you about to say?"

"I also saw Ollie with five or six older boys. I didn't spot Jace, but I might have missed him in such a large group." She rubbed her forehead. "Oh, Becca, I truly apologize. Being older, I should have checked on Ollie and Jace. We were having such a wonderful time with the girls."

"It's fine. Ben is probably with Captain Cobb. I'll get him, and then we can find Ollie. Hopefully, Jace is with them too." Rebecca placed an arm around Martie's shoulders. "You stay here with Edie and Nellie. I'm unsure where Cordelia has wandered off to, but you're the only one who can keep the sisters together until I'm back. Stay by the blanket."

"We will." Martie ushered Nellie and Edie toward the picnic blanket, her hands on their backs.

Mr. Mooney rejoined Rebecca, accompanied by Caroline. "I dispatched men to scout Main Street and the side roads between here and the boardinghouse. Another group headed east from here."

"Thank you, Mr. Mooney. I'm going to the wharf to find Ben and get his help locating Ollie. The girls mentioned they last spotted him heading toward the riverfront, and I'm hoping Jace is with him."

"Where's Simon?"

"He returned to Hogue House for a nap. He's been busy helping at the ranch and standing in for the sheriff."

"Okay, I'll join you."

"I'll stay with Martie and the girls." Caroline smiled, giving Rebecca's hand a reassuring squeeze.

Rebecca and Mr. Mooney rushed to the wharf, catching Ben on his way back from the dock. After filling him in on the situation, they moved along the riverfront at a clipped pace toward Lee Creek until they encountered a group of boys.

"Ollie." The boys' heads whipped around at Rebecca's sharp tone.

Ollie's eyes went wide. "Becca."

"What do you think you're up to? Where's Jace?"

"We left him behind at the courthouse. I told him to stay with Edie on the picnic blanket."

"He's not with Edie. You were supposed to watch him." She put her hands on her hips. "Now he's gone, and we've arranged a search party for both of you. If you boys know what's best, you'll return to your families this instant."

The boys scattered, abandoning Ollie to face Rebecca alone.

"Becca, I'm sorry. I didn't know. I thought he'd stay with Edie." Ollie lowered his gaze. "He was all fired up about your cooking, so I told him to eat as much as he wanted."

"Did he mention his brothers at all? Did he say where they could be?" Ben stepped closer.

"No. He went on and on about the food and his dog."

Rebecca folded her arms. "Think, Ollie. Did he give any clues as to where he might go?"

"Hold on." Ollie's brows furrowed, and he worked his mouth side to side. "Wait. He mentioned Oscar enjoys splashing in the creek and wished the dog would get better so they could go soon."

"The creek." Ben stroked his chin. "Lee Creek."

"Becca, how much trouble am I in?" Ollie kicked at a loose stone, avoiding eye contact with her.

"Oh, this is beyond my responsibility." Eyebrows raised, she pursed her lips. "Half the town is hunting for you and the Drake boy. I'll hand the matter over to Simon."

"No, please don't."

"Should I bring Nicholas into this? With the sheriff away, those are our only options right now." Rebecca's jaw tightened. She didn't want to scare Ollie, but she wasn't about to let this slide either.

Ollie's lip drooped. "I prefer Simon."

"Mrs. Brandt and Martie are with the girls on the picnic blanket. Head back to the picnic and stay close to them, okay?" Rebecca eyed him narrowly. "We'll search for Jace along the creek."

"Follow me." Mr. Mooney guided the way to Lee Creek.

"So much for my siblings stepping up and taking responsibility," Rebecca muttered.

"I never said taking responsibility would come without mistakes." Ben tipped his head, scanning the area along the creek.

"I'll say." Mr. Mooney shook his head, picking his way through tall grasses. "The most memorable lessons in responsibility come on the heels of error. Young Ollie is about to learn a lesson he'll never forget. Mark my words."

"I agree." Ben elongated his stride to avoid a muddy patch, then reached back and offered his hand to Rebecca. She hesitated only a moment before taking it, her fingers slipping into the old familiarity with surprising ease. "This could be a significant step toward manhood for Ollie."

"I didn't expect him to pick Simon to deliver his consequences." Mr. Mooney clicked his tongue.

"Mr. Mooney, you mentioned yesterday how good Simon is with kids." Rebecca's brows furrowed. "That's why you wanted him to locate these Drake boys before Nicholas could."

"Being Simon's younger brother changes things entirely." Mr. Mooney scratched his chin. "Nicholas is likely to be lenient with Ollie because he has a soft spot for you, while Simon will consider the impact on the family's reputation. I wouldn't want to be in Ollie's shoes right now."

Ben glanced away, twisting the narrow band of metal on his hand slowly and deliberately at the mention of Nicholas. "I wouldn't want to be Simon in either situation. However, he'll gain a valuable lesson, nonetheless."

Rebecca's gaze rested briefly on Ben's hands. Yesterday, Mr. Mooney had asked what Ben needed, and she couldn't say. Now it occurred to her more than anything he needed a lifeline. And by gifting the ring, Levi had tethered Ben to some shared faith, some unspoken resolve between men she would never understand, but knew he needed.

Cupping her hands around her mouth, Rebecca drew a deep breath and shouted, "Jace."

Ben grabbed her arm. "Maybe we ought to avoid shouting his name."

"Why?" Mr. Mooney stopped, turning to face them.

"Simon and I talked to him this morning, but he wouldn't share where his brothers are." Ben rubbed the back of his neck. "Their father's instructions were to keep their whereabouts secret because he feared a 'bad man' might find them. The boys might be apt to hide if they hear us coming."

"Everything about this is so odd." Rebecca tugged at her ear. "Do you think there is something bigger going on here?"

"What are you trying to say?" Mr. Mooney tilted his head.

"I don't know. I can't piece it all together yet. It's an odd sense I can't explain."

"You know who else experiences that?" Mr. Mooney dipped his chin. "Justin. You both get it from your mother. Her intuition was always spot on." He clicked his tongue. "I bet it'll be the same for you. I always trust Justin's gut. It's never been wrong so far."

"I don't know what good it does us if I can't make anything of it."

"Give it time. It'll come together."

"I hope it's not too late when it does."

"Let's keep going." Ben pressed on. "I haven't spoken with Simon since our talk with Jace, but I suspect the boys might be camping out rather than staying in the usual spots."

The trio proceeded along Lee Creek, pausing now and then

to listen. Occasionally, Mr. Mooney pointed out animal tracks. He was a far more skilled tracker than Rebecca realized. She appreciated his presence for his tracking skills and as a buffer between her and Ben.

A twig snapped to their right, and they froze, listening. They exchanged glances, waiting for another sound. Leaves rustled, and a bush trembled. Rebecca swallowed hard and steadied herself.

Simon, accompanied by Noble, pushed through the underbrush. Rebecca, Ben, and Mr. Mooney let out a collective sigh.

"Simon." Rebecca released an uneven breath. "Weren't you home, napping?"

"Some folks arrived at the house asking if Jace had returned." He stroked Noble's neck. "No one had any idea which direction he might have gone."

"We chose the creek since Jace mentioned splashing in a creek with Oscar." She scratched Noble behind the ear. "What brought you here?"

"Nothing quite as solid as that." Simon rolled his head from side to side. "I just considered where a young boy might have the most fun. The creek is where I would go."

Ben scanned the surroundings. "This would be the perfect area to set camp if you needed to leave four boys alone for a few days."

"Or longer." Simon plucked a blackberry from a nearby bush and ate it. "Plenty of berries through here."

"Pretty smart. They have access to fishing and hunting, with nearby water for drinking and bathing." Mr. Mooney pointed toward the creek. "It would be ideal if they don't camp too close and a storm doesn't crop up."

The group resumed their movement alongside the creek. With Simon's horse and their larger number, remaining quiet grew more challenging. They progressed at a more cautious pace than before. After fifteen minutes, Rebecca stopped, silencing them with her finger to her lips and gesturing to her ear. They all paused.

Sounds echoed across the distance. Laughing, yowling, arguing. Singing?

> *"All around the mulberry bush*
> *the monkey chased the weasel.*
> *The monkey thought it was all in good fun,*
> *Pop! goes the weasel."*

Broad smiles flickered between them as they exchanged glances. Simon pointed, and the others nodded and followed. As the noise escalated, Simon paused to secure Noble to a tree and signaled for the stallion to remain quiet. Noble's head bobbed in response. He gestured with two outstretched fingers for Ben and Mr. Mooney to flank the boys. Then he instructed Rebecca to hold her position while he circled to the far side.

The three men crept toward the boys from three directions. Rebecca eased closer, careful not to give herself away. She paused and crouched behind a bush where she could see all four boys, poised for the men's ambush. The boy she recognized from the mercantile yelled at two slightly taller boys caught up in a wild tussle. Jace sang loudly, striking one of the brothers with a stick every time he hit the word "pop" in the song.

How could they endure this for days at a stretch? What kind of parent abandoned such a rowdy bunch?

The boys' laughter lifted toward the sky, free and wild. She wished she could bottle it before life chipped it away.

Simon's hand shot up, signaling to Ben and Mr. Mooney. The trio rushed in, each nabbing one of the brothers. Jace darted toward her, and she leaped from behind the bush, sweeping him off his feet and into her arms.

"Gotcha." She grinned and hugged him closely. Then she

placed a kiss on the top of his head. "Listen, you mustn't hit your brothers with sticks, okay?" She waited for his nod. "Hungry? I can fry some chicken for dinner."

"Fried chicken?" He smiled brightly, but then his expression changed. "Oh no, we'll be in big trouble when Pa finds out we gave our hiding spot away."

"I'm sure your pa will be pleased to hear you've been taken in by a family who'll keep you safe. Let's get those brothers, okay?" She scooted him toward the center of their camp. "Are you going to introduce us?"

"Those are the twins, Cason and Jesse." He pointed to the taller two boys.

"You gotta stop calling us twins." Jesse crossed his arms like he wasn't scared.

Jace stuck his tongue out. "Pa calls y'all twins."

"He's fooling around." Cason wiped his face on his sleeve. "My pa and their pa was brothers, but my pa died. Uncle Cal took me in, and he calls us twins because me and Jesse are the same age, but we ain't real twins. I'm their cousin."

"Oh, I see." Rebecca's gaze drifted to the smaller boy in the shadows. "We met at the mercantile, but I didn't get your name."

"Didn't give it."

"He's Hayden." Jace grinned. "He might be smaller than those guys, but he's the oldest and he brought us apples and peaches."

He tugged Jace close to him. "Shouldn't have led them here, Jace."

"But we're gonna have fried chicken. I done my part. I hunted up fried chicken."

Chapter Twenty-Four

Ben sank onto a tree stump in the forge and rubbed his face in exhaustion. He stretched his back, the ache familiar. Not unlike the night he lost Sean. A night ending with a younger brother asleep on each side of the fire, unaware of the blood on Ben's hands. He had sat like this, trying to breathe through the weight on his chest.

Ben leaned forward, his elbows on his knees. He remembered Sean's words.

"You'll be all right, Doc," Sean had said, as if Ben were the one dying.

He raked a hand through his hair and exhaled.

"I haven't forgotten you," he whispered. "But I don't know how to carry you."

The silence answered. Outside, the wind stirred.

Ben reached for a bent nail left behind in the dust, rolling it between his fingers. *Lord, how long will we have to sit together in this place?*

He drew a medical bag in the dirt using the nail, then erased it, letting the silence settle and do its work. It didn't fix anything but kept him from splintering.

After wrangling the four Drake boys, he couldn't help but think of Sean. It had been no easy feat. He and Simon had taken the brothers—and cousin—along with Ollie, to Mr. Fremont's to care for the pony, the cow, two pigs, and several chickens. The five boys also weeded and watered the garden, gathering any ripe produce they found and taking it in the house to Mrs. Fremont. Relief bloomed on her face as she thanked them each with a slice of sweet bread.

While there, the twins continually snuck into the hayloft to test their slingshot, ignoring Simon's and Ben's repeated warnings. Jace attempted to sneak the barn cat into the wagon. Hayden, however, determined to finish the work. He took a special liking to Mr. Fremont's horse, Missus. Ollie remarked that getting all the Drake boys focused on a task simultaneously was akin to herding cats, even though Ben and Simon continually had to warn him against chasing the pigs through mud puddles.

Upon returning to Hogue House, Rebecca insisted the four Drakes and Ollie take a proper bath. Trying to run those boys through a washtub was quite the adventure, but she wouldn't allow any of them, including him and Simon, to eat until everyone cleaned up. Ben stifled a yawn and wiped his face.

The forge door opened with a slow creak. Little Jace stepped in and closed the door behind him. As he turned around, his eyes widened at the sight of Ben.

"Oh, I didn't know anyone was here."

"Why are you sneaking around, Jace?"

"Miss Rebecca wants us all in the upstairs bedroom. But I gotta see Oscar."

Ben stood and waved him over. "Come on."

He crouched beside the boy. Jace petted the dog and spoke to him in hushed tones. The boy was the most subdued he had been all day. Oscar remained very still.

"Mr. Ewing, do you think Oscar will be all right? He usually licks me when I pet him, but now he's just lying there."

"He's very weak." Ben wrapped his arm around the boy. "But since he's made it this far, I have every reason to believe he will recover. It will require time for him to regain his strength. Don't expect him to have the vitality he had before, though."

"What's vitality?"

"Energy, liveliness. He may be unable to keep up with you as he used to. You will need to be patient with him."

Jace leaned over and hugged the dog. "I can do that."

The door creaked open again, and they turned to see Hayden, the oldest Drake boy.

"What are y'all doing?" he whispered.

"I want to stay with Oscar." Jace frowned.

"You can't stay out here tonight." Hayden went to his brother's side, taking his hand. He stared toward the door, on guard. "Miss Rebecca has been real nice to us. I can't remember when I had so much food. She gave us clothes with fewer holes. I didn't like the tub much, but I reckon she saw it as a kindness. She wants us to sleep in real beds, so we're gonna do it."

"I guess it's rare for you boys to sleep in a bed." Ben rubbed his back, thinking of the months he'd spent sleeping in unlikely places.

"Eh, who needs a bed? Pa usually comes by a hay bale, and we got blankets when we need 'em." Hayden hitched a shoulder.

"What kind of work does your father do exactly?"

"He's been followin' a man for someone, trying to figure out where the railroad is going."

"So, your father is a railroad man? A surveyor, perhaps?"

"Pa don't work for the railroad. He works for a fella with a fair amount of money who wants his son back."

Ben scratched his jaw. "The man your father works for is missing his son? Does the son work for the railroad?"

"I don't think so. I think the son wants a train or something like that. I didn't understand." Hayden fiddled with a loose thread on his shirt. "Every time the son pulls up stakes, so do we. Pa's gotta follow him, or he don't get paid. He should get a lot of money when this job is done. He says we might build us a cabin somewhere and have pigs and a cow."

"Hayden, is your father a detective? Does he conduct investigations?"

"Pa is just Pa, Mr. Ewing. He don't go by titles or anything."

"Jace tells us your father is worried about a bad man. Can you tell me more about that?"

"Don't know much about him. Pa has warned us to stay out of sight of the bad man while he's gone, but I've never seen the man. We try not to draw attention when we visit the town. But we haven't done so good at it lately." Hayden pressed his lips together. "I've asked Pa who the bad man is. All he says is the man talks smooth but has a dark side. Says I'll know him if I ever see him."

"Hmm." Ben stood and gave the boys a reassuring pat on the back. "Hayden, you sure worked hard at the Fremont place. Especially taking care of Missus."

"I'm gonna be a cowboy when I'm grown." He pulled Jace close, tucking him under his wing. "If I do hard work now, I'll be good at it later when I have more horses."

"We should head inside. Oscar will be fine on his own for the night. Simon will check in on him, and I will too. We'll ensure he gets some water and see if he can eat a little chicken."

"If he don't eat Miss Rebecca's fried chicken, there's no hope for him. It's the best I've ever tasted." Jace grinned.

As Ben followed them out of the forge, the hairs raised on his neck. He turned. Nothing but a cat slinking across the street. He stood there a moment longer, uneasy. The street was too quiet.

"You coming, Mr. Ewing?" Hayden held the door open.

Ben joined them on the porch and followed them into the

main house. Simon and Levi sat in the parlor with Ollie and the twins, teaching them to darn socks. Rebecca entered from the dining room.

"Did you say goodnight to Oscar?"

"Yes, ma'am."

"All right then. I'll take you all upstairs and tuck you in." She gestured to Ollie. "Ollie, you come too." Rebecca led the way as the boys trudged up the front staircase.

"Levi, when did you get here?" Ben settled beside Levi on the settee while Simon occupied the nearby chair.

"I haven't been here long. You seem tired, my friend."

Ben brushed his hair back. "I didn't picture things unfolding this way when Rebecca asked me to join her for church and a picnic."

"It's been an exciting few days, to be sure. They haven't been restful at all." Simon stood and stretched. "I know this isn't what you expected when you came home."

"I don't recall it being this way when I was here before."

"It's always been a spirited town." Simon rubbed his jaw. "You were busy with your medical practice, so, understandably, you don't recall the hustle and bustle of the boardinghouse. It can get lively and unpredictable here, day in and day out. You do much whittling, Doc?"

"Can't say I have."

"Perhaps you can pick it up. How about joining me?"

"I don't own a knife."

"That's fine. If Rebecca finds one lying around, she puts it in a tin in the pantry. So, make sure to grab one on your way out. Levi, you coming?"

Levi stood, holding a Bible. "I think I will."

Ben and Levi followed Simon to the backyard fire ring, where they made themselves comfortable on log stools. Levi handed the Bible to Ben.

"What is this?"

"It's a Bible. Rebecca mentioned you needed one when she left church this morning."

"You didn't need to go to all this trouble. I'm sure you're eager to get home."

"No trouble." Levi waved off the comment. "Since Justin's absence, I've been yearning for male camaraderie. Dawn has visited our house more frequently. It's a little like a never-ending ladies' sewing circle."

"How can I repay you for this?"

"My gift to you, my friend." Levi pressed his palm to his chest. "A man cannot live a full life without it."

"I appreciate it." Ben pulled it to his chest, patting it, and then set it on the empty stool beside him. "I'll treasure it."

Simon grabbed a bucket of wood scraps and sticks from the shed, allowing Ben and Levi to select a piece before he chose one for himself.

"Since this is your first time, let me explain a couple of basic cuts." Simon demonstrated. "First, you have your rough cut. You're going to push the knife away from your body freely. When using a rough cut, make sure no one is in your circle." Simon traced a circle in the air around himself, about an arm's length wide. "A more effective technique is the push cut. You can use the thumb of your opposite hand to control the knife's range of motion. This method ensures safety both for you and those nearby."

Ben mirrored Simon, tossing wood chips at his feet.

"There you have it. For now, there's no need to make anything. Practice your technique." Simon resumed whittling. "This is what I do when I need to wind down at the end of the day."

"You appear to be a jack of all trades." Ben grinned. "Were those boys mending socks?"

"That's precisely what they were doing." Simon chuckled. "I picked it up from Justin when he corrected some of my errant ways. So, how did your conversation with Ollie turn out?"

"He didn't share much information about the spyglass, but we established some boundaries and expectations between men."

Simon raised an eyebrow. "Oh?"

"He fears I might hurt Rebecca again." Ben kept his eyes trained on the blade he held.

"Mm." Simon nodded, flicking wood chips from the edge of his knife. He rotated the piece of wood and resumed whittling, employing varied techniques. "At the Fremont place, he mentioned you and Rebecca enjoyed a conversation on the picnic blanket before wandering off together. Did you have a nice chat with her?"

"She asked about California, and I think she deserves to know, but I couldn't tell her." Ben placed his knife and stick on the stump next to the Bible and rubbed his face. "I only ever wanted to protect her, so I didn't invite her to come to California with me. It was the right decision. I knew it would be difficult, but I never imagined how bad things would get."

"You need to talk about it. I understand if you can't talk to Rebecca about it, at least not yet." Simon's hands stilled. "But Levi and I are here and willing to listen."

"She used to look at me like she saw something sacred in me, something worth holding on to. Now I see doubt in her eyes. It's like I wandered off the map and lost my place. Not just with her, but with God too. If she knew the whole truth, I don't know if she would consider me beloved now. I'm not sure God wants me either.

"What is the truth, Doc?" Simon leaned back slightly.

"Where do I start?"

Levi handed him the Bible. "Begin by inviting Jesus."

Ben hugged the Bible, lowered his head, and offered a silent prayer. Afterward, he placed the Bible on the stool.

"Now, start from the beginning." Simon pointed with his chunk of wood.

Ben recounted what he had confided to Rebecca during the picnic. He turned the nail in circles around his finger, taking a few deep breaths. *Lord, sit with me in this moment. Please grant me the courage to share the rest of this story.*

"Your wish to leave medicine is related to Sean's death." Levi leaned forward as he whittled. "What happened to him?"

"Sean's passing didn't drive my desire to leave medicine. I've seen men die before, even by violent means, though never someone I'd grown close to." Ben sat on the stump, grabbing the stick and pocketknife. He carved the wood in quick strokes, then paused and shifted on the stump. "It was what happened afterward."

"Take your time, Doc."

"Before his death, Sean's father discovered a profitable vein but turned down a wealthy man's offer to purchase the rights. This man greased some palms after Sean's parents died to secure the claim for himself." Ben hunched forward, resting his elbows on his knees.

"I'm concerned the new businessman in town is up to similar tricks." Simon bit his lip. "Busted up a fight in the saloon yesterday with one of his associates. The other fella involved claims he's being pressured into selling his property to him."

"I've heard something along those lines." Levi acknowledged. "What did Sean do?"

"He found it difficult to provide for his siblings after losing the claim. They had no money to live off." Ben turned his palms up. "I did my best to help, but we struggled to provide food and shelter for five people. The cost of everything in California was much higher."

"Many people lost more than they gained during the Gold

Rush." Simon shook his head. "John Slade lost his dry goods store and is now struggling to make a living as a farmer."

"Sean determined to reclaim at least some of his family's gold. Before I caught him, he had been pilfering nuggets from the claim for weeks." Ben's voice neared a whisper. "I urged him to stop. He could not cash in what he'd taken without the tycoon learning about it." He stood, stretched, and then paced around the fire pit.

Levi gripped his knife and stick in one hand. "Sounds like the odds were against the boy."

"Headstrong. Committed to being the man of the family. It was a formula for trouble." Ben rubbed the back of his neck. "He wanted to take a stand like his father would have."

Levi lowered his eyes. "Sometimes the thing we can't let go is our undoing."

"He returned to the claim the following evening shortly before dusk, and I trailed him. In my rush to keep pace, I failed to realize his siblings had followed us." Ben returned to his seat and resumed whittling. He trained his eyes on the end of the stick. His hand trembled as his strokes slowed.

"The tycoon was lurking, and when Sean came up with a nugget"—Ben cleared his throat—"he fired."

His breath shallowed. "His body ..."

A chill swept over him. "I rushed to catch him, and we fell." His grip loosened around the knife and stick. "Sean's sister screamed." His voice faltered as he tightened his jaw, grinding his teeth. "That's when I realized the children were there. They saw it all."

"Ben." Simon's fingers curled against his knees.

The house door swung open as Rebecca backed out, pulling it closed. Turning, she froze. She tucked her chin, glancing from one man to the next. "Oh, I didn't know anyone was here."

Simon joined her in a few strides, took her by the elbow, and ushered her toward the door. "Can we talk?" He called over his shoulder to Ben and Levi, "I'm going to get a glass of water. I'll be right back."

Ben paced around the circle, arching his back and steadying his breath.

Levi gripped his shoulders as he passed. "You're doing well."

Simon returned without Rebecca, handing a glass of water to Ben. "I asked her if we could have some time undisturbed. A little fellowship among men."

"I dream about it. It haunts me." Ben took a sip. "I can't go on." He gave the glass to Simon and moved to the opposite side of the fire pit.

"Another time, then." Levi rested his hand on Ben's shoulder. "You can share the rest later. Just remember, you're not alone in this."

Simon approached, placing his hand on Ben's other shoulder. "You have brothers."

Ben's gaze fell to his hands. With an unsteady breath, he turned the nail around his finger. A comforting warmth enveloped him. "And Jesus."

He stepped out from their hands and toward the oak grove, pushing his hands through his hair. In the distance, the first fireflies of the evening glowed. He strode across the fire ring to his seat, and the other men followed.

"The children stood behind me as the gunslinger approached, declaring, 'I'll put an end to these thieving brats once and for all.' I was the only thing standing between him and those kids." Ben rested his elbows on his knees, rubbing his hands together. "I lunged at him, dislodging the revolver. We grappled, fighting for control of the gun." Ben shoved his hands through his hair, grasping handfuls of curls. "I seized the handle, rolled—" He paused, swallowing hard. "And pulled the trigger."

A cold shudder coursed through him. His voice caught in his throat, and he choked a whisper, "I killed him."

Chapter Twenty-Five

The morning sun broke through the upstairs windows as Rebecca hurried down the back stairs and into the kitchen, snagging an apron from the hook near the pantry. She put it on, tied it around her waist, and stopped at the counter. A stack of clean plates waited on the counter nearest the pantry, while a cast iron skillet lay upside down at the opposite end. A few utensils rested at the bottom of the wash tub in the sink.

Her brow furrowed as she examined the counter more closely. A plate of biscuits rested on the kitchen table. She tilted her head and pressed a fingertip to her temple, following the hushed tones coming from the dining room.

Rebecca peeked around the corner. Nellie and Edie played Whist at the far side of the dining table. She pulled the chair nearest her and sat down.

"I apologize for missing breakfast." Her shoulders sagged. "Where is everyone?"

"Martie is reading in the parlor. I win those." Nellie swept two cards from the center. "Simon took Ollie and the Drake boys to the Fremonts, and Cordelia and Ben left soon after."

"Oh, I suppose I should thank Martie for preparing breakfast." She patted the table as she rose.

"Martie didn't make breakfast." Nellie set down her last card with a casual flick.

Rebecca paused. "Who did?"

"Dr. Ewing started it, and Simon lent a hand." Nellie took the following two cards and passed them to Edie.

"It was so good." Edie tallied the cards she had amassed. "I think I'm in the lead now."

"There's gravy behind the biscuits, but the boys finished the bacon." Nellie offered an exaggerated pout. "Sorry, we tried to save you some."

"It's okay. You don't know where Ben or Cordelia went?"

The girls shook their heads.

"All right, I'll check with Martie." Rebecca rounded the table and stepped into the parlor.

Martie lounged in the ivory Gainsborough chair, her feet resting on a small footstool.

"Martie, can you tell me where Cordelia and Ben have gone?"

"Mm?" Martie kept her eyes on the page.

"Cordelia and Ben?"

Martie traced her finger along the page momentarily before glancing up. "Ben mentioned needing wallpaper, but I didn't quite follow. And Cordelia left without a word. I assume she went to Brandt's tailor shop since I noticed her speaking with Mrs. Brandt at the picnic."

"Oh, why didn't anyone wake me when you noticed I overslept?"

"Ben was up early making breakfast, and when Simon came down, he pitched in too." Martie marked her place in the book with a ribbon and shut it. "They both suggested letting you sleep in. I thought it was a great idea, although I need to stop by

Gray's Café today to inquire about a job. We decided I would stay with Nellie and Edie until you woke."

"Did Simon discuss his plans with you? Why are Ollie, Nellie, and Edie not in school?"

"Simon believed a day off was justified after the unexpected events of the weekend."

Rebecca released a puff of air. "So, when he returns with all the boys, I'll have to stay with the kids."

"I don't think so. Simon thought it was fine for Nellie to stay and keep an eye on Edie until he came back with the boys." Martie set her book on a side table. "He assured me he would take care of everything here once they finished at the Fremonts'. We're free to leave whenever you wish."

"Really?"

"That's what he said. He believed you might have some matters to attend in town." Martie traced the edge of her book. "But he asked me to check with you before I went."

"All right, then." Rebecca blinked as if emerging from a dream. "I'll head upstairs to clean the boys' room and change into something nicer for town. Then we can go together."

"Sounds wonderful. However, you don't need to be concerned about the boys' room. Simon had them tidy up before they came down for breakfast."

"He's doing well with them, isn't he?"

"He is. It's like a sneak peek of what kind of father he would be." Martie's eyes brightened. "He gave Hayden and Jace the option to stay here, as they weren't at fault for the incident involving Mr. Fremont or the search party. They enjoyed visiting the Fremont place yesterday and jumped at the chance to go. Bringing Ollie along as a consequence for losing Jace seems to be doing him good."

"I agree." Rebecca glanced toward the stairs. "I didn't have a chance to journal last night. Would you mind if I take time to do it this morning in case I miss the chance again this evening?"

"I don't mind, but surely today will be calmer than this weekend." Martie leaned on the arm of the chair with her chin on her hand. "I wish I had caught the journaling bug from Mama as you did. I'd much prefer to read, though."

"Give it a few years. You may discover a love of both." Rebecca squeezed Martie's hand.

Grateful for a few moments of peace, Rebecca climbed the stairs as her thoughts drifted to the pages of her journal—and the questions she hadn't had time to untangle.

She glanced at her room, then toward Ben's. She crept down the hall and quietly cracked open his door. All the clothing Simon had lent him was neatly folded on Mr. Perry's old bed. Ben's side of the room was impeccably tidy, showing no evidence of his presence. Shutting the door, she went down the hall to her room.

She retrieved her journal, went to the kitchen, poured coffee, and stepped outside. Opening her journal, she flipped to the back pages and traced her fingers over the fishhooks. With Simon watching the kids, could she spare time for a fishing trip? She turned to a blank page. Better not. She had to focus on finding boarders. And then there was the spyglass. After the conversation with Captain Cobb, she and Ben hadn't had a chance to discuss their thoughts.

She smiled. He'd had some shining moments the last couple of days. Fleeting glimpses of the man she had first been drawn to. Even with his discomfort in the medical situation, he remained attentive to Jace and Oscar. His warm and unexpectedly insightful advice regarding her siblings and encouragement to practice self-compassion resonated within her. After the picnic, he engaged with the boys as much as Simon had.

Yet he'd been difficult to read after his time whittling with Simon and Levi. Had he finally shared the details of his California experience? His early departure from the boardinghouse after breakfast raised more questions. Was he leaving? The Whipple Expedition departed in July to explore western routes for the railroad. Might he be eager to sign on with another survey team heading west? Why wasn't he wearing the clothes Simon had given him? They were undoubtedly in better shape than his.

She shook her head and shoulders, dismissing thoughts of Ben Ewing. After licking the tip of her pencil, she scrawled a word at the top of the page. Mama.

She remembered how Mama used to sit at the table with her journal, Bible opened beside her, lips moving in silent prayer. Rebecca asked if she prayed while writing, and Mama answered, "Writing is how I listen to Him." That memory comforted her, like warm hands wrapped around her own. Rebecca had written ever since, but did she listen?

Sometimes, when the house was quiet, Rebecca still heard her humming hymns in the kitchen. Not words, just the hum. A soft, steady comfort filling the corners of the home. Mama's faith hadn't shouted. It had shown up quietly at sickbeds, in journaling, while folding laundry.

"Let Him hold you in the hard things," she used to say.

Rebecca touched the page again. Maybe her own ache, this weight she carried, didn't have to be shouldered alone. Perhaps it was something she could hold with the Lord instead of merely surviving it.

Mama would never have left Van Buren. She had moved from one house to another, even living on the steamboat with Pa. But once they settled and constructed the boardinghouse, Mama declared she would remain in Van Buren forever. She had created a life connecting them in ways they had never experienced before. And wasn't their family all the better because of it?

The mountains and rivers of the West no longer held the same charm they once did. With Hogue House's fate uncertain,

Rebecca was hesitant about moving down the street, let alone relocating across the country. However, change was in the air. Justin had married and was growing his horse ranch. Ivajohn was on the verge of marriage. Cordelia often spoke of attending teachers' college, alternating with dreams of a prosperous husband. Simon longed to become a lawman. How had she never realized they wouldn't remain together forever at Hogue House?

She nibbled the end of the pencil.

Mama prayed through every change, even the ones she didn't want. Rebecca hadn't inherited Mama's steady faith. Hers was wobbly, too tied to results. But maybe, if she started bringing her fears to the Lord instead of tucking them into journals, she'd find what Mama found, Peace before answers.

The back door flew open. She gasped. The twins raced out, tripping over each other and tumbling down. They glanced up at her with sheepish grins.

"Hello there, Miss Rebecca."

"Good morning, Jesse. Good morning, Cason." She resolved to use their names whenever possible. Her mother often referred to the Hogue children by their names and unique nicknames intentionally. She wanted her kids to feel recognized, not part of a faceless group. "You're back early, aren't you?"

The boys scrambled to their feet, chuckling and nudging one another. "Yes, ma'am."

"The doctor showed up, and Simon decided it would be best to return later to finish our chores for the Fremonts." Cason lifted a slingshot. "So we were gonna see who can shoot the farthest."

"I see."

The back door swung open again, and Simon poked his head outside. "Boys, let's get moving. You can do some stable chores before returning to the Fremonts'."

"Aw, Mr. Simon, can't we work on our aim?" Jesse pointed to

Cason and the slingshot. "We don't know how far this thing can shoot."

"We'll set aside time to do it later this afternoon."

"Will you do it with us?" A smile bloomed on Jesse's face. "I bet I can shoot farther than you."

"We don't bet." Simon walked over and mussed the boy's hair. "But I'll practice with you. You may be surprised how good I am with a slingshot. I can show you a thing or two. Now, hurry up. Ollie will show you what I want done."

They took off running, the slingshot bouncing in Cason's pocket as they disappeared around the side of the house, already arguing about who would carry the feed bucket.

Simon slipped to the corner of the house, checking if the boys had gone to the stable. He turned to Rebecca. "I should have taken the slingshot to keep them from getting distracted during chores."

"I'm sure they would discover other distractions." Rebecca smiled.

"You know, I don't think they're driven to misbehave. It's curiosity." Simon squinted and rubbed his neck. "They have an unquenchable desire to explore how things work and test the limits. Like wanting to know the range of their slingshot. The challenge is helping them recognize when exploring their curiosity is appropriate."

"And where it's appropriate."

"Being in town with a green-broke pony was certainly not the place." Simon grinned. "I hope they didn't disrupt your writing too much. I'll let you get back to it."

"Can you spare a moment?"

"Sure." He straddled the tree stump next to her. "I don't want to take away from your journaling, though. I know time to write was always important to Ma."

"Martie expressed a desire to have inherited the desire for journaling from Mama."

193

"I enjoy seeing you with a journal. It's comforting, as if part of her lingers among us." Simon crossed his arms over his chest. "It's important we allow you time for this."

Rebecca rubbed her temple with the end of the pencil. "I haven't seen Mama's journal since I can't remember when."

"Since before she died. It's okay to say it."

"Do you remember she kept it in an old wooden box?"

"The one with flowers carved on it?"

"That's the one." She closed her eyes, trying to visualize its location in their father's room. "I haven't seen it in forever. It used to be on the dresser in Pa's room, but I haven't noticed it there for years."

"I believe he moved a few of her belongings to the lost and found room."

"Why would he do that?" Rebecca's face pinched, and she recoiled at the thought of her mother's belongings abandoned in the dusty old room.

"He felt her absence profoundly for so long." Simon patted his arm. "Having her most treasured belongings close by was hard for him. What makes you dislike the lost and found so much?"

"It's just so sad and unsettling." An image of a cameo ring with a sentimental inscription formed in her mind. "Those items likely carry significant meaning, yet no one has claimed them. It's the place where legacy and heritage are long forgotten. The place where legacy and heritage go to die."

"Mm. That's a rather bleak perspective." Simon pulled a face.

"How do you see it?"

"Perhaps people don't seek these items because their bond with loved ones is far more profound than the objects they've touched or shared." He raised his hands toward the sky, then let them fall to his knees. "Even so, the lost and found symbolizes hope for those who have endured sudden farewells or longed for more meaningful relationships with loved ones. If these items find their way back to their rightful owner or someone cherished, it might bring peace and comfort, a means to hold close what was lost."

"That hadn't occurred to me." Her heart warmed. "You sound more like Levi every day."

"He's one of the wisest men I know." Simon smiled, the sun highlighting his blond hair.

"I've been reflecting on our family's history in the boardinghouse." Rebecca pulled the open journal close to her chest. "Have you ever considered we might not all be living here one day?"

"Well, sure." He chuckled. "We'll all grow up eventually and likely start our own families. We can't stay in this house forever."

"I suppose I never considered a time we wouldn't all be together until now." Her voice dropped as she hugged the journal tighter. "I don't want it to change."

"Everything changes, Becks." He squeezed her hand.

"Justin once shared the same sentiment with me. I expressed my frustrations about the Forty-niners and the town's expansion, lamenting how the river, creek, or any of the places I used to explore had changed. He said it was never going to stay the same."

"What brought all this on?"

"I think it started with Edie. She can't remember what Mama looks like, so I reminded her of the portrait above the mantle."

"She'll always find it there."

"But she asked who would get Mama's portrait when we've all grown and moved out." Rebecca rubbed the journal's smooth leather cover. "And that's when it hit me. We won't always be here. What will happen to Hogue House? What will happen to all the things we've shared here?"

"Hmm. I haven't given it much thought. I guess I assumed one of us would stay."

"Who?" She searched Simon's eyes. "If Hogue House doesn't stay in the family, there will be no mantle with a portrait to return to."

"We've got time to figure it out. Don't fret about it now." Simon patted his knee. "Now, since we haven't had much time to talk, how are things going with Ben?"

"Okay, I guess."

"What's the matter?"

"Who says anything is the matter?"

"You gave me your holding-back answer." He arched an eyebrow. "What aren't you saying?"

"Did you know he left early to go to the mercantile for wallpaper?

"Yes. He told me."

"Don't you find it odd?"

"It's for the portrait silhouette project he has planned for Edie. I will teach Ollie and Hayden how to make the frame for it. What's so strange about it?"

"What time did he leave? How long does it take to ask Mr. Mooney about scrap wallpaper?"

"What's going on here? What's bothering you?" He propped his elbows on his knees.

She held her breath.

"What is it?"

"He left the clothes you loaned him in his room. What if he's leaving again?" She tucked her chin. "The Whipple Expedition left in July. What if he decides to join the next big venture west?"

"The military expedition? He would never catch up to them."

"I'm sure private survey teams are going west. Remember the gold prospectors left in waves. Why wouldn't these railroaders do the same?"

"I only gave him two changes of clothes. It's all I could spare.

Didn't Martie do the wash on Saturday? I'm sure she washed his clothes." Simon took one of her hands in his. "He won't leave, especially without discussing it with you. He's probably found odd jobs in town."

"How can I be sure?"

"There are only two things Ben has wanted since he met you. To provide for you and to protect you. He thought he was doing both by taking the doctor position for the survey team going to California."

"You're defending what he did?"

"No, but I understand wanting to protect and provide for your loved ones."

"Shouldn't we have discussed it, though? Isn't it something we should have decided together?" Her brows furrowed. "Shouldn't I have had a say in our future together?"

Simon leaned back, arms crossed. "You mean how our family listens to me when I talk of wanting to be a lawman?"

"Simon, that's not fair." She dropped the journal to her lap. "We're only interested in your well-being. Going off half-cocked seeking revenge on Billy Kinder won't make you feel better."

"It's not about revenge."

"Justice then."

"It's not even about justice." He rubbed the back of his neck. "Not entirely."

"What then?"

A howl rose from the stable. Simon stood, massaged his neck, and sighed.

"I'd better go see what's going on." He tweaked her nose. "Don't worry about Ben or the boardinghouse. It'll all work out, Becks."

"Don't call me Becks," she whispered. She couldn't bear to tell Simon about Baas and the boardinghouse's uncertain future. A tear rolled down her cheek as Simon disappeared around the corner. She wiped it away and closed the journal, tucking it into the belted pocket under her skirt, a small but reassuring weight against her side.

She tried to reassure herself Ben was tethered—to the ring, to Simon and Levi, to the boys. But she had learned long ago even the surest ties frayed without a word.

Chapter Twenty-Six

Ben browsed the aisles of Mooney's Mercantile, patiently waiting for others to depart. Olivia Pratt flashed him a smile from behind one of the wooden shelves, and he responded with a nod.

"Dr. Ewing, I haven't seen you in quite some time." She grabbed a can and added it to her basket.

"It's been some time. I've only recently returned."

"I'm surprised you didn't find other accommodations." She glanced down her narrow nose. "Especially in light of your history with Rebecca."

"Ah, yes. Well, Justin invited me."

"Justin? You do know he no longer resides at Hogue House?" She sniffed. "He has begun a horse ranch near Levi."

"Uh, yes, but I don't think he has an extra room." How could such a petite woman be so intimidating?

"He has a barn, doesn't he?" She grabbed another can. "Or many church families could offer you shelter. I'm surprised you're being so thoughtless with our Rebecca."

"Mrs. Pratt." Sam beckoned her to the counter. "I've got the remainder of your order ready to go."

She shot Ben a sharp nod, scrutinizing him before heading to the counter with Sam. Taking a deep breath, Ben nervously fiddled with his shirt button. Just breathe. He expected Rebecca to have staunch support, especially from Olivia Pratt. Though he didn't know much about women, he noticed they often united in solidarity like no other group when one of them suffered at the hands of a man.

He shifted closer to the counter, hoping for a discreet word with Mr. Mooney once he concluded with Mrs. Pratt. Although Simon had assured him Sam would provide any leftover wallpaper at no cost, Ben planned to offer a small token of appreciation in return. He was thankful Captain Cobb permitted him to clean the deck during the picnic and had invited him back this morning for more work, however menial. Despite the captain's loyalties to the Hogue family, he had shown Ben remarkable grace.

"Keep an eye on the new businessman in town." Mrs. Pratt patted Sam's hand. "I hear he's already bought several properties at the top of Main Street. I wouldn't be surprised if he aims to acquire the entire town. My Martin mentioned some of these, ahem, *gentlemen* plan to buy up whole towns before the railroad arrives. I like our town as it is."

"I've heard he's a smooth talker. Has a charm about him. Always gotta watch those types." Sam loaded her items into a box, glancing toward the door.

"Have you received any word from the sheriff? Did he send a messenger?"

"No news yet."

Mrs. Pratt stroked her necklace. "I do hope he captures this Cutter-Doyle gang soon. We're fortunate they haven't passed through town." She leaned closer to Sam, lowering her voice. "Wouldn't it be something if he returned with Billy Kinder after all this time? I know it would give the Hogues comfort to see justice served for Mahala's murder."

"Mrs. Pratt." Sam cleared his throat. "It was an accidental shooting."

"It was a deliberate act of murder. He may have intended to target the Memphian instead of Mahala. Yet, it's all the same." She tilted her head down.

"Billy's connection to the outlaws is rumored. There's no way to know his whereabouts." Mr. Mooney lifted the supply box. "Shall I carry these out for you?"

"Yes, the horse and buggy are right there." She indicated toward the window. "My Martin is at the saddlery."

She gave Ben a forced smile as she left. Another woman smiled and nodded while placing a list on Sam's counter before leaving. Ben moved to the counter as Sam came back in.

"Morning, Ben. What can I do for you?"

"I heard you might have leftover wallpaper scraps. I want to assist Edie with a special project."

"What are you thinking?" Sam tapped the counter.

"Uh, we're creating a silhouette portrait." Ben rested his hands on the counter. "The silhouette will be plain paper, so we need something to help it stand out."

"I have just the thing." Sam slipped behind the curtain and emerged with a red flocked wallpaper. "What do you think?"

"Oh." Ben took some coins from his pocket. "I meant to pay, but this seems quite lavish."

"Nonsense." Sam pushed Ben's hand aside. "I'll do anything for little Edie. Keep your money."

"I insist, Sam." Ben extended his hand. "I did some tasks for Captain Cobb and want to settle my dues. It's important to me."

"That's all." Sam took a penny from his palm. "I refuse to accept another cent. Eventually, I'll toss these scraps if no one else wants them. Not much use for this sort of thing around here."

"May I ask who placed the original order?"

"The new businessman you heard Mrs. Pratt talking about. Name on the order is Baas."

"Baas? The hotel owner?"

"You know him?"

"You don't? Didn't he come by to pick up his order?"

"No, he sent a man to fetch it. When did you encounter him?"

"We met briefly at the picnic yesterday."

"Funny, I didn't see anyone unfamiliar there." Sam ran his fingers over his stubbled jaw. "Except for the Drake boy, of course."

"Ollie and I took a stroll around the square. Baas approached me at the back side of the courthouse after Ollie returned to Rebecca."

"What did he have to say?"

"He asked me to visit the hotel today to discuss a job."

"What type of work would you do at a hotel?"

"I'm not sure." Ben rubbed his jaw. "Though I'm hard up for cash, I can't imagine working for someone like him."

"Did he exhibit some unpleasantness?"

"On the contrary, he certainly exudes charm, as you've mentioned." Ben folded his arms across the counter. "I've known men like him in California. For them, nothing is more valuable than money. Keeping a safe distance from him is advisable."

"I've never been fond of smooth talkers."

"Sam, can we package this paper and tie it with a bow? I want it to be special for Edie." He retrieved another penny from his pocket. "For the ribbon."

"Not necessary." Sam raised his hand. "I'd be glad to. Are you going back to Hogue House right away?"

"I'm hoping to find Rebecca in town. I thought I'd invite her to lunch at Gray's. They're open for business, right?"

"Indeed, they are. Fine idea. Enjoy your lunch, and I'll have this ready shortly."

"One more thing. I didn't notice any newspapers. Have you already sold out?"

"Wasn't worth reading today. I returned them to the newspaper office."

"Oh. Nothing newsworthy happening?"

"Not worth your time." Sam took the wallpaper and vanished behind the curtain.

Ben grimaced as he turned to leave. Spotting Levi on the boardwalk, he quickened his pace to catch up. He bumped Levi with his shoulder.

"Well, hello." Levi shaded his eyes from the sun. "How are you faring this morning?"

"I'm managing fine." Ben chewed on his lip. "Some light is starting to break through the boulder in my cave."

"Making progress. I like to hear it."

"How are you?"

"Praying for rain." Levi wiped his brow. "The crops need it sorely."

"I didn't see a garden at your place."

"Justin and I share a garden. It's on his property."

"Seems you have a solid partnership."

"We certainly do. I guess we've been partners since he was about sixteen." Levi clapped his hands together. "What brings you to town?"

"Captain Cobb offered me a little work. Nothing long-term, but he welcomed me to stop by daily until he departs."

"Good. Good." Levi pointed to the mercantile. "Have a little chat with Sam?"

"I stopped by to buy a wallpaper sample for a project I'm working on with Edie."

Levi chuckled. "Perhaps a little something to take the place of the spyglass?"

"A silhouette portrait." Ben adjusted his shirt as sweat trickled down his back. "While discussing the idea with Rebecca yesterday, she caught me off guard."

"Oh? How's that?"

"She offered to help me find the spyglass owner."

Levi halted abruptly, a broad, toothy grin emerging. "You don't say. What prompted this change of heart?"

"She discovered Ollie had been hanging out at the riverfront after school with a group of boys. She's concerned about him and thought the spyglass might give her an eye into his world since he found it by the river. Yesterday's events didn't help, though. Ollie leaving Jace unattended."

Levi whistled. "She still seemed plenty aggravated when I spoke with her."

"Overall, she handled the situation gracefully." Ben's tone warmed. "She didn't raise her voice or give a lecture. Instead, she was plain-spoken, to the point, and handed the matter to Simon."

"She second-guessed herself a bit yesterday evening." Levi shook his head. "Turning it over to Simon was wise."

"Oliver balked at the suggestion but fell silent fast when she mentioned the alternative was Nicholas."

"Good for her." Levi nodded with a smile.

"Having Mr. Mooney along was a relief. I'm not certain I can handle being alone with her at length. I worry I'll misstep." Ben's eyebrow quirked up. "By the way, did you know Mr. Mooney is a skilled tracker?"

"Mr. Mooney is a man of hidden talents." Levi nodded slowly. "So, how is the spyglass search going?"

"Yesterday, we spoke with Captain Cobb and Captain Horn. They didn't mention a missing telescope but noticed a few passengers using a spyglass." Ben paused as a scruffy figure with blond hair and pockmarked cheeks sauntered past.

"Something wrong?" Levi glanced around.

"Let's step into the livery for a moment."

"Did you throw a shoe?"

Ben checked his feet. "Throw a shoe?"

"Did Pickle lose a shoe? Did you leave him at the livery?"

"A shoe. Yes." Ben nodded slowly. "Pickle lost a shoe. Let's check on him, shall we?"

Ben seized Levi by the shoulder and shoved him into the livery stable. Inside, he peeked through a crack in the door.

"What has gotten into you? You all right?"

"Have a look." Ben guided Levi to the opening. "Do you see the fella with blond hair? The one with the marked face."

"I see him."

"He may have observed Rebecca and me while we spoke to the captains yesterday." Ben crowded Levi to get another peek. "She would have more insight than I do. I had my back to him, but while he was moving crates he almost dropped one on me. That's when Horn showed up and scared him off."

"If you believe this search may become risky, ask Rebecca to bow out."

"You've been here a little over three days, and you're putting Rebecca at risk?" A deep voice interrupted the conversation, startling Ben and Levi. They spun to see Nicholas step out from the shadows.

"Nicholas, we didn't see you." Ben faltered.

"Is Rebecca in danger?"

"No, I don't believe so." Ben stepped back as Nicholas approached. "Some peculiar things are happening around town, but isn't that typical for a town this size?"

"You've already stirred up the gossips." Nicholas poked him in the chest. "If I find out she's in danger—"

"Listen, Nicholas." Levi wedged himself between Ben and Nicholas. "Ben would never put her in danger. None of us would. But you must acknowledge since the railroad discussions started, there seem to be more suspicious people around than usual." Levi spoke over his shoulder while keeping Nicholas at arm's length. "Add a category to your list of possible spyglass owners. Could belong to a railroad surveyor or someone similar."

Ben laughed uneasily. "Levi, this might not be the best time."

"Ben, is our friend still out there?"

He stretched his neck to peek through the hole. "I can't see him. Might have moved on."

"Nicholas, my friend, why not let us get out of your hair and put this behind us?" Levi gave him a light pat on the chest.

"Go ahead." Nicholas stepped back. "But I'm watching you, Doc."

Ben gulped. "I'd expect nothing less."

As the pair emerged from the livery, Ben scanned the street in one direction while Levi checked the other.

"I don't see him." Levi lowered his voice, casting another glance down the road.

"Me neither." Ben patted him on the back. "I asked Nicholas to keep an eye on Rebecca while I was in California. He's done his job well. Perhaps to my detriment."

"Nah. Don't let him fool you. His loyalty to you is plenty strong, even though Rebecca outranks you." Levi gestured toward the courthouse. "You might want to see the clerk about the spyglass. You never know who might come asking."

"Right. Railroad capitalists and clerks are being added to the list." Ben ran his hand through his hair. Then he raised his finger, indicating the nail around it. "I forgot to mention that I remembered while searching for Ollie and the Drake boy. I remembered to ask Jesus to sit with me."

"I noticed it helped with our conversation last night too." Levi gave Ben a reassuring pat on the shoulder.

They continued down the block until they reached Pickle. Ben stopped, unbuckled his saddlebag, and took out the Bible.

"Look. I decided I'd better carry it with me."

"You're going to be all right." Levi smiled. "Remember Isaiah 54:10."

"Levi." Ben examined the Bible in his hands. He quieted his voice. "What happened to Mahala Hogue? Mrs. Pratt mentioned at the mercantile Billy Kinder killed her. How is that possible? I knew him. He was a good kid."

Levi's demeanor darkened. "A man from Memphis came to town and clashed with Billy's brother at the saloon, killing him. Billy vowed he would shoot the man on sight if they crossed paths again."

Inhaling deeply, Levi cast his eyes down. He took a few steps toward the mercantile and pointed. "It occurred right there, just below the mercantile. Billy saw the man in the street. It was crowded that day. Farmers bringing their goods and steamboats arriving. It was busy."

His gaze shifted from the mercantile door to the location of the incident. "Justin and Mahala had finished shopping. Justin paused to speak with a young woman while Mahala moved into the street as Billy shot his revolver. She went down. Didn't make it through the night."

A metallic tang flooded Ben's mouth as his stomach knotted. He turned away from the mercantile.

Levi clutched his shoulder. "Nothing could be done. Rebecca has repeatedly gone through your medical books, questioning what she could have changed." Levi locked onto Ben's eyes. "You couldn't have saved her either. She wouldn't have survived even if a doctor had been by her side."

"But I could have ..." Ben's knuckles whitened as he gripped the Bible. "I could have been here for Rebecca."

"You can't change the past. There was a purpose for your time in California." Levi gripped his shoulder. "What would've happened to those children without you there?"

Ben closed his eyes. He held the hands of a young girl and

her two brothers. Sean's final words echoed. *Send them east to my aunt.* Had he not been at Angels Camp, would the children have reached their destination safely? Perhaps they wouldn't have survived the night without him. But keeping them alive had forever changed him, just as trying to save her mother had changed Rebecca.

"Ben."

He opened his eyes.

"You can't change the past." Levi lightly shook his shoulder. "You can only go forward from here."

Ben let out a heavy sigh. "There are days it seems like I'll never escape it."

"You won't. But God will use this to help you become a better man." Levi patted his shoulder. "I need to find Allie. We'll talk again soon."

Ben placed his Bible in the saddlebag and scanned Main Street for the one face he longed to see. Carriages and horses lined the street. A group of women exchanged glances with him, whispering behind their hands. A few men passed, shaking their heads. Had news spread about the spyglass search?

His eyes wandered farther up Main Street until they fell upon honey-colored hair. Several people blocked his view. He shifted to the other side of Pickle, stroking the gelding's neck. His heart sank. Rebecca walked arm-in-arm with Nicholas Franks, with Martie following closely as they entered Hildesheim's Bakery.

Chapter Twenty-Seven

Rebecca slid a list across the counter to Conrad Hildesheim. "We won't require as many baked goods today, Mr. Hildesheim. Most of the boarders have moved."

"I've heard." He snatched the list and turned swiftly, his footfalls heavy as he retreated to the shelves at the back. Her stomach tightened as his brusque demeanor caught her off guard. The good-humored German baker had lived with them for years and never been snappish.

"Does he seem ill-tempered this morning, or is it just me?"

"He's usually a ray of sunshine." Martie tilted her head. "It's certainly not his usual chatty disposition."

"You seem a little off today as well. Though to be fair, you've never been very chatty." Rebecca turned to Nicholas with a grin. "I was quite startled to see you coming up the street. I thought someone might have been hurt. You never said what brings you out today."

"Folks keep telling me I should get out more." He made eye contact, then his gaze darted away. "Say I need more sunshine. Personally, I could do without the heat."

"If you find a way to beat this heat, let us know." Rebecca narrowed her eyes at him. "Now, do you want to tell me the real reason you met up with us?"

He shifted his weight as his eyes swept the storefront window before returning to her. "Where are you headed after this?"

"I have to visit the mercantile."

"Best you go straight there." He tugged the curtain back to view Main Street. "There's been some tension in town today."

"Oh? Is it safe to be here?" She raised an eyebrow. A creeping unease had taken root inside her, low, steady, unshakable. Not knowing how to interpret it left her exposed, off-balance, and unable to shield her family in the way she usually would. "Is there news of the Cutter-Doyle gang?"

"Nothing to report." Nicholas forced a smile. "No concern for safety. No more than usual anyway."

Mr. Hildesheim slid a brown package, tied with twine, across the counter. He silently accepted her coins and returned to the back of the bakery. She paused momentarily, adding the package to her basket.

Mr. Hildesheim peeked from the back. "Goot day, Miss Hogue." And he vanished.

The terse dismissal left a bad taste in her mouth. She linked arms with Martie. "I suppose he wants us to leave."

She squinted as she stepped into the sunlight and scanned the street. "We're off to the mercantile."

Nicholas caught her shoulder. "Perhaps I should accompany you."

"Nicholas Franks." She stepped back onto the boardwalk. "What is going on?"

"Who says anything is going on?"

"When we're working together, you remind me how desperately you wish to return to the saddlery." She poked his chest. "You never take a moment to chat afterward, and I don't see you anywhere in town. And now I can't shake you. Enlighten me."

"I don't—"

Frustration simmered as she nudged his chest once more. "Careful."

"I don't want folks to misunderstand."

"Misunderstand what?"

"I want to make sure they grasp the situation between you and Doc Ewing properly."

"Never you mind what others think of us." Her face tightened. "If anyone gets the wrong idea, I can set them straight. But unless you came to visit, perhaps it's best you head back to the saddlery and leave my personal affairs to me."

Nicholas reddened. "Yes, ma'am."

With a forlorn expression, he turned toward the saddlery.

"What in the world has gotten into Nicholas and Mr. Hildesheim today?"

"I don't know." Martie's eyes widened. "I have never seen Nicholas behave like this. I've seldom seen him at all. However, Simon says he's sweet on you. Perhaps he's jealous since Ben has returned."

"Sweet on me?" Her head snapped around. "Mr. Mooney thinks the same thing. Do you suppose it's true?"

Martie tilted her head, her mouth pulling to one side. "Well, I do now."

"I simply do not need another thing to deal with." Rebecca sighed. "Let's hurry to the mercantile before he rethinks his decision to accompany us."

They crossed to the boardwalk on the other side of the street. A few women from church averted their eyes when Rebecca smiled and nodded. Her brow furrowed as the women hurried past, their faces set in uncomfortable lines. She'd always known small towns bred gossip, but this was different. She was the subject now. Her heart sank. Did they think her too forward, too bold in her relationship with Ben? Had they heard of the spyglass search and presumed a wedding was forthcoming, as Horn had? A gentleman met her gaze and then crossed to the opposite side of the street.

The sting of whispered judgment pricked her heart. She breathed deep, recalling Mama's words. *You don't have to carry their opinions to Jesus. Just carry your own heart.* One step at a time. One prayer at a time.

"Nicholas and Conrad aren't the only ones out of sorts today." She opened the door for Martie to enter first. She lowered her voice and added, "I hope Mr. Mooney is in a better mood."

"Hello, girls!" He smiled warmly. "What brings you by?"

A wave of relief washed over Rebecca, but it was fleeting when a mother with two young children glanced at her and quickly left. She furrowed her brows in confusion as she watched them rush out the door.

"Mr. Mooney, am I missing something?"

"How do you mean?"

"We—or I—are receiving odd looks today. Which is to say, people are avoiding making eye contact with me."

"Hmm. I don't believe that's the case." His expression turned serious. "There's been a lot of tension since the sheriff left. Plus there's chatter about the railroad and the spyglass. And don't forget about those Drake boys' missing father." He lightly patted the counter. "People are a bit jittery, that's all."

"I'll have to take your word for it."

His generous smile returned. "So, do you have anything in your basket I could add to my store?"

Rebecca passed the bakery parcel to Martie and placed the basket on the counter. She took out several items and arranged them.

"I brought several sets of tea towels and potholders, a few aprons, and a selection of candles."

Martie drew in a breath. "Becca, these candles are stunning. When did you make them? How did you do this?"

"Sometimes I can't sleep. When I don't know what to write, this relaxes me." She traced the curved loops of a candle. "Mama showed me how. I dip the candles in various colors and then carve the wax before it sets completely."

"I don't carry anything like this in my shop. My candles are basic pillars, tapers, votives, and tealights." Mr. Mooney examined a candle, rotating it in his hands. "This displays fine craftsmanship."

"Oh, it's nothing." Rebecca's cheeks warmed.

"No, I'm serious." He gestured toward the curves and added, "This is as exquisite as Levi's metalwork."

"You think so?"

"I know so." Mr. Mooney gathered the tea towels, potholders, and aprons. "Just a moment. Let me place these on a shelf with similar items."

The bell chimed as Caroline Brandt entered. "Hello, Rebecca. I thought I spotted you through the window."

"Did you enjoy the picnic yesterday?" Rebecca shifted her gaze from Caroline to Mr. Mooney and back again.

"Oh, I did. I can't remember the last time I've had such a delightful and lively experience." A wide smile bloomed on Caroline's face. "Martie, what do you think of *Jane Eyre*?"

"It's mysterious and swoony. I've never read anything quite like it." Martie placed her hand on her chest. "Sad, but so beautifully written, like walking through fog with a candle."

"Sounds intriguing. I'm glad it suits your fancy." Caroline joined them at the counter and picked up one of the candles. "Sam, where have you been hiding these?"

"Becca made those." Martie grinned.

"My dear girl, you made these?" Caroline scrutinized the

candle from every angle. "And you've been keeping them to yourself?"

"It's something I dabble in when I have the time."

"Well, make more time for this, dear." She selected two candles from the collection and left some coins on the counter. "Sam, I'll take these two candles in addition to my fabric purchase."

"Caroline, no. It's too much."

"I'm getting a bargain. Once people discover these, they will fly off the shelf." She leaned past Rebecca to catch a glimpse of Martie. "I hope she shows you how to make these. She may need help keeping up with demand, mark my words."

"That's kind of you to say."

Sam returned to the front and picked up a crate from behind the counter. "Here's your fabric. Let me wrap those candles to keep them safe."

He quickly wrapped them in brown paper and secured the bundle with string, placing it atop Caroline's crate. Then, smiling at her, he slipped three pieces of butterscotch into the box. She gazed at him, moon-eyed.

"Mr. Mooney, do you have any newspapers left?" Rebecca grabbed a piece of butterscotch and pushed a penny across the counter.

"No papers today." His gaze remained fixed on Caroline.

Rebecca glanced at Martie, who bounced her eyebrows playfully.

"Mr. Mooney."

"Hmm?"

"We should be going. Martie needs to talk to Mrs. Gray about a job."

"Hmm." He looked into Caroline Brandt's adoring eyes.

"Okay, then." Rebecca drummed her fingers on the counter, glanced at Martie, and pointed to the door. She picked up her basket and followed Martie. "It's time for us to leave."

She moved past Martie to open the door, triggering the bell's chime.

"Rebecca." Caroline kept her eyes on Mr. Mooney as she scooped up the coins. "Make sure to take your money."

"Kindly apply it to the boardinghouse tab." She exited behind Martie.

Once on the boardwalk, the sisters burst into laughter. They doubled over, leaning on one another for support. Rebecca pressed her hand to her side, trying to catch her breath.

"I hope they end up as a couple." Martie straightened, folding her hands under her chin. "They are so adorable together."

"Maybe I ought to give them the spyglass." Her delivery fell flat.

Martie pressed her palms to her cheeks. "Does Ben have it?"

Rebecca nodded as she approached the notice board. Her fingers brushed over the cluttered papers. "My note about our vacancies is gone."

Martie accompanied her, furrowing her brow. "Are you sure?" She shuffled through slips of paper, her fingers pausing as she scanned. "There's no mention of the boardinghouse here. Let's check with Mr. Mooney."

"No, I think I know what happened to it." Baas loomed fresh in her thoughts.

"Would someone have taken it? Perhaps they'll inquire about a room."

A chill crept down Rebecca's spine as she recalled the unsettling conversation with the man, and she wrapped a protective arm around Martie. The way he had unexpectedly appeared, his breath on the back of her neck. His charming but treacherous smile, especially when he mentioned Cordelia. His proposal wasn't just a business proposition. It was a maneuver designed to unsettle her. But she wasn't ready to give up Hogue House without a fight.

"The wind must have knocked it down." Rebecca clenched her jaw, trying to push the unsettling thoughts away. "Let's get you to Gray's." She tried to sound casual, but the pit in her stomach remained.

Chapter Twenty-Eight

A sliver of shade offered a brief respite from the heat as Rebecca strolled down the side street with Martie. She took a deep breath, welcoming the enticing aroma of Annetta Gray's cooking, which overshadowed the typical scents of dust and manure, mingled with the crisp, earthy fragrance of the river. Occasionally, Gray's Cafe evoked memories of Mama's meals. The delightful scent caused Rebecca's stomach to growl.

Martie giggled. "You should have had more than coffee for breakfast."

"Rebecca. Martie."

The girls glanced toward the familiar voice.

Ben jogged toward them. "I thought I had missed you."

Rebecca's heart lifted. He was here. He hadn't gone anywhere. However, there was no guarantee he hadn't spent the morning asking about survey teams.

"Where have you been?"

"I've been searching for a job." Ben wiped his mouth with the back of his hand. "I helped Captain Cobb a bit yesterday and this morning. Lent a hand at the dry goods store during a rush and did some sweeping at the carpentry shop." A spark of pride lit his face.

"It sounds like you've been quite busy." Rebecca glanced his way, her voice warm but measured.

"Some jobs took half an hour or less, but Captain Cobb kept me a while." His chest puffed. "Simon mentioned you'd be coming to town, so I've been wandering all over trying to find you. I'd like to take you to lunch, and it seems you were heading to Gray's anyway."

He took them both by the arm and ushered them to the café. Rebecca had just started to push the door open when it slammed shut from the other side. She yelped and jumped back, hand flying to her chest.

Ben moved in front of her with eyes narrowed on the door, holding his arm out in a protective manner.

"What was that?" Martie rushed to the window, but the curtains were tightly drawn.

Inside, muffled voices rose, then Annetta Gray's voice crackled with irritation and the others fell silent. Chairs scraped. Dishes clattered. Footsteps thudded across the hardwood floor.

"Hello? Everything all right in there? Open the door." Ben banged his foot against it.

Rebecca pressed her palm to her forehead. "Has everyone in this town gone off their rocker today?"

Ben took a step back and regarded her with curiosity. "Is there anything I should be aware of?"

"It's been a day. I don't want to talk about it," she muttered, rubbing her temple. She stepped forward again and knocked firmly. "Annetta Gray, are you open for business?"

The door swung open with a whoosh, and Mrs. Gray welcomed them with her familiar broad smile. "Rebecca, dearie, what a surprise to see you here twice in one week. You don't usually brave the summer heat alongside the hot café kitchen. I wasn't expecting you until after first frost."

Rebecca widened her eyes and shook her head vigorously, a knot of unease forming in her chest. She couldn't fathom what to do if Mrs. Gray brought up Baas. She had told no one about their meeting, hoping to discuss it with Eliza Dawn the first moment they could manage alone. But with Mrs. Gray's cheery nature, she feared the woman might inadvertently spill the details of their conversation.

A quiet breath escaped her. Could she trust Mrs. Gray to keep her secret? The idea of Baas's name circulating made her stomach churn. She couldn't explain why, but she suspected a connection between him, the strangers near the outlying properties, and the rumors of the railroad. But no one, not even Ben or Martie, could know that yet. Not until she understood how all of it connected to Hogue House.

"Mrs. Gray, are you able to seat three?" Ben attempted to peek around her.

Mrs. Gray side-stepped to block his line of sight. "You want to eat?"

He nodded.

"Here? Today?"

Rebecca propped her hands on her hips. "Mrs. Gray, are you open for business, or aren't you? I'm suddenly famished."

Mrs. Gray waved her hand behind her. "If I remember correctly, you're not fond of the heat in my kitchen during summer."

"Winter is generally my favorite season to savor your tasty dishes, but today, the scent from your café reminded me of Mama's cooking." Rebecca smiled politely.

"It does, doesn't it?" A gleam of excitement lit Martie's eyes. "Plus I want to talk to you about a job."

Rebecca shot a sharp glance at Martie, subtly nodding to Ben.

"It's for the experience, not because we need the money."

Martie's eyes glinted at Rebecca. "Given all her duties, Rebecca hardly has the time to teach me to cook."

Mrs. Gray glanced behind her before swinging the door open. "Come in. I have the perfect table for you."

Rebecca surveyed the room. Patrons sat rigidly, eyes fixed ahead, as motionless as river turtles on a log. Silence filled the air. Tables perfectly straight and aligned. Everything unnaturally in order, contrasting sharply with the usual café atmosphere.

"I thought we were supposed to find our own seats." Rebecca traded glances with Martie.

"New way of doing things. More orderly. I seat everyone as they come in now." Mrs. Gray showed them to a front table in the far corner, away from the other patrons.

"Is that so?" Rebecca settled into the corner chair to get a clearer view of the room. "Why did you slam the door in my face? What was all the commotion?"

"I beg your pardon, dearie. It couldn't be helped." Mrs. Gray wiped her face with her apron skirt. "The fool cat from the livery slipped in through the back door. Set off a commotion, everyone trying to shoo it away before it wandered across the table and onto someone's plate. You know how cats can be. They don't give a mind about no one but themselves."

"The livery cat?" Ben tapped his fingers rhythmically on the table.

"The livery cat." She licked her fingertip like a pencil. "Now, what'll you have?"

"I'd like sweet tea and the special." Rebecca surveyed the room as Mrs. Gray pretended to jot the order on her hand.

"One water, one special."

"I requested sweet tea."

"Of course you did." Mrs. Gray chortled. "Checking to see if you were paying attention, dearie. What'll you have, Doc?"

"Is there a menu board available?" He scanned the room.

"Two sweet teas and two specials, it is." She stuck her finger behind her ear like a pencil.

"And you, Miss Martie?"

"A job?"

"Follow me, dearie."

Martie followed Mrs. Gray to the kitchen. Midway through the dining area, a man set some coins on the table and got up to leave, his plate untouched. As Mrs. Gray scooted by, she nudged the back of his knee, saying, "Sit. Eat. You're not leaving until your plate is empty."

The man sitting at the table closest to the kitchen unfolded his newspaper. As he did, Mrs. Gray snatched it from his hand while passing by. Martie turned back to Rebecca, eyes wide, hands hovering midair. Rebecca rubbed her temple in response.

"That's the only newspaper I've seen today." Ben leaned closer and spoke quietly. "Mr. Mooney mentioned he took the mercantile copies back to the newspaper office because it wasn't worth reading."

"Are you serious?" Rebecca crossed her arms on the table and leaned closer. "He told me there were no papers today."

Mrs. Gray moved between the tables, bringing them two glasses of water. Rebecca and Ben shared quizzical glances.

"Mrs. Gray, why did you take the paper from the gentleman over there?" Rebecca dipped her chin toward the man.

Mrs. Gray remained focused on their table. "Paper? No. No newspapers today."

"Are you certain? It resembled a newspaper." Ben leaned around her.

"Old edition." She smiled, nudging into place. "No paper available today. Sam Mooney will tell you that."

Before either could speak again, she disappeared.

"This is giving me a headache." Rebecca rubbed her temple again. "Let's talk about something else."

Ben's expression tightened. "I hesitate to mention it now, but I wanted to discuss the spyglass."

"Yes, we haven't had the opportunity to exchange information since I offered to help you."

"You have information?" Ben perked up.

"I'm sorry to get your hopes up." She drank some water. "No, I don't."

"Oh." He sipped his water. "This morning, Captain Cobb mentioned he spoke with the other steamboat captains regarding it."

"Good." A bit of tension eased from Rebecca's face. "What leads do you have?"

"None. All the captains' telescopes are accounted for." Ben tapped the table. "Levi assisted me in compiling a list of other options, though."

"I want to hear it." She turned her glass in circles.

"He recommended we inquire with the doctors, sheriff, railroad investors, court clerk, and military scouts. Additionally, we should consider the passengers Captains Cobb and Horn referred to."

"Dr. Pernot attended the picnic yesterday. His telescope is accounted for."

"Oh, I wasn't aware he was there."

"He arrived at the square while we spoke with the captains. With all the chaos afterward, I didn't get to introduce you."

"Remove him from the list." A hint of pleasure played at Ben's features, the tension she'd grown used to nowhere in sight. "The sheriff is away, and as far as I know, so is the other doctor. What's his name?"

"Dr. Dibrell."

"We won't be able to ask them until they return."

"Sam had a thought." Rebecca tapped the table. "I mentioned the sections won't extend, and he suggested we disassemble it for cleaning. I'm unsure if there could be additional engravings on the other parts, though. Cleaning it might not be beneficial."

"It's not a bad idea. We can take care of it once we're back at the boardinghouse." Ben smiled. "It makes more sense than wearing out our shoes and horses."

Martie arrived at their table with two plates of smoked ham and potatoes. She set the plates down and leaned to whisper in Rebecca's ear.

"Ben, if you'll excuse me, I'm needed in the kitchen." Rebecca took the napkin from her lap and placed it on the table.

Ben stood, wearing a slightly pained expression. "Something medical?"

"No, nothing of the sort." She smiled at his relief as he pulled her chair out. "One of the girls needs to talk."

On the way back, Martie whispered, "She's been like this all day."

In the back corner of the kitchen, Sarah sat on a stool in tears. Rebecca glanced at Martie and lifted her hands in a small, helpless gesture, unsure what to do.

"I can't believe I'm saying this," Rebecca murmured, eyes shut and hand covering her mouth, "but I'm better in a medical situation. No one knows what is wrong with her?"

Martie shook her head. "She cried so hard most of the morning, no one could understand her."

Rebecca pressed her palms against her skirt and took a deep breath. How she wished for some visible sign of the problem. Martie gave her a nudge. She moved close and crouched in front of Sarah.

Placing her hands on Sarah's knees, she held the girl's attention. "I'm unsure how to help, but I'd like to try. Can you tell me what's wrong?"

Sarah took a shaky breath and released a trail of indistinguishable words and intermittent sobs.

"Look into my eyes, Sarah." Rebecca patted her knee. "I need you to breathe with me. Let's slow down. In." Rebecca inhaled slowly through the nose. "Out." She released a long breath.

As Sarah mimicked Rebecca's breathing, her sobs quieted. Rebecca continued the pattern for a few minutes. Sarah's shoulders dropped, her back straightened, her chest opened, and her chin lifted. Rebecca stood and rubbed her back.

"There, now. That's better." Rebecca helped her to her feet. "Now, can you tell us what's wrong?"

"I'm being kicked out of Bradley House." Sarah wiped her tears away, sniffling. "I have nowhere to live."

Rebecca glanced at Martie. "Did you know this?"

"I understood 'no home.' I wasn't entirely sure what she meant, but I thought maybe?" Martie laid her hand on Rebecca's wrist. "We have a need. She has a need. Can something be worked out?"

"Perhaps?" Rebecca folded her arms across her chest, cradling her cheek with the other hand. "In the past, we've had Dawn and one other young lady. It's worth considering."

"I agree." Martie nodded.

"Take heart, Sarah." Rebecca grasped her hands. "We have room at Hogue House. When you've finished here, gather your things and come to the boardinghouse, okay?"

"Thank you." Sarah threw her arms around Rebecca.

"I'm happy to help." Rebecca peeled away from Sarah and hitched her thumb toward the dining room. "I'm going to eat, and I'll see you later."

She wandered back to the table, sat, and placed her napkin in her lap, shaking her head.

Ben set his fork on his plate. "Everything all right?"

"I think it will be. It seems Sarah has been ousted from Bradley House. This day has been so unusual, I didn't think to ask why." She cut her ham into bite-sized pieces. "We're going to try to accommodate her at Hogue House."

"There's certainly plenty of room." Ben scooped a forkful of potatoes.

"True. However, traditionally, one end of the hall has always been for male boarders while the other has been for family." She took a bite of ham, followed by a sip of water. "Since we have male tenants on one end, we can put her in the lost and found room. We did the same thing with Dawn so she could have some privacy."

"Perhaps the boys and I could move to the bunkroom."

"Nonsense. It would be far too cramped for five people." She took another sip of water. "I'm not going to worry about it now. Let's finish our meal."

Ben's gaze traced the line of empty tables between them and the other diners. He shook his head. "It certainly has been an odd day."

"I can't wait to get home. I've had my fill of town." Rebecca traced the edge of her glass. "This evening, I plan to have a glass of tea before I take my journal to the grove to enjoy some fireflies and moonlight."

Ben smiled. "I've always been fond of fireflies. They bring a bit of hope to dark places."

His sentiment tugged at her heart. She found herself wanting to share a bit of hope with him. But something inside her whispered *not yet.*

Chapter Twenty-Nine

Rebecca placed a plate of cookies and two cups of tea on the kitchen table, taking the chair opposite Ben. They stared at the spyglass.

"These are also called gentlemen's telescopes because large estate owners use them for hunting." Ben shifted uncomfortably.

"Interesting." She scooted the plate toward him. "I got these spiced butter cookies from Hildesheim's bakery, though Conrad didn't seem happy to have my business."

"Maybe Nicholas did something disagreeable?" Ben picked up a cookie, pausing to lock eyes before taking a bite.

Rebecca quirked her head. "Why would Nicholas have anything to do with it?"

"I saw you on his arm at the bakery." Ben's jaw flexed.

"So, you've been spying on me?"

"I wasn't spying. I happened to see you while running errands." He tapped the package Mr. Mooney had wrapped so neatly. "Uncommon for Nicholas to wander about town, particularly during business hours."

"I agree." Rebecca reached for a buttery treat.

"Did he mention why he wasn't at the saddlery?"

"Both he and Conrad acted strangely. Who can say why?" She sipped her tea. "Besides, their behavior was no more unusual than that of anyone I met today."

"I experienced something similar." Ben sat back, crossing his arms. "I noticed women sneaking glances and whispering behind their fans."

"Men walked across the street, seemingly to avoid me. Did you experience it too?"

"Yes, or shaking their heads as if I'd done something wrong." Ben pushed his hair from his forehead. "I wondered if it was because I'm back. They know how you and I parted." He flicked his thumb across his fingers. "I anticipated they would be protective of you, considering my return. The whole town adores you."

"Funny way of showing it." Rebecca grabbed another cookie and pushed the plate to the middle of the table. "No matter the problem, we can't do anything about it right now. Let's focus on the matter at hand." She brushed away crumbs, took a clean towel from a nearby drawer, and spread it across the table.

"I should have considered cleaning it earlier." Ben raised his arms as Rebecca tucked the towel underneath them. "However, it's been such a long time since I've owned a spyglass, I'm out of the habit of maintaining one."

"Pa cleans his regularly. Not often, but consistently. I've never paid attention to how he does it. Where do we start?"

"We'll begin at the eyepiece and proceed toward the barrel's wider end. First, I'll need to separate the stuck sections. It may take a bit of force."

"Will it damage the telescope?"

"It can withstand reasonable pressure, but I'll be careful." Ben sipped his tea and then removed the cap from the barrel of the spyglass. He braced the spyglass between his knees, gripped it beneath the eyepiece and around the barrel, and gave a solid twist. The metal groaned faintly. He wiped his hands on his pants and renewed his grip, twisting again. The first section began to budge, and he continued working it back and forth until it slid free.

They both sighed in relief.

He continued the process with the second section. After a few moments it extended with a soft *pop*.

"This is its full length?"

"I believe so. Telescopes are classified according to the number of sections that extend from the barrel, making this one a two-draw telescope." He pointed to the newly exposed sections. "Now, let's disassemble it." He removed the eyepiece and the first lens cartridge, setting them on the towel. "This lens cartridge contains two lenses, one located at each end of the cartridge."

"How many cartridges are there?"

"This telescope features two cartridges, an eyepiece cartridge and an erector cartridge. The piece at the end of the barrel is two lenses glued together." He unscrewed the next coupling ring, removed the erector cartridge, and laid the pieces on the towel. Lastly, he removed the lens piece from the barrel. "Tiny bits of grit and sand may be causing the jam. Thankfully, you found the oil for your father's telescope. We'll search for markings as we clean it, though I doubt the other pieces have any."

"What's the method for cleaning it?"

"First, we will clean all the lenses. Then we will clean and oil the metal tubes."

"Okay, let me get a couple of soft cloths, and I'll help." Rebecca returned to the table, handing him a fabric swatch and keeping one for herself. She cleaned the lenses of the erector cartridge while Ben focused on the eyepiece cartridge. She wiped one lens, but when she turned the cartridge around to polish the other one, she dropped her cloth.

"Ben, I discovered something. It's a tiny, folded piece of paper." She freed the wedged paper and opened it.

"What does it say?" Ben leaned closer.

"I can't make it out. It makes no sense."

"Let's see. It might just be poor handwriting." He reached for the paper. "I'll give it a try."

"It's not bad handwriting." She pursed her lips, shaking her head. "It's nonsense."

"I don't think it's gibberish. It could be a code." Ben scrutinized the note. His finger traced the rows of letters as she leaned over his shoulder. "Notice the gaps between these clusters of letters? This suggests that these groupings represent words, likely pointing to a type of alphabet code."

"Rebecca!" A shrill, pitchy voice echoed from the entryway.

"Ivajohn." Rebecca sprang from her chair and hurried through the dining room, joining her sister in the parlor. Ivajohn had red eyes, and her dark hair was disheveled. "Ivajohn, what's the matter?"

Ivajohn raised the newspaper high. "How can you ask what's wrong?" She shook the paper. "This is a stain on our family. Emil's mother is considering canceling the wedding."

Ivajohn puddled on the settee, engulfed in tears and sniffles. Rebecca hurried to her, wrapping an arm around her sister. Ivajohn pulled away from the embrace, waving the paper in Rebecca's face. Rebecca's eyes darted around, trying to read the headline. Pressing fingers to her temple, she seized the paper with her other hand. At the top, bold letters proclaimed:

Proprietress or Mistress?

Her mouth was coated in cotton. Her finger swiftly brushed over the words. Waves of nausea and dizziness washed over her. *Lord, I can't carry this alone.* The article disclosed Ben's living situation and implied he was "trading favors" for services at the boardinghouse. She crumpled the paper, squeezing it repeatedly.

"Ivajohn, where did you get this newspaper?"

"Mrs. Turner requires her daily newspaper, so when Mr. Mooney had none available, she visited the dry goods store and found one there."

"This is a lie. You know it's not true."

Ivajohn sobbed. "I tried to tell her."

"Is everything all right? Is there anything I can do?" Ben stepped into the room.

Ivajohn leaned over the back of the settee. "Move out."

"Ivajohn." Rebecca's tone flattened. "Ben, we've identified the reason behind the unusual reactions we encountered today." She passed him the paper.

A crimson hue spread up his neck as he read. "Who would publish something like this? I'm going straight to the newspaper office to demand a retraction."

"A fit of rage will only make things worse." Rebecca covered her mouth with her hand, trying to keep her composure. "I can't believe Mr. Clarke would print such a thing. Perhaps his brother might. But Anslem Clarke is sincere and warm-hearted, even if a bit blunt. Dawn has been quite content working for him since he took over the paper from his brother."

"Then what do you suggest?"

"Let me think." She tugged on her ear, her mind already racing for options. A knock sounded at the front door. Rebecca held her breath and didn't move, the knock landing like the final straw. She motioned Ben to put the paper away. "It's likely Sarah from the café. Maybe letting her have a room will help mitigate the harm caused by the paper."

Rebecca opened the front door. Sarah stood, bag in hand, her countenance considerably brighter than at their last meeting. Her face radiated hope.

"We're all here, Rebecca." Sarah handed Rebecca her carpet bag.

All?

Rebecca leaned out the front door, mouth agape. Her heart lifted. And sank. It was hope and chaos both, storming her doorstep. The Bradley House women, including Paulette Bradley, gathered in the yard while Nicholas Franks stood beside his fully loaded wagon beyond the fence.

Rebecca raised a finger to Sarah and shut the door between them. Leaning against the it, she shook her head. Turning to Ben, she tented her hands against her mouth, then lowered them to her chest.

"Ben, go clean out your room."

Chapter Thirty

"You want me to leave?" A wave of confusion rolled through Ben before he managed to clamp it down.

"Not leave. I need you to move." Rebecca motioned him toward the front window. "Look."

He hooked the rose-patterned curtain with his finger, drawing it aside to glimpse five women in the yard and Sarah on the porch. Nicholas waved from the road. Ben released the curtain and stepped back.

"What are they doing here? I thought Sarah needed the room."

"I did too." Rebecca's gaze remained fixed on the door. "But Nicholas's wagon is full. They've all come with bags. It appears they intend to stay." She turned to Ivajohn. "It may get rather cramped. I understand if you need to go, but I'd appreciate it if you could stay so we can finish our conversation."

"I don't believe Mrs. Turner wants me at the parsonage, so I guess I'll stay here." Ivajohn dried her face. "Maybe I could wait in the study?"

"It might be the quietest place." Rebecca clasped her hands together, then turned to Ben. "Since Simon is at the Freemonts',

I could use your help gathering the women in the dining room. We'll need to go over room assignments and figure out how to make this work. Then you can assist with moving the Drake boys' things. Thank goodness Martie returned early and went for a stroll with Nellie and Edie."

"Of course." Ben nodded. "Anything you need."

"After they're settled, would you mind checking for any leftover biscuits from this morning? And maybe offer water or tea? I'd like to speak with Nicholas a moment while you get them settled."

"I've got it." He started toward the entry. "Ready when you are."

Rebecca opened the door to find Sarah waiting, her smile bright and hopeful. Rebecca took her carpet bag and handed it to Ben. "Come in, all of you. We'll meet in the dining room and sort things out there."

Once the women filed inside, Ben ushered them toward the dining room. Paulette Bradley's bonnet sat unusually low on her forehead. When he tried to sneak a glance at her face, she turned away.

"I'll join you shortly." Rebecca waved as she stepped outside.

In the dining room, Ben motioned to the chairs. "Ladies, make yourselves comfortable. I'll be right back with refreshments."

Sarah tugged at his sleeve, offering a quiet, "I can help."

He gave a grateful nod, and together they carried biscuits from the kitchen and poured glasses of water and tea. A few polite smiles and pleasantries passed between them, but an undercurrent of tension lingered beneath the surface.

Having taken care of the Bradley House women, Ben excused himself. He approached the front parlor window and lifted the edge of the curtain to check on Rebecca. Nicholas stood close, one hand gently cupping her face as his thumb brushed her cheek. She clasped his hand with both of hers, nodding slowly.

She turned to the house. He dropped the curtain and moved aside, blending into the wall. That was it. Nicholas had finally staked his claim, and she had accepted. A courtship? A proposal? Maybe it was time to take Mrs. Pratt's advice and consider lodging with a church family. He had been foolish to think he belonged at Hogue House. Naive to believe he could be part of Rebecca's life again. Five years had passed, and too much had changed.

He returned to the dining room as Rebecca entered the front door. As she stepped through the door from the parlor, she apologized to the women for the delay. She stood beside Paulette Bradley, rubbing her shoulder before sitting beside Ben.

"While I stepped out, did Ben take care of everyone?" Rebecca rested her hand on his shoulder.

As Ben rose, nods and expressions of gratitude circulated the table. "Would you like some water?"

"Could you bring my tea from the kitchen table?" She scooted her chair so he could pass.

"Of course." He stepped out and returned with both their glasses. He set hers in front of her, then sat on the other side of Sarah. Rebecca shot him a questioning glance but said nothing.

"Okay, there are six of you, Ben, the four Drake boys, and seven of us Hogues until Pa returns from Missouri. Paulette, do you know how long you'll need to stay?"

Paulette tucked her chin. "Indefinitely."

"What happened?" Rebecca's expression tightened as she leaned forward, concern edging her voice.

All the women began explaining at once. Sarah, crying, held onto Paulette's hand tightly. Viv, fiery green eyes flashing, slammed her hand on the table. Bess and Lucy shook their heads in bewilderment while Judy crossed her arms in defiance.

"Ladies, ladies." Rebecca waved her hand. "Let's focus on room assignments. You've had a lot to deal with, whatever it was." She tapped the table in front of Paulette. "We can discuss things privately later."

Paulette's glass was nearly empty, so Ben fetched a pitcher from the kitchen, refilled her water, and placed the pitcher on the table. Despite his efforts, he couldn't see her eyes. The other women had either come without bonnets or removed them upon entering. He suspected Paulette concealed something. Some information? Or perhaps an injury?

"Ben, let's put you, Ollie, and Simon in Pa's room. We can get two cots from the bunkroom. The Drake boys can move to Ollie and Simon's room, where they'll either share beds or make two additional pallets on the floor." She took Paulette's hand. "This arrangement leaves three open rooms at the opposite end where the men typically stay, and no one has to sleep in the lost and found room."

"I don't want to impose on Ollie and Simon. And I'm uneasy about staying in your father's room." Ben stood.

"Nonsense. You're practically family." Rebecca waved him off. "Simon and Ollie won't mind. I sent Nicholas to check on Martie and the girls. They should be back soon, and he can assist with unloading his wagon. Now, let's get you all settled in."

Practically family.

The phrase landed like a weight in Ben's chest. Not long ago, he'd been foolish enough to wonder if a future with Rebecca might be possible. Now that she had accepted Nicholas, her words seemed to redraw the lines. Family. Did she think of him as a brother?

He waited for the women to disperse before gathering the Drake boys' belongings. Soon enough, the upstairs corridor became a flurry of footsteps and voices. Approaching the middle of the hall, he bumped into Rebecca as she ascended the stairs. The sweet scent of honeysuckle momentarily overwhelmed his senses. Her blue eyes met his gaze, lingering longer than he anticipated. Her eyes, even tinged with exhaustion, sent shockwaves through him. The ache in his chest deepened. He muttered a ragged "excuse me" before continuing to the new room, carrying more than the Drake boys' things.

He stepped inside, closed the door, and let the boys' packs fall to the floor. Slumping onto the bed, he paused to gather his thoughts. He couldn't recall Hogue House ever being so full. Had it been this crowded after the gold prospectors arrived in town? Had Rebecca ever been burdened with so many at once?

He returned to his old room, grabbed the pile of clothes Simon had loaned him, and made his way toward Mr. Hogue's room. Before he reached the door, Rebecca stepped into the hall face-to-face with him.

"I was simply—" She gestured toward the room cattycorner from the Drakes' as she sidestepped past him. "That's my room."

"If I remember correctly, your father's room is opposite yours."

She nodded.

"I planned to place the clothes Simon lent me inside before unloading the wagon."

"Oh, great. As Captain Cobb often says, 'All hands on deck make short work.'" Her cheeks rounded.

Ben grunted in agreement, stowed his items in Clayburn Hogue's room, and went to the wagon. Nicholas acknowledged him with a flick of his chin and threw a carpet bag at him, hitting his chest with a thump. Ben set it down, poised to catch another. After collecting three bags, he started for the house when a fourth bag hit him in the back.

He turned to glare at Nicholas. "Is there a problem?"

"Not at all. Catch these next two bags, and I'll join you." Nicholas grunted, tossing two more bags from the wagon. He jumped down to collect his share. "I take it you've seen the paper by now?"

"I have." Ben gathered his three bags.

"What are you going to do about it?"

"What can I do?"

"Move out."

"I'm considering it."

"Do more than think about it."

As they reached the door, both men attempted to push through simultaneously. Neither gave way until Sarah and Judy arrived from the opposite direction, heading out to the wagon. At that point, Ben conceded the right of way to Nicholas. Nicholas carried the bags to the top of the stairs, dropped them off, and then came back down, jostling Ben as he passed.

Ben wandered the hallway with three bags, asking every woman he met if they could help him find the owner and room before placing the bags beside the respective doors. As he headed toward the stairs, he searched for Paulette Bradley but couldn't spot her. Upon reaching the top of the front staircase, he glanced back one last time and collided with Rebecca as she ascended the stairs. He stumbled backward, gripping her forearms, and they tumbled to the floor. Their eyes met, and they remained still. Her warm breath tickled his neck, and he tensed in response.

"It's fortunate we're moving in." Viv's green eyes flashed. "Or folks might start believing today's newspaper article."

Ben scrambled to his feet, apologizing as he extended his hand to Rebecca. "Wagon's nearly empty. If you can spare me, I'll reassemble the spyglass. Then I've got an appointment in town. Possible job opportunity."

Rebecca smoothed her skirt. "Of course. I don't want to hold you up."

"What do you want done with the coded message?" He nodded toward the kitchen, careful not to meet her eyes too long.

"I'll tuck it inside my journal for safekeeping."

Ben returned to the kitchen, swiftly reassembled the spyglass, then made for the stable. Moments later, he emerged with Pickle, guiding the horse wide around the wagon out front. As much as he dreaded speaking to Ambrose Baas, putting a little distance between himself and Rebecca might do him good. Perhaps the ride would help clear his head.

"Cutting out, Doc?" Nicholas dropped a bag on the ground. "How far are you going this time?"

Ben ignored the man's questions as he continued on his way. After a few minutes, he reached the hotel and tied Pickle to a post. He paused, taking in the three-story structure, and his heartbeat quickened.

He spun the ring on his finger. "I'm unsure what you expect from me, Lord. Should I stay in the cave? Truth is, the thought of returning to medicine downright hollows me." The nail bit into his finger as he spun it, a small, necessary pain keeping him anchored. "This Baas fella sets me on edge, so a role elsewhere would be much appreciated."

He stroked Pickle's neck, more for his steadiness than for the horse. "Okay, buddy, wish me luck."

Ben stepped into the opulent lobby, trying to shake the uncertainty in his mind. The recent conversation with Baas had left him more unsettled than he cared to admit. There was something in Baas's charm, his calculated warmth. It didn't sit right with him. Despite the polished exterior, Ben sensed more lurking underneath.

He approached the front desk, where a rigid man greeted him. He led Ben to the third floor and through a narrow hall to an extensive study. The room smelled of fine cigars and polished wood, a space designed to impress with a subtle air of extravagance.

It was decorated in Empire style and divided into two areas by a wide rectangular arch. One side contained a small library with shelves along one wall, featuring two green leather accent chairs and a small table. The other side boasted a large mahogany desk topped with a green leather inset. Canted legs curved gracefully into bronze lion's paw feet. A striking bronze grizzly bear sculpture was positioned in one front corner, while an ebony dip pen rested in a green marble base on the opposite side.

A narrow table next to the window displayed a collection of frames. He approached and examined them. Three contained photographs while two stood empty. One of the photos captured his interest. It featured Baas with Captain Sterling Reed in front of the *Valiant*.

The door opened behind him, and he turned, holding the photograph of Captain Reed. Ambrose Baas entered, one hand tucked in his pocket while the other hung loosely at his side. He crossed the room, selected a figurado cigar from the box at the end of the table, and lit it.

"A recent acquisition." Baas took the photograph from Ben and returned it to the table.

Ben's gaze drifted to the two empty frames. "Planning to add more?"

Baas followed his line of sight. A slight smirk tugged at the corner of his mouth. "Oh, yes. Some things are worth waiting for. Those are reserved for accomplishments of a more ... personal nature."

"I'm glad you came. I thought you might let the opportunity pass you by." He turned back to the cigars. "Cigar?"

"No, thank you." Ben wondered if the recent acquisition referred to the ship or its captain. "As a hotel proprietor, what led you to venture into the steamboat industry?"

"Mr. Ewing, you have it wrong." Baas puffed on his cigar as Ben raised an eyebrow. "Since you appeared unsure about your future in medicine, I thought the more common title was in order."

"I'm still getting used to 'mister.'" Ben sat near the

bookshelves with a view of the clouds, giving temporary relief from the sun. "Please continue."

"I started with steamboats. Lost the financial backer for my first vessel." He took another puff from his cigar. " So, I won my first steamboat in a card game. Now I own an entire fleet of them."

"And the hotel?"

"This isn't my first. I began acquiring hotels some years ago. It complements my steamboat endeavors when passengers disembark and stay at one of my hotels." Baas seated himself behind his desk. "The owner of the first hotel I attempted to buy withdrew last minute. Undeterred, I took a risk and won my first hotel in a horse race."

"Sounds like a haphazard approach to business."

"I expand my business with strategic decisions." Baas's lips curled in an unnatural smile. "However, if traditional methods fall short, I resort to practices that amuse me. If a venture is destined to fail, it should at least be adventurous and entertaining. Regardless, I'm not left empty-handed for long."

"I suppose if life doesn't offer enjoyment, accumulating wealth seems pointless."

Baas's words about steamboats, hotels, and fortune confirmed what Ben already suspected. The man didn't deal in simple business. There was something else beneath the surface. But Ben was more interested in the implications of the offer.

"Now I have a fortune in fine stories. I do love a good tale." Baas snuffed his cigar. "So, Mr. Ewing, I assume there's a story that explains why you want to move away from medicine. Care to share?"

"Not especially." Ben tried to keep his expression neutral, though the weight of Baas's gaze measuring his response set him on edge.

"If you don't share, how can I persuade you to return to it?"

"Why hire a doctor?"

"It's the fashionable thing to do." Baas held his palms up. "Doctors this far west cover a wider region and are often unavailable when needed. By hiring an in-house doctor, I'll ensure my patrons receive timely medical attention."

"Do your patrons often require medical attention?"

"That's the charm of it, *Doctor*." Baas winked at his use of the title. "In this profession, injuries are uncommon. Most issues we deal with are merely indigestion, fainting spells, and mild ailments. You'll rarely require treatment beyond a tonic and spring water."

"Mm." Ben nodded slowly. "It's an interesting proposition."

"Lounge in your first-floor study adjacent to the hotel's health salon. Indulge in the luxuries the hotel provides. Socialize with guests while listening to elegant music in the lobby or enjoy complimentary meals at the hotel café." Baas clapped his hands, folding them together. "Why, just this morning, I engaged a talented pianist."

"Health salon?" Ben tilted his head. "Doesn't the hotel have a proper infirmary?"

"Mr. Ewing, we cannot casually use crass words like 'infirmary' or 'medical office.' Too closely tied to diseases such as cholera, influenza, and scarlet fever. We don't want to drive guests from the hotel. Our health salon is intended for well guests to enhance their health further."

Ben rose, rubbing his hands together. "Could I have time to consider it?"

"Until the end of the week." A smoke ring wafted between them. "After that, I must take care of business out of town. I'll find a doctor elsewhere if I don't hear from you before then. I can't promise your position will be secure when I return."

"Fair enough. I'll let you know my answer soon." Ben grasped the doorknob.

"Are you able to find your way out?" The clouds shifted. The late afternoon sun cast Baas in silhouette. And Ben knew.

That same shape. It was the same boxy, broad-shouldered build he'd seen outside Hogue House the first night he went to Rebecca in the grove.

"I am."

Ben descended the staircase, his mind buzzing with thoughts about the man, his offer, and what he could have been doing at Hogue House. There was daylight enough left, but Ben couldn't shake the unease settling in his stomach. As he approached the front door, he stopped in his tracks.

A familiar voice drew him back. He paused, hearing it again, a voice rich with charm and feigned laughter. He scanned the room until his gaze landed on Cordelia Hogue. She sat at the piano, her fingers ready to play, while a gentleman leaned over and talked to her. She looked … different. The soft silk taffeta dress in fairest pink suited her, but the way she seemed so at home unnerved him.

He shook his head in disbelief. What had she gotten herself into? He crossed the lobby in determined strides. "Excuse me, sir, might I have a word with the lady?"

"Wait your turn, pal."

Ben slid the nail ring back and forth, setting his composure. "Excuse me, I'm the hotel doctor and must speak with the young lady."

Cordelia's cheeks flamed as the young man left. Her expression hardened, and she spoke through gritted teeth. "Ben Ewing, what do you think you are doing?"

"I could pose the same question to you." He waited, knowing the more he pushed, the further she would dig in her heels. But he couldn't leave her at the mercy of whatever game Baas played.

She eyed him with a mixture of amusement and disdain. "I'm here at Baas's invitation. He's been most kind to me. You should be more open-minded, Ben. You know, Rebecca wants us all to find work. I'm doing my part to make sure I'm not burdening anyone."

The sting of her words drove deeper than he cared to admit.

"That's not what this is about. You're playing with fire, Cordelia. You don't know what you're getting into." He took hold of her arm. "Come back to Hogue House with me."

"You are causing a scene. I know exactly what I'm doing." Her voice honeyed. "Ben, darling, keep this between us, and I'll support your attempts to capture Rebecca's heart."

His stomach twisted. Was that what everyone saw? A man chasing after the past, clinging to what he'd lost? "I'm not out to win her affections."

"Aren't you? Isn't she the true reason for your return?" She brushed a tendril of hair behind her ear, her eyes narrowing as she met his gaze. "And wouldn't it benefit your case to have the backing of all the siblings? I could help sway things in your favor."

"I refuse to engage in your games, Cordelia." Ben tapped the piano. "If you won't come with me, at least be honest with Rebecca about what you're doing here."

He stood, composed and motionless, a battle smoldering in his chest. He couldn't save her. Not by force. And certainly not by playing along. The tension between them crackled, but she stood before he could say anything further, smoothing down her dress.

"Well, I think I'll stay a little longer. I'll see you back at Hogue House." She offered him a teasing smile. "And don't worry. I can handle myself with Mr. Baas."

Ben clenched his jaw. Cordelia was naïve, blind to the danger. But it was all too clear to him. It was only a matter of time before it played out, and Cordelia would be in over her head.

Chapter Thirty-One

Ben was relieved to find Nicholas's wagon gone when he returned. After grooming and caring for Pickle, he entered the forge. Oscar noticed him immediately, lifting his head and perking up his ears. Ben knelt next to the dog, giving him a scratch along the neck.

"You're improving."

Oscar wagged his tail in agreement.

The door creaked as the twins stepped inside. They paused at the sight of Ben. "When did you return, Mr. Ewing?"

"Not long ago. What are you boys doing?"

Jesse lifted the bucket he carried. "Miss Rebecca let us keep a bucket of scraps beneath the back stairs. She says it's time to bring it to Oscar."

"She gave us this too." Cason raised a bowl. "Do you think he might be ready to stand and eat?"

"Only one way to find out." Ben patted Oscar's head. "It won't hurt to try."

Cason set the bowl beside Oscar, and Jesse filled it with scraps from the bucket. Oscar tried to stand but wobbled and collapsed back to the ground. On his second attempt, he fared better but remained somewhat unsteady.

"Is it okay if I support him by lifting him?" Cason crouched by the dog and placed his hands underneath.

"As long as he accepts the help. If he growls or becomes agitated, let him be. Tuck your hands inside his front legs so you're not pressing on his stomach while he eats." Ben showed him where to place his hands. "I thought Oscar was Jace's dog. Why isn't he out here?"

Jesse thumped the bucket. "She thought this old bucket might be too heavy for him, so we volunteered to handle it."

"Let's swap." Cason nudged Jesse, and they changed positions. "Oscar is a big dog, and he's getting heavy."

"Is Oscar a big dog?" Jesse spoke in a babying tone. "Hims a good boy. Getting strong, aren't you?"

"Do you boys miss your camp?"

"Nah, we're sleeping better here." Cason scratched the back of his neck. "Jesse and me ain't told nobody, but we think someone's been sneaking around trying to find our camp. So, we've been taking turns staying awake through the night to keep watch over the place. Here, we don't have to worry about protecting our brothers."

Ben crouched next to them, his arms resting on his knees. "What leads you to believe someone is closing in on your camp?"

Jesse scratched his head. "While hightailing it back from town after Mr. Fremont's accident, we spotted something. A shadowy figure in the woods. So we decided to take a different path back to camp."

"Could you describe it? Was the figure tall and slim or short and stout? Can you use descriptions like that?"

"It was a long, skinny shadow." Cason switched spots with Jesse again. "We're real sorry about Mr. Fremont. We rushed because we had seen this shadow before and were trying not to take long in town."

Jesse wrinkled his nose. "That's all true, except the shadow wasn't long and thin. It was short and somewhat square."

"No, it wasn't." Cason shook his head.

"Was so."

"Don't really matter what kind of shadow it was. I reckon we'll know exactly whose shadow it was before long."

"Why's that?" Ben rested his arm across his knee.

"Because we set traps." A broad grin pushed up Jesse's cheeks. "Not gonna matter if we're there or not. Someone gets in one of those, we'll see what shape their shadow is."

Oscar let out a whimper as Cason's hand narrowly avoided the snake bite. After Cason released Oscar, the dog limped back to its bed. The boys gently stroked Oscar's head, and the dog fell asleep within moments.

"Okay, boys. It's time to go back inside the house. Do you know where Miss Rebecca is?"

"She told us to leave the bucket here and return through the front door." Cason toed the dirt floor.

"I think she's got one of them new women in the kitchen doing woman things." Jesse's eyes grew wide.

"What do you mean by 'woman things'?" Cason hit him on the arm.

"Cut it out." Jesse rubbed his arm. "I'm not sure. Things boys shouldn't get involved in."

"Could be we're too loud." Cason pursed his lips.

"We're too loud?" Jesse slowly shook his head. "I ain't heard loud until we returned to a house full of women. Mr. Ewing, ask me tomorrow about missing camp. I might give you a different answer."

Ben chuckled. "All right, why don't you boys go to bed? Use the front door as Miss Rebecca instructed."

Once the forge was quiet again, his thoughts turned to what the boys had said. He had anticipated their stories would match the shadowy figure he had seen behind the Hogue property. The short, boxy shadow he now knew to be Baas. He never expected them to have differing descriptions. Scratching his head, he started to believe Rebecca's intuition was accurate. Something unusual was undoubtedly going on. Yet he struggled to determine whether it connected to Ambrose Baas. With news of the Cutter-Doyle gang in the area, it was better to cast the net wide for now.

He petted Oscar one last time before exiting the forge and heading to the back of the boardinghouse. Mindful of what the boys had told him, he paused to listen at the door. He could hear two muffled female voices, which sounded calm enough, prompting him to knock. The voices ceased. Moments later, Rebecca opened the door.

"Ben, why are you knocking at the back door?"

"I didn't want to disturb you. I was in the forge with the twins. Did you ask them to come in through the front door?" He moved aside to maintain the occupant's privacy.

"Yes, I did."

"I was going to enter through the front, but I wanted to check if you needed anything first." Ben shuffled the dirt with his shoe. "If all is well, I'll go to the other door."

"Hold on a second. Please don't go." She stepped inside, leaving the door slightly ajar. Whispers were exchanged. After a brief discussion, she came back out.

"Please come in. I'd like to hear your thoughts on an injury if you don't mind."

Ben stuffed his hands into his pockets with a quick scan of the weathered oak where he had seen Baas before. Nothing appeared out of sorts. He then nodded and followed Rebecca into the kitchen. Inside, Paulette Bradley sat at the table, her chair angled sideways, the drawn curtains behind her shielding her from the outside world. Ben stayed by Rebecca's side.

Rebecca lifted a lamp from the table. "Paulette, close your eyes." She brought the light closer. "What do you think?"

These examinations always left Ben's insides quivery. Rebecca's presence eased some of the discomfort. Having another woman with medical training present was a great benefit when assessing female patients. He paused to consider the sensitivity of his words.

"Mrs. Bradley, I apologize for the questions I must ask." He paused, and she gave a brief nod. "Did someone hit you? A man?" His brow furrowed in response to her nod. "When did this happen?"

"Two days ago." Her words were barely audible.

"Would you like to hold the lamp, Ben?" Rebecca extended it toward him.

His hands were steady, but acted as if they might start shaking at any moment. "It would be easier if you held it." He turned back to the patient. "Mrs. Bradley, I will ask you to open your eyes shortly. But first, have you experienced any blurred vision?"

She shook her head.

"Slowly open your eyes. Take your time." As she did, Ben examined them closely and caught a grimace on her face. "Is the light painful for you?"

"Not any more than normal."

Ben pulled at Rebecca's arm while gesturing toward the back door.

"Paulette, we need to step outside for a moment." Rebecca accompanied Ben out the door.

"The swelling and bruising are consistent with her injury. I was reluctant to touch her face. I assume you did. What was your impression?"

"It didn't feel as though anything was broken. It appears the injury is confined to the swelling and bruising we observed." Rebecca brushed her cheek close to her eye. "However, I am worried about the possibility of a concussion."

"I agree. It's difficult to be certain about it."

"Rest?"

"And observation." Ben nodded. "Steer clear of further injuries."

Ben re-entered the house behind Rebecca. She knelt by Paulette's side. "It's as you and I discussed. It's good you're staying here. We can keep a close eye on you." She took Paulette's hand. "You mentioned this man showed up with a signed deed from your husband and expelled everyone from your boardinghouse. Can you tell us his name?"

"Caine. Isom Caine."

"Mrs. Bradley, can you describe him?" Ben sat across from her.

"He was tall and thin, with unkempt, coal-black hair hanging across his forehead in an unflattering way." Paulette sucked in a breath. "His breath reeked of whiskey."

"He showed up out of nowhere to evict you?" Rebecca returned to the kitchen counter, resting her palms on the wooden top.

"I don't know how, but he located my husband." Paulette turned to Ben. "It's been over two years since I've seen or heard from him. Almost ten years since he ran off, but he reappears time and again, seeking money for his next scheme. No idea what Caine offered, but he sold me out."

"Mrs. Bradley, did Caine act alone? Was anyone accompanying him?" Ben's gut tightened.

"To my knowledge, he was alone. Didn't have anyone with him when he came in and showed the deed." She rested her fingers on her cheek. "When we balked at leaving, he brandished a revolver. Struck me with the handle. Said I needed to get my girls in line."

Rebecca returned to Paulette's side and helped her from her chair. "You must be tired. Why not turn in for the night?"

Paulette vanished up the staircase near the pantry. Rebecca faced Ben, massaging her forehead. Watching her, he remembered. It wasn't her strength that first drew him. It was her mercy.

"My heart goes out to her. How could someone swoop in and take her home so unexpectedly?"

"There is a particular breed of men who take advantage of widows and women with absent husbands. It happens more often than we're aware." Ben drummed his fingers on the table. "Your intuition seems correct, even if you haven't put it all together yet. I talked to the twins in the forge. They mentioned rushing back to their camp on Friday because they feared someone might uncover its location."

"Who?"

"They didn't know. They only saw a shadowy figure, yet it occurred twice."

"Did they provide any additional details?" Rebecca tucked loose strands of hair behind both ears.

"Cason characterized the figure as tall and thin, whereas Jesse described it as short and stocky. Their descriptions starkly contrasted with each other. And each young man was adamant about what he saw."

"Do you believe they possibly saw two individuals? And one of them might be Caine?"

"Honestly, I'm not sure what to think, but it seems reasonable." Ben ran his hand across his chin. "Rebecca, there's something I haven't shared with you."

"What is it?"

"A few nights ago, I believed I saw a figure hiding in the shadows near Hogue House." Even now, he thought he heard a branch creak outside, though no wind stirred. "That's why I went looking for you in the oak grove that first night."

"Why didn't you tell me?"

"In California … well, I'm constantly reliving past events. I questioned whether I saw someone or if it was merely a figment of my imagination, a scene from the past." He traced the wood grain on the table. "When I asked the boys to describe what they'd experienced, I hoped their insights would either validate or disprove what I saw."

"How would you describe what you saw?"

"The figure was boxy. Or at least I think it was." Ben tapped his forehead, hesitating. "But it was such a momentary glance."

It could only have been Baas. Same build, same broad-shouldered silhouette had stood in front of the window in Baas's office. But saying so would open a door he wasn't ready to walk through—not without betraying Cordelia. He wanted to give her the chance to be honest with Rebecca. And he wasn't sure what Baas was after. Not yet.

"At this stage, all we can do is remain vigilant and keep our eyes trained on the shadows." Rebecca leaned back in her chair.

"I left California to escape the shadows." Doubt gnawed at Ben's heart. "Yet it appears they always find me." He placed his palm on his forehead and sighed. "And often, the shadows seem tied to change and money."

"In what way?" Rebecca leaned forward, resting her chin on her hand.

"The Gold Rush exposed an unprecedented level of greed. I witnessed depravity and violence like never before. The railroad attracts the same caliber of individuals. Economic progress and the pursuit of wealth will threaten the value of human life."

"That's a very bleak view of things."

"Hope was scarce in California." Ben folded his hand on the table.

They remained quiet. The oil lamp flickered, glowing onto

the metal reflector behind it. Rebecca's hand brushed his, her touch light but lingering.

"This isn't California. There will be light again."

He stared at their hands, a warmth stirring in his chest despite the ache. She believed there would be light. And maybe, just maybe, he wanted to believe with her.

Chapter Thirty-Two

"Ivajohn!" Rebecca's hand flew to her chest. "Ben, I'm so sorry. With everything going on, I forgot she was waiting in the study. I wouldn't blame her if she decided to sneak out and head back to the parsonage."

She hurried to the study, pausing to gather her thoughts before entering. As she stepped inside, she saw Ivajohn asleep on the divan. She repositioned a chair closer and nudged her sister's shoulder.

Ivajohn moaned, partially opening her eyes. She peered around the room through narrowed slits. "Ugh. So, it wasn't a dream. I'm still here."

"I apologize, Ivajohn. I didn't anticipate being inundated with boarders all at once." Rebecca lifted her hands in mock surrender. "However, this does nicely solve the issues caused by the newspaper article, doesn't it?"

"Except there hasn't been any retraction issued, and even if one is published, the ideas about you and Ben are already circulating." Ivajohn placed her arm on her forehead. "What should I do? Mrs. Turner will prevent the wedding from happening."

"Don't fret, dear sister. Everything will turn out fine."

"It doesn't matter anyway." Ivajohn sat up. "I don't believe I'm suited to be a pastor's wife."

"What are you talking about?" Rebecca sat on the divan next to her, rubbing her back. "Why would you say such a thing? You and Emil are so well-suited."

"Being a pastor's wife involves more than complementing your husband." Ivajohn's brows knit together. "You need to manage the household and minister alongside him. Emil relates effortlessly to everyone. I struggle to bridge those divides. I value people as much as he does, but I'm awkward and out of place."

"I sense there's more to this than the newspaper article."

"Mrs. Turner called me a wallflower. She believes I am timid and weak. She has been overly critical ever since she arrived." Ivajohn buried her face in her hands. "I'm at a loss. I can't seem to make her happy."

"How long will she be here?"

"After the ceremony, she intends to visit Emil's brother in Shiloh."

"You mentioned you're unable to please her. Tell me, who is it that you should be pleasing?"

"Emil?"

Rebecca clasped Ivajohn's hands gently. "Could I tell you a story Emil shared with me?"

Ivajohn nodded.

"He recounted a missionary expedition involving a young girl who strayed from her tribe, and you came across her. The girl hesitated to return to her people, as some had adopted the faith, but she had questions she was afraid to ask." Rebecca rubbed Ivajohn's hands. "You willingly heard her inquiries, showing quiet compassion. Some from her tribe told her that embracing the faith meant abandoning her native language, a prospect she dreaded. You reassured her God understands every language and would not ask her to forsake the tongue of her heritage. Moreover, you assured her He speaks the language of her heart, a language that transcends words.

"Other missionaries might have demanded she reject every part of her people's heritage and culture." Rebecca squeezed Ivajohn's shoulders. "I'll ask again, who is it that you're meant to please?"

"The Lord." Ivajohn's expression brightened.

"During our childhood, I noticed instances where you displayed subtle defiance, especially with Justin and me. You firmly set boundaries, making sure we recognized the limits. Firm, yet never unkind." Rebecca rested her fist in her palm. "You might have to stand your ground with Mrs. Turner in a similar manner."

"Oh, I don't know if I can."

"You are one of the most capable women I know." Rebecca squeezed her knee for emphasis. "If you'd prefer to stay here tonight, your old bed is ready in our room. However, if you want to return to the parsonage, I'm sure Simon can take you home."

"Thank you, Rebecca." Ivajohn embraced her. "I'm sorry about the newspaper. I can't comprehend why Mr. Clarke would permit such untruths to be published about you."

"It would not shock me if he was unaware until the paper was published this morning."

"How could he not know? If he didn't approve it, how was it printed?"

"I'm uncertain, yet I have an idea. Some men will chase progress relentlessly, disregarding even a woman's good name." Rebecca moved toward their father's globe and slowly rotated it. "There's a connection to the railroad, I'm sure."

"What will you do? So many have seen it." Ivajohn folded her hands in her lap.

"First, I'm going to take stock of my friends." Rebecca tapped her lips. "Mr. Mooney didn't sell any papers today. He returned them to the newspaper office. And Mrs. Gray collected the papers that came through her door." She let her hand fall to her chest. "Then perhaps I'll take a lesson from Levi by way of Ben. I may sit with the Lord in this before I try to pray it away. But after that, I'll speak with Dawn since she works for the newspaper."

"I think I'll do the same. If it's all right with you, I'd like to pray more in the study before I ask Simon to take me home."

"Take your time." Rebecca spun the globe, exited the room, and shut the door behind her, leaning her head against it. Just like Mama. She used to press her forehead to the pantry door and pray until the tears came. After silently praying for her sister, she headed upstairs.

A sister with wedding blues, six new female boarders instead of men, four unruly but big-hearted boys, and a doctor in distress. Rebecca shook her head. How did Mama manage such a large family, especially with the boardinghouse bustling? She longed to discover her mother's secret for holding everything together. At the top of the stairs, she caught sight of the lost and found door.

She would have to overcome her disdain for the cave of lost legacy and heritage and find Mama's journal. She pressed her hand to her chest, urging the ache within to subside. The room was fuller than ever, crowded with forgotten things, stories no one remembered, and pieces of the past shoved aside. Once a small collection above the bunkroom, the lost and found had taken over an entire room inside Hogue House. If it kept growing, where would it stop? It swallowed space meant for the living. For legacy.

In that way, it was no different than Baas's proposal.

He wasn't after land alone. He was after history. Home. Her home. Mama's legacy. Mama's memory. And if Rebecca wasn't careful, everything that mattered might be buried beneath his ambitions—just as Mama's journal was buried somewhere inside this room. If she didn't fight for it, it could all be lost forever.

She would like to believe the arrival of the Bradley House women was a light in the darkness. But something told her Baas would not give up until he got what he wanted.

She turned away from the lost and found. Finding Mama's journal would be better left to the light of day. Better to meet shadows with sunlight and Jesus at her side.

Chapter Thirty-Three

Rebecca balanced a laundry basket on her hip as she walked down the hallway toward the back stairs. She stopped a few steps away from the lost and found. While she dreaded the task of sifting through the items inside, another part of her was excited about the possibility of finding Mama's journal.

"Oh, is there laundry?" Judy greeted her at the top of the stairs. "I'll handle it."

"That's not necessary."

"It is necessary. This is why room and board are cheaper at Mrs. Paulette's." Judy took the basket from her. "We all contribute to the chores. It lightens the load for everyone, both financially and otherwise. Martie mentioned you enjoy writing, yet you've found it challenging to carve out time lately. We'll help you make time for it. Focus on what you must do, and don't stress about the laundry."

"Thank you, Judy."

Judy disappeared down the stairs, balancing the basket on her hip.

Rebecca had been surprised to find the women of Bradley House bustling in the kitchen long before the rest of the household had risen. Having woken up earlier than usual, she had hoped to enjoy some quiet time journaling in the kitchen. Instead, she found a whirlwind of activity as the women prepared breakfast, set the table, and cleaned the kitchen in anticipation of the others waking. Viv and Martie took the younger Hogues to school before heading to work.

Since the dining room was crowded, Rebecca and Paulette had breakfast in the kitchen while discussing lodging arrangements for the women of Bradley House. Paulette proposed a plan similar to the one she offered the Bradley House women. In exchange for taking on extra chores, the women at Hogue House would pay fifty cents less than their male counterparts. While Hogue House would incur a minor financial loss from the rent, Rebecca's chores would significantly decrease.

With Judy tending to the laundry, Rebecca stood alone in the quiet corridor, heart already turning toward the room she'd been avoiding. Her feet heavy, she shuffled to the lost and found. She reached for the doorknob, then hesitated, pulling her hand back. Adjusting her skirt, she glanced both ways down the hall. She turned the knob, stepped into the room, and leaned against the closed door.

Trunks, furniture, and countless forgotten items cluttered the space. A weightiness filled her heart. She could never grasp how Eliza Dawn regarded this room as a treasure trove. It was a graveyard, full of old relics laid to rest. She traced her finger along a trunk and picked up a silver hairbrush resting on top. Was it passed down from mother to daughter, or maybe a gift from a groom to his new bride? With care, she placed it back in its spot. Nearby, a christening gown lay folded in a crate. Had a baby ever worn it, or was the child lost too soon? Her fingers brushed over the gown.

With her eyes shut, she envisioned her mother's journal in a wooden box adorned with carved flowers. It rested on the highboy dresser in her father's room not long ago. Now, it lay forgotten somewhere in this room. Locating it would be like having one more conversation with her mother.

Rebecca opened her eyes and shifted items from pile to pile with quiet determination. The edge of a wooden box carved with delicate floral designs peeked through the top of a faded carpet bag. She lifted the box and hugged it to her chest, heart fluttering. With trembling fingers, she lifted the lid to check for the treasure she sought. Nestled inside was a leather journal worn soft by time and memory. A piece of her mother's faith, preserved and waiting. It resembled her own journal. Cradling the box close, she carried it down the hall and tucked it securely under her bed for safekeeping.

She hurried downstairs to the kitchen, where Paulette and Judy prepared to do the laundry. "Paulette, do you need my help with the wash? Did you find everything you needed?"

"Everything is ready outside." Paulette lifted a large basket. "We're gathering the baskets, one for Hogue House and another for Bradley House. Judy and I will make quick work of this. When they return home, the other girls will take the laundry from the lines."

"You're a blessing, all of you." Rebecca wrapped her arm around Paulette's shoulders. "I'm off to town now."

In the stable, Rebecca saddled Truly and noticed Pickle's stall was vacant. Ben had once again left the boardinghouse early, likely to visit Captain Cobb in search of additional work. The possibility Ben might pursue a position with a railroad survey team lingered in her mind. She couldn't shake the feeling he might be tempted to venture west again. Perhaps not so far as California, but well beyond the territories. She hoped Mr. Mooney was wrong about this intuition thing, which he claimed her mother gifted her. She wanted to be wrong. Just this once.

As she stopped in front of the newspaper office to tie Truly to the hitching post, movement across the street caught her eye. Ben stood in front of the hotel, speaking with a dark-haired woman. She clung to his elbow as he escorted her to the entrance. When he opened the door, she lifted her face to say something to him. She was unmistakable. Cordelia. She laughed and placed her hand on Ben's chest before entering the hotel.

The blow of it landed first before anger rose, fierce and heated, to shield the rawness beneath.

"Good morning." Eliza Dawn joined her at the hitching post, wearing a notepad on a string slung from shoulder to hip.

"Is it?" Rebecca pointed toward the hotel. "Did you see them?"

"Ben and Cordelia?"

"So you did notice them entering the hotel together?" Rebecca crossed her arms.

Eliza Dawn glanced beyond her. "I'm sure it's not what you think."

"What do I think?" Rebecca clasped her hands together tightly. "Please, tell me, because I don't know *what* to think anymore. My name is smeared across the newspaper's front page while Cordelia strolls into the hotel at his side in broad daylight." She pumped her squared fist. "What am I supposed to think?"

"Well, I'm not sure." Eliza Dawn took her by the elbow, leading her toward the boardwalk. "I can guess why you're here today, though. Mr. Clarke?"

"You better believe I am."

"He's waiting for you." Eliza Dawn pushed open the door to the newspaper office. "Don't pay them any mind. Let's take care of business."

Eliza Dawn led her to Mr. Clarke's office. "Mr. Clarke, I trust you are acquainted with Miss Rebecca Hogue."

"Miss Hogue." He offered his hand.

She set her chin and clasped her hands in front of her. "Mr. Clarke."

He cleared his throat. "I sincerely apologize for the article published yesterday regarding Hogue House."

"Let's be clear, Mr. Clarke. The article was specifically about me, not Hogue House." Rebecca moistened her lips. "It resulted in an extremely uncomfortable and disconcerting day, to put it mildly. Furthermore, it remains to be seen how this article will affect my reputation, family, and business in the future. Therefore, along with a retraction, I deserve an explanation for how this happened."

"Miss Hogue, I guarantee a retraction will be issued immediately, and the matter thoroughly investigated."

"When you say a retraction will be issued immediately, do you mean it is in this morning's edition?"

"No, it will be published in tomorrow's paper."

"Unacceptable. It allows the whole town forty-eight hours to run my reputation into the ground." Rebecca advanced, invading his personal space. "Publish the retraction in a special edition this afternoon."

"We print daily. Unfortunately, it's the best I can do."

"Mr. Clarke, your reputation as a sincere and warm-hearted man assures me that you mean no harm. This separates you from your brother and his rival, who have historically used their newspapers to exchange insults. That's not the sort of publication you're associated with." She rested her hand on his arm. "Surely, you recognize the benefits to both our reputations in publishing a special edition."

"Mr. Clarke, won't you consider this? I'm happy to volunteer for the typesetting to offset the expense," Eliza Dawn pleaded with uplifted palms.

"If I make a concession this time, I will have to produce

special editions for everyone who objects to any little thing printed about them." Mr. Clarke crossed his arms, resting his chin between his thumb and forefinger. "While I am sympathetic to your plight, it's not sound business practice."

"Good day, Mr. Clarke." Rebecca halted at his door. "I will inform Sam Mooney his boycott of your paper will need to continue for at least a month. Then we'll see how sound your business practice is."

"Miss Hogue, please hold on." Mr. Clarke stepped closer and rested against the door. "I can't guarantee anything. We'd need sufficient articles and ads to fill the pages, but I will do my best to print an afternoon edition."

"In turn, I will request Sam Mooney do everything possible to end his boycott once the retraction is published. Thank you for being open to reason."

"I'll see you out." Eliza Dawn moved past Mr. Clarke to accompany Rebecca. "Shall we take a stroll?"

"All right." Rebecca crossed her arms. "I don't understand why he was so obstinate. My reputation could be permanently damaged by this."

"Mr. Clarke intended to release a special edition before your request." Eliza Dawn rubbed Rebecca's shoulder as they walked. "I hoped to prevent any doubts regarding what you've heard about his character. He was heartbroken that such an incident occurred at his newspaper."

Rebecca stopped. "What? What was that all about?"

"With this being Mr. Anslem Clarke's first year at the paper, he cannot let his staff view him as someone who wavers. However, it was skillfully handled, suggesting a mercantile boycott of the paper. Sam commands great respect, and other businesses might join in, withdrawing their support and advertisements."

"You were part of this?"

"Yes, we created a plan yesterday. While we need to finish writing the articles, Mr. Clarke and I will manage the typesetting ourselves. He's not willing to risk the retraction being mishandled." Eliza Dawn sidestepped a young boy running down the boardwalk. "His investigation of how this happened is ongoing. He knows the typesetter is at fault, but the motivation behind his actions remains unclear."

"I know who is responsible, and I think you'll find the typesetter's motivation is financial gain."

"You know who is responsible?"

"Ambrose Baas. I'm sure he bribed the typesetter to alter the front-page article."

"The new hotel owner? But why?"

"He wants Hogue House."

"What's his interest in Hogue House if he already owns the hotel?"

"I'm uncertain. I believe it could be connected to the railroad in some way." Rebecca hugged her upper arms. Mr. Mooney had encouraged her to trust her instincts, even when the full picture hadn't yet come into focus. A few more pieces, and it would all add up. Hopefully. "Several small mysteries have surfaced recently. There are those shady individuals you mentioned lurking around various properties. Annetta Gray gave me a cryptic warning regarding Baas. Paulette Bradley has been removed from Bradley House by a man named Caine. Moreover, it appears that the father of the Drake boys may be missing." Rebecca lowered her voice. "Also, we discovered a coded message hidden within the spyglass."

Eliza Dawn retrieved a pencil from her skirt pocket and hurriedly wrote on her notepad. A steamboat's whistle echoed a tune in vibrant, resonant tones. One long, two short, one long. Another whistle sounded, producing a deep, haunting, almost spectral timbre.

"Sounds like Captain Reed will be landing the *Valiant* shortly." Eliza Dawn's ears perked with interest. "I'm curious which ship sounded the second whistle." Then she slowed, pressing a hand lightly to her stomach. "Between you and me, my stomach hasn't agreed with anything this morning. Maybe it's all the excitement." She offered a faint laugh, though a telltale glow warmed her cheeks.

"You're not keeping your notepad around your neck anymore. What prompted the change?"

"I followed Simon into the saloon to get the story about a brawl when an uncouth oaf grabbed the string around my neck." Eliza Dawn slipped the pencil into her pocket and rubbed the area beneath her chin. "Needless to say, it was quite a precarious situation. I figured wearing it this way would be safer."

"It would be safer to avoid those stories." Rebecca stopped to face her sister-in-law. "Honestly, Dawn, I don't understand why you and Simon are so attracted to trouble."

"I understand your concerns about Simon." Eliza Dawn grasped her shoulder and met her eyes. "He has a unique ability to calm people. His involvement in such matters benefits the town. I've never encountered a man better suited to be a lawman than your brother. He is fair and compassionate, yet steadfast and just. It seems like he might've found his calling."

"I'm unsure whether my family can embrace the life of a lawman for him. I don't know if I can accept it."

"Rebecca, you hold the key. If you embrace it, your family will follow suit." Eliza Dawn leveled her gaze, voice steady with conviction. "He won't find happiness until he chases his passion. It's how he wants to contribute to the town."

"I'll give it some thought." Rebecca's heart pinched. "My family has given up so much already."

"I know they have." Eliza Dawn squeezed her hand. "All I'm asking is you give it some thought. For Simon's sake."

"I promise I will." Rebecca strolled along the boardwalk. "For now, I'm going to check with Mr. Mooney about some items I crafted for the mercantile."

"Do you have items for sale at Sam's store?"

"Yes, some potholders, tea towels, aprons, and candles." A subtle prickling sensation raised the hairs on her neck as if someone watched her. A quick scan revealed nothing out of the ordinary. She rubbed the back of her neck, dismissing the feeling. "Mr. Mooney offered to stock them on our behalf while the boardinghouse is struggling. Though I've agreed to lodge the Bradley House women, Martie and I decided to continue our original plan since we're unsure how long the women will be with us. So she is working at Gray's Café, and I am creating items to sell at the mercantile."

"Are your candles the new carved pillars Caroline has showcased in the tailor shop window beside her hats?"

"She bought two the day I delivered them to Mr. Mooney."

"They are beautiful." Eliza Dawn clasped her wrist. "I had no idea you made decorative candles."

"How is Cordelia managing with her?" Rebecca laid her hand atop Eliza Dawn's. "Is she getting along or acting peevishly?"

"I didn't see Cordelia during my visit."

Rebecca halted. "She wasn't there?"

"Perhaps she was in the back. I'm not sure."

"That's odd." Rebecca's gaze wandered up the street toward the hotel. "Considering we saw her and Ben together at the hotel earlier." She paused, recalling another moment. "And now I think of it, they were both missing from the picnic at the same time. Their whereabouts have been unaccounted for more than once of late. Maybe something is going on between the two of them."

"Oh, come on. You know better." Eliza Dawn gave her a reassuring pat on the shoulder. "Cordelia had eyes for Ben for about half a minute when he lived here before. Her interest faded once she learned he was compensated with chickens and goats. He's in an even worse position now. Not her type at all."

"It doesn't make sense, does it?"

Eliza Dawn coiled her arms around Rebecca's arm, leaning against her shoulder. "Now, I'm eager to learn more about this coded message."

Chapter Thirty-Four

Ben guided Cordelia through the hotel lobby to her designated dressing room. She opened the door and urged him to come in, but he politely declined, choosing instead to stay at the threshold while she provided a brief tour. A stunning pink silk taffeta gown hung gracefully in one corner from a custom-made valet stand designed for formal attire. Opposite it stood an ornate dressing table topped with a large mirror. Cordelia squealed with delight, snatching an item from the table and hurriedly presenting it to him.

"Oh, Ben. Isn't it exquisite?" She showcased a tortoiseshell hair comb embellished with seven graduated carved coral cameos set in gold. "What a truly enchanting gift. It matches the gown perfectly. Baz is such a charming and generous man."

"Mr. Baas—pronounced Boss, not Baz—is not what you think, Cordelia."

"Baz is a nickname for his middle name, Sebastian." Cordelia enclosed the comb in her hand. "It's how his closest friends address him."

"I wish you would reconsider your employment with him.

You'd be safer to forego any dealings with the man." Ben crossed his arms. "I wouldn't even be here if not for you."

"I could say the same. Had you been covering your room costs from the beginning, Rebecca might not have urged me to find a job."

"I'm sure it's unnecessary now that Rebecca and the Bradley House women have reached an agreement."

"I love playing the piano at the hotel." Cordelia's expression grew radiant. "Moreover, this goes beyond a professional relationship. Baz spoils me. And I enjoy it."

Ben leaned against the door frame. "Will you not reconsider?"

"If you want to play the role of a mother hen, why not wait in the lobby?" She nudged him through the door and slowly closed it, flashing a coy smile.

Ben leaned against the door, twisting the nail around his finger. "Lord, I may have to accept this medical position to keep an eye on her. I hope You'll stay close to me, okay?"

Ben arrived at the front desk and patiently waited while the clerk handed keys to two men ahead of him.

"We hope you enjoy your stay, gentlemen. Miss Cordelia Hart will perform in the lobby shortly, and the hotel café features excellent dining options."

"Cordelia Hart?" Ben approached the counter. "Why the name change?"

"Tugs at the hearts of the gentlemen. While in the lobby, captivated by Miss Cordelia's skills, they will certainly catch the aroma from the café and be inclined to spend more money with us."

"Ah. I see."

"How may I assist you, Dr. Ewing?"

"You may dispense with the title for the time being. I'm unsure about the position." Ben flattened his palm on the counter. "Might I visit the infirmary?"

The gentleman's eyes grew darker.

"Pardon. I meant health salon." Ben tapped the counter. "Could I view the health salon and the connected office?"

The man handed Ben a key and pointed toward the corridor near the front desk. Ben proceeded and unlocked the door. The room was spacious, including a sitting area, storage space, and limited exercise equipment. The sitting area featured a slender bookcase and two Rococo Revival chairs matching the lobby's decor. Against another wall, two jump ropes dangled from hooks above a dumbbell rack and weighted ball. A counter spanned the length of the third wall with shelves displaying bottles labeled "imported spring water." A glance into the office revealed a large carved desk, a slender table by the window, and a globe. There appeared to be little medical equipment in either space. If this represented all Baas intended to offer, it suggested medical care wasn't the primary goal. What was his angle? How could a health salon, as he referred to it, generate additional revenue for the hotel?

After leaving the salon, Ben returned the key to the front desk. "Thank you. I'll relax in the lobby while contemplating Mr. Baas's proposal."

"Please take advantage of the complimentary meals at the café. Enjoy a bite while you're here."

"Thank you for the offer, but I prefer not to take advantage of Mr. Baas's generosity until I've decided about the position."

"Suit yourself."

Ben lounged on a settee by the window facing the piano. Cordelia appeared from the dressing room, prompting the men to rise as she glided through the sitting area. Her gown danced gracefully as she moved through the space, showcasing her elegance. The coral comb in her hair contrasted beautifully with her dark tresses. A young man accompanied her to the piano, leaning close to whisper, to which she responded with a shy giggle.

Ben shook his head and turned to view the street, tucking his hand into his pocket. His fingers brushed the spyglass. He had grown so accustomed to carrying it, he had forgotten it was there. He should have left it at the boardinghouse. There wasn't much point in carrying it with Dr. Dibrell and the sheriff out of town. Unless they happened upon the captains' passengers, there was no one to ask about it. No more leads unless they could decipher the coded message Rebecca had discovered. Though codes weren't his strong suit, perhaps he could make sense of the communication given enough time.

Nicholas Franks appeared on the other side of the boardwalk. Ben scanned the street for Rebecca. The door to the mercantile opened, and she came out, smiling and waving. Nicholas took a package from her while pausing to chat.

Ben turned away, his eyes falling slowly shut. His fingers brushed the spyglass just as Rebecca's had brushed his hand the night before, light but lingering. She hadn't offered answers then, only a sliver of hope amid shadows. And for a breath or two, if felt like something shared between them. But across the street, she smiled at Nicholas like hope had already found a new home.

The mellow piano music eased his spirit. Cordelia Hogue, despite her flaws, was undeniably talented. A young man lingered by the instrument, watching her intently. Ben joined her on the piano bench. She shot him an unspoken warning, which he met with an easy smile. He locked eyes with her admirer and nodded, prompting the young man to retreat.

Cordelia spoke through clenched teeth. "What do you think you're doing, Ben Ewing?"

"I'm keeping an eye on you, like Justin or Simon would if they were present."

"I don't require an additional brother."

"On the contrary, you don't seem to have enough brothers." Ben leaned in, their shoulders touching.

A young man burst into the hotel, shouting, "Dr. Ben Ewing! Is Dr. Ben Ewing here?"

"There's your cue, Doctor." Cordelia grinned slyly.

Ben stood and approached the boy. "I'm Ben Ewing."

"Doc, you need to hurry. Mr. Baas is at the wharf. There's been an accident."

"I—" Ben's heart catapulted into his throat.

"Hurry up, Doc." The boy waved toward the door. "No time to waste."

Ben's feet trudged heavily, like wading through mud. He followed the boy with Cordelia close on his heels. On the street, most people carried on as usual, though a few noticed the commotion. From across the street, Rebecca cast a casual glance his way. In the distance, five sharp whistle blasts pierced the air. The warning signal for danger.

Ben halted. "Wait. I don't have a medical bag."

"What's happening?" Rebecca hurried over with Nicholas beside her.

"A duel took place at the wharf." The boy shoved Ben forward. "Doc doesn't have a medical bag."

"I'll fetch my horse. I have supplies packed in my saddlebags." Rebecca dashed off in the opposite direction.

The image of Sean twisting and collapsing resurfaced in Ben's thoughts. A duel. His hands trembled. His feet remained frozen in place.

"Ben, quit dawdling." Cordelia raised the taffeta layers. "Baz is injured. He could be bleeding to death."

"Come on, Doc." Nicholas took him by the arm. "Rebecca will catch up."

Simon met them at the dock. "Ben, a steamboat duel injured several passengers. I've sent someone to fetch Dr. Pernot and Levi. We'll need all the help we can muster."

"Steamboat duel?" Ben croaked. "I don't understand."

"It's a steamboat race," Simon clarified as they navigated the dock in a tight cluster.

"How could a race lead to an injury? Did the boiler explode?"

"No, Ben. A steamboat duel is a competition where captains wield their steamboats like weapons to push each other off course as they vie for first landing." Simon shouted over the din. "They rammed each other."

"How could anyone be so reckless with passengers on board?"

People rushed scattershot down the boardwalk, crowding from every direction. The noise and turmoil reigned. A burly dockworker shoved past, almost sending Cordelia into the water. Ben steadied her, pulling her close.

"We should fall back. There's no way through." Ben attempted to turn back, but the path had disappeared. "Cordelia, you shouldn't have come."

"I need to check on Baz. I've got to see he's all right."

"Simon, what's the plan?" Ben drew Cordelia closer. Protecting her came too easily, even when she made it difficult to want to. But he had to do it. For Rebecca. "We need to get her out of here. Rebecca will also be at risk. She'll never reach us."

"I'm going for Rebecca." Nicholas turned back.

"Take Cordelia with you." Ben seized his arm. "Get her to safety."

"No, sir." Nicholas removed Ben's hand from his arm. "What I'm about to do requires raw force. I can't assure my safety, let alone hers."

Nicholas grunted as he turned, crouched low, and plunged into the crowd. He quickly vanished among the mass of people, yet a ripple of motion along the wharf signaled his progress. In contrast, Ben, Simon, and Cordelia found themselves trapped in a deadlock, unable to advance or retreat. Ben's throat tightened.

A clanging bell echoed near Water Street, drawing closer. The ripple effect initiated by Nicholas reversed, traveling down the boardwalk toward Ben, Simon, and Cordelia as people halted in reaction to the bell. Levi's commanding voice resonated through the area. Though Ben couldn't make out his words, individuals began to form a path from the riverbank toward them. Levi, Rebecca, and Nicholas became visible as a route emerged down the wharf's center. Levi handed the bell to Nicholas, who continued toward the end of the dock, clanging as he went. Simon followed Nicholas while Levi barked orders to the wharfmen. Though the tension in Ben's chest lessened, his hands shook.

"I heard there was an accident." Dr. Pernot hurried toward them, carrying a medical bag.

Levi directed Ben and Rebecca toward town. "You two set up a medical tent by Water Street. Dr. Pernot, accompany me. Nicholas and Simon are clearing the path ahead."

Ben let Cordelia go, and they followed Rebecca to Water Street. Townspeople showed up with supply-laden wagons. They fashioned sunshades from wagon sheets, and sheltered patients, grouping them based on the severity of their injuries. Cordelia was assigned to a tent for the walking wounded, where she comforted them by mopping their brows with a damp rag. Meanwhile, Ben directed Mrs. Pratt and a few other women in cleaning and bandaging less severe lacerations at a nearby tent before he joined Rebecca at the third station, which catered to the seriously injured.

"How is everything going here?" He approached her while she attended to a man with facial lacerations.

"It could be a lot worse." She cleaned the blood from the man's face. "Currently, there are a few broken bones and some deep cuts. If we act swiftly, we can prevent loss of life or limb. Can you keep up?"

"I'll give it my all." He swallowed past the knot in his throat.

"Would you rather we work together, or should I tend to someone else?"

"I doubt your hands will be steady enough for stitching. Are you able to set bones?" She wiped her brow with her arm. "Conrad Hildesheim and several other strong men are ready to help steady patients."

"Set bones." He hesitated as he surveyed the patients in the tent. "I'll get started."

"He goes first." Rebecca indicated a young boy. "Inform the men of your needs. They assisted in organizing the medical supplies, so they are familiar with the location of everything."

As Ben prepared to set the boy's broken arm, two men stepped in to lend aid. Conrad Hildesheim steadied the child's torso as a ruddy-faced man draped himself across the boy's legs. Despite his racing heart and trembling hands, Ben spoke to the child in soothing tones.

"Say, Doc, wouldn't it be better to approach it from a different angle?" The ruddy-faced man massaged the boy's legs. "Maybe get a different grip there? Like this?" He demonstrated an alternative hold with his hands.

"Are you a doctor, sir?"

"No, I wouldn't call myself a doctor, but I do study a little of this and a little of that."

"Well, I am a doctor." Ben winced at his unexpected declaration. The words caught him by surprise but once spoken, they took root somewhere steady inside him. "At least for the moment. And I've done more than my fair share of this."

In one quick motion, Ben set the bone. A brief wave of nausea swept over him as the boy cried out, but it soon faded. He took a damp cloth from a nearby bucket, wrung it out, and gave it to Conrad, instructing him to remain by the boy's side until needed elsewhere. Conrad gladly obliged, and Ben moved on to other patients.

Within a few hours, they'd treated dozens of patients, aided by several townspeople willing to learn how to handle minor cases. Ben was reminded of his early days under his father's instruction as he staggered into the bushes twice to expel the contents of his stomach. He soaked a cloth in a nearby bucket and wiped his forehead. Rebecca had labored diligently, seldom pausing to rest. She spoke to him only briefly to discuss patient care.

"Sir. Doctor." A man on a nearby blanket lifted his hand and let it drop.

Ben approached him. "How may I assist you?"

"The lady doctor. She was going to find out about my family." The man rubbed his forehead. "I was waiting on the pier for their arrival when the accident occurred. I never saw whether they got off the boat."

"You weren't on the boat? How did you sustain your injuries?"

"When the *Valiant* collided with the *Caprificus*, the hotel owner, Baas, cheered for the ship's captain." The man shut his eyes. "I informed him my wife and children were aboard the *Valiant* and insisted he apologize. He declined, so I poked him in the chest. He clocked me, and I fell. I'm uncertain what I hit my head on, but I sustained a gash."

"I know someone has been jotting down the patients' names." Ben gently squeezed the man's shoulder. "I'll ask if Rebecca managed to locate the list. For now, relax."

Ben stood and turned, running into Levi.

Levi gripped his shoulders, steadying them both. "How are you doing?"

"I'm okay. I've had better days, but I've also seen worse." Ben gestured for Conrad to sit with the man while he spoke to Levi. "Join me?"

"Sure." Levi strode several feet with Ben.

"This gentleman reported getting into a skirmish with Ambrose Baas on the dock." Ben blinked hard. "He claims Baas cheered the captain of the Valiant for ramming the other vessel."

"It's worse, I'm afraid." Levi wiped his hand across his mouth. "After Baas injured the man, he was heard saying he was only sorry Captain Sterling hadn't crippled the *Caprificus*. He is backing Reed's action to claim the victory at any cost. Says the reputation for the fastest ship will earn more money in the long run."

"Have you spoken to Baas about it?"

"No one has seen him since he made those comments." Levi shook his head, squinting against the sun. "He disappeared in the crowd."

"I knew Baas was bad news the moment I met him. He reminds me of Carraway." Ben paused. He couldn't bring himself to refer to Carraway as the man he'd killed. "The man who shot my friend Sean. Have you seen Rebecca? Her patient is asking about his family."

"She may have gone aboard the *Valiant*. There's a small number of passengers who haven't disembarked yet." Levi leaned around Ben, surveying the dock. "I saw her on the dock with Nicholas."

A sudden howl erupted from the far end of the wharf. Captain Cobb shouted for assistance. Ben and Levi hurried toward him, overtaking Simon on the dock. Captain Cobb waved them past his ship, directing their attention to the *Caprificus*. A man hung precariously from the starboard side with a rope twisted around his ankle.

Chapter Thirty-Five

Ben rushed the deck alongside Levi and Simon. Together, they worked hand over fist to haul the man topside. The rope slipped, and the man dropped a few inches. They froze.

"Sir," Ben shouted from the railing. "Sir, take the rope."

"I can't. If I move, it'll come undone."

"Keep calm, bend at the waist, and grab the rope." It swayed. "Hold steady. We'll haul you up."

The wind gusted, increasing the rope's sway. The man howled. Levi and Simon attempted to stabilize the rope to no avail.

"Sir, what happened?"

"The rope cinched tighter."

"We're bringing you up." Ben signaled to Levi and Simon with a nod. The three of them strained to hoist the man while he thudded against the ship.

Once close enough, Ben's fingers found a grip on the man's waistband. Levi and Simon each held onto a leg while Ben seized the man's shoulder with his other hand. They all toppled backward as the man fell onto the deck. Simon took the knife from behind his back and cut the rope from the man's ankle. Ben examined him, gently moving the ankle.

"You'll need to stay off it for a few days, but it should heal on its own. Should we carry you off the ship?"

"No, sir. I'm part of the crew." He gestured to shipmates gathered around. "Could you boys help me to my quarters?"

A couple of men propped him up as he hobbled away. Ben, Levi, and Simon walked down the gangplank to the dock, where they met Rebecca and Nicholas. Ben fell in step with Rebecca as the rest of the group moved ahead. Something in her posture made him hold back a step. Tight shoulders, eyes straight ahead, her stride brisk. She hadn't acknowledged his presence. Perhaps it was the weight of the day. Or maybe something had shifted, and he'd missed it.

"Today has been quite eventful." He gently reached for her elbow, holding her back from the others. "Did you notice the man who assisted Conrad and me with the young boy earlier?"

"I saw two men helping you, but I didn't get a good look." Her tone flattened, almost clipped. "Why?"

"I didn't notice then. Too focused on the boy. But the man had a ruddy complexion and tried to show me how to set the bone." Ben scanned the area for the scruffy blond wharfie who had followed him into town. "However, he admitted he wasn't a doctor."

Rebecca placed her hand on her lower back, still not meeting his eyes. "Do you believe he's Captain Cobb's passenger, the one carrying the spyglass?"

"He certainly matches Captain Cobb's description."

"Do you think he hung around?"

"We should check, but maybe it's best not to bring up the message."

"Absolutely." Rebecca stepped away, already gazing beyond him. She rushed to the end of the dock where Nicholas stood waiting. "Nicholas, you don't have to wait for me. I'll swing by the saddlery on my way home."

Ben and Rebecca returned to the medical tents, though she kept a half step ahead like she wasn't quite walking *with* him. Conrad and Mrs. Pratt oversaw a small group of townspeople caring for the few remaining injured. A few people stopped to speak to Conrad as he discharged patients to loved ones taking them home. Meanwhile, Mrs. Pratt kept track of a list of passengers and the injured, trying to help reunite those who had been separated due to the accident.

Ben approached Conrad and asked, "Do you recall the man who assisted us with the young boy? Is he here?"

"Ja, he is vith Mrs. Pratt at zee second tent." The German baker pointed the way.

"Thanks, Conrad." Ben and Rebecca strolled toward Mrs. Pratt's tent. "It's reassuring to see the third tent vacant. I suspect most of those left might be deckhands and dockworkers."

Her voice was polite but distant. "I understand you're eager to leave medicine, but you managed yourself admirably today."

The words were kind. Her tone, less so.

"I felt like a beginner once more. I struggled to manage my stomach." Ben nervously flicked his thumbs against his fists. "It was awkward. I hope my disappearances into the bushes went unnoticed."

In one corner sat the ruddy-faced man, alternately cooling two men with a damp cloth. Ben beckoned him to join them outside the tent, and he politely excused himself from the patients.

"I apologize, but I missed your name earlier." Ben rested his hand on the man's shoulder.

"Danville. Anthony Danville." The man fanned himself by tugging at his shirt.

"Mr. Danville, first, thank you for lending a hand today. Your support greatly improved our efficiency and effectiveness, and having volunteers like you makes a significant difference." Ben shook his hand.

"I was pleased to be here."

"Second, were you a passenger on Captain Cobb's ship, the *Resilient*, last week?"

"I was. It was an enjoyable journey. I boarded in St. Louis and encountered beautiful sights throughout the trip."

"Using your spyglass?" Rebecca tilted her head.

"Yes, of course." He took the instrument from his pocket. "See? It's a three-draw created by Ronchetti in Manchester."

"It's a lovely instrument." Rebecca's expression fell. "We wondered if you lost one, as we found one missing an owner. But here you have it."

"Could it possibly be an H.V. Laun spyglass?"

Ben turned to Rebecca, hoping for a shared spark of enthusiasm. But she only gave a quick nod.

Ben squeezed Danville's shoulder. "Yes. Are you familiar with the owner?"

"Perhaps. I was birdwatching by the riverfront on Thursday with my precious gem." He patted his telescope. "While I was there, a couple stepped off a ship and chatted with me. It turns out the gentleman shares my passion for birds and telescopes." Danville bounced on his toes, his face radiant. "He owns an H.V. Laun spyglass. Actually, he has two of them. He collects telescopes and reportedly features a variety of makers in his home collection."

"Are they staying at the hotel? Do you remember their names?"

"They didn't mention their accommodations." He rubbed his chin. "I'm awful with names. I think it was Talcott, Talbert." He squinted, searching the depths of his memory. "Talton, Talbut? I apologize. I can't quite remember the name."

"It's all right." Ben pumped the man's hand. "I appreciate it,

Mr. Danville. This has been quite helpful. We won't keep you any longer."

Ben guided Rebecca by the elbow, walking opposite the medical tents. "What a break this is. Can you believe it?"

"Quite the break." Her tone dripped with sarcasm. "We have Captain Horn's description and possibly half a name. And no clue where to start searching for this couple."

"But Horn's man with the bulbous nose is undoubtedly the owner." Ben enthusiastically pounded his palm. "This wraps up the afternoon nicely, doesn't it?"

"Mm. You may continue enjoying your day as you were before all the excitement."

"What do you mean?"

"I saw you enter the hotel with Cordelia." She cut her eyes at him. "Then she comes out right after you in a flounced silk gown. Do you know what impression that leaves? And this was after I spent the morning at the newspaper office trying to fix the fallout from yesterday's article."

"*You* spent the morning working to fix the situation?"

"Yes, while you and Cordelia did who knows what at the hotel, I was trying to restore my tarnished reputation." She stopped, hands on her hips. "By the way, where did that dress come from? You know what, never mind. I need to get home. Dinner is at six, assuming you and Cordelia can tear yourselves away from the hotel." She stormed off, vanishing in the distance. He pressed his hand flat over his heart, trying to calm the heavy thud behind his ribs.

"Simon and I took a moment to visit with Captain Cobb." Levi appeared at Ben's side with Simon. "What did we miss? Is everything all right?"

"I don't believe so." Ben scratched his head.

Levi raised an eyebrow. "What went wrong? It appeared all sunshine and roses for a while."

"Then things clouded up real quick-like." Simon nudged Ben's shoulder.

"We've discovered an exciting lead with this telescope. It's likely linked to one of Captain Horn's passengers who arrived on Thursday." Ben rubbed the back of his neck, brow furrowing. "All that's left is to find this couple and confirm whether it belongs to the husband. Anthony Danville, the man we spoke to a moment ago, provided a name. Or at least a potential one."

"Sounds like a boon." Simon clapped once, folding his hands together. "What's the issue?"

"Rebecca saw me at the hotel this morning with Cordelia."

"You know, for a man who survived California, you sure picked a fine way to get yourself scalped at home," Simon added with a lopsided grin

"Ambrose Baas hired Cordelia to play piano in the hotel lobby."

Levi dug his toe into the ground, shaking his head. "And Cordelia is hiding this from Rebecca."

"Yes, I've tried to persuade her to leave, but she refuses." Ben pinched his upper lip. "I encouraged her to be truthful with Rebecca. She fears Rebecca will pressure her to resign. And she should." He ran his hands through his hair. "I didn't say anything because I hoped Cordelia would eventually be honest with Rebecca."

"You were allowing her room to grow." Levi clicked his tongue. "Aw, Ben, I hate to say it, but you're in a no-win situation. Cordelia needs to grow, yet she lacks motivation. She's not ready. I'm sure she feels she's living in Rebecca's shadow."

"So her dress isn't from Brandt's shop?" Simon tilted his head and squinted one eye.

"No, Baas has appointed a dressing room and supplied the dress. Today, there was jewelry on the dressing table."

"Why?" Levi cupped his elbow in one hand while tapping his lips with the other. "It can't be merely to acquire a pianist."

"I'm not sure. There must be an angle, but I can't nail it down." Ben lowered his gaze, his voice measured. "He's also offered me a job as a doctor. I haven't accepted yet, but I'm contemplating it because it would allow me to watch over Cordelia. This morning, she accused me of being a mother hen and an additional brother."

"Thanks for having my back, brother." Simon patted his shoulder. "Baas knows the right bait to reel her in." Simon's lips flattened. "She has aimed to marry well for as long as I can recall."

"It may be wise to explain to Rebecca your presence at the hotel with Cordelia, given that she noticed you together." Levi's voice held a quiet gravity. "Cordelia had her opportunity to share."

"I agree. Staying silent will only deepen the divide between you and Rebecca." Simon crossed his arms, shaking his head. "If the gap grows any larger, I might be unable to help you."

"I only wish I understood Baas better." Ben pressed his hand to his chest. "It's not very helpful to say I'm trying to protect Cordelia like I would a younger sister when I'm unclear about what dangers I'm guarding her against."

"Baas is a polarizing figure. Sometimes, he's an enigmatic charmer. Other times, he's pompous and contentious. There's no in-between with him." Simon pointed toward the *Valiant*. "He played the instigator in this steamboat incident. A few brawls have erupted involving people who allege his employees exercise strong-arm tactics to coerce them into relinquishing property. However, he distances himself enough from these events that when questioned, he claims these individuals acted independently. They weren't following his orders."

"That is, until today's incident." Levi jabbed his palm with his finger. "He publicly declared his intention to obliterate the

Caprificus. His goal is for his steamboat business to succeed no matter the cost."

"He would employ the same aggressive tactics with the hotel." Ben raised an eyebrow. "However, I don't understand how acquiring land would help his steamboat line or the hotel. Did those individuals involved in the saloon incidents own any property nearby?"

"Two of them do, and two do not." Simon brushed the dirt from his hands, glancing toward the wharf.

"Where are the properties of the two who don't?"

"One business is located farther up Main Street from the hotel." Simon drew a rough map in the dirt, approximating the properties' locations with his toe. "The other individual has some property a short distance from Main Street."

"Something doesn't add up." Ben rubbed his hand across his face.

"Baas made a mistake today, revealing his intentions on the dock. He's starting to slip up. Whatever he's planning will soon come to light." Levi patted Ben's shoulder. "Let's help Mrs. Pratt and Conrad with these last few patients so they can go home."

"Simon, hurry!" A young teenager raced toward them, sliding to a halt. "Ollie's in trouble!"

"I will remain with Mrs. Pratt and Conrad. You both go." Levi set his hand on Ben's back, giving him a steady shove forward.

Chapter Thirty-Six

"We didn't know what to do, Simon." The boy twisted the brim of his cap in his hands. "It's our fault. When we heard the steamboat's whistle signaling danger, we took the opportunity to sneak down to the riverfront as soon as the teacher let us out."

Simon kept pace beside him, his voice steady and low. "Ollie decided to stick with you, even after facing consequences for the same issue just two days earlier?"

"It's not his fault. We pressured him."

"Where is he? What kind of trouble is he in?" Simon gritted his teeth, lengthening his stride.

Ben tapped his thumb against the banded nail while struggling to keep pace with the two. His thoughts raced. Rebecca had already gone home. If Ollie was hurt, could they reach Dr. Pernot before he left the wharf for the day?

"He believed this man was shadowing Rebecca."

"Wait." Ben hop-stepped to keep pace. "Following Rebecca. Do you have a description?"

"Real ugly. Leathery, pock-marked face."

"Stringy blond hair?"

"That's him." The boy nodded breathlessly. "Ollie believed he was tailing Rebecca, so he confronted him, and they fought. Hurry."

"How far?" Ben's gears turned. "How far away is Ollie?"

"Not too far. Right around the first slight bend."

"Go back." Ben stopped, nudging the boy toward the wharf.

"Ben, what are you doing?" Simon hesitated. "We can't stop now. I need to reach my brother."

"We have to prepare for any medical situation." Ben urged Simon forward. "Go on, Simon. I'll follow closely behind, but he's got to go back."

Simon nodded and sprinted as quickly as his legs could go.

"Listen closely, kid. This is crucial." Ben tightened his grip on the boy's shoulders. "Go back. Locate Levi, Mrs. Pratt, or Conrad, any adult you encounter. Tell them to summon Dr. Pernot." Ben wiped the sweat from his forehead. "If Pernot isn't at the wharf, instruct them to gather medical instruments, hot water, and soap if available. Do you understand?"

The boy's eyes widened, and he nodded.

"Move. Quickly. Do everything I said."

Ben observed the boy momentarily as he dashed back toward the wharf. Then, he ran full split to catch up with Simon. As he rounded the bend, he spotted Ollie on the ground. Simon cast aside the scruffy wharfie as a taller, dark-haired man attacked him from the tree line. The wharfie scrambled to his feet and rushed Simon. Fire ignited in Ben's belly as he charged the man, sending him sprawling. Ben straddled the wharfie, landing a right hook across his jaw. Once, twice, three times, and the wharfie lost consciousness.

Simon dodged the dark-haired man. The man's knees brushed the ground before he sprang up beside Ben. The scent of cheap whiskey made Ben's stomach churn. Simon and the whiskey-soaked man faced off, crouched and circling each other.

"Ben, grab Ollie and go."

"But Simon—"

"I'm fine." Simon gritted his teeth. "Ollie's been stabbed. Go. Now."

Ben rushed to Ollie, tearing his shirt open. Ben's stomach dropped. Blood pulsed in sluggish spurts from a narrow slash above the boy's hipbone. He tore a piece from Ollie's shirt and pressed it against the wound. Ollie groaned in response.

"Ollie. Ollie, hold this. Press as hard as you can." Ben's stomach twisted into knots as he scooped the boy into his arms. He sprinted down the riverbank, muscles battling the pain. As he approached the medical tents, Levi and Conrad hurried to take Ollie from him. He collapsed to his knees, gasping for air. As he rose, Mrs. Pratt drew near.

"Benjamin, dear, there are clean water buckets here." She led him to the tent's edge. "In her rush to leave earlier, Rebecca forgot her instruments. Captain Cobb supplied hot water, and Levi soaked them."

"Where's Dr. Pernot?"

"He went home soon after you and Simon vanished. Where's Simon?"

"He asked me to get Ollie to safety and take care of him." Ben gazed into the distance. "Said he wouldn't be long."

Mrs. Pratt squeezed his elbow. "I'll say a prayer, dear."

She gave him a small piece of soap, and he cleaned his hands in a bucket. Levi and Conrad placed Ollie on a makeshift table and removed his shirt. The red stain on Ollie's side triggered a wave of nausea, prompting Ben to inhale slowly through his nose.

"Levi, apply pressure to the wound until I'm ready." Ben took another deep breath. "I need to familiarize myself with the supplies. Explain to me how you've arranged everything."

Mrs. Pratt guided him through the suturing supplies, clean cloth strips, and other items they believed he might require.

"We aimed to keep everything as fresh, organized, and clean as possible, according to Rebecca's preferences."

"You've done an excellent job. Thank you." Ben wiped his brow with his forearm. "I guess we don't have ether or chloroform."

"No, we don't."

"I don't know the extent of the wound." Ben joined Levi. "But I'll need to work as quickly as possible."

"We're here for you. Whatever you need, ask." Levi leaned in and lowered his voice. "How are your hands?"

"Don't ask." Ben's voice went quiet. "If I step away, reapply pressure to the wound." Ben glanced around the group. "Conrad, you'll have to hold him down. Mrs. Pratt, I need you to keep the instruments and towels within reach for Levi and me."

"Vee are ready." Conrad grasped Ollie's shoulders while Mrs. Pratt nodded in agreement.

Ben grabbed a fresh rag from Mrs. Pratt's instrument board, a small wooden plank covered with a clean cloth. "Okay, Levi, show me."

Ben cleaned the blood from the wound, trying to evaluate the situation more carefully. He inhaled roughly, battling the queasiness in his gut. Nausea bullied his stomach, and he stepped away. He doubled over beyond the medical tent, his stomach spasming against his will. After it eased, he shut his eyes momentarily to regain his composure. A cool, damp sensation rested on his forehead. He opened his eyes.

"You're not alone, brother." Simon dabbed a rag behind his ears and down his neck.

"You're okay. You made it."

"I did. I need you to work on my cheek next." Simon smiled. "But make it pretty, okay?"

"Sure. May I have another minute?" Ben shut his eyes as Simon went to the medical tent with the others. "Lord, I can't stay in this dark, damp cave any longer. Ollie needs me." He stared at his trembling hands before closing his eyes again. "Be with me in this new place. Hold me together with Your love and the compassion Levi spoke of. I can't face this alone."

He flexed his fingers once, twice. A steadiness filled him, not his own. Strength poured through him from the Rock, the fortress, the cave. A wave of tranquility engulfed Ben as he examined his hands once more. They remained steady. He went to the medical tent. He met Mrs. Pratt's gaze, and her expression softened.

"Ollie, focus on Conrad. He will breathe along with you, all right?"

Ollie nodded and hissed through his teeth when Ben touched the wound.

"Good news is the blade entered at a shallow angle just above your hip bone. It's a long wound, but not very deep, and thankfully, no vital organs affected." Ben flexed his jaw. "On the downside, it will require a lot of stitches. Also, it's just above your waistband, meaning wearing pants will be uncomfortable for a while."

Ollie kept breathing along with Conrad, inhaling sharply through his teeth and exhaling with emphasis.

"You're doing well, Ollie." Ben fought off a slight wave of lingering nausea. "Let me know if you need to take a break."

"You're doing excellent as well." Levi rested his hand on Ben's back. "I've never seen stitches this impressive."

Ben laughed nervously. "How many stitches have you seen put in?"

"Allie is always sewing." Levi winked.

"Mrs. Pratt, I forgot—" Rebecca halted, her eyes snapping to the makeshift table. "Ollie?" Her breath caught and she locked gazes with Ben. "What happened?"

"I'm okay." Ollie hissed, eyes flicking away from Conrad. "It's nothing. Doc says it looks worse than it is."

A rush of footfalls on packed earth broke through the tension.

"Ollie! Where is he?" Ivajohn's voice cut through the air as she flew toward them, windblown and wide-eyed. "Someone stopped me in the street and said he was stabbed."

Ben's throat tightened. One hand faltered. Levi patted his back, whispering, "Even if the mountains walk away and the hills fall to pieces—"

"He's here. He's safe." Simon stepped between the sisters and the table. He gathered them in his arms, guiding them to the foot of the table. "Let Ben finish. He's doing well."

Ivajohn's gaze landed on some bloodstained cloths dropped near the table. Her breath grew ragged. "He's just a boy," she whispered. "Just a boy…

Rebecca put an arm around her, drawing her close.

"I know. But he's strong." Simon gripped her elbows. "You'll only distract him. You can stay here if you're calm. Otherwise, we'll take a walk."

"I can't just stand here." Rebecca released Ivajohn and stepped forward, but Simon held out a hand to block her.

"You have to let Ben do this." Simon took her hand. "Listen. Ollie and the other boys came from school when they heard the emergency signal from the steamboats. He ran into some trouble. "

"I don't understand. What happened to him?" Rebecca leaned into Simon, attempting to get closer, but he held fast.

"He believed someone was following you. A man with a scarred face."

She drew in a sharp breath. "The dockworker."

"They struggled. I got there as the man pulled out a knife and stabbed Ollie."

Rebecca's hands pressed to her mouth.

"He'll be all right." Simon rubbed her fingers. "Let Ben do his job."

"His hands." Her whisper reached Ben, causing his right hand to tremble slightly.

Levi leaned close. "Even if the mountains walk away and the hills fall to pieces …"

Ben met Levi's gaze, drawing a steadying breath. "His love won't walk away from me. His peace won't fall apart. The God who has compassion on me says so."

He closed his eyes as if sealing the words inside. Opening his eyes, he focused on the boy. "About ten more stitches, Ollie. You with me?

"I'm tired, Doc. And hurting." Ollie's breathing matched Conrad's again. "But I'm with you."

Ben's needle moved with care, his hands steady again. "Mrs. Pratt, once I finish, we'll need something to cover the wound. Otherwise, his waistband will irritate it."

"I'll handle it." Rebecca slipped away from Simon, collecting the necessary items from the medical supplies.

Ben tied the final stitch and massaged Ollie's shoulder. "You are among the most courageous patients I've ever had."

"If I had followed Simon and Rebecca's rules, I wouldn't have been your patient." Ollie grimaced.

"Simon might allow this one to slide." Ben winked. "Ready to load up and go home?"

"Home." Ollie closed his eyes. "I like the sound of that."

"Me too."

Chapter Thirty-Seven

Rebecca entered Pa's room, holding a water bowl, while Ollie dozed. She settled beside him on the bed and gently wiped his forehead with a cool cloth. He opened one eye, shut it again, and licked his lips.

"I'm sorry, Becca."

"It's me who should apologize."

"Why? What did you do?"

"I shouldn't have joined the foolish spyglass search." She wet the cloth again, wringing the excess water into the bowl. "The man you fought wouldn't have followed me if I hadn't been involved, and you wouldn't have encountered him. I should have returned the spyglass to the lost and found as planned. Then none of this would have happened."

"Ben mentioned you thought it would bring us closer together."

"It was an absurd idea."

"Was it?" He offered a faint smile. "Thanks to the spyglass, I have you all to myself right now."

A tear rolled down her cheek while a half-giggle escaped her lips. "I guess I can't argue with that."

"I wouldn't have talked to Ben either." Ollie took the cloth from her and placed it on his chest.

"I heard you told Edie not to call him Ben if he asked."

"Yeah, I was sore at him for hurting you." Ollie shifted with a grunt. "But I'm starting to see things differently. He might be okay. I'm grateful he brought me back to the wharf and took care of my injuries."

"I'm sorry I wasn't there for you."

"Becca, you can't always be there for us." He grasped her hand. "You're kinda frustrating, trying to shield us all the time."

"I've heard this quite a bit recently. I suppose I've smothered everyone since Mama's passing."

"That's not it." Ollie squeezed her hand. "Sometimes, we want to support you. We're a family, and protecting each other should involve everyone, not just one individual. You don't allow us to protect you like you do for us."

"Oh, Ollie, you've grown up before my eyes." She leaned forward to kiss his forehead.

Pa's room door creaked open. Martie entered with a tray of food, and Simon followed. A moment later, Ivajohn slipped in behind them, her eyes swollen and red-rimmed.

"I couldn't leave yet." Ivajohn wrung her hands. "I had to see you once more." She reached Ollie's bedside and brushed a damp curl from his forehead. "You gave us quite a scare, baby brother."

"Heaven knows we can't afford to lose a brother. The girls outnumber us six to three." Simon chuckled, nudging Ollie's shoulder.

Ollie half-laughed, pressing a hand to his side.

"How are you doing?" Ivajohn sniffed.

"Better now." He yawned. "But it stings when I laugh."

Simon moved to the far side of the bed as Rebecca scooted aside so Martie could set the tray on the bedside table.

"Would you like some stew?" Martie sat poised, ready to feed him.

"Is there any cornbread? I'm so hungry." He yawned. "And I'm tired too. I can't decide which I want more, food or a nap."

"Hey, hero." Simon pretended to jab his arm. "I'm proud of how you handled Ben's medical treatment, but don't ever scare me like that again."

"Yessir."

"You make me feel like an old man." Simon pressed his hand to his heart as if injured. "And now I sound like Justin."

"Oh, don't." Ollie laughed. "Don't make me laugh. It hurts."

A knock sounded at the front door. Rebecca started to leave, but Ollie seized her hand. She hesitated and then drew closer.

"What is it?"

He gestured with his chin to his siblings. "The spyglass brought five of us closer. It's not so bad."

"I suppose not." She mussed his hair. "Make sure to eat and get some rest. I appreciate you trying to protect me."

As Rebecca descended the front stairs, a quick prayer of gratitude arose in her heart. The day had the potential to be far worse. For a time, she had put aside the issues with Ambrose Baas. She rested in the gift of having most of her siblings gathered safely under one roof. A satisfied smile spread across her face as she opened the front door and found Nicholas on the porch.

"Nicholas." Rebecca blinked in confused surprise. "I haven't had the chance to clean my medical equipment since we returned home. Is Dr. Pernot not available?"

"I didn't come regarding a medical issue." He shifted his weight, hands fidgeting before one lifted halfway as if to reach for her, then dropped back to his side. His gaze darted up, met hers briefly, and fell again.

Rebecca's cheeks warmed. Her smile faded as she took a small step back. "I apologize if I've given you the wrong idea."

"Rebecca Hogue, I've been sweet on you for a while." He brushed his finger over his lips. "But I'm smarter than I appear. I've got enough sense to know there will never be anything romantic between us."

Her cheeks grew hotter with embarrassment. "So why are you here, Nicholas?"

"Before leaving town to track down the Cutter-Doyle gang, the sheriff designated me as his deputy." He avoided her gaze. "I need Simon."

"Is there trouble in town? Did another fight happen?" She rested against the door. "How severe is it this time?"

"You're mistaken. I don't require Simon's assistance." He gradually lifted his gaze to meet hers. "I need Simon to accompany me. To the jail."

She stared at him with a blank expression. Then she shook her head as if to clear water from her ears. "I don't think I heard you right. Did you say you're taking Simon to jail?"

"Yes, ma'am."

"What is the charge?"

"There's been a man cut up pretty badly. His body was found at the riverside." Nicholas ran his teeth over his lip. "Simon's knife was found nearby. Where is he?"

"He's upstairs with Ollie."

Nicholas took a step over the threshold.

Rebecca pressed her palm firmly against his chest, shoving him back. "What do you think you're doing?"

"I'm going to get him."

"I don't think so." Rebecca blocked his way, her jaw set like stone. "After all we've done for the town. After all Simon has done—someone's accusing him of murder?

"I'm sorry, Rebecca." He lowered his head, backing out of the doorway. "I can't go without him. Another man claims Simon also injured him. There's one dead, one injured."

"He deserves a moment with his family before you take him." Rebecca's gaze fell to the floor. "I'll get him."

Her stomach dropped. She turned without a word and ascended the stairs, each step heavier than the last. Simon's knife? A man dead? She paused at the bedroom door, taking a deep breath before pushing it open. Simon sat in a chair next to the bed, reading a dime novel aloud with Ivajohn over his shoulder while Martie was nestled beside Ollie.

Rebecca didn't speak.

Simon's eyes met hers. "What's wrong?"

She opened her mouth, but nothing came out. Her throat burned. She stepped inside and closed the door. "Simon," she rasped. "A man is dead. And they found your knife."

"What? That's—no." Ollie sat up fast, groaning and clutching his side as Martie steadied his bowl. "Simon wouldn't—"

"Nicholas is downstairs." Rebecca's voice was low but urgent. "He's come to take you in."

Martie gasped. One hand shot to her mouth. "Take him in where?"

"To jail." Rebecca's voice cracked. "For questioning."

Ivajohn stood, frozen behind Simon, white knuckles curled into the shoulder of his shirt. Her brows drew tight, lips parted but speechless.

Simon folded his hand over Ivajohn's before prying her fingers free. He stood slowly, as if the room tilted under him. "You believe I didn't do this."

"With everything in me." Rebecca crossed the room, reaching for his hand and giving it a squeeze. "But I have to walk you down."

Ollie tried to rise. "I'm going too."

"No," Simon said firmly. "Ivajohn and Martie, stay and take care of him."

Martie nodded, blinking back tears as she folded an arm around Ollie.

Ivajohn finally found her voice, steadying herself on the back of the chair. "This can't be real."

Rebecca led him downstairs, her grip tight around his fingers.

Simon hooked the thumb of one hand in his pocket. "Nicholas, why would you ever think I'd kill someone?"

"I hope I'm mistaken, Simon, but the knife discovered near the body resembles yours." Nicholas shifted, holding out his hand. "Let me see your knife, and I'll happily head home for the night."

Simon reached for the knife sheathed at his back. He glanced at Nicholas and then at Rebecca. "It appears I've misplaced it."

Simon stepped out the door, yet Rebecca clung to him. She stifled her tears as Simon released her hand.

"I'll go. It's a formality. I didn't do it, and my name will be cleared." Simon forced a smile, though it didn't reach his eyes. "He's just doing his job. It'll be fine, Becks."

"Don't call me Becks," she whispered as he crossed the lawn with Nicholas.

As Ben and Cordelia entered through the front gate, they ran into Nicholas and Simon. Cordelia's skirts swished with pointed precision as she passed, not bothering to acknowledge Nicholas. She and Ben joined Rebecca at the door, watching Simon mount the extra horse Nicholas had provided.

She stared after them as they disappeared down Cane Hill, each hoofbeat pounding like judgment in her chest. Simon's absence left a raw edge, like someone had torn a page from Mama's journal and left the binding ragged.

"Where is he going?" Cordelia placed her hands on her hips.

"Jail."

"Ha-ha. Very funny."

"This isn't a joke." Rebecca turned to face her. "Nicholas is taking Simon to jail."

"Isn't this a fine kettle of corn?" Cordelia threw up her hands dramatically. "Pa's been gone barely a week, and the entire family is unraveling in your hands. Our family name has been tarnished. We've welcomed vagabonds and women into our home. Martie and I have had to find work. And now Simon is getting arrested." Cordelia crossed her arms and tapped her foot. "What's next, Rebecca?"

"Not a word, Cordelia." Rebecca swept past her. "We both know you did not get a job. A flounced dress, yes. A job? No."

Cordelia gasped. "Well, I—"

"Don't act like Caroline Brandt made the gown you wore today." Rebecca rubbed her forehead. "I'm going upstairs to see Ollie. Then I'm going to the grove."

"I'd like to check on Ollie as well." Ben ascended the stairs after Rebecca.

The twins dashed through the corridor at the top of the stairs with Paulette on their heels. Rebecca quickly stepped aside, bumping into Ben. Paulette seized Jesse by his collar, tickled him briefly, and then guided him toward his room.

"Finish folding your clothes, and then you can visit Oscar." She gestured for Cason to come along. "You as well, young man." She addressed Rebecca and Ben. "We apologize. We'll try to be more cautious."

Paulette stood by the bedroom door, watching the boys complete their task. With a steadying breath, Rebecca closed her eyes. She couldn't remember the boardinghouse ever being this crowded. No matter where she turned, she was bound to bump into someone. Each time Edie expressed a desire to climb a tree, Rebecca wanted to climb up right behind her.

Rebecca took a few steps toward Pa's room but hesitated. Turning back, she nearly collided with Ben again. Her breath hitched as she pressed her hand below her collarbone, fingers splayed as she tried to smooth away the spike of tension.

"I didn't realize you'd be so close behind me." She exhaled sharply, trying to collect herself. "Listen, Ben, I need space. I'm not ready for more questions. Or reassurances."

"I'll catch up with you once I check on Ollie."

"I'd rather you didn't." Her tone softened, but her stance held. "I need air, not company. My thoughts are all jumbled, and right now I don't trust what might come out of my mouth."

"There's something pressing I need to talk to you about."

She sighed in exasperation. "If it's about the spyglass, don't bother. It's been nothing but heartache, and I'm done chasing answers with it."

"It's not about the spyglass."

"Fine." She sighed, and her shoulders drooped. "Come find me outside when you're done with Ollie."

Chapter Thirty-Eight

Rebecca nestled her journal and the intricately carved wooden box under her arm as she stepped out the back door. Viv, Bess, and Lucy gathered around the fire ring, engaged in conversation and laughter. As Rebecca inhaled, her ribcage constricted, resisting her lungs' need to expand. The more space she sought, the less room there seemed to be.

"Good evening, Rebecca." Viv's emerald eyes sparkled. "Will you join us?"

"I'll just—" Rebecca gestured toward the far side of the fire ring, offering a quick nod and a tight smile.

"Well." Viv faced Bess and Lucy. "No matter what you think, a man with a touch of danger is alluring to me."

"Oh, Viv." Bess clucked her tongue. "Aren't you always testing the limits?"

"You'll be lucky if you don't end up in a boot yard one day." Lucy shivered and crossed her arms.

"We'll all find ourselves in a graveyard eventually." Viv chuckled as she leaned in. "I believe we should enjoy ourselves along the journey."

Rebecca averted her gaze and rolled her eyes. The back door creaked open as Ben emerged. He encroached upon the girls' space, took a wide stance, and crossed his arms.

"Good evening, ladies." His gaze lingered on Rebecca. "This area is closed to everyone for the rest of the night."

"To be sure." Viv's gaze trailed from Ben to Rebecca as she rose. She glided past Ben, whispering over her shoulder in a not-so-quiet tone, "Don't do anything I wouldn't do."

Ben assisted Lucy and Bess in getting out of their seats by holding their elbows. He shot a warning glance at Viv. "I'm going to do precisely what you would do—go inside."

He acknowledged Rebecca with a nod while leading the three women inside. The latch clicked shut behind them. Rebecca sighed deeply as she set her journal and box on a stump nearby. Turning slightly, she propped her feet on a stool beside her, adjusting her skirt for coverage. She wrapped her arms around her knees.

How had everything gone so wrong in a few days? She should have informed Pa about their struggles since Conrad's departure. Their family always celebrated with tenants when they reached their goals, particularly when starting a new home or family. Usually, filling the empty rooms at the boarding house didn't take long. However, Conrad, Captain Cobb, and Pastor Turner vacated their rooms around the same time, complicating the task with the need to fill multiple rooms. Although she wasn't keen on the railroad coming, it would bring many workers needing accommodation.

It would also bring many items for the lost and found room. She longed for this spyglass search to turn out as sweet as apple pie, as Levi's and Justin's searches had. Yet life had taught her hopes and dreams are best left by the wayside. Of course, expecting the search to result in true love was nonsense. *But Lord, was it too much to ask for our family to be drawn closer together?*

Instead, Cordelia and she grew more distant. Ollie was

injured, and Simon in jail. How could Nicholas Franks believe him capable of murder? He was a far less clever man than she had given him credit for. But it didn't matter. The boys wouldn't have encountered trouble if she hadn't yielded to Ben's desire to locate the spyglass owner.

A pair of arms wrapped around her neck, and she stiffened.

"Surprise," Edie whispered in her ear. "We sneaked up on you."

Rebecca's heart lifted at the three smiling faces and one wagging tail before her. "Oscar, you're out of the forge. I don't think I've ever seen a dog smile before."

"He's real slow and doesn't jump around, but he's stronger." Jace patted Oscar's head.

Rebecca rubbed the dog's back. "Well, you've taken excellet care of him."

"My brothers have too." Jace beamed. "We haven't fought with each other near as much since coming to Hogue House. Do you think something good can come from bad things?"

"I've pondered that very thing." Rebecca pressed her lips together, thinking. "Let's hope so."

"I saw Simon leaving with Nicholas." Edie placed her hands on her hips and tilted her head. "They got work to do?"

"I think they're attempting to solve a crime." It wasn't a lie, but it also wasn't wholly truthful. Yet Rebecca would go to great lengths to safeguard any semblance of innocence in these young souls.

"How long will he be gone?"

"I'm afraid I don't know. This might take some time, sweet pea."

"Okay. Let's put Oscar to bed." She bumped Jace with her shoulder. "Do you mind if we stay up a bit longer to read? I want to share the shipwreck book with Jace."

"For a little while. Only a few chapters, not the entire book."

Rebecca watched as Edie and Jace skipped back to the forge

hand-in-hand. After a moment, Edie let go of Jace's hand and dashed back to Rebecca, enveloping her in a comforting embrace.

"I love you, Becca. I'm real glad you took all these boys in." She stroked Rebecca's hair. "I like having a friend who's fascinated by shipwrecks. Tomorrow we'll climb trees together. But don't worry, I'll make sure no one spots me up there."

"I love you, too, Edie." Rebecca's heart swelled with mixed emotions. Joy, sadness, concern, and love. She held Edie even tighter. "I love all of you so much."

Edie skipped ahead with Jace as Oscar poked along behind them. Rebecca took her pencil out of her pocket and picked up her journal. Opening the book to a blank page, she stared at the emptiness. She tucked the pencil inside, closed the journal, and dropped it onto her lap. Mama's box rested on the log beside her. She reached out and traced the flowers with her fingers.

As the door creaked ajar, Ben peeked outside. She let out a sigh.

"Too soon? I'm interrupting."

Rebecca stiffened but nodded politely, placing her journal atop the wooden box. "C'mon. Let's get this over with."

"After Nicholas visited, I wanted to check on you." Ben exhaled and smiled tightly. "What crime does Nicholas think Simon committed?"

Rebecca's lungs trapped air like a vacuum. "Murder."

"Mur—" Ben's voice came too loudly. He shifted to a whisper. "Murder? Is the man daft? Who?"

"I'm not sure. Who did Simon fight by the river?"

Ben closed his eyes, his brows raised, and rubbed the back of his neck. "The wharfman was there. You know, the one with oily blond hair and a scarred face. As I arrived, Simon had already thrown the man off. Then a taller, thinner guy emerged from the woods. They were about to take Simon on together, so I rushed at our wharfie and knocked him out." Ben moved around as if rehearsing for the event. "Simon knocked the second man off balance next to me. He reeked of whiskey. Once he steadied himself, they circled each other like two bobcats ready to tie into it." Ben bent down and circled a stump. "At that moment, Simon told me Ollie had been stabbed. He insisted I take Ollie and leave, so I did."

"I wish you could have stayed with Simon. He needed a witness." Rebecca rubbed her hands together "But you made the only choice you could. I would have made the same decision if I were in either of your shoes."

She shut her eyes tightly. Lifting her chin, she reopened them. "Ben, I'm not sure how to fix this."

"Me neither." He sat across from her, clasping her hands.

She released a short breath. "You had something to tell me?"

"I want to discuss Cordelia and me."

She freed her hands and rubbed her neck, attempting to ease the pain in her throat. "It's none of my business. You are free to pursue any relationship you want. I hold no claim over you, regardless of our history."

"A relationship? With Cordelia?" Ben let out a short, incredulous laugh. "You're completely mistaken about this situation."

"But I saw you arrive at the hotel together." Rebecca crossed her arms, bracing herself. "She was on your arm."

"She was on my arm, indeed. I was merely being a gentleman, attempting to protect her. From herself. A full-time job, I must say." Ben held up his hands, exasperated. "Do you know where we had come from moments before?"

"No. Where?"

"The newspaper office. We believed we could persuade Mr. Clarke to print a retraction quickly." Ben spread his hands in a helpless gesture. "And we were successful. This afternoon, I found a paper at the hotel with the retraction on the front page."

Rebecca laughed.

"You find it humorous?"

"I was at the newspaper office when you two entered the hotel." She wiped her cheeks, smoothing away the tiredness. "I spoke with Dawn after I met with Mr. Clarke. He always planned to include a retraction in a special afternoon edition."

"It appeared to be a tough pitch when we met him."

"His brother was a tough man. As he follows in his brother's footsteps at the newspaper, he's trying to show his staff he's not to be taken lightly."

"I understand." Ben rose and paced around the stump where he had been sitting. "I visited the hotel because Ambrose Baas approached me at the picnic and offered me a position as a doctor in the hotel's health salon."

"You accepted a position as a doctor after shying away from medical issues all this time?" Heat crept up Rebecca's neck.

"I have yet to accept the position formally." Ben rubbed his neck. "I visited him the day the Bradley House women came. Being here felt constricting, and honestly, I was a bit jealous watching you with Nicholas."

"You observed us?"

"I served refreshments as you recommended. You took a while to return, so I checked the window to see if you were coming." He paused, gazing into her eyes. "You weren't." He resumed his pacing around the stump. "Anyway, after I met with Baas, I found Cordelia playing the piano in the lobby. Baas hired her. She plays in a lovely gown while the men fawn over her. She is pleased as pie."

"I was right after all. The dress didn't originate from Brandt's, and she's not employed there." Rebecca rubbed her forehead.

"I've pretended to be interested in the doctor position to follow her to work and keep her safe. I've asked to inspect the facilities, spent time in the lobby, and found ways to stall the job offer. But I'm nearly out of options to avoid it." He faced her. "I spoke with Simon and Levi today and realized I should have told you about Cordelia earlier. It's like taking the position with the military survey team to California." He rested his hands on her knees. "This is a problem we should address together, and once again, I left you out of it. I hope you can forgive me."

She bowed her head.

"Rebecca?" He leaned back, resting his hands on his knees.

"I've treated my family the same way." She closed her eyes tightly. "When Mama died, we felt so much pain. Since then, I've tried to shield them all, including Pa." She hugged herself. "I haven't shared this with anyone, but the boardinghouse is in trouble. Our payments to several local businesses are overdue. They've been patient because Mama always went out of her way to help others. They all benefited from her kindness. However, they can't show that level of understanding forever." She buried her head in her hands, rubbing her face.

"You'll be able to catch up. I'll take the hotel job." Ben held her hands. "With the rent from the Bradley House ladies, along with my income and Martie's earnings, plus Sam selling your things, you'll get back on track."

"It's even worse." She locked eyes with him. "Ambrose Baas wants Hogue House."

Ben froze, the air between them tightening like a noose.

Chapter Thirty-Nine

"Baas wants Hogue House. Why?" Ben raked his hand down his face. "How does hiring Cordelia help him achieve that?"

"I think he plans to propose to her so she can convince Pa to draft a testament naming her as the sole beneficiary of the boardinghouse."

"It's a long game." Ben blew out a slow breath. "I question whether patience is one of his virtues. He's likely to act to secure Hogue House sooner rather than later."

"I hadn't considered that." Rebecca stood, gripping her collar. "If a will bequeaths Hogue House to Cordelia, then Pa isn't necessary. What will we do?"

"Sit down and let's think about this together." Ben took her hand. "This man is entirely focused on his enterprises, the steamboat line, and the hotel. We must uncover the link between those businesses and his desired properties."

"Does he want more than one property?"

"Recently, Simon has stepped in to break up a few saloon brawls. The individuals involved indicated Baas's associates attempted to force them out of their properties."

"Ben, how did we miss this?" Rebecca clutched the stump for support. "Isom Caine, who expelled Paulette Bradley from her home, must be working for Baas."

"Do you recall Paulette's description of Caine?"

"Tall and thin with unkempt hair."

"Coal-black hair." Ben stood, pressing his palm against his forehead. His muscles tensed. "The second attacker Simon encountered must have been Caine. We need to talk to Simon. It's essential to find out if the wharfie remained unconscious when Simon returned to the medical tent after he was free of the attackers."

"Do you think Caine murdered the dockworker?"

"I'd wager on it, even though I'm not a betting man." Ben tapped his fist against his lips. "It's got to be the railroad."

"If the railroad arrives, his steamboat service will suffer a loss in passengers." Rebecca stood and paced. "He's expanding his ventures. Hotels, steamboat line, and railroad."

"Perhaps acquiring additional businesses which stand to gain from the railroad's arrival in town."

"Like Gray's Café? Mrs. Gray cautioned me about him." Rebecca clasped her arms tightly across her chest. "We should check with the clerk's office tomorrow to find out if they have any details on potential railroad routes through Van Buren."

"I agree."

"I'm so overwhelmed." Rebecca shook her hands. "I don't know what to do with myself."

Ben spun the ring on his finger. He moved two stumps closer together and sat, waiting for Rebecca to sit with him.

"Let's follow Levi's advice."

"Invite the Lord to sit with us." She offered a faint smile.

"When he offered that advice, he asked me to imagine my hard place in life." He flicked his thumb over the ring. "I pictured myself in a cave. Since then, I've made a habit of inviting the Lord into my cave."

"You sit with Him in a cave?"

"It symbolizes the difficult, dark moments in life." Ben rubbed the nail ring thoughtfully. "Levi said I should stay in the cave until the Lord moves. Then I should follow Him. Today, I realized it was time to leave the cave."

"Where did you go?"

"At first, I thought He might be leading me into the doctor's position Baas offered. I did invite Him into the moment as I followed Cordelia into the hotel, but I have no interest in the role Baas is offering." Ben shook his head, almost ruefully. "I didn't truly leave my cave until Ollie needed me to stitch him up."

"This whole idea of sitting with the Lord in hard places is working for you."

"You think so?"

"I do. You went straight from the hotel to setting bones at the wharf, then to rescuing Ollie and stitching him up."

"I can't claim I went to the wharf following the Lord. It wasn't even on my mind. I only went where summoned, hesitantly at that."

"Maybe that's part of it." Rebecca's gaze softened, a thoughtful crease forming above her brow. "It's about trusting He's there as you move forward and take the next action."

"This is a worthwhile moment to reflect on." Ben shut his eyes. "Lord, we invite You into these shadowy areas. We don't know what lies ahead in the coming days, but help us abide with You and move only when You move."

They sat in silence for a few moments, eyes closed. Ben opened one eye to peek at Rebecca, then shut it again. A rustling from the oak grove drew their attention. They stood to get a better view. As Rebecca moved closer, the sweet aroma of honeysuckle enveloped him. He shielded her with his body as she slipped her arm around his chest. The moonlight shimmered on a redhead.

"Am I seeing a Drake before me?" Ben summoned the most paternal tone he could muster.

"Apologies, Mr. Ewing." Hayden stepped out from the grove, rubbing his hands on his pants. "I saw Jace leave the forge door ajar, and Oscar managed to escape." The dog trailed closely behind. "I figured it was best to get him back since he's not yet strong enough to defend himself against other animals if he roams at night."

Rebecca rested her head against Ben's back, her hand pressing into him. He covered her hand with his, gently rubbing it with his thumb. He pinched the bridge of his nose with his other hand.

"I'll put him up and secure the door. Then I'll attempt to get my brothers to bed." Hayden scratched the back of his neck sheepishly. "I'm sure Mrs. Paulette will help. She's kinda taken with us, I think."

"Until morning, Hayden."

As the boy vanished into the forge, Ben and Rebecca laughed softly. He gazed into the grove, checking for anything hiding in the distance. A small light blinked on and off, tracing a path through the underbrush. He quietly indicated it to Rebecca.

"A firefly." She moved toward it, and he followed. "I've been watching this little fella for a few nights. I didn't make it out here last night. I missed him."

"You know, they flash to draw a mate's attention."

"I was unaware." She crept through the trees, crouching.

He crouched alongside her as they followed the twinkling firefly. "He will keep his little light shining until another firefly responds with its flickering light."

"Then what happens?" Rebecca turned, almost nose to nose with him. She gave a soft, self-conscious laugh.

Her breath stirred the air between them, light and warm. The fragrant aroma of honeysuckle muddled his thinking. His gaze dropped, lingering for half a heartbeat on her mouth. Pulse drumming, he ached to pull her nearer.

"No more flickering?" she whispered.

She was so close he could almost breathe her words. The night seemed to hold its breath with them.

"They drift into the moonlight"—his voice grew raspy—"and live happily ever after."

He grasped her hand, brushing his lips across her fingers. The brush of her skin against his jaw was featherlight, sending a shiver down his spine.

"I regret leaving you." He pressed his cheek against her hand. "I wanted to keep you safe. Protecting you has always been my only desire." His thoughts went fuzzy as her fingers traced along his neck. His hands trembled faintly, and his fingers enfolded hers, delaying her touch. His eyes locked onto hers. "I promise I will never leave you again. Ever."

She raised her chin to him. A shaky breath filled his lungs. He stood, lifting her to her feet and tucking her beneath his arm. He turned her toward Hogue House, willing his legs to move. It required all his willpower to resist getting lost in this moment.

"You are caught in the greatest battle of your life. I don't want to take advantage of your need for refuge from the challenge. I don't want you to doubt yourself—or me."

Chapter Forty

Rebecca tucked the final hairpin in place and retrieved the wooden box from under her bed. Cordelia remained covered in the opposite bed. Following her talk with Ben, Rebecca was okay with Cordelia sleeping in. It was best she didn't keep working at the hotel.

She lifted the box lid and removed her mother's journal. Initially, she had hesitated to read it, but interruptions had also played a part. Part of her was eager to uncover her mother's secrets to raising a family, while another feared she might not measure up to her mother's legacy. Mama always knew exactly what to say and do for her children.

She glided her fingers over the cover, snagging the edge. Her eyes shut, she inhaled deeply, and flipped to a random page. Upon opening her eyes, she trailed her finger down the page and halted at a name.

Benjamin Ewing.

Her breath hitched, and she glanced out the window. The sun dared to peek over the horizon into the oak grove, hinting at the coming changes. Change wasn't unfamiliar, was it? It had been woven into their lives for longer than she realized. Only it seemed more unsettling with Mama gone. She shifted her gaze back to the page.

> *Ben Ewing left for California today. While I understand his reasons, my heart aches for Rebecca. He thinks leaving is the way to provide a better life for her. I wish he could recognize she would be happy living simply and exploring the wilderness with him. But there's more. I sense he aims to discover the kind of man he is, to determine if he is worthy of her. Yet, I worry he may come to know more about who he is not rather than gaining insight into his true self. As a mother, I feel helpless. I have no remedy to mend her shattered heart, no sacred words to soothe her wound. Frequently, I find my role is limited to listening, providing comfort, and praying. I teach them and minister to their hearts as I can, but ultimately, I must place them in the Lord's care.*

Rebecca tucked the journal back into its box under her bed. Maybe she resembled her mother more than she realized. Mama's secrets were straightforward. Listening, offering comfort, praying, and entrusting her children to God's care. These were all things her children could do as well.

If only Mama could witness Ben's growth under Levi's mentorship. Ben now recognized he needed to partner with her regarding Baas's influence on Cordelia. He took the lead in inviting Jesus into their situation through prayer. His restraint and patience in the grove were remarkable. Her breath quickened at the memory of his closeness. He exemplified more patience than she possessed. With prayerfulness, partnership, and patience, what more could a woman desire in a man?

Rebecca came down the front stairs, Viv stopping her before she could get out the door.

Viv. Her coy words with Ben hadn't been forgotten. They lodged somewhere in Rebecca's ribs, stubborn and unshakable.

Don't do anything I wouldn't do.

But Ben hadn't taken up the banter. Perhaps there was nothing to worry about. Even so, she didn't like it.

"Rebecca, you didn't come down for breakfast." Viv twirled a dark curl behind her ear. "Can you let Ben know Edie asked about a gift for your sister? Something about a silhouette portrait?"

"Oh, yes." Rebecca winced. "Unexpected things keep popping up. Let her know we'll try to get to it tonight. And please tell Paulette and Judy how much we appreciate them watching the younger children and taking care of Ollie. We're trying to protect them from gossip."

"Of course." Viv nodded her assurance.

Rebecca met Ben outside the stable, where he had their horses ready to go. Together, they rode to the court clerk's office and went inside to inquire about possible railroad routes. One proposed line ran very close to Bradley House, but Hogue House sat several blocks away. They thanked the clerk and set on their way.

"Gray's Café is around the corner. Do you want to visit Simon while I speak to Mrs. Gray? If I speak with her alone, she might be more forthcoming with information." Rebecca smiled faintly, steeling herself for the task ahead.

"It sounds like a good plan. Do you want to meet back here?"

"In about half an hour?"

Ben agreed and they headed in opposite directions. Rebecca went to the back door of Gray's Café and knocked. She could hear light chatter, clanging dishes, and the patter of feet. No one came to the door.

She banged again. "Open up. It's not the livery cat."

Annetta Gray yanked the door open. "My goodness, aren't we making quite the habit? If you'd like to be seated, go around the front and seat yourself."

"Mrs. Gray, I need to ask you some questions about Ambrose

Baas."

Annetta came out and shut the door behind her. "What makes you think I know anything about Mr. Baas?"

"You warned me about him the day we had lunch together. Why?"

"I don't trust anyone new in town. You know that, dearie."

"Mrs. Gray, has he made an offer on your café?"

"He threatened my George. It was a veiled threat, but a threat nonetheless." Mrs. Gray wiped her hands on her apron. "He intends to own all eating establishments in town, so his passengers have the best dining. Said it would be terrible if we fell on hard times because one of us was injured in an accident of some sort. Perhaps fishing. We ain't had fish at the café since."

"Mrs. Gray, would you be willing to tell Nicholas? He's been deputized by the sheriff."

"Oh, dearie, no." Mrs. Gray wiped her apron again. "You would have to gather a crowd of business owners before I would cross Ambrose Baas. I've heard he's in league with the Cutter-Doyle gang. Don't know if it's true or not."

"But Mrs. Gray, we have to stand up to him."

"So he aims to have your boardinghouse too? I suspected as much." Mrs. Gray rubbed her ear. "I knew when poor Sarah said this Caine fella was ousting the Bradley House women, he must work for Baas, and he'd be coming for you and yourn next. I've got to get back inside, but you be careful, dearie." She slipped inside the door.

Rebecca scanned her surroundings, paranoia creeping up her spine. Every time Baas had approached her in town, he had been undetectably quiet. All clear.

She crossed the street on the backside of Gray's and rounded the corner to the saddlery. Ambrose Baas stepped out of the attached livery. He gripped her by the arm.

"Miss Hogue, our saddler isn't in today. It seems he has a

special prisoner in jail." He backed her into the shadows of the livery's awning. He leaned close, breath hot on her ear. "You shouldn't have taken in those Bradley House women. Don't think the income they provide will save you."

"I know you're trying to buy property along the possible railroad routes." She forced an unnatural calm in her voice, though her heart pounded in her ears. "Hogue House isn't on any of those routes. It's a waste of your time and money."

"I want Hogue House for the sport of it. It's a little matter of payback." He let his fingers trail lightly along her collarbone. A casual gesture, almost absent-minded, yet too familiar. "It's too bad Cordelia couldn't perform in my hotel today. Her melodious tunes soothe my mood. I find I'm a bit more irritable than usual. And while I'm thinking of it, where is the good doctor?"

"Stay away from my family and our boardinghouse."

"I expect to see your sister at the piano before the evening meal. I think my guests would quite enjoy an evening performance." Baas squeezed her face and turned loose, disappearing in the shadows behind the livery.

Rebecca slid to the ground, shaking. She steadied her breath and leaned into the building to pull herself up. Then she hurried beyond the courthouse to the jail. She entered, shut the door, and pressed herself against it. Three men stared back at her.

"Rebecca?" Nicholas rounded the desk, but she held up her hand.

She pressed her eyes shut and swallowed tears, setting her composure before speaking. "Don't come any closer. I do not need your help."

Opening her eyes, she pressed her hand down her skirt. Ben sat on a stool outside Simon's cell. She joined him without so much as a glance back at Nicholas. Ben rose and motioned for her to sit.

"You look pale. What happened?"

Lord, I'm drowning. If only I could sense Your presence now. Something within her quieted.

"It's Baas. He wants Cordelia to play this evening."

"Did he say what he'll do if she doesn't come?"

"No, but he asked where you were." She couldn't keep her breath from shaking as she spoke.

"Nicholas, you've got to let me out of here." Simon stood, gripping the bars of his cell. "My family is in trouble."

"I'm sorry, Simon." Nicholas lowered his gaze, voice tight. "My hands are tied."

Ben's eyebrows furrowed. "Simon, we need to know about the man who stabbed Ollie."

"Someone stabbed Ollie?" Nicholas rubbed the back of his neck, his voice cracking slightly. A heavy silence fell over the jail office.

"The man you claim was murdered." Rebecca glared at him.

"Aw, Rebecca." Nicholas pounded his fist. "I can't hear this. Retaliation is a motive. I'm stepping outside. I'll come back in when this conversation is over."

"I'm so sorry, Simon." Rebecca's eyes widened. "I didn't think."

"It's okay. What do you need to know?"

"I charged the wharfie, knocking him down." Ben glanced at Rebecca, then returned his attention to Simon. "Then I struck him until I knocked him out. I landed three right hooks."

"I was otherwise occupied and didn't catch all of that. But I knew you put him out of commission." Simon crossed his arms.

"When Ollie and I left you, he was down. Still unconscious. Did he regain consciousness while you fought the dark-haired man?"

"No. But the dark-haired fella told Nicholas I stabbed both of them. He said he got away, but his friend didn't. Only I never took my knife out."

"We think the man you fought is Isom Caine. He's the man

who took Bradley House. Is it possible he could have taken your knife while you struggled? How did the fight end?"

"He might have. When you left, we were circling. Then he launched at me, and we scuffled for several minutes. Then suddenly, he broke off and ran for the trees. I was worried about Ollie, so I didn't give chase."

"He probably waited until he was sure you were gone and doubled back." Rebecca rubbed her hands together. "We've got to figure out how to implicate Baas and Caine in all this."

Chapter Forty-One

Ben adjusted his collar as he and Rebecca stepped off the packed dirt road and onto the boardwalk bordering the courthouse square. The sun beat down, glinting off the windows as a wagon creaked by.

"You probably don't want to hear this." Ben ran his hand through his hair. "But the telescope may be connected to everything."

Rebecca bit her lip. "What makes you say that?"

"Cason said the shadowy figure he saw was tall and thin. Maybe Caine." Ben tapped his fist against his mouth. "Hayden mentioned their father works for a man searching for his son, and the son wants a train. What if Horn's passenger with the spyglass is that man?

Rebecca fanned away a little puff of dust as they approached the square. "If the son is Baas, do we even want to find the owner of the spyglass?"

"Rebecca. Ben." Eliza Dawn waved, hurrying toward them. "What brings you to the courthouse?"

"Research." Rebecca flicked her fingers in a loose wave. "You?"

"Picking up notices for the newspaper. Slow news day, aside from people claiming they've seen Billy Kinder. Not exactly print-worthy without proof." Eliza Dawn tapped her notepad. "Need help?"

"We're trying to eliminate our last lead on the spyglass." Rebecca exchanged a glance with Ben. "There was a couple on Captain Horn's boat. The husband had a spyglass, pointing out landmarks to his wife."

"Not that the description helped much." Ben shook his head. "Bulbous nose. Chatty wife."

Eliza Dawn's face lit up. "I know exactly where they are."

Rebecca blinked. "How is that possible?"

Eliza Dawn laughed, brushing a hand across her middle as if steadying herself. "I guess I have a knack for being in the right place at the right time lately. I stopped by the mercantile to check on your candle sales." Eliza Dawn grinned, tapping her temple. "The couple you're describing was there. The wife fawned over your candles. They might be there even now."

Rebecca grabbed Eliza Dawn and kissed her cheek. "You're the best."

She and Ben rushed to their horses and galloped up Main Street, catching the couple as they stepped out of the mercantile.

"Pardon me, sir." Ben stepped forward. "Were you passengers on the *Coffee No. 7* last week? Do you happen to own an H.V. Laun spyglass?"

"Ah, another spyglass enthusiast." The man smiled, smoothing his lapels. "I own two."

"Did you lose one?"

"Afraid not. I have one in my pocket. The other is on loan."

Ben's shoulders slumped. He wiped his brow and glanced at Rebecca.

"Sir, would you mind?" Ben held out the telescope. "Perhaps you'll notice something we missed."

"Gladly." The man took the spyglass from Ben and turned it over carefully, frowning at the tiny initials carved into the lens cap. His expression tightened. "Where did you find this?"

"My brother found it near the riverfront." Rebecca pointed.

"These initials, M.E.T." He pointed to the letters. "Marsden Emery Talbot."

Ben's brow furrowed, and he shook his head. "Anthony Danville mentioned meeting a couple. Their name was Tal-something. This is yours?"

Mr. Talbot's face shadowed. "In a sense. May we speak privately?"

"You can follow us to my family's boardinghouse." Rebecca gestured up the street.

The Talbots climbed into their carriage and followed them up Cane Hill. At the boardinghouse, Rebecca slipped inside, quietly asking Paulette and Martie to keep everyone out of the forge a while. She returned with a water pitcher, tin cups, paper, and a pencil.

Inside the old forge, Ben placed the spyglass on the table. "So this belonged to you?"

"I entrusted it to a man named Calvin Drake." Mr. Talbot picked up the spyglass, extending the sections. "We've been searching for my wife's son. Her estranged son."

Mrs. Talbot laid a hand gently on his arm. "It wasn't your fault, dear. My son didn't have much guidance growing up. You could have given him everything, but he needed more than we could offer."

Mr. Talbot sighed. "When he started making reckless decisions, I hired Mr. Drake to track his movements. We've been following his trail ever since. The last word we received said Drake was headed here."

"Your stepson is Ambrose Baas?" Ben's hands pressed into the table.

"I am sorry to say he is." Mr. Talbot dropped his gaze. "I

backed out of supporting his steamboat venture after Captain Hogue dismissed him for dishonorable conduct."

Mrs. Talbot dabbed at the corner of her eye with a handkerchief.

"We never dreamed he would spiral like this." Mr. Talbot spoke in hushed tones. "Pushing the railroad schemes, targeting businesses."

Rebecca poured water into the tin cups, passing one to Mrs. Talbot. "You are awaiting another message from Drake."

"We were." Mrs. Talbot folded her hands tightly.

Mr. Talbot twisted the spyglass again, then frowned. "It's missing."

Ben tapped the table. "The coded message isn't in the telescope anymore. But we have it."

Ben withdrew the slip of paper and slid it across. Mr. Talbot took a piece of paper from his vest pocket, studied both, then scribbled quickly on the blank sheet.

At last, he pushed the translated message toward them:

Baas secured three properties on Van Buren Main Street. One by coin, two under pressure. Pushing harder before rail plans go public.

Hogue House not on route, but he wants it. And her. Not for profit. For payback.

Watch for his second, I. Caine. Tall, thin, coal black hair, butchered haircut. Always in the shadows and twice as cruel.

—C.D.

Ben stared at the message, the pieces aligning at last. Calvin Drake had been hired to track Baas. The spyglass passed through him. The Talbots were Baas's family. And the coded note, hidden in the lens, confirmed it all. Baas had pressured two landowners into selling and bought another outright, just ahead of the railroad announcement. He wasn't after Hogue House for profit. He wanted it for retribution. For legacy. The whole trail—Drake to Talbot to Baas to the railroad—now formed a single, unbroken line.

Before Rebecca could react, Martie burst through the door.

"Rebecca! We can't find Edie and Jace. They went out back earlier to climb trees, and now they're gone."

Paulette rushed in behind her, wringing her hands. "I should've let the twins go with them. I thought they needed to finish chores first. I ..." Her voice broke.

Ben was already moving, grabbing his hat. "I'll find Nicholas."

Rebecca nodded. *Lord, please let them be nearby. Let this be nothing more than childhood mischief.* Still, her mind spun through worst-case scenarios.

REBECCA SCANNED THE GROVE, her skirts brushing against the grass as she moved. Where would Edie go? What tree would she think perfect for climbing? The fireflies flickered in the early dusk, the grove bathed in soft, silvery light. It should have been comforting. Instead, their restless dance kindled unease, flashing like frantic warning lights as the shadows stretched, long and menacing.

She moved toward the clearing where she had sat with Ben just days ago. He'd seen a shadow that night, a boxy figure moving among the trees.

Could it have been Baas?

She pushed aside a low-hanging branch and gasped.

At the base of a tall tree, Edie's book lay abandoned across gnarled roots. She darted forward, scooping it up, and froze.

A rough hand clamped over her mouth. Another arm pinned her against a broad chest.

"Hush, now." A low voice rasped. "Not a peep."

Terror exploded through her, but she forced herself to steady.

Breathing deeply, she recalled the words from her mother's journal. Listen. Comfort. Pray. Trust.

The man's breath was hot against her ear.

"I never meant to hurt your family. I've tried to watch over you."

His grip shifted slightly, loosening against her mouth.

She twisted her head but couldn't get a glimpse of her captor. "Where are Edie and Jace?"

"I'd never hurt Edie." The voice was thick with emotion. "That little girl's gonna carry enough hurt without her mama."

"Why are you here?"

"To help. Maybe to ease the burden of my sins." Essence of peppermint did little to mask his smelly breath. "I paid your feed bill."

Rebecca blinked, confused. The words didn't make sense. Not here. Not like this. Who would ease her burden this way? And why now?

Her voice dropped. "What are you trying to repay?"

The man didn't answer at first. His breath hitched. "There are things you can't take back. But sometimes—sometimes you try to tip the scale. Even just a little."

Rebecca stiffened. Her heart pounding, a chill crept through her bones. Her thoughts snapped back. "Edie and Jace. Do you know where they are?"

"Caine took them. He's bad. Been huntin' those Drake boys, tryin' to get at their Pa."

"You know Mr. Drake?"

"He's in hiding." The man's arm tightened. "Stay still."

"My foot's falling asleep." Her voice came out hoarse. "Pins and needles."

He let her shift ever so slightly.

"Where are Edie and Jace?" she whispered.

"Caine's got 'em in the old shack on the bluff. Root cellar underneath. Caine and one other fella."

Rebecca closed her eyes. "You're risking a great deal by telling me this."

"Don't seem right, leavin' it undone." There was something heartbreakingly familiar about the voice. "I owe your ma."

There it was. Confirmation. She could trust the information he gave her. She inhaled.

"Nicholas is deputized. He can help us get them back."

"No. Don't leave Simon unguarded. I can't protect him if Nicholas leaves the jail."

Rebecca nodded slowly.

"You trust me to keep my eyes shut?"

"Yes." He released her. She heard him step back, footsteps crunching on the leaves.

She whispered into the darkness, "Billy."

The footsteps paused.

"I know you didn't mean to kill Mama." Tears slid silently down her cheeks. "I forgive you."

A soft sound, half-sob, half-sigh. Then the leaves rustled as he fled into the falling night.

Rebecca pressed Edie's book to her chest and ran. They had to save the children. And time was running out.

Chapter Forty-Two

Rebecca drew Truly to a halt beneath the trees near the bluff, her heart pounding. They had picked their way slowly through the woods, each hoof step muffled by pine needles and packed earth. She slid the shutter over the face of her lantern, burying the flame. The old shack with a slanted roof and warped walls loomed ahead, Edie and Jace imprisoned in its cellar.

"Should we wait for Drake?" Rebecca whispered.

"I wish you'd let Nicholas join us." Ben rubbed the back of his neck, his voice tight. "I don't like this. Two against one, and I'm not sure I'm fit for these odds."

"If Baas has ties to the Cutter-Doyle gang, I can't risk Simon being unguarded." Nausea rolled in her gut as she secured the lantern and dismounted. "I'm only okay leaving the boardinghouse because Paulette fetched Levi."

"Thank heaven she did." Ben's voice was low and rough as he dismounted. "If Levi hadn't been there, those Drake brothers would have followed us here. I don't know what he said, but it worked." Tightness pulled at his chest as he thought of Sean's siblings, hiding in the shadows. "They were determined to save their brother."

"Siblings may not always see eye to eye, but they can be fierce protectors."

"And this messenger?" Ben's eyes narrowed. "How do you know he can be trusted?"

"I can't say without putting him in danger." Rebecca pulled her journal from her pocket, clutching it to her chest. Mama's lessons. Listen. Comfort. Pray. Trust. She repeated them silently. "There will come a day when I can tell you everything."

Ben twirled the nail around his finger. "We'll give Drake ten more minutes. Then we move."

Rebecca nodded, her jaw taut. She slid the fishhooks from the journal, wedging them between her fingers. In the distance, the small shack gave no sign of life, except two lanterns hanging from a post on either side of the door. Beyond it, a dim shape moved near the bluff's edge.

Ben stiffened, his empty hands curling into fists. "There. Tall, lean. I think that's Caine."

A second figure lurked in the shadows closer to the shack. Rebecca's stomach turned. "There's another. Between us and the cellar."

Ben's jaw flexed. "We'll circle wide. I'll draw their attention. You get the children."

With a roar, Ben exploded from the trees and charged toward Caine. They collided in a flurry of limbs and fists. Caine grunted, staggering under the force. But the guard didn't draw off.

Rebecca sprinted toward the shack, darting behind the rain barrel. The guard spun and followed her. She held her breath as he crept closer. Baas stepped from the shadows, his eyes fixed on Ben and Caine. The guard hesitated, distracted.

Rebecca's knuckles tightened around the fishhooks. She'd only ever used them for fishing. But she had to reach the children. Lunging, she raked the fishhooks across his face. He bellowed, grabbing for her wrist. She spun, wrenching free, then thrust her elbow backward into his abdomen. As he stumbled, he reached for her hair.

A crack split the air. The guard collapsed without a sound, blood blooming beneath him. Rebecca stared, breath caught. Crawling low, she made for the cellar.

"Going somewhere, Miss Hogue?" Baas moved toward her, revolver raised, eyes trained on her.

Slowly, she turned. Baas had saved her.

No.

Claimed her.

Edie and Jace's muffled cries set her heart on edge.

Rebecca rose to her feet, fishhooks nestled between her knuckles. Her toes edged backward, drawing Baas away from the shack and closer to the bluff's edge.

"Come now, darling." He sneered, step by step closing the gap. "No one needs to get hurt."

"Don't you know?" Rebecca's jaw clenched as her fingers flexed. Her voice was steady, even bold, as she circled, edging closer to Caine and Ben. "I don't cooperate with bullies."

Baas lunged.

She sidestepped, diving low, and drove the hooks deep into his forearm. He howled, blood dotting his sleeve. Pain slowed him, his movements turning sluggish and uncertain.

Ben swung hard, catching Caine squarely. Caine staggered, but as he twisted, light glinted off the blade in his hand. Rebecca's breath caught as he lunged toward Ben, thrusting twice. Ben growled in pain. Rebecca's eyes darted from Ben to Baas as she tried to stay out of Baas's reach.

"Ben. Ben, talk to me." She dodged as Baas came at her, his steps uneven, his reach off-target.

"Move." Ben barked. Then, gripping his shoulder, he rammed into Caine. Together they barreled into Baas as Rebecca leaped out of the way. All three men tumbled over the bluff, disappearing into the darkness.

"Ben!" Rebecca dropped to her knees, scrambling to the cliff's edge.

Below, Ben clung to a narrow ledge with one hand, holding Baas with the other.

"Let him go!" Panic clawed her throat.

"I can't." Ben strained. "He'll die."

Rebecca worked her fingers down the cliff face, barely grazing his. She choked on a breath.

Lord, please. I won't lose him too.

It wasn't only Ben's life slipping through her fingers. It was everything she hadn't known how to hold before. She edged forward, desperation tightening her grip. She pulled with all her strength, but it wasn't enough. Ben's fingers slipped.

"Don't let go, Ben." She tightened her grip. "I won't let you go again."

Then hands. Another pair, gritty and scarred, reached out from beside her and locked around Ben's arm.

"I'll get them." The voice was low. "But we've got to move."

Billy Kinder.

Together, they hauled up Ben and Baas, their bodies bumping and scraping the rock face. They collapsed, gasping. Baas clutched his bleeding arm while Ben dragged himself upright. Kinder rose, disappearing into the shadows.

"Are you hurt?" Ben brushed Rebecca's hair from her eyes.

"Me?" She glimpsed his shoulder and thigh. "You're bleeding."

"It's fine." He tried to rise. "Where are the children?"

"I'll get them." Rebecca squeezed his hand. "Rest."

A man jogged toward her, a rifle slung over one shoulder. She froze. He raised his hands in the air. "You all right, ma'am?"

"Drake?" Her voice cracked.

"I am." He touched the brim of his hat. "Let's get those kids."

Rebecca nodded and led the way. At the cellar, she flung the door open. "Edie! Jace!"

Two tear-streaked faces peered up from the dark. They flew into her arms, sobbing. She wrapped them tightly, murmuring prayers of thanks. A moment later, Drake crouched beside them. Jace froze, then launched into his father's arms.

"Pa!"

"I've got you, buddy. I've got you now." Drake lifted him high, hugging him fiercely. "I found Baas's horse in the trees." He cradled Jace. "I'll take him to the jail." He turned to Ben. "Caine?"

"Gone. Over the edge." Ben's voice graveled. "Didn't resurface."

Rebecca's throat tightened. "Then we can't clear Simon. No one can testify—"

"Kinder wanted to give you this." Drake pressed a piece of paper into her palm. "A witness statement signed by him. Along with information I can provide, we should be able to clear Simon's name." Then Drake let Jace slide off his lap and went to secure Baas, leading him to the horses.

Rebecca's knees nearly buckled. She pressed the paper to her chest. "Thank the Lord."

She eased herself under Ben's arm, helping him stand. He managed a wobbly smile as he leaned on her. His eyes shone weary but bright from a dirt-smudged face, and blood stains dotted his shirt and pants.

Edie wiggled her way under Ben's other arm. "You look plain awful, Dr. Ewing."

He chuckled. "I *feel* awful."

"Don't worry." Edie grinned. "Rebecca will take care of you, and I'll help."

Rebecca took Drake's place. "You held on."

He leaned close to her ear. "I told you, I'm not leaving again. Not when I've finally found home."

Somewhere nearby, a firefly lit the shadows. Rebecca glanced at the children. At Ben. At the trail of light winding into the trees like a question not yet answered. Some stories weren't finished. And this night wasn't through with them yet.

Chapter Forty-Three

The lamps along the jailhouse boardwalk flickered against the late hour, casting trembling shadows across the dirt-packed street. Most of Van Buren had gone quiet, but not the dear souls gathered near the jail. Rebecca sat beside Ben on the bench outside, his wounds bandaged but in need of stitching. They had stopped by Hogue House to drop off Edie and Jace with Paulette, but Ben insisted on coming with Rebecca to gain Simon's release.

Rebecca glanced down the boardwalk where Ivajohn, Cordelia, and Martie sat on another bench on the other side of the jailhouse entrance. She let her head drop back against the wall, her gaze skyward, as she crossed her arms and sighed. Patting her knees, she stood and paced to the end of the boardwalk. Around the corner, Baas sat slumped against the side of the building with Levi standing guard over him.

She turned back to Ben. "I don't understand what's taking so long." Rebecca paced. "They've been in there over an hour."

Ben tugged at her fingers. "Sit down. You're wearing me out."

She sat, cradling his face in her hands. "Why didn't you stay at Hogue House? These wounds need more than bandages. And you need rest." She bit her lip. "I had forgotten how stubborn you could be."

"I want to go home." He shifted uncomfortably. "But it's not home without my family. The whole family."

Down the boardwalk, Mrs. Pratt arrived and stopped to talk to the three sisters. Their restrained voices seemed more fitting of a graveside service than a much-anticipated homecoming. Mrs. Pratt leaned in, hugging Cordelia.

"Have you spoken to her?" Ben's gaze followed Rebecca's as his thumb brushed lightly over her knuckles, grounding her.

"Not yet." She sighed. "I dropped Edie and Jace off with Paulette. Then I asked Levi to come and guard Baas. I couldn't stand the thought of him being inside the jail with Simon. The whole town thinking Nicholas had two criminals locked away." She shook her head. "It needs to be a clean line when his name is cleared. Simon comes out. Baas goes in."

"Be patient. They'll get it sorted." Ben squeezed her hand. "You should talk to her."

"It can wait."

Ben tugged her chin toward him. "I meant what I said. When we're finished here, we all go home—as family. Now go."

"Stubborn."

"You're one to talk." He gave her a nudge as she stood, and she swatted his hand away.

Rebecca walked down the boardwalk. "Excuse me, ladies, could I have a moment with Cordelia?"

"Of course, dear." Mrs. Pratt gave her shoulder a squeeze and leaned in to whisper, "Lead with grace, dear. You'll be fine."

Rebecca pressed a smile. "Thank you, Mrs. Pratt."

Rebecca sat next to Cordelia, folding her hands in her lap. A few straggling passersby glanced their way, but Rebecca kept her eyes forward, unflinching. *Just breathe*, she coached herself, unsure of how to begin.

Cordelia stared into nothingness. Then she spoke, her voice raw. "Rebecca, I … I didn't know. Everything turned upside down and it's my fault."

"It's not your fault." Rebecca grimaced. "This was coming to our doorstep no matter what. It's progress."

"I think …" Cordelia paused. "I think I've been jealous of you. You're so much like Mama, the way you care for everyone. I could never fill her shoes. Never be enough." Her voice cracked over the word "enough."

The ache in Rebecca's chest swelled. She took Cordelia's hand.

"You're not meant to be Mama. No more than I am." Her voice stayed steady, even as her throat tightened. "She wouldn't have wanted that."

Cordelia blinked hard, struggling.

"Mama would want us to grow into our own shoes." Rebecca smiled faintly through the sting in her chest. "Find the truest version of yourself and be her. Be fully her, and it will be enough."

Cordelia gave a shaky laugh. "That sounds like something Mama would've said."

"She did. To herself." Rebecca squeezed Cordelia's hand. "In her journal. We should read it together when we get home. Her words aren't for me alone."

"Maybe I'm ready to walk in my own shoes." Cordelia focused on her hands, inhaling slowly, then lifted her chin. "It's time I stop trying to be someone I'm not."

Tears spilled down Cordelia's cheeks. Rebecca pulled her into a fierce hug, holding on tightly as the lanterns glowed warmly along the street. Rebecca cradled Cordelia against her shoulder and kissed the top of her head.

Mr. Mooney, Caroline, Mrs. Gray, and Eliza Dawn joined Ben at the opposite end of the boardwalk. Rebecca signaled Mrs. Pratt and the sisters to remain with Cordelia. Then she turned and crossed to the end where the others stood. As she approached, Eliza Dawn wrapped her in a hug.

"Thank goodness you're all right. Oh, I'm all teary-eyed. I don't know what's come over me." Eliza Dawn dabbed at the corner of her eye, then lifted the notepad hanging from the string over her shoulder. "Fine reporter, I am."

Rebecca smiled, a glimmer of understanding lighting in her chest. Eliza Dawn's emotions were about more than the drama of the past few days. There was a hint of new beginnings in the air, and Rebecca would hold them close to her heart for now.

Before she could respond, Mr. Mooney shifted.

"There's news." He glanced at the others. "Some of the town's leaders are meeting right now to organize a formal railroad company. Decided it wasn't safe to wait in light of recent events." He raked his teeth over his lips. "The Little Rock and Fort Smith Railroad. They're setting it up and moving ahead, whether we like it or not."

Mrs. Gray folded her arms tightly. "I hope they remember folks like us when they lay their tracks. Baas nearly crushed my family in the name of progress."

"At least now it's in the open." Caroline folded her hands primly. "Perhaps it will make coercion and underhandedness more difficult."

"I agree." Mr. Mooney squeezed her hands. "It's a chance for honest men to be part of it. Done right, it could be a blessing instead of dividing the town."

Rebecca blew out a slow breath. "We've seen what ambition without conscience can do. We'll pray they move forward with wisdom. In the meantime, we'll hold fast to hope."

The jailhouse door creaked open, and Nicholas stepped outside, followed by Drake. Nicholas held up a piece of paper, unfolding it. "This alone is enough to clear Simon. Drake gave a statement as well. Air tight. I'll keep these documents safe until the sheriff's return."

Drake patted Ben on the back. "He's cleared. It's over."

Nicholas's eyes met Rebecca's. The soft dip of his chin and the tenderness in his eyes landed like a mixture of apology and acceptance, a man attempting to right something that could never be fully mended. Rebecca's throat tightened, but she offered a faint nod, her fingers curling against her skirt, anchoring herself. Then, without another word, Nicholas turned and stepped back inside.

Moments later, Simon stepped into the lantern glow, a free man.

"Simon." Rebecca folded him into her arms, pressing her cheek to his. She stepped back to give him space, though one hand stayed anchored to his sleeve.

Simon met Ben's gaze. An almost imperceptible nod passed between them, some language between men Rebecca couldn't fully comprehend, but knew it was forged in hardship, sealed in faith. Rebecca gripped Simon's hand one last time, her heart thick with gratitude and ache all at once.

They had survived the shadows. Together.

"Billy Kinder signed the witness statement that set me free." Simon rubbed his neck as if trying to shake off the confusion lodged within.

"I know." Rebecca's voice was low and steady. The ache behind his question tugged at her, and she wished she had an answer that would hold.

"He was right there, and the three of you didn't bring him in?"

"He saved Ben's life." Rebecca's hands curled into balls at her sides. "He saved Edie. We wouldn't have known where to find the children without him."

"It doesn't make sense." Simon glanced away, jaw tight. "He killed Ma, Rebecca. And then he saved Edie, a child. How am I supposed to carry both?"

He paused.

"I'll find him. If it's the last thing I do, I'll find him."

Rebecca let go. She blinked against the sting in her eyes as Levi rounded the corner with Ambrose Baas. Drake joined Levi in quick strides as Baas shuffled forward, bitterness etched into the lines on his face.

A slight tremor passed through the group as a woman stepped from the shadows, gray hair braided and looped neatly, eyes pinned to Baas with trembling restraint. Her husband steadied her with a hand on her back.

"Ambrose." One word. Spoken softly, without accusation. Without pity. A name spoken like a wound.

Baas faltered mid-step. The shift in his posture was unmistakable, though he didn't look up. A man who had once been someone's son.

Baas lingered, eyes pressed shut. Slowly, he unfettered his eyes, lingering on his mother's expression. A sorrowful, wordless disappointment scrawled across her face, but in the deep lines, something softer. A mother's undying love. Baas's breath stilled.

"You had a choice, son." She touched his hand lightly and he glanced away. "You always did."

Baas's jaw clenched. His gaze drifted to Rebecca and his eyes softened as though a veil lifted. The shadow of storm clouds rolled away and something clearer took its place. Rebecca couldn't name it. Regret? Sorrow? The unraveling of pride? A man aching for redemption? Whatever it was, it was the first crack in his façade and Rebecca wondered if healing might find him too.

Levi urged him forward.

Nicholas emerged with irons.

"Ambrose Baas, you're under arrest for crimes of coercion, property fraud, and attempted kidnapping," Nicholas said, loud enough for any passersby to hear. He ushered the man inside, slamming the door behind them.

Ben rose and grunted, swaying slightly, and Rebecca quickly slid beneath his arm.

She paused. "What are you doing?"

"I'm going in. I have questions." He gritted his teeth as she helped him inside.

Nicholas nudged Baas into the cell and the door clanged shut with finality. Baas sat on the cot's edge, unflinching, elbows on his knees. He fixed his eyes on the floorboards. Ben and Rebecca stood just beyond the bars with a lingering need to understand.

"Why the children?"

Baas lifted his eyes, the fire replaced by something hollow. "You think I planned all that?" He dragged a thick hand down his face. "Caine was a spark thrown too close to kindling."

"You gave him the match."

A muscle in Baas's jaw jumped. "He took it further than I intended. I guess I turned a blind eye one too many times."

Silence stretched.

Ben and Rebecca turned to leave.

"Rebecca ..." Baas's voice faltered and Rebecca paused. "I never meant to harm the children. I only wanted what Hogue owed me."

Her jaw tightened, but she didn't look back. She heard the plea in his voice, but not every wound was hers to tend. Some healing belonged to Jesus alone. She walked out the door with Ben, letting it close behind them.

Ben squeezed her hand and whispered, "Home."

She nodded, her throat tight, a silent prayer of thanksgiving stirring in her chest. "Home."

Hogue House waited, along with the work of mending. No fireflies tonight. Only lanterns flickering in the dark. And somehow, enough light to find their way home.

Chapter Forty-Four

The sun peeked over the horizon, the long night finally coming to an end as Ben slid from the saddle, muscles aching, with Simon there to steady him. The Drake boys spilled into the boardinghouse yard to greet their father with Oscar's tail wagging in the background. A weight lifted from Ben's chest. Four brothers, all safe with their pa. He slumped onto a barrel outside the stable, images of Sean and his siblings filling his thoughts.

The Hogues flooded around Simon, all talking at once and sharing warm embraces, laughter, and tears. Ben closed his eyes as he leaned against the stable wall and smiled, the sun warm on his face. After years of wandering in darkness, the light broke, and he could breathe again.

Martie rushed to the fence. "Justin and Pa are coming!"

A whoop went up. Rebecca pressed her hand to her heart, meeting Ben's gaze. She pushed through the throng of siblings toward him. As she passed Levi, she tapped him, motioning to Ben. Levi disappeared into the house.

"You." She poked Ben's chest gently. "Come with me."

He chuckled under his breath. "You always were a little bossy."

"For your own good." She teased, tugging him gently into the forge.

Levi returned with Simon and Eliza Dawn, both carrying supplies. Rebecca covered the forge worktable with a clean sheet. The faint tang of iron clung to the wood beneath it, a quiet reminder that this was a place for shaping what had been broken and forging something new. Levi and Simon helped Ben up before Simon took his station at the door, keeping the rest of the world at bay. Eliza Dawn lingered in the sitting area for propriety's sake.

Rebecca washed her hands and gathered the items she needed from a small medical satchel. Ben stripped off his shirt and grimaced as Levi helped him lie back. Eliza Dawn respectfully turned her back, keeping her distance as Levi cut the pant leg away just above the injury.

Rebecca drew a sharp breath at the sight of the gash. Ben's gaze followed hers to the wound, angry and red, but not dangerously deep. Her cool, steady fingers traced his skin.

"This will hurt."

"Hurts already." He smiled weakly.

She cleaned the wound, then threaded her needle and began stitching, the bright laughter of children beyond the door keeping him afloat. It was time to shine light upon the remaining darkness between them.

"Becca."

"Mm?"

"About California."

Rebecca waited.

"I killed a man." Ben's voice was low and rough.

Her hands paused, then resumed sewing. "You told me about Sean."

"He died in my arms." Ben closed his eyes. "But I never told you"—he took a shaky breath—"I killed the man who murdered him."

His eyes found hers, shadowed and worn.

"I was protecting Sean's brothers and sister, but it was more than that." The ache knotted at his throat. "I was furious. At the man. At myself. At God. I was overtaken by darkness. I stopped believing the light could find me."

Rebecca continued to work in silence.

"I promised Sean I would send his siblings to their aunt in the east. I sold everything I had to get those children to safety. I had nothing left to return home to you."

Rebecca knotted the first wound carefully and lowered her gaze to the cut fabric along his thigh. She hesitated. Her hands trembled momentarily, then steadied. Levi helped roll Ben onto his side so she could reach the wound more easily.

"If you hadn't gone"—she tugged the needle gently—"you wouldn't have saved Sean's siblings. And if I had been with you in California, I wouldn't have been at Mama's side when she died."

His breath caught.

"God knew." She met his gaze. "He knew where we needed to be. I can see that now."

His hand fisted on the table beside him as she stitched in silence until the final knot was tied.

"You're home, Ben." She smoothed her hand over his shoulder. "With family."

He captured her hand, pressing it to his chest. She leaned closer, eyes shining, and brushed the curls from his forehead. His breath tangled with hers as lips lightly brushed lips.

He hadn't planned to kiss her.

He just did.

Soft, hesitant. More whisper than assurance, more ache than resolution.

Everything stood still. Then he lifted his gaze, studying her expression. She didn't retreat. Her hand stayed pressed against his heart. And somehow, it was enough.

Another round of cheers went up in the yard, and Justin entered the forge.

"Sheesh, Doc. I guess the fallout was a little worse than I anticipated." Justin glanced from Ben to Rebecca. "I hope she didn't hurt you too bad."

Ben opened his mouth, but Simon slipped in first, leaning against the doorframe with a smirk. "Didn't I say we'd have to live with the fallout? Inspired Doc to a new profession, though. Pig farmer."

"Pig farmer?" Justin scratched his head.

"Mm-hmm. And as soon as that shoulder's better, he will practice hog tying you."

Justin clucked his tongue. "In my defense, Doc, I didn't think it would involve stitches."

"Stitches to the heart." Simon's playful grin softened to brotherly approval.

Ben shook his head, the corner of his mouth tugging upward. "Reckon I'll survive. Might even call it worth it."

Simon pushed off the doorframe and tossed Ben a mock salute before disappearing into the yard, Justin trailing after him with a hearty laugh.

The forge door closed, leaving Ben and Rebecca in the hush again.

Ben exhaled, threading his fingers through hers once more.

"Go," he murmured. "Your family's waiting."

She lingered a beat longer before slipping away, the warm scent of honeysuckle lingering in the air.

Ben leaned his head back against the table and shut his eyes.

He had kissed her.

She had let him.

And the world hadn't shattered. It had settled.

Darkness gave way to light. Not all at once, but like sunrise through mist. California. Baas. Regret. It was all losing its grip, one mercy at a time.

~

IN THE FOLLOWING DAYS, rumors spread fast. Baas's business interests crumbled. Merchants withdrew secret agreements. River captains distanced themselves. And Paulette Bradley regained ownership of Bradley House through a careful petition and the quiet help of friends.

Some said Isom Caine hadn't survived the fall from the bluff. Others claimed they glimpsed a thin, dark figure slipping through the trees near Fort Smith, vanishing like a shadow at sunset. And though no one could prove it, whispers grew louder that Billy Kinder, outlaw and ghost, had been spotted riding hard along the old stage roads, always a day ahead of the law.

Chapter Forty-Five

The late afternoon sun lit Hogue House in a warm, autumn glow as laughter tumbled like a babbling brook. Edie and Jace raced toward the big oak in the backyard. Hayden, Jesse, and Cason gave chase as Oscar bounded behind them. Cordelia, Martie, and Nellie replenished trays of cookies and tea. Sam and Caroline shared a plate of cookies on the front steps, a little closer than "friends" might.

Rebecca stood at a distance, soaking it all in. The wedding had been simple, sweet, and everything Ivajohn and Pastor Turner had hoped for. Ben joined her, leaning his good shoulder against a tree and rubbing his thumb against his injury on the other shoulder.

Rebecca brushed his hand away. "Don't scratch. It won't heal properly."

"I could use a distraction." His hand slipped to the small of her back, pulling her close.

She smiled, savoring the stillness beside him.

"You're quiet." His breath fell soft on her ear.

"Trying to hold on to this moment."

Circling back to them, Edie edged beside Ben, tugged at his

sleeve, and whispered in his ear when he bent close. Ollie stood in the distance, brandishing a wooden frame with a swatch of red flocked paper. Ben took Edie's hand.

"You'll have to excuse me." He smiled at Rebecca. "I forgot I have a small obligation to tend to."

And he disappeared into the forge with Edie and Ollie.

Allie and Eliza Dawn slipped through the crowd toward her, grinning.

Allie bumped her with her hip. "How's that fading memory?"

"Much clearer than it once was." Rebecca hugged herself.

"Clear as the view through a spyglass?" A warm glow accompanied Eliza Dawn's sheepish grin.

Rebecca took her hand and whispered, "Clear enough to see you might want to stop worrying about whether or not you're able to have a child."

Eliza Dawn froze, searching Rebecca's face. "You think—"

Eliza Dawn glanced at Allie, who nodded her agreement. Tears welled in Eliza Dawn's eyes. She squeezed Rebecca's hand, eyes scanning the yard until they found Justin. She gave Rebecca a quick hug and went to join him.

"With the Bradley House women moving out and the Drake boys moving in, how will the boardinghouse fare?" Allie rubbed her shoulder.

"Well enough for now. The Talbots are staying with us temporarily until the judge hears the case." Rebecca sighed. "I'll have wares at the mercantile. Martie will join Caroline, making hats at the tailor shop."

"And Cordelia?"

"Cordelia is set on teacher college." Rebecca turned to face Allie. "Says she needs time away from home to figure out who she is. Maybe she's right."

"And what about you and Ben?"

"I'm not sure. We haven't had a chance to talk about it."

"Take some time. Get to know each other again. It will be worth it." Allie hugged her close and whispered, "And fun too." With a wink, she was gone.

Rebecca eased over to the forge, peeking through the window. As Edie sat on a stool, Ben crouched low, charcoal in hand. A small candle cast her shadow on a piece of paper at the far wall.

"Sit still. Chin up." Ben moved slowly and carefully.

Rebecca rested her chin on the window ledge, warmth blooming in her chest. When he finished, Ben mounted the silhouette onto the crimson background Ollie provided. Edie took the finished gift, holding it to her chest, a rare treasure. The three reappeared from the forge just as Ivajohn and Pastor Turner emerged from the house.

Edie presented Ivajohn the gift with a small curtsy. Ivajohn drew the child into her arms, wiping away tears before climbing into the wagon. As it rolled away, Ivajohn flung the bouquet over her shoulder. It hit Simon squarely in the chest, igniting cheers and laughter. Send-off whoops, hugs, tossed handfuls of flower petals. Rebecca moved through the well-wishers with feather-light steps, floating on the first true joy to settle over Hogue House since Mama's passing.

Edie hugged Ben around his middle. "Thanks for your help, Dr. Ewing."

"You can call him Ben now." Ollie puffed up his chest and stole her nose. "He's one of us."

Edie squealed and chased after him, snatching at his thumb stuck between two fingers.

Rebecca took Ben by the hand, leading him toward the fire ring. She glimpsed Eliza Dawn and Justin at the opposite end of the ring as they rounded the corner. She slowed, drawing Ben to a stop in the shadows of a nearby tree, allowing the scene to unfold unseen.

Eliza Dawn's hand rested on Justin's chest, his fingers

wrapped around hers as she spoke. His eyes wide, he brushed her cheek with the back of his fingers. Eliza Dawn rested her head against his chest, and he wrapped his arms around her. Then, lifting her chin, he kissed her forehead, joy clinging to them like a soft new light.

"Good news?" Ben whispered.

"The best." She took his hand, slipping between the forge and the shed.

They strode through the grove behind Hogue House, each step slow and deliberate. Ben clasped her elbow, guiding her around a briar patch. His touch lingered.

She found the fallen log where they'd first spoke upon his return and sat. He joined her, resting his hand lightly against her back.

"Everything all right?"

"It's hard to go back to normal." Her voice faltered. "After everything we've been through."

Ben brushed a strand of hair from her forehead. "Close your eyes, Becca."

She did.

"Where is He?"

She inhaled deeply, the earthy, sweet scent of the grove.

"I don't see Him."

"Again. A little farther."

"He's at the edge of the grove." She smiled. "With our firefly friend."

"You're not alone." He pressed his forehead to hers. "You never were. He's been there through all the hard places."

Rebecca opened her eyes, tears rolling gently. "I wonder," she whispered, "if sitting with Him in hard places is always meant to be solitary."

"Sometimes, it's just you and Him. No one else can walk that path." He traced the edge of her jaw with his knuckles.

"But sometimes"—he cupped her hands between his—

"when you've walked through hard places with someone you love, you can sit with Him together. And you point each other to the Light when one of you struggles to see it."

"Even if it flickers like a firefly?"

Ben smiled. "Especially then."

A tiny firefly floated between them, tracing a crooked line in the air. Ben smiled and followed its trail as it danced before Rebecca's face, haloing her in a shimmer of living light.

Slowly, he tipped up her chin and kissed her. A kiss weighted with all they had lost, all they had survived, and all they dared to hope for.

When they drew apart, Rebecca whispered, "I'm glad you're home."

Ben brushed her hair back, his voice raspy. "Home. Where light flickers in the darkness."

Above them, two little fireflies blinked, circling one another, then drifted together into the sacred shadows.

Epilogue

Choctaw Nation, near Fort Coffee
Early Spring, 1854

Early morning mist clung to the prairie grass as Rebecca washed her hands in the wooden bowl beside the field tent. She stood and stretched, her hand at her lower back. Beside her, Ben adjusted the bandage around a man's shoulder while an elder Choctaw healer murmured instructions in low, rhythmic tones. They had spent the better part of the winter volunteering at a small encampment near Fort Coffee, treating fevers, pulling teeth, setting bones. It had been humbling work.

Ben passed a warm compress to the healer, who nodded in approval. Rebecca smiled at the quiet rapport that had grown between them all, grateful for the exchange of knowledge and the shared weight of compassion. She tucked a small bundle of herbs into a pouch and placed it with the other supplies she had gathered.

A horse snorted beyond the tent.

Simon.

He dismounted with practiced ease, his coat lined with dust and cold resolve. He had come to escort them back to Arkansas to ensure safe passage before pursuing his next lead. He finished cinching his saddle as the morning light broke across the horizon.

"You about ready?" Simon tied off the last saddle strap with a practiced flick. His voice was even, but his eyes already scanned the horizon.

Rebecca placed her hand on his arm. "Won't you come home with us?"

"I'll ride as far as the state line to ensure your safety." He gave a half smile. "Then I'm heading toward Sallisaw Creek. Word is Billy Kinder was seen north of there."

Rebecca tucked a few more bundles of herbs into her saddlebag before she and Ben made their farewells to the Choctaw healer. They rode hard for a few hours before stopping at a quiet bend in the Arkansas River. Ben dismounted, then reached up to help Rebecca down from Truly. Eliza Dawn's baby was due any day now, and urgency pressed at Rebecca's spine. Yet, they lingered in the hush, hearts full with the weight of what they had left behind.

She turned to Simon, seated atop Noble. "You won't stop and eat with us?"

"No time to lose."

Ben's gaze was steady. "Don't ride so hard you forget what you're riding for."

Simon paused. "I haven't forgotten."

Rebecca reached for his reins, steadying Noble. "Promise me it's forgiveness you're chasing, Simon. Not only justice." Her voice caught "If it's anything else, it'll consume you."

"I don't know what I'm chasing. Not exactly." Simon stared past them, as if searching the horizon for something only his soul recognized. "But I'll know it when I find it."

"I hope it's mercy." She squeezed his hand.

"Take care of yourself, Becks."

Rebecca blinked hard. "Don't call me Becks," she murmured, too soft for him to hear.

Simon held her gaze a long while before turning his horse and riding to the east. He disappeared over the horizon. Her heart thrummed the rhythm of Noble's hoofbeats as Ben wrapped his arms around her.

Rebecca laid her head back against his shoulder. "Will he be all right?"

"I don't know. All the stillness has gone out of him." Ben hooked his chin over her shoulder. "It's like he can't make sense of the two. Billy Kinder with a gun, and Billy Kinder holdin' a cracked compass, tryin' to find his way home."

She buried her face in his collar. "I wish I knew he wasn't riding straight into more sorrow."

"Me too." Ben pulled her closer.

Their embrace lingered and he brushed her hair from her forehead. "I've been meaning to ask you something."

She tipped her head, teasing. "Don't you need to ask Pa's permission first?"

Ben laughed, low and warm. "Already done."

"When?" She blinked.

"Before we left Van Buren." His eyes twinkled. "But there is someone else's blessing I need."

"Oh?" Rebecca frowned, confused.

Ben's thumb traced her fingers. "Ollie."

She tilted her head, brows knit together, and Ben chuckled.

"We had a manly understanding once, he and I. Remember? At the picnic. Seems only right to finish what we started."

Her heart lifted with a shaky laugh. "I'd nearly forgotten."

Ben leaned closer, voice roughened by tenderness. "You've carried so much for so long, Rebecca Hogue. Let me carry some of it with you."

Their foreheads touched. Their breaths mingled. She tipped

her chin up, and he kissed her—a kiss that deepened as Rebecca rose onto her toes, arms winding around his neck. She rested her head against his chest, his heartbeat steady in her ear.

She whispered, "I'm glad you're home."

"But we're not home yet."

She'd spent too long tying the word home to walls and doorways. Maybe it had always been something softer. Something closer. She patted his chest. "You are home."

Acknowledgments

Writing a story like *Fireflies in Sacred Shadows* doesn't happen in isolation. I'm deeply grateful for the people who helped bring this story to light.

To my family, whose patience, prayers, and willingness to pick up dinner duties made room for this story. Your love steadies me.

Thank you to those who prayed me through dry spells, encouraged me with truth, and reminded me why I write. There are too many of you to name, and each of you is priceless to me. You helped me rest in the sacred beauty of walking through hard places together.

To the dear friends who helped me battle doubt with steady encouragement, thank you for the check-ins, brainstorming sessions, retreats, laughter, and gentle nudges forward. Callie Bradford, Jenny Carlisle, Sheila Daniel, Linda Dindzans, Heather Greer, Melissa Nesbitt, Kathy Vernich, and Ellen E. Withers, you have each stood beside me, and I'm deeply grateful. Your presence made the journey lighter and the work more joyful.

To my series editors, Amy Anguish, Linda Fulkerson, Suzie Waltner, and Heidi Glick, and the publishing team—thank you for handling this story with such care. Your insight and excellence made it stronger.

Special thanks to Judy Smith and Anthony Wood, whose name suggestions, drawn from a Mason jar, sparked the creation of Isom Caine. When those two names came together, the character stepped fully into my mind, shadowed and sharp.

Thank you for lending your names to a figure who became a vivid part of this story.

A heartfelt thanks to those who preserve history. Clara B. Eno's *History of Crawford County* opened doors of inspiration. And to the unnamed archivists, cartographers, and researchers whose quiet work made this story possible, many thanks.

I'm deeply grateful to the Grant County Library for placing *Of Faith and Dreams* on their shelves, to the Saline County Library and Bookish Emporium for faithfully championing local authors through meaningful events, and to the churches and women's groups who continue to share clean and Christian fiction like *Of Faith and Dreams*, *A Gift for All Time*, and now *Fireflies in Sacred Shadows*. Your support helps deliver stories of resilience rooted in faith and grace to readers authors could never reach alone.

Chapters on Main in Van Buren has become a touchstone for me. It's often the first place I slip into when I arrive in town and the last place I linger before I leave. Their coffee brims with imagination, their shelves invite discovery of new and used treasures, and their people are as warm as the stories they share. Chapters is both a starting point and a steady presence— a shining reminder of why stories and community matter so much.

Finally, to every reader who picked up this book in search of faith, hope, or resilience—this story is for you.

About the Author

Tonya B. Ashley writes stories that speak to the weary and the wandering—faith-filled fiction rooted in family, redemption, and the sacredness of suffering. Whether she's unraveling a love story beneath flickering fireflies or tracing grace through grief, Tonya's writing leans into the belief that hope still flickers in the darkest places.

She is the author of *Of Faith and Dreams*, Book One in the *Lost and Found* Series, and *Once Lost, Now Found*, a prequel novella featured in the collection *A Gift for All Time*. Her newest novel, *Fireflies in Sacred Shadows*, can be read as a standalone or as part of the *Lost and Found* series.

When she's not writing, Tonya enjoys time with her family, connecting with students, reading in a hammock, and junk journaling with a creative cup of coffee.

Author's Note

As a child, the woods around my home and visits to my great aunt's farm fed my imagination. I never imagined a city could do the same—until I wandered into Van Buren. The town's fascinating history and charming character inspire creativity every time I visit. In the Lost and Found series, I strive to weave together fiction and history thoughtfully, combining facts with creativity while carefully respecting the town's past.

My fictional version of Van Buren, Arkansas, is based on an 1888 map, which is the oldest one I've found. Even though the novel is set in 1853, this later map influenced the placement of landmarks such as Hogue House and Main Street.

Historically, the Little Rock and Fort Smith Railway was established in 1853 with John Drennen as its first president. However, the first train from Little Rock did not reach Van Buren until June 24, 1876. Although I found no evidence of land grabs in Van Buren's development, such tactics were common during the railroad expansion across the country. In 1887, railroad tycoon and "robber baron" Jay Gould took control of the Little Rock and Fort Smith Railway, which inspired some fictional elements in this story's business dealings.

The novel pays respectful homage to two of Van Buren's early real-life physicians. Dr. Dibrell is mentioned by name, and Dr. Henri Pernot, who arrived in Van Buren in 1852, makes a brief cameo appearance. Van Buren hosted several doctors throughout the 1800s; some stayed only for a short time, while others became deeply involved in the town's community. Since this story focuses on a fictional doctor, the character of Ben Ewing naturally provided an opportunity to honor the town's rich medical history.

The character of Eliza Dawn "Dawn" Hogue is fictional, but real people inspired her presence at the Arkansas Intelligencer. Brothers George and Anslem Clarke each served as editors of the *newspaper* in the early 1850s. George Clarke was described as brilliant but impulsive and is said to have once published work by a thirteen-year-old girl from Fayetteville. It's easy to imagine a woman like Dawn working at the printing press. When George left Van Buren in 1853, his brother Anslem became editor and was also given a cameo role in the novel. Described as straightforward and warm-hearted, it seems likely he might have kept this fictional female reporter on staff. Anslem managed the paper until his death in 1859. The *Intelligencer* soon shut down afterward.

All other characters, businesses, and events are entirely fictional but reflect the types of enterprises and community figures that might have been present on Main Street during this time.

While writing this novel, I was thrilled to finally find a copy of Miss Clara B. Eno's *History of Crawford County, Arkansas,* available online. Her work opens doors of curiosity, reverence, and creativity. Van Buren's true history is rich enough to stand on its own, but it also sparks the imagination and invites storytelling, both real and fictional. It has been a joy to imagine this "Wild West before the Wild West" town and the people who may have called it home.

If you ever visit, dear reader, be sure to ride the trolley and the train, stop by the Drennen Scott House, explore the town, and enjoy coffee and books at Chapters on Main. You'll be glad you did.

—Tonya B. Ashley

Citations

1. Perspective Map of Van Buren (1888)

Henry Wellge. *Perspective Map of Van Buren, Ark., County Seat of Crawford County, 1888.* Milwaukee: Norris & Wellge, 1888. Library of Congress. https://www.loc.gov/item/75693085/.

2. Van Buren and the Little Rock & Fort Smith Railroad

Encyclopedia of Arkansas. "Van Buren (Crawford County)." Central Arkansas Library System. Last modified May 27, 2022. https://encyclopediaofarkansas.net/entries/van-buren-868/.
Encyclopedia of Arkansas. "Little Rock and Fort Smith Railroad." Central Arkansas Library System. Last modified August 6, 2021. https://encyclopediaofarkansas.net/entries/little-rock-and-fort-smith-railroad-6487/.

3. Dr. Henri Charles Pernot & Dr. James Anthony Dibrell

Arkansas Studies. *Sidney Austin Pernot Papers, 1873–1955.*

Arkansas Studies Institute Archives. https://arstudies. contentdm.oclc.org/digital/collection/findingaids/id/4813/.

Find a Grave. "Dr. James Anthony Dibrell (1817–1897)." Accessed April 30, 2025. https://www.findagrave.com/ memorial/38145760/james-anthony-dibrell.

4. Arkansas Intelligencer and the Clarke Brothers

Library of Congress. *Chronicling America: Arkansas Intelligencer (Van Buren, Ark.), 1842–1859.* https://chroniclingamerica.loc. gov/lccn/sn82016488/.

5. Clara B. Eno and Crawford County History

Encyclopedia of Arkansas. "Clara Bertha Eno (1854–1951)." Central Arkansas Library System. Last modified January 11, 2023. https://encyclopediaofarkansas.net/entries/clara-bertha- eno-2701/.

Also by Tonya B. Ashley

Of Faith and Dreams—by Tonya B. Ashley

Lost and Found series—Book One

When Van Buren, Arkansas, is inundated with Forty-Niners seeking to outfit themselves with horses before heading west, Justin Hogue sees it as the perfect opportunity to step out of his father's shadow to establish a horse ranch. The same influx of prospectors ushers in a competitive horse trader who wants him out of the way. Further complicating things, Justin is challenged with a new tenant at the Hogue family boardinghouse.

Eliza Dawn is an independent, headstrong seamstress who claims to follow the prospectors west to sell her garments. Justin believes she's hiding something. After all, a few dollars for shirts isn't worth the risk. So, he keeps his distance until a mysterious letter and an intriguing ring unite them in searching for an unknown prospector.

Can they find one man in a thousand before the gold expeditions leave town? What will put Justin's dreams at greater risk–conflict with the horse trader or Eliza Dawn's secrets?

Get your copy here:

https://scrivenings.link/offaithanddreams

~

A Gift for All Time

A Collection of Three Christmas Novellas

A beautiful hand-carved nativity set travels from its original home in Germany to a riverboat in Van Buren, Arkansas, in the mid-1840s, then to Mexico, Missouri, at the beginning of the American Civil War. More than a century later, it resurfaces in a tiny town in the Arkansas River Valley.

Three stories tell of the impact this treasure has on the families who own it. God's love survives tragedy, turmoil, and even abandonment. His love is the gift for all, for all time.

https://scrivenings.link/agiftforalltime

Stay up-to-date on your favorite books and authors with our free e-newsletters.

ScriveningsPress.com

www.ingramcontent.com/pod-product-compliance
Lightning Source LLC
Chambersburg PA
CBHW061917130726
47908CB00017B/1662